The Return
of the
Laramie Kid

by Bill Vaznis

THE RETURN OF THE LARAMIE KID

by Bill Vaznis

ISBN - 978-0-9894592-1-1

Thunderchicken Advertising, LLC
P.O. B ox 684
Lima, NY 14485

Printed in the United States

The text type was set in Georgia Regular

DEDICATION

To Bev...my inspiration

The Return of the Laramie Kid

Prolog   **13**

The Kid From Ft. Laramie   **15**

Chapter One: The Fire   **29**

Chapter Two: A Friendship Is Born   **37**

Chapter Three: The Buck   **43**

Chapter Four: A Friend In Need   **49**

Chapter Five: The Rendezvous   **53**

Chapter Six: The Rescue   **57**

Chapter Seven: A Few Hours Later   **63**

Chapter Eight: Moses Sheridan   **65**

Chapter Nine: An Old Friend   **69**

Chapter Ten: The Nelsons   **79**

Chapter Eleven: Strangers in Camp   **85**

Chapter Twelve: The Silver Bullet   **89**

Chapter Thirteen: Riding Lessons   **97**

Chapter Fourteen: Boys to Men   **105**

Chapter Fifteen: Clayton's Father   **113**

Chapter Sixteen: The Truth Be Told   **117**

Chapter Seventeen: A Promise No More   **121**

Chapter Eighteen: The Roundup   **131**

Chapter Nineteen: The Water Moccasin   **137**

Chapter Twenty: A Decade of Statehood   **145**

Chapter Twenty-One: The Shooting Match   **149**

Chapter Twenty-Two: Dancing Water   **157**

Chapter Twenty-Three: Miss Anabell   **163**

Chapter Twenty-Four: Dueling Hatchets   **173**

Chapter Twenty-Five: Brocken Arrows   **181**

Chapter Twenty-Six: The Grifters   **193**

Chapter Twenty-Seven:
The Judge Packs a Pair of Navy Colts   **199**

Chapter Twenty-Eight: Back at the Ranch   **211**

Chapter Twenty-Nine:
The Secret Room and the Secret Within   **215**

Chapter Thirty: Finally, The Truth Comes Out   **225**

Chapter Thirty-One: The Conflagration   **229**

Chapter Thirty-Two: A Time Fot Reflection   **235**

Chapter Thirty-Three: Bull and the Hatchet   **243**

Chapter Thirty-Four: The Picnic   **251**

Chapter Thirty-Five: The Decision   **257**

Chapter Thirty-Six: The Laramie Kid Rides Again   **261**

Chapter Thirty-Seven:
Revealing Evidence at the Courthouse   **269**

Chapter Thirty-Eight: Back at the Secret Room   **275**

Chapter Thirty-Nine: Mathew Brady   **279**

Chapter Fourty: Judge Alexander Reinststed   **289**

Chapter Forty-One: Death Revealed 295

Chapter Forty-Two: Texas Gold 301

Chapter Forty-Three: Outside Vachel's Compound 307

Chapter Forty-Four: Goliath Does His Death Dance 313

Chapter Forty-Five: One More Scare 319

Chapter Forty-Six: Inside Vachel's Compound 323

Chapter Forty-Seven: The Traitor 329

Chapter Forty-Eight: Wagons, HO! 333

Chapter Forty-Nine: Red Dog's Moment in the Sun 339

Chapter Fifty: One More Favor 343

Chapter Fifty-One: The Celebration 347

Chapter Fifty-Two: The Premonition 353

Chapter Fifty-Three: Saturday Morning on the Praire 355

Chapter Fifty-Four: News from Colbey 367

Chapter Fifty-Five: The Calm Before the Storm 371

Chapter Fifty-Six: Bull and Davis Team Up 379

Chapter Fifty-Seven: Reinett's Prophecy Comes True 389

Chapter Fifty-Eight: A Father's Revenge 395

Chapter Fifty-Nine: A Son's Revenge 397

Chapter Sixty: Your Rose is my Rose 401

Chapter Sixty-One: Good-Bye 407

PROLOG

He couldn't sleep. The funeral was wearing heavily on his mind, and after tossing and turning fitfully for hours, Will slipped out of bed and quietly dressed before stepping outside in the cool nighttime air. He crossed the yard under the cover of darkness, and entered the main barn through a side door. Once inside he struck a wood match, and while the flame was still high slid it under the glass globe to catch the kerosene soaked cord afire. Whoosh!

After adjusting the wick, he held the lantern up high and disappeared into the bowels of the barn. A few minutes later, while running his hand along the top of an oak carrying beam, he found what he was looking for...a latched metal box holding among other mementos a yellowed newspaper clipping from the Colby Tribune dated July 18, 1865.

The author, a young dime novelist at the time, had interviewed all the witnesses he could find after the hanging, then several days later wrote out the course of events in great detail and exactly as they occurred.

Will set the lantern down on a barrel head, hooked his reading glasses over his ears, and then sat down on a oak bench to read the account one more time.

THE KID FROM FT. LARAMIE

by Ned Buntline

The Kid from Ft. Laramie became suspicious when seven gruff-looking strangers rode into town that afternoon, one at a time and from the same direction—five minutes apart—and tied their horses to the railing across the street from the bank. Each slipped through the swinging doors of the Lucky Seven Saloon without incident, but once inside, they spread out around the bar as if their movements were planned well in advance.

The Kid had seen a couple of the men before, but he couldn't remember when or where. He put his beer down and stared down the street, trying to think. Something wasn't quite right...he could feel it.

Inside the saloon, Lilly walked over to one of the men, burly and unshaven in a black hat. "Buy me a drink cowboy, and I might show you a good time!"

"What's your name?" he asked without looking at her.

"My name's Lilly, handsome, what do they call you?" she replied with a smile and a gentle touch to the man's arm.

The man in the black hat grabbed a bottle of whiskey off the bar and took a long swig before turning around and looking at her directly. "Well, you talk like a Yankee whore, Lilly, and I don't drink with Yankee whores, and I don't fuck Yankee whores, either. I just shoot 'em!" And with that he grabbed her long golden hair with his fist and shoved the barrel of his revolver into her mouth. "Now, Lilly dearest, tell me the truth. Are you a damn Yankee?"

Terrified, Lilly shook her head no, but the man in the black hat was not convinced. Turning his face away, he pulled the trigger anyway, scattering her brains and blond hair against the mirror behind the bar. He looked at what was left of her nose and lower jaw with contempt and pushed her away, letting her collapse to the floor in a lifeless heap.

The other six men pulled their guns and told everyone to get on the floor if they knew what was good for them. Flabbergasted, each customer dropped to the floor without question.

The killing was designed to bring all the righteous men to the saloon, and within a few minutes, a storekeeper wearing a white long-sleeved shirt and black vest, along with the sheriff and his young deputy Steve Sweeney, burst through the swinging doors.

"That's all of you this town has?" laughed the man

with blood and bits of shattered bone on his shirt. "Yankee sympathizers!"

"What's going on here," demanded the sheriff. "Who shot, and what the hell is wrong with Lilly?"

"I shot her by accident, Sheriff! But you I am going to shoot you on purpose. And with that he raised his pistol and shot the sheriff and storekeeper square in the head before turning his aim on the young deputy. "Now, son, you are going to do exactly as I tell you...or I will kill you, too. Understand?"

The deputy was so scared all he could manage was a stammering "yes".

"You'll do...I think," he said quietly to the deputy. "Jack, cover these Yankees, and if any one of them moves, shoot him and the two guys closest to him in the fucking head. Somebody grab the deputy and take him with us. Tom, you and Mike step outside and cover the street. The rest of you follow me."

The Kid from Ft. Laramie heard a single shot and figured it had to be nothing but trouble. Then he saw Pete Wilkins, who owned the Mercantile, the sheriff, and his young deputy run into the saloon followed quickly by two more shots.

"This is it," he muttered to himself, as he stood up and put his beer down before double-checking each pistol and levering a cartridge into the chamber of his Henry. Then he pulled a tin star from his shirt pocket, pinned it to his vest, and stepped out into the middle of Main Street.

Four men soon crossed the street and went directly into the bank. The man in the black hat noticed a familiar big red stallion tied to the hitching rail in front of the bank, but didn't give it a second thought.

Once inside the bank, the robbery went down quickly. "Do as you are told and you might get to go to church tomorrow," yelled the man in the black hat. "Tell them what will happen to them if they flinch, Deputy."

"He just killed the sheriff and Pete Wilkins," stammered the deputy. "He shot them both in the head! PLEASE do what he says!"

The man in the black hat pointed his pistol at the employees. "Now, each of you face the wall and drop to your knees. NOW!"

The bank manger and three tellers, terrified out of their minds, dropped to their knees. The deputy caught the eye of the young female cashier as she eased herself to the floor, and the man in the black hat caught the exchange.

"You two know each other? Oh, I get it. She's your gal, huh Deputy?"

The vault was still open, and within one minute it and the three cash drawers were emptied into three large grain bags, and three of the robbers were rushing out the front door and onto the street carrying the cash and shooting wildly at anything that moved.

The man in the black hat told the female cashier to get up and stand next to the deputy. "He's your man, huh Miss? Well, he ain't much of a man! Put your arms around him and kiss him good-bye! Go ahead, KISS HIM!"

And with that the man in the black hat aimed his pistol at the deputy's face and, after a long pause, said "BANG KID" and backed out of the bank laughing like hell.

The young deputy had clearly pissed his pants.

Tom and Mike stood in front of the saloon as the others exited the bank. Something else caught Mike's eye however. He looked down the middle of Main Street and watched in disbelief as a lone lawman with twin cross-draw Colts and a Henry held at port arms walking directly at him, his tin star flashing in the early afternoon sunlight.

"We got trouble, Boss!"

The man in the black hat looked down the street and saw the badge, too.

"Kill him!"

Tom and Mike drew their pistols, but it was too late for them. The Ranger gunned them both down with a hail of gunfire from his Henry and then shot Jack in the throat with a single shot as he rushed through the swinging doors to help. Two more rifle shots through Jack's rib cage ensured he would not survive the day.

Rattled at the sudden turn of events, and the fact that three of their comrades were already dead or dying, two of the robbers threw their grain bags loaded with cash across their saddles and started to mount up for a quick getaway out of town. The Henry barked twice, dropping both horses to the street with spine shots, exposing the two robbers to additional gunfire. Before they could draw their pistols however, two more rifle shots echoed down Main Street, and both men were suddenly lying prostrate in the street next to their bellowing horses, each man bleeding profusely from a slug hole in the center of his chest.

The third robber wanted nothing more to do with this lone lawman, dropped the money bag, and dove for cover behind a watering trough as the man in the black hat frantically emptied his pistol in the general direction of the Ranger, missing him entirely, and then jumped on his horse for a quick getaway.

The Ranger raised his rifle to shoot, but his aim was blocked by the saloonkeeper running out the swinging doors and into the street with his scatter-gun mounted firmly against his shoulder. He saw the robber hiding behind the water trough and without hesitation filled him with two loads of 00 buckshot, killing him instantly.

The Ranger ran to his mount, slipped the Henry into the scabbard, and within seconds rode after the man in the black hat. He raced past the bank and livery stable and down the middle of Main Street in hot pursuit before catching sight of the escaping bandit just as he reined in his mount to duck down a long alleyway that led to the outskirts of town.

The Ranger cleared the alleyway with ease and now leaning low over his saddle repeatedly slapped the red stallion's hindquarters right to left with his reins.

"C'mon Big Red, giddy up! We can catch him!"

With fire in his eyes and eagerness in his heart, the red stallion broke into a full gallop. He was born to run, and as he had done so many times in the past, soon put the Ranger within easy pistol range of an escaping bandit.

The man in the black hat, sensing the Ranger's presence, abruptly turned his mare into a precipitous ravine. Grasping the rear of his saddle for support, and then leaning as far back as he dared, he forced the mare down the steep and rocky slope.

Without breaking his stride, Big Red leaped over the edge of the ravine, and with the Ranger's stirrups high on Big Red's neck, began his own downward spiral with wild abandon.

When the man in the black hat reached the bottom of the ravine however, he dug his heels into the mare and forced her to climb back up to the rim of the ravine where he quickly dismounted and took cover behind a small pile of rocks.

The Ranger was trapped! Cornered at the bottom of the ravine, he slid off Big Red and quickly took cover himself.

"If you know what's good for you, Ranger, you will turn around right now," yelled the man in the black hat as he reloaded his pistol, "and go back to town. You ain't gonna take me alive!"

"I have no intention of taking you alive," yelled the Ranger. "You are going to die right here, right now, Robertson."

The man in the black hat crouched lower and out of sight behind the rocks. How did the Ranger know his name? That voice, and then the sight of the big red stallion, the same stallion hitched earlier in front of the bank, jarred his memory—and his heart began to race. This was no ordinary lawman cornered at the bottom of the ravine. He was a Texas Ranger, the same Texas Ranger that nearly took his life two years earlier near the Mexican border.

Robertson held the high ground, but he wanted to run nonetheless. His mare had wandered only a short distance away, but he would have to cross open ground to get to her. And the Ranger was a crack shot. Damn, thought Robertson, he just gunned down five of his men in town, single-handedly!

Robertson peered back over the rocks, but could not see the Ranger. The red stallion had held his ground, and the Ranger's Henry rifle was still secured in the scabbard, so he figured the Ranger was pinned down behind some nearby rocks and could not get to him. He slowly lowered his head once again behind the rocks and tried to figure out a plan to get away.

The Ranger was going to kill him, that he was sure of, even if he raised his hands and gave up. There was no forgiveness for what he did in town a few hours earlier, or along the Mexican border a few years back. None.

Once Robertson caught his breath, he peered into the ravine and yelled down to the Ranger. "One of us is going to die today."

But he got no immediate answer.

Then from uphill and behind him came the response. "That's right, Robertson. You! You are going to die!"

The Ranger had wasted no time climbing out of the ravine. As soon as Robertson eased out of sight, the Ranger did the unexpected. Instead of moving down the ravine and away from Robertson to safety, the Ranger scurried back up the ravine toward Robertson and crawled out over the rim to safety. Robertson had him cornered, but he took his eyes off the Ranger long enough for the Ranger to escape the ravine and turn the tables.

And now Robertson was going to die.

"You have no jurisdiction for what happened along the border. There are no courts, no jails," pleaded Robertson.

"That's right. There are no warrants out for you, and there is no place I can take you to be hanged, legally anyway, for butchering that unarmed Mexican family.

But bank robbery is a hanging offense here in Colby, and you are doomed to swing, Robertson. Doomed."

Robertson gripped his pistol and wiped a bead of sweat off his forehead with the front sight. He was scared, and for good reason. This Ranger was someone he feared. He had a well-earned reputation for torturing his prisoners for days before jailing them. Word had it he even skinned one cowpoke alive for raping a young Mexican girl outside San Antonio. That guy died several days later after allegedly confessing to the crime.

"I'm going to shoot you in the knees like you did Juan's son, and then laugh as you did when the boy cried for his father's help," boasted the Ranger. "Then I am going to gut shoot you like you did Juan's wife before taking you back to Colby for a righteous hanging."

Robertson began to shake. He remembered shooting the Mexican's wife in the belly just to watch her bleed. The expression on her husband's face had flamed his passions, egging him to shoot the boy, too.

Robertson would have stayed to watch the agony, but witnesses had summoned the Ranger. He ran down an alley and hid in the hayloft above the livery stable while the Ranger searched furtively for him. A few hours later he stole a horse and left town under the cover of darkness, leaving the Ranger to care for the carnage the man in the black hat had created.

Now it was Robertson's turn to be tortured. It was his time to die, and he was terrified. With eyes bulging, Robertson contemplated his next move. He spun the cylinder on his pistol to be sure it was still loaded, and then he checked it again. Sweating profusely and shaking like a calf about to be slaughtered, he peered carefully up the hill between the rocks.

Suddenly, the Ranger fanned the hammer on his Colt, sending a cylinder full of bullets at Robertson. Twang! One ricocheted through the rock pile, tearing off a piece of Robertson's right ear. Screaming, Robertson stuck just his hand over the rocks and emptied his pistol aimlessly up the hill in a desperate effort to kill the Ranger.

After the hammer fell on his last bullet, Robertson turned around and saw the Ranger standing six feet away with a pistol aimed directly at his face. He had circled around and come up behind Robertson, who was now cowering in absolute terror. He dropped his pistol and raised his hands over his head, but it was to no avail.

"This first one is for Juan's son," screamed the Ranger as he cocked the hammer. Robertson covered his eyes with both hands and in a loud, piercing, high-pitched shrill cried out, "No! No! Please," just as the Ranger dropped the hammer.

The blast echoed off the rocks and down through the ravine, but the shot had gone off over Robertson's blood-soaked head, striking the ground beyond. Missing on purpose, the Ranger looked down at Robertson's quivering body with a broad smile.

The man in the black hat had clearly pissed his pants.

The Ranger stepped forward and struck Robertson in the head several times with the butt of his Colt, rendering him unconscious for the moment. A loud whistle brought Big Red out of the ravine, and a few minutes later Robertson was hogtied with the Ranger's lariat and bound belly down over Robertson's saddle for the ride back to town.

Two days later Robertson was hanged in Colby just as the sun was setting, blubbering hysterically as they dropped him unceremoniously from the scaffolding. When he stopped kicking, there was a sigh of relief among the townsfolk in his passing.

Nobody laughed.

It seems Robertson relished killing innocents with a certain brutality and then rejoiced by laughing about it for weeks and even months afterward. In a twisted sort of way, the mockery was a ritual designed to thwart his own mortality. It did not work. Robertson was buried before sunrise the following morning in a shallow unmarked grave far, far from town.

Nobody cried.

Will unhooked his glasses and with a sigh slid them back into his shirt pocket. Then carefully folded the newspaper clipping, placed it back in the metallic box and hid it once again out of sight atop the oak carrying beam.

Dawn as still several hours away, and Will would need all the rest he could get to make it through the next few days.

He extinguished the flame and hung the lantern on a peg near the barn door before walking back across the yard to the ranch house. Relieved, Will settled back into bed, with Reinette none the wiser, knowing in his heart that someday the Laramie Kid would ride again...and soon fell fast asleep.

The Return of the Laramie Kid

CHAPTER ONE
The Fire

It had been a long day. The red sun was now hanging motionless in the sky like a giant fiery sphere, prolonging the extreme sadness that engulfed the grief-stricken couple. As the last carriage left the ranch, Will and his wife Reinette walked back to the family cemetery, alone but arm in arm, to say good-bye one more time.

For the last few days she had been strong, thanking friends and neighbors for their kind words and acts of sympathy. She even managed a smile now and then as she stood stoically in the parlor listening to all the good intentions, thankful however that the reverend and his wife were standing close by in case she needed them to shush a curious neighbor.

As the mourners finally left the ranch that evening in ones and twos and small family groupings she felt more relieved than burdened. A funeral could be physically taxing as well as emotionally draining. After several days of receiving mourners, there were clothes to wash, the good china to be put safely away, and the floors were a mess with the company and all. She would tidy up in the morning she reasoned, but first she had to help her grandson get into his bed clothes and climb under the covers. He was only seven years old and didn't understand why his mother and father had to die.

"It's God's will," his grandmother said as she tousled his hair, "and they are now together in heaven smiling down on us. Someday you will see them both again."

Clayton still didn't understand who God was or anything about heaven. He only knew he missed both of his parents terribly. He could barely remember the fire that morning and waking up in the dark to his mother's screaming. The next thing he recalled was someone wrapping him up in an old blanket and carrying him and his friend Jason through the smoke and fire and down a flight of stairs to the street below.

There he and Jason were handed off to a kind old woman who rushed both boys through throngs of onlookers and fire fighters to the far side of the street and then around the corner where they could not witness the carnage. Clayton cried out frantically for his mother and father as he tried to look back at the fire, but the old lady turned his head away.

All Clayton could hear that night was men yelling and horses snorting as nearly 100 volunteers struggled to save those poor souls still trapped within the burning timbers. Terrified, he struggled to free himself from the arms of the old woman. He had to find his parents, he had to go back to the hotel, but the kind old woman held him tightly, trying to sooth his fears and those of his friend Jason who just stood there whimpering in the dark.

As the commotion lifted an old man rushed up to the old woman's side. It was her husband, Bob. "Anybody else get out?" she asked in a whispered voice.

Before she could quiet him with a single finger over her lips, the old man blurted out that there were no other survivors. "Nobody got out except these two kids, and an Indian and his squaw. Keep the boys away, Sarah, it is not something they should see...or smell."

Those words sent a cold chill through Clayton's body. He knew without hearing any more that his mother and father did not escape the blaze. He closed his eyes in despair and wept uncontrollably.

Clayton seemed to be in a daze over the next few days, but was grateful when neighbors and family friends knelt down to give him a big hug and offer him their heartfelt condolences at the cemetery.

That's all Clayton could remember of the fire and the funeral, at least for the time being. Right now he just wanted to go to sleep.

"It has been a long day, Clayton," said Reinette softly as she tucked him safely into bed. "Try to get some rest." Clayton looked into his grandmother's moist eyes and saw that she too was very sad.

Reinette kissed him on the forehead, and picked up the lantern, its flickering light casting dark eerie shadows on the walls and ceiling. When she closed the door to Clayton's room, she could hear him sobbing.

Holding back her own tears, she entered the parlor where she found Reverend Marstall making some additional notations in the family Bible before returning it to its right-ful home on the mantle above the fireplace.

Jacob Wilfred Alexander

Beloved son of Wilfred & Reinette Alexander

Born June 15, 1840

Died August 23, 1865

John Wilfred Alexander

Beloved son of Wilfred & Reinette Alexander

Born July 14, 1842, in San Antonio, Texas

Died May 22, 1870, in Colby, Texas

Sally Marie (Lister) Alexander

Beloved wife of John Wilfred Alexander

Born June 11, 1843, in San Antonio, Texas

Died May 22, 1870, in Colby, Texas

Clayton John Alexander

Beloved son of John & Sally Marie Lister Alexander

Born September 28, 1862

She had known the reverend and his wife Elizabeth since she was a child. In fact, he had married her and Will over 30 years ago just several days' ride from here in Texarkana, the same year they bought the old Alexander ranch from Will's favorite uncle, George W. And he had also officiated at her son John's wedding to Sally Lister just eight years ago. Was that all it was, she thought to herself. Only eight years ago?

"I'll stop by later in the week, Reinette," said the reverend as he gathered up his hat and coat. "And I'll have another talk with the boy. It's going to be tough on him, but we'll make sure he gets through it okay. I'll be around whenever he needs me. I owe it to John and his brother. They were both fine God-fearing men."

"I'll walk you and Elizabeth to your carriage, Reverend," said Will as he glanced at Reinette, as if to ask permission. Once outside, Will mentioned to the reverend what both he and his wife Elizabeth already suspected: Reinette was in shock over the inexplicable loss of her second son and his wife. She would need her husband now more than ever if she was to grieve properly and heal from the ordeal. Indeed, the pain of losing both her sons cut deep to the bone. And even with Will's support it would take a long time before she could be her old self again. In the meantime, they had a grandson to raise.

As the reverend's carriage disappeared from sight, Will and Reinette found themselves once again approaching the oak grove where the family cemetery lay sheltered from strangers' eyes. But as Reinette neared the picket fence she could not hold it in any longer, and her pent-up grief began to spill. She knelt down and rearranged the flowers that had been carefully positioned around the three fresh graves, placing several additional floral pieces on two nearby graves, as if the five occupants were now somehow joined in the hereafter. Only then could she sob, and she did so uncontrollably until the sizzling red orb slipped behind the distant hills and darkness began to close in.

After wiping her face with a lace handkerchief, she rose to her feet, but only with the help of Will who was having trouble wiping his own tears away. She had barely spoken to him during the funeral, just a faint yes or no when the occasion required it, and even then their eyes only met for a brief moment before she would lower her head and look away. He knew she was angry with him, as if it was his fault their two sons and daughter-in-law were now gone.

He grabbed both her shoulders and faced her head-on. "We'll get through this Reinette, just like we've gotten through all our troubles. We have to be strong, for the boy's sake. We have to give him the strength he is going to need to make it in this world."

"You never mind giving him strength," snarled Reinette as she tore loose from Will's hold. "Both of our sons are gone! Jacob died in a shoot-out with those cattle rustlers no one now remembers, and John died with everyone thinking he was nothing but a worthless saddle tramp. Neither of our boys will ever get the honor they deserve.

"And why? So they could wear a star for you? So they could go out and get killed, and for what? To protect our neighbors, many of whom could care less what happens to anyone else? For law and order you told me, for justice. Well, Wilfred Jacob Alexander, let me tell you a thing or two. Our grandson is not going to follow in your footsteps. He is not going into law enforcement like his father or his uncle, either. You hear me? I want you to promise me right now on our sons' graves that you will retire from the bench from this moment on and that you will not encourage Clayton to become a peace officer. Please Will, I couldn't bear the pain of losing Clayton, too! He is all we have left."

Will knew his wife was desperate by the tone in her voice. If she lost Clay, it would be the death of her. There was no doubt about that. And he could not for a second bear the pain of losing her, too.

Will stepped back and lowered his head, looking her straight in the eyes. "I promise you, Reinette. I promise you with all my heart."

And that was all that was said. The next morning Will dropped his homemade tin badge on the kitchen table and took his pistols out to the barn. He would need a gun while working the ranch, but he would never again pack his twin custom 1851 Navy Colts in public. This move was against his better judgment. The West was not safe, at least not yet, and a gun was often the only difference between good and bad. A promise is a promise nonetheless, one that he would stand true to, no matter what, but it was a decision he would one day regret.

CHAPTER TWO

A Friendship Is Born

Nearly ten years had passed, and Clayton was starting to fill out. He was tall and square-jawed like his father and grandfather, but he had the fair skin and cobalt blue eyes of his mother, a look that had not gone unnoticed by the girls in school. They would tag along behind him and Jason, teasing them both with childhood laughter.

School would resume in the fall, but until then he was going to kick up his heels with his boyhood friend Jason. They had the whole summer to enjoy!

Will had encouraged their relationship despite the rumors in town that Jason's Indian father had been suspected in starting the fire that killed Clayton's mother and father and several other townsfolk. An angry mob lynched Gray Eyes before the sheriff could launch an investigation. But Will and Reinette did not believe the accusations, and told Jason in no uncertain terms that his father was not responsible for the fire.

Jason's white mother Louise died within a year of the fire and was buried aside Gray Eyes in the Alexander family plot behind the ranch house. Soon thereafter, Jason went to live with his aunt outside a convent in Texarkana.

When she suddenly passed, Will and Reinette asked Jason to stay with them and Clayton at the ranch. He and Clayton were growing up fast, and they had a lot in common. Jason would have chores to do, and he was expected to maintain good grades when school resumed, but they would pay him, too, for his labors and deposit a portion of his weekly earnings in the bank for him. Jason wanted to be a lawyer, something frowned upon by some white folks, but with the help of Will and Reinette, he had a good chance of attending a big university when he graduated from high school. He would need all the money he could scrape up to help defray the cost of tuition, room and board, plus books and other living expenses if he had any hopes of obtaining a law degree. Fortunately, working on the ranch for the Alexander's would help.

They also gave him something he never had before —his own room. As the summer dragged on, he would lay down atop his bed after his chores were completed and ponder his future for hours at a time wondering what it would be like to be a lawyer. The white man still looked down on Indians, and tales of mistreatment were common around town. Often told with hilarity, ranch hands would brag about how they had employed liquor to dupe an old man from his money, or how they once used their horse to drag a "young buck" down the street at the end of a rope for gazing at a passing school girl a little too intently.

These men had no honor, thought Jason to himself. And they contributed little to the community. Hell, if cattle ranchers did not need bodies to mend fence lines and punch cows for market, these guys would go hungry if left to their own devices, or worse, freeze solid on the open prairie come the first winter storm.

And then a smile transposed on Jason's face. What decent woman would want one of these cowboys? They generally had only enough money to get drunk, and they stunk so bad even their horses shook their heads and blew snot out of their noses when one walked by a little too closely.

Yes, he would use the law to get justice, and he would do so with a keen mind and a sharp tongue. He would only use violence as a last resort to defend himself or a friend. In the meantime he would bide his time and be thankful he was living with the Alexander's, who treated him with kindness and respect.

"Your father was a great and loyal friend to me and my son, John," Clayton's grandfather told Jason the day he moved in at the ranch. "We never had to ask, but could always count on him to do the right thing at the right time. When you get a little older, I will tell you more about him, things you need to know. Things that will make you proud to be his son."

Those words were reassuring to Jason. All he ever heard from the white townsfolk was that his father set fire to the hotel that killed Clayton's mother and father and several others. And when they told the story there was fire in their eyes that brought shame to Jason's heart.

Suddenly, there was a knock at his door.

"Who is it?" he asked.

"What do you mean, 'Who is it?' It's me. What, have you got a girl in your room? Open up! Let's go hunting!"

Jason snapped out of his depression and smiled. Clayton was becoming his best friend, and the thought of him sneaking through the brush again trying to skewer a buck with a bow and arrow "Indian style" was just too funny for him to imagine. It's not that Clayton is a bad hunter, it's just that he had not yet learned to be a dead shot with a bow and arrow—or a rifle for that matter.

Click. Jason turned the key and opened the door.

"Well, I don't see her. Dancing Water must be hanging around Red Dog these days. You spend too much time in your room daydreaming and not enough time courting her!"

Jason tossed a pillow at Clayton and laughed out loud.

"Get your boots on and grab your bow. Moses told me they have been seeing a couple of big deer feeding in that strip of trees and brush along the creek bottom a few miles out of town.

"They're whitetails, too. Moses told me they have been showing up around her quite regularly ever since he became ranch foreman. He has seen them back east in Missouri and says they are a lot tougher to get close to than mule deer. Let's go and try to get one."

The two scrambled side by side down the stairs, each trying to knock the other to the floor, until they got outside where they raced to the barn like a couple of jackrabbits. Once inside, Jason went to the far stall and saddled Smokey, the roan Will gave him soon after his arrival at the ranch.

"Isn't it time you rode Red Cloud?" Jason shouted to Clayton from inside the stall, "or is he just too much horse for you?"

"Well," said Clayton, his voice rising, "he won't even let me slip a bridle on much less saddle him."

Indeed, the red stallion would not let Clayton approach too closely. When Clayton reached for the bridle hanging on the opposite wall, Red Cloud reared up again and again making it impossible for Clayton to get close enough to slip the bit in the horse's mouth.

"It's useless," said Clayton as he gathered up his bow and arrows. "I'll ride the mare instead."

"What about Red Dog?" asked Jason.

"What about him? The last time he bow hunted with us he got mad because we teased him about missing. If he was here we would ask him to go with us, but he's not so let's not. At least not this time."

As the two rode out the front gate, Clayton spotted Will walking toward the barn. "I'll be right back," he told Jason. "I think it best we let Grandpa know where we are going."

Clayton dismounted and walked into the barn, but could not find Will. He called his name out several times, but got no answer. Where could he have gone? Clayton thought to himself. He ran around the outside to the corral, but there was no one to be seen. He walked back inside the barn and then over to the mare. He gave up his search and was soon riding back to the front gate.

"That's odd," Clayton said to his friend. "I saw Grandpa go into the barn, but when I got there he was nowhere to be found. He was not in the corral, either. I wrote a note for him inside the barn and left."

The Return of the Laramie Kid

CHAPTER THREE

The Buck

There was not a cloud in the sky as the two rode out, but the air had a bitter nip to it. Autumn was closing in fast, and soon the boys would be back in school. But school was the last thing on their minds on this day. They were going deer hunting!

A few hours later Jason and Clayton were hobbling their horses. Each pulled a pair of deer hide leggings and a pullover shirt from their saddlebags along with a pair of soft-soled moccasins. After changing into their hunting attire, they scampered off toward the creek. Soon they were looking for tracks and other deer sign along the water's edge where the earth was soft and moist.

"Here's another place where deer are crossing from one side of the creek bottom to the next," explained Jason as he pointed to several fresh heart-shaped hoof prints he spied along the banks. "These are all does and fawns however. Let's work our way up river a bit. It's time for the bucks to rub the skin off their antlers. If we can find a few places where saplings are clean and shiny from the rubbing, we'll know there are bucks in the area."

Clayton nodded in approval. Suddenly, a doe broke from nearby cover and sprang across the creek in great bounds with two smaller deer just behind her, their white tails swinging back and forth in mad confusion until they reached the safety of the far shore and disappeared behind a green wall of brush.

"Wow! Do you believe that?" whispered Jason. "They were bedded down right in front of us and we didn't see them!"

"Let's go up the next bend and then split up," suggested Clayton, his chest heaving from the excitement. "You can take one side and I the other. Maybe we will push a few deer across the creek and into each other. I'm itching to get a shot."

"Do you have enough arrows?" chided Jason. "You can have some of mine if you want. I'll only need one sharp one to get my deer!"

"Very funny. I won't miss today!"

As they inched their way around the next bend, they could see another trail the deer used to cross the creek. The trail was lined with several rubbed saplings, the sign they were looking for. The water was shallow here, and Jason decided he would sneak on over to the other side and hunt the far strip of tall cottonwoods.

"I'll go slow up alongside the creek until I reach the deep pool where we fish once in a while. I'll wait for you there. Whistle to me if you get a shot, and I'll cross back over and help you find your arrow!"

Clayton glared back at his friend in mock anger and then started pussy-footing up stream. Soon he was left alone with the sounds of small birds winging through the brush and chirping insects flying overhead in the blue, cloudless sky.

As he swung one leg over a dead fallen log, he spied another freshly rubbed sapling a few yards up the deer path he was following. When he approached the thigh-sized tree, he could see yet another rub gleaming at him just ahead through the brush.

He slowed down even more now, stopping often to lower his head and stare into the shadows for a twitching ear, a bit of antler or the white throat patch of a white-tail buck staring back at him. A swaying sapling 20 yards up ahead caught his attention for a moment, and then it stopped. Clayton stooped down low, and after picking out a few places he could step into without making any noise, inched forward a yard or two without taking his eyes off that sapling before pausing once again.

The sapling started to sway back and forth once more, but this time Clayton could see the head of a whitetail buck, his ears laid back, and the whites of his eyes in clear view, raising and lowering his head as he peeled the bark off the sapling and the dead skin off his rack.

Clayton's heart started to pump faster, and sweat coated the palms of his hands. This was the opportunity he hoped for. He still couldn't shoot however. He had to close the distance a few feet to an opening along the trail where he could thread a shaft.

When the buck resumed rubbing, Clayton reached the clearing without spooking it. Then in one fluid motion he pulled an arrow from the quiver strapped to his back and dropped to one knee.

The buck snapped his head up and looked around, testing the air for danger, and then resumed his rubbing. That's when Clayton slid the arrow onto the bow string, picked a tuft of hair just behind the buck's near shoulder to aim at and brought his bow to full draw. When his finger touched the corner of his mouth, he released the shaft.

The buck jerked its head around, but it was too late for the arrow was already en route to his vitals. At least that is what Clayton surmised, but an unseen branch deflected the shaft at the last moment and sent it ricocheting through the brush.

The buck snorted loudly and bolted through the thick cover with his tail tucked tightly between his rear legs, cracking dead branches with every leap before disappearing along the riverbank.

Clayton was devastated. He waited several minutes after the buck ran off before he stood upright, shaking his head in disbelief. The last time he saw his arrow it had careened off a sapling some 10 yards behind the buck and then skittered along the ground under a carpet of dead leaves and other forest duff for several yards before disappearing entirely from view.

He was sure he could retrieve it so he walked over to the exact location the arrow disappeared and started looking under the leaves, but to no avail. He broadened his search by walking in ever larger circles trying to catch a glimpse of the turkey feathers used for fletching or to feel the arrow's shaft under his feet. He looked in the weeds, under dead logs and inside piles of dead brush, but still no arrow. What was he going to say to Jason?

Crack! A dry twig snapped behind Clayton. He turned around expecting to see Jason, but instead another man came into view, towering over him by a good foot or so, even in moccasins.

"What are you doing here, boy?" bellowed the man, his hand resting on his holster. "This is private property, and we don't allow nobody messing around."

Startled, it took a few seconds for Clayton to gather his senses and fathom what was going on. He had seen this man in town several times before, usually either going in or leaving the saloon. He always looked disheveled, like he slept in his clothes, and he stank whenever Clayton walked past him on the boardwalk.

His friends called him Bull, probably because he was broad-shouldered Clayton reckoned. But he also had a reputation for being a troublemaker around town, a role Bull obviously relished.

"Private property?" declared Clayton. "Since when?"

Suddenly the man stepped forward and with a huge right hand landed his bare fist on Clayton's face, knocking him directly to the ground.

"Don't sass me, boy!" bellowed Bull again, pointing his finger at Clayton. "Now git, or I will rap you with my fist again!"

Clayton rubbed his face. His left eye was already swollen, cutting off his vision somewhat. He reached for his hat and back quiver and stood up, a bit wobbly at first, and draped the quiver over his shoulder. He could see that several of his hunting shafts were splintered, but his bow, still on the ground, did not look to be damaged.

As he brushed the dirt off his hat and squared it back on his head, he turned and looked Bull straight in the eye. "I know who you are," Clayton said bending over now to pick up his bow. "They call you Bull. Not because you are strong or mean-tempered, but because you smell like a dead bull buffalo rotting on the prairie."

Bull slowly lowered his right hand and placed it on the butt of his pistol. "Boy, I *told* you not to sass me!"

CHAPTER FOUR

A Friend In Need

Jason crossed the creek and then looked back just in time to see Clayton disappear around the far bend. Then he too began sneaking in and out of the thick brush looking for a racked deer.

It didn't take long. Almost immediately a spike buck stepped into view only to disappear almost as quickly into the thick underbrush. Jason slowly pulled an arrow from his back quiver and took a few steps forward in the hopes of getting a shot, but the buck was long gone. Undaunted, Jason walked a few feet into the shadows and remained motionless for almost 10 minutes before slipping the shaft back into his deer hide quiver and moving along. You never know, he thought to himself. Another deer might have been nearby.

There were plenty of tracks and droppings on his side of the creek. Jason even spied a few lonesome rubs on a deer run he had come across, but the deer seemed to have moved up stream farther or had bedded down on one of the many grassy bluffs overlooking the creek. He followed the pathway without incident toward the creek where he sat down to take a breather. That's when he heard Clayton's arrow ricochet through the trees and the buck snort and then high-tail it through the cottonwoods.

Jason laughed to himself. Clayton had missed again! He waited in case the deer crossed the creek nearby before he moved upstream to shallow water where he could easily wade across the stream. He climbed the banking and followed the path toward Clayton's position when he heard another voice. A man's voice, and it did not sound friendly.

Jason kept a low profile and moved quickly but silently along the path until he came to a point in the trail where he could see Clayton facing Bull head-on.

When Bull's right hand dropped to the butt of his revolver, Jason's heart began to race wildly and his palms grew sweaty. Clayton was in trouble, big trouble, and he had to do something—and do it right now. He instinctively reached over his shoulder, pulled a wooden shaft from his quiver, and attached it to his bow string in one fluid motion. Stepping out in the open where he could get a clear shot at Bull, he yelled.

"Bull, that six-shooter moves one inch from your holster, and I will send this shaft clean through your fat belly causing your innards to spill all over the ground. You will be nothing but coyote bait by morning, if you live that long."

Bull spun around to face this new adversary, and when he did, Clay pulled an arrow from his quiver and nocked it.

Bull had not counted on the half-breed showing up, but he was not about to back down, either. He kept his hand on the butt of his pistol and hunkered down ready to draw.

"This is private property, and I'm telling you boys to git and git right now if you know what is good for you."

Clayton felt sick to his stomach, and his heart was throbbing in his throat. Bull sounded meaner than ever, and for the first time in his life he knew he was in trouble. Real trouble. He had to think fast.

"No good can come from this, Bull. Calm down, and we'll back our way on out of here."

There was a sense of honesty in Clayton's voice, a sense of reason that Bull picked up on. He doubted he could get them both before one of them sent an arrow through his gizzard. He relaxed a bit and stood up, then motioned for the two boys to skedaddle.

The confrontation ended nearly as quickly as it had begun, and soon Clayton and Jason were back at the horses. Neither said a word until after they stuffed their moccasins and hunting clothing back into their saddlebags and mounted up.

Clayton was the first to speak. "Something isn't right, something is going on. Bull is protecting that section for a reason, and I'll bet it isn't good."

Jason eased Smokey up alongside the mare and blessed himself. "I agree. But what could it be?"

They both turned in their saddles and looked back in time to see Bull climb up a bluff to where his horse was hobbled. Just then another rider appeared from out of the shadows. He looked somewhat familiar, but at that distance they could not make out his identity. There was something odd about the manner in which he filled the saddle, as if his right leg did not fit the stirrup properly. It appeared the two men were having a heated conversation when Bull mounted up and the two rode off in different directions.

"Whatever is going on up there," Jason said in a low tone, as if the two men on the bluff could hear him, "they don't want anyone to know about it."

"I agree," whispered Clayton, not taking his eyes off Bull. "I wonder what it could be?"

CHAPTER FIVE

The Rendezvous

Bull climbed the bluff to where his horse was hobbled and was stowing his moccasins in his saddlebag when he heard another horse come up behind him.

"I didn't hear any shots," the man on the bay said. "What happened?"

"I caught the two of them along the river hunting deer. I scared them good. They won't be back here again."

"I told you to kill both of them, didn't I? When I give you an order, I mean for you to follow it, without thinking."

"And I told you I would take care of it," barked Bull in return. "The two of them don't have a clue what is going on. The boy is retired judge Wilford Alexander's grandson, and the half-breed lives with them on the family ranch. If I had killed them there would be a dozen deputies out here poking around. Is that what you want, boss?"

The man on the bay scowled. He knew Bull was right, but he didn't like his orders being ignored, either. He had hired Bull to do some of the dirty work that needed to be done. He didn't like hired gun hands standing up to him.

Not one bit. But for some reason he trusted Bull's judgment.

Bull mounted up and looked over his shoulder at the man. "Anything else?"

"No. Take a different route back to town," said the man in a mild conciliatory tone. "I am not going back to the ranch until sundown, and then I am going back to town myself."

Goliath slithered along the rocky outcropping with careful determination, but stopped suddenly when he felt the pounding of a horse's hooves clip-clopping up a nearby trial. The horse would pass close by, too close for Goliath's comfort, and he froze. Normally he would coil up and send out a warning by rattling his tail, but this day was different. He would hold his ground and if left unmolested would let the large animal pass by unharmed.

The horse soon came into view, and Goliath could see that it had a human rider, a danger he had long ago learned to avoid. He dared not move now for fear he would be spotted. Instead, Goliath let the blinding sun and his natural skin tones camouflage the full length of his nine-foot eight-inch body.

The horse and rider's attention was momentarily diverted by the sounds of rocks rolling off the hillside and crashing into the dead brush below. By the time the horse and rider looked back up the trial, they were safe and well past Goliath's striking range.

Goliath remained still however for he felt the tremors of another animal, a smaller and less fortunate critter padding towards him along the same rocky outcropping. It was a young coyote, and it too was on the hunt. It also had remained motionless in the brush so as not to be seen by the horse and rider, and when Bull passed by the coyote, it scurried away to safety in the opposite direction—and into big trouble.

Goliath was hungry. He had not eaten in several days and needed a meal soon to maintain his 32 pounds of bone and muscle and scaly skin.

The hapless coyote never saw the rattler until it was too late. Goliath had coiled up and struck the young song dog's left flank once with lightening speed as he padded unknowingly past the serpent. The coyote yelped and jumped back after the strike, but it was too late for him. With a triangular shaped head twice the width of a man's clenched fist and twin fangs nearly two inches long, a measured dose of lethal venom had already entered an artery and was pumping quickly through the coyote's bloodstream as he tried to make good his escape. It was to no avail however, for the young song dog was already dead on his feet.

Goliath did not move after the attack, but let the frightened prairie wolf flee the scene under his own power. Several minutes later he flicked his forked tongue in and out to locate flecks of scent from the fleeing coyote. He tracked it this way for almost 75 feet until he came upon the still-warm body of the young coyote. Goliath slithered around to his victim's head and poked it several times to make sure it was dead. Then he unhinged his lower jaw and opened his mouth wide over the pup's face, and two hours later Goliath had completely swallowed the deceased song dog head first. He instinctively retreated then to a dark enclosure where he could digest the juicy dog at his leisure.

The Return of the Laramie Kid

CHAPTER SIX

The Rescue

On the way back to the Colby ranch, Clayton and Jason met up with Reinette. She was taking the buckboard into town for supplies and had spotted the boys riding in the opposite direction, probably heading for home. She stopped in the shade to see if the boys wanted anything special before she resumed her mission.

"I saw the note you left Will," she said as she shielded her eyes from the glaring afternoon sun. "Did you see any deer?"

Clayton and Jason looked at each other and shrugged their shoulders. They had already decided to keep quiet about their encounter with Bull until they could talk to Moses more about it. Moses was foreman and the best ranch hand on the payroll, and both boys had come to rely on his opinion.

They dismounted and tied their horses to a nearby bush where Smoky and the mare could rest a spell. It had already been a long day.

"We got a shot, but the arrow ricocheted into the

underbrush," said Clayton somewhat sheepishly as he moved out of the sun and into the shade.

"What do you mean, 'we'?" laughed Jason. "It was you that missed, not 'we'!"

Reinette smiled. She loved the camaraderie the boys had developed. She hoped it would carry them through the next several years until they were both out of school and well on their own. She worried less when they were together, knowing they were looking out for each other.

Jason poured some water out of his canteen and into his cupped hand for the horses. Then he took a swig himself before offering the canteen to Clayton. Soon they recounted their hunt that morning to Reinette, leaving out the details of course that might cause her unnecessary concern. Her inquiry as to the welt on the side of Clayton's head went unanswered until she again asked Clayton what was wrong with his face.

"Deer hunting is a rough game," Clayton replied in playful sarcasm. "I got knocked to the ground by a stinking bull while looking for my lost arrow. It doesn't hurt much, just my pride got injured."

Clayton knew he was only telling half the truth, and he wanted to change the subject before the real truth came spilling out of his mouth.

"Where did Grandpa go this morning?" asked Clayton, thinking himself quite clever at the diversion.

"I don't know where Will went to, but he's around somewhere," replied Reinette as she faced forward and straightened herself out in the seat. She then turned to face the boys again. "I'll be back in time to finish making supper.

There is a bottle of jam and a few biscuits on the shelf next to the stove. That should hold you until I get back. I was planning on a venison roast, but I guess we will have to wait," she said jokingly before slapping the reins.

The buckboard creaked, and Jake and Big Jim moved out of the shade and into the sun. Suddenly, the two steeds reared up and tried to break free, their eyes bulging with fear. Reinette tried to control the horses, but they were bucking wildly now with their front legs flaying the air in a frantic effort to get loose from their harnesses.

"Grandma, what is going on?" yelled Clayton. "Tighten up on the reins or they will break away!"

That is when Jason spotted the trouble. A foot-and-a-half-long viper had slithered out of the sun looking for a bit of shade and had spooked Jake and Big Jim. Both steeds reared up again on their hind legs and then broke into a gallop, taking the buckboard and Reinette down the road at a frightening pace, running over the hapless snake's body, and crushing its head in their mad dash for safety.

They were a quarter mile down the dusty road before Clayton and Jason could mount their horses. By then a big lead had developed. They could see Reinette trying to calm the horses, but Jake and Big Jim were at a full gallop now and would not stop until they were totally spent from the run. The road up ahead was rough with ruts, and the boys feared the buckboard would throw a wheel or even tip over if they could not catch up to it in time.

Suddenly, from a cloud of dust on a bluff above the road, a dark red stallion appeared. Its rider slapping the reins on the horse's flanks back and forth as horseman and stallion weaved their way down the bluff in unison, and then onto the road between the runaway buckboard and the two boys who were trying to catch up.

"Who is that guy on the big red horse and fancy Mexican saddle?" yelled Clayton as Jason pulled up alongside.

"I don't know," shouted Jason. "I have never seen him before! Look at him go. He rides like the wind!"

Dressed in wool trousers, with a double bandoleer crisscrossed over a sky blue cotton print shirt, and a gray sombrero, the mysterious rider leaned low over the saddle and with twin pistols cross-mounted and glistening in the afternoon sun, pushed his stallion even faster. "C'mon Red Cloud, giddy up!"

Horse and rider soon came off the bluff and with clumps of crimson dirt flying in the air behind them, galloped up a slight incline and onto the cart road. Red Cloud was in top form now as he gathered up speed, quickly closing the distance behind the runaway team.

As the buckboard rounded a bend, Reinette screamed, pulling back hard on the reins. It was no use. She knew the perils ahead on the road and braced herself against the corner of the seat with her foot on the brake. When the brake gave way, all Reinette could do was hold on...and pray.

Then out of the corner of her eye, a flash of blue and a rider on a big red stallion galloped up and alongside of Big Jim. He reached out, grabbed the reins, and slowed the buckboard down as if he had done this a hundred times before.

When the buckboard rolled to a stop, the rider quickly dismounted and eased Reinette to the ground. "Oh, Will, thank God! I couldn't stop the rig, and I feared we were going to wreck just up ahead."

She wrapped her arms around Will, wiped a few tears from her face, and then stepped back, putting her hands on her hips. "What on earth are you doing out here?"

Will dusted himself off and gazed down at the ground before looking into Reinette's eyes. "It's John's birthday. I could not let it pass without wearing John's clothing and taking Red Cloud for a ride around the ranch."

Reinette hugged Will again. "I know...I know. I miss him too."

Jason and Clayton caught up to the rig and jumped off their horses.

"Are you all right Grandma?"

"Yes, I am fine thanks to Will."

They looked over and were surprised it was Will who was riding the red stallion.

"Grandpa, where did you learn to ride like that? That was incredible! It was as if you and Red Cloud are a team!"

Will just smiled and looked over at Reinette. "Red Cloud is a special horse. He knows I will not put him in harm's way without good reason."

"I have never seen that silver-studded saddle before, either," blurted out Clayton suddenly, still excited from the near disaster. "Where did it come from? And what are you doing in that shirt?"

"Not now, boys. And not a word of this to anyone, understand? I will explain everything to you when you get older. Let's get back to the ranch and have some supper. I am hungry as a bear. By the way, did you boys get a deer?"

Will tied Red Cloud to the buckboard, climbed on board,

and immediately sat down next to Reinette for the short ride home. Clayton and Jason just looked at each other in awe as they followed them back to the ranch. What was he doing dressed like that? And where did he get those old twin Navy Colts and the Mexican saddle?

Could it be? They had heard rumors about Will being associated with the Texas Rangers, maybe a secret Ranger, but they were just that, rumors. Clayton and Jason had never seen Will pin on a star, and never had they seen him with that saddle or those particular Navy Colts for that matter. Clayton and Jason shook their heads and tried to put that notion out of their heads.

At least for the time being.

CHAPTER SEVEN

A Few Hours Later

They soon arrived back at the ranch, tired but glad the ordeal ended without anyone getting hurt. Reinette wasted little time talking after Will helped her out of the buckboard. She went straight into the house, cleaned herself up, and then busied herself in the kitchen preparing supper.

Everyone was hungry, that she was sure of, and she already had a big meal in mind. She left a large pan of beans laced with brown sugar and bacon strips simmering on the stove next to a cured ham set to a low boil in another cast iron pot. The fire had long gone out, as she knew it would, but the pan was still warm to the touch. She pulled some kindling from the wood box next to the stove and soon had a warm fire blazing in the pit under the four removable metal plates.

She hung an empty pail under the pump a few steps from the stove and filled it halfway with water. A short trip to the root cellar produced an apron filled with potatoes from her garden and a pair of yellow squash. Reinette soon had the potatoes and squash heating up on the stove while the beans and cured ham simmered nearby. Supper would be ready in 30 minutes she reckoned. She stepped outside in the cool air and told Moses before returning to the kitchen to set the table.

In the meantime, the boys put the horses up in the barn and after wiping them down stowed their saddles, bridles, saddlebags, and other gear in the tack room. They then sat down on a bench and examined their archery tackle, vowing to repair Clayton's arrows, at least those that could be salvaged, before they went deer hunting again. They would talk to Moses about their confrontation with Bull in the morning.

As they walked out of the barn and toward the ranch house, Clayton and Jason could see Will and Moses unhitching Jake and Big Jim.

"You need any help, Grandpa?"

"No thanks, you boys go and get ready for supper. We'll be in shortly."

As Clayton and Jason disappeared into the ranch house, Will turned to Moses. "Take care of Red Cloud and stow the saddle and other gear while I change out of these clothes, okay? I think Clayton and Jason are wondering what they really saw on the road to town earlier this afternoon. I do not want them to know the truth about me. I made a promise to Reinette."

CHAPTER EIGHT

Moses Sheridan

Moses was up and out of bed and outside doing chores by pink light. As ranch foreman, he enjoyed this quiet part of the day. It gave him an opportunity to mull over the previous day's events as well as plan for the work that had to be completed during daylight hours.

He inspected Red Cloud for any injuries he might have incurred on yesterday's ride through the wild country with Will, and was pleased the horse was none the worse for the encounter. Moses was one of the few people who could approach Red Cloud without the stallion getting fidgety and rearing up. All it took was a few soft words and a gentle caress along his flanks and Red Cloud would turn his head toward Moses' body and whinny. It was as if Red Cloud understood Moses' heart, trusting him implicitly and knowing that above all he would always try to do right.

After checking on the stock, Moses returned to the bunkhouse to clean up for breakfast. While washing his hands he looked up into the mirror. Moses didn't know how old he was for sure, but he thought he was in his late forties or early fifties. Gray hair and crow's feet around his eyes wouldn't let him think he was any younger even though the scars on his face and neck had dimmed somewhat with the passage of time.

A couple of fist fights defending himself from drunken cowboys accounted for a scar under his left eye and another on his lip, and a fall from a horse into a barbed-wire fence several years ago left a 10-inch scar on his neck that took longer than usual to heal due to some sloppy suturing. Nonetheless, he was still lean and fit thanks in part to a life-time of hard physical work, and at nearly six foot even, he was nobody to tangle with without reason.

Moses' parents were long dead, but he had an older sister back east who worked as a servant at a girl's finishing school. They had lost touch with each other years ago after Moses' wife and baby girl died in childbirth.

Moses rinsed his hands, looked back into the mirror, and began to reminisce. He was an angry black man back then. He had suffered the slurs and physical abuse of racism growing up, and when Martha died, he drifted south through St. Louis and Springfield, Cairo and Memphis, and then over into Ft. Smith, Arkansas, looking for a new start. A stopover proved to be a life-changing event for Moses for it was here that he learned how to stay focused and get the job done even when dealing with rowdy men.

Hungry after not eating for more than two days, and exhausted from walking all day and sleeping fitfully under the stars, Moses entered Ft. Smith hoping to find some-thing to eat and a place to rest his weary body. At least for a few days. He was heading for Texas, and he was going to get there no matter how long it took. A sign near the livery stable led him to take a job as an orderly in Dr. Carl Roger's clinic. Room and board and a friendly staff soon helped make Moses feel welcome.

He was fascinated with the various procedures Dr. Rogers performed, but he was even more enthralled with the manner in which Dr. Rogers talked to his patients. He always seemed to say the right words to help put a patient at ease.

"You have to calm the mind before you can heal the body," Dr. Rogers once told him. "Most people nowadays only see a doctor when they are desperate. They need to know that you are capable of doing the doctoring, and that means you have to first earn their trust before you can do any fixing.

"You know what I am talking about, Moses. I have seen you work with some of the patients, the ones that are scared, like Mike Nelson's boy, when he broke his leg falling off his horse. You have a smile and an easy manner about you, and the kid liked you from the git-go. What did you say to Bobby again, "We don't shoot teenage boys with broken legs, just their horses." That got a hearty laugh out of him and we were able to quickly set his leg."

Yes, Moses knew what Dr. Rogers was talking about, and it was good to hear it from somebody else, especially a prominent white man who was not a racist. It confirmed for him that it was not the mere color of a man's skin that made him good or bad—Lord knows he'd had dealings, good and bad, with most every race—but rather how he interacted with other people. Indeed, it was amazing how far a man could go when dealing with others by first offering up a little respect.

It was a lesson that would soon save Moses's life.

CHAPTER NINE
An Old Friend

Moses worked for Dr. Rogers for nearly eight months, running errands, helping sick folk in and out of bed and easing the worries of others, but the drive to move on never faded. He did not miss being hungry and cold at night, but he did miss life in the open and under the stars. He liked sitting next to a crackling fire, roasting a rabbit he snared earlier in the day or maybe a fat raccoon he caught descending from a den tree as the day's light was fading. He liked being on his own, free to do as he pleased and taking care of himself frontier style.

He about made up his mind to talk to Dr. Rogers about leaving the clinic when he returned from the apothecary that afternoon. It would not be an abrupt departure, but rather one that would give everyone time to say good-bye. He would especially miss the reading and writing lessons Dr. Rogers gave when time allowed. Moses was already feeling poorly about his decision.

As he neared the far side of Main Street, he heard footsteps running up from behind and a familiar voice call out his name.

"Moses! Moses Sheridan!"

Moses turned around and came face to face with the likes of Jimmy Grant.

"What! I don't believe it! Jimmy Grant!"

Moses grabbed Jimmy's extended hand, shook it fervently for several seconds, and then stood back to get a full view of his friend. "I never thought I'd ever lay eyes on you again! What in the dickens are you doing here in Ft. Smith?"

"What are you doing in Ft. Smith?" echoed Grant.

"Well," stammered Moses, "I help out at Dr. Roger's clinic out near the hotel. Been here since last fall. What about you?"

Jimmy laughed heartily, obviously thrilled to see a familiar face in the middle of nowhere. A face he had not laid eyes on since, well, since before the war.

"I just got into town. I've been riding for a few ranches in the Indian Territory for two years now, but I'm done with that. I wants to go back home for a spell and see my family."

"Listen," said Moses, grinning from ear to ear, "I need to finish this errand for Doc, but then I'm free for the rest of the day. Can ya meet me later? We can eat at the hotel and catch up on all the news."

"Yup, sure can!" replied Jimmy. "I'll see you at six o'clock." And with that both men went their separate ways each looking forward to seeing the other in a few hours.

At the hotel later the two men ate heartily and talked about their early years for hours. It was good for both of them to look back at their childhoods, and find out what happened to their friends and neighbors.

"It's been more than a couple of years now," said Jimmy as he pushed himself back from the table. "But the last I knew, the Davenport brothers, Ezrah and Ike, both died in the war. Nobody knows for sure where, but most believe it was at Gettysburg. Young Peter Gooden got hisself drowned swimming with some friends at night. They didn't find his body for several days. His funeral was terrible sad."

"Lord, I remember Ike and me fishing with our cane poles one spring evening," Moses chimed in after draining the last from a cup of coffee in a single gulp, "catching a mess of bullhead at the mouth of one of the feeder creeks. His momma fried them up the next day and we ate every last one of them! You were there, too, as I recall, and so was big Ed Ryan."

"Yeah, Ryan was there. But that was after you whooped that bully behind the hardware store. He thought you'd turn and run, but instead you hit him first and so hard you broke his nose and busted a tooth off right at the gum line, splitting half his upper lip wide open as I recall. He had it coming though, no doubt about that, and that no-good-for-nothing never gave you no trouble after that day. In fact, Ryan never gave nobody worry when you were around.

"You never did back down from nobody, Moses. You always held your own even when the other guy was mus-cled up and a mite bigger. I always respected you for that, although at times I wondered if you might be a bit touched!"

Moses tilted back in his chair and laughed. He did not see himself as crazy in the head however. He knew that if he backed down from someone like Ryan, the bully would own him. And no man, black or white, likes the thought of being owned. But Moses also knew he had to pick his fights carefully. Discretion was always the better part of valor.

Jimmy folded his hands and leaned across the table. "You're gonna love this, Moses. The last I heard, Ryan married Betty Burton and is helping Mr. Helms out at the livery stable. Back then he was big and fearfully mean, but we have growed some since then, and today he barely stands over five feet tall. And he don't give nobody any lip. You cured him of that!"

The two men talked on for several more hours before agreeing to meet for an early breakfast the next morning. Later Moses smiled as he lay in his bed thinking about all that transpired that evening. Imagine, Jimmy Grant, right here in Ft. Smith. What are the chances?

The next morning Moses and Jimmy met again. There was plenty of banter and lots of laughs as they ate and reminisced.

"You been traveling alone all this time?"asked Jimmy. "Eh gads, you musta been awful lonesome at times."

Moses nodded his head. "Sometimes it ain't bad to be lonesome. I met up with a younger black last summer just outside Cairo on my ways south to Memphis. He seemed reasonable enough, at least at first. Asked where I was heading and if he could tag along for a few days. I told him south, and that I didn't mind much if he came along. I didn't know he was aiming to bushwhack me and take my pouch though."

"How come you trusted him so easy?" asked Jimmy as he leaned forward across the table. "You was always the cautious one, especially when it came to strangers."

"We had talked a bit in town around the livery stable a couple of times where I got a few hours work every other day or so," replied Moses, "enough for a grub stake, but I was still surprised to see him on the trail. I had mentioned to him I was just passing through town on my to Texas, but didn't think much of it until later.

"What happened?"

"The kid was real likeable at first, telling me funny stories and all. Called himself Poco. After a few days I got used to having him around. Then one morning just as the sun was rising I caught him pawing through my pouch. He found my wife's wedding ring and was holding it up to the sky and admiring it."

"What'd ya do?"

"I asked him real firmly what in the hell he thought he was doing! That's when he pulled a pocket pistol from under his shirt and pointed it at my face. 'Old man', he said sarcastically. 'You just lay right there and you'll be just fine. I'm taking this ring and the money you made tossing horse shit out the livery stable. You owes me this for keeping you company these past days.'

"Without saying another word the kid took my boots that I had drying next to the fire and tossed them in the brush, then took off running down the trail. He was long gone by the time I got up and put my boots on."

"You're lucky he didn't cave your head in, Moses!"

"Yeah, I know. But that wasn't the last of it. I gathered up my goods and began to follow the trail the kid took when six white men rode up directly behind me, real unfriendly like."

"What'd they say? What'd they want?"

"They was real mad, you could tell. 'You seen a young buck nigger, about half your age old man?' asked one of them. When a white man calls you that, you knows you are in big trouble. 'He stole some cash from one of the store keeps, and word has it he was last seen heading for Memphis. He goes by the name Poco.'

"Without hesitation I told them the truth," said Moses, "and what had just happened to me. Then I pointed out the direction I last saw Poco. One of the riders dismounted, grabbed my pouch and dumped the contents on the ground. Then he turned around and hit me twice in the head with his pistol. 'You'd better not be lying or we'll hang your black ass right next to Poco's when we catch up to him! Understand old man?'

"I was terrified. I can hold my own against most men one-on-one, but there were six of them and they meant business. I averted my gaze and kept my head low and they rode off in the direction Poco ran off to. I thought I had seen the last of them, but two hours later they came riding back dragging Poco stark naked behind one of the horses. He was already half-dead. I identified him and then they showed me my wife's wedding ring and I told them that was it. That was the ring he stole from me."

"Tell me they gave it back to you," said Jimmy, his voice rising.

"No, they did not. They put Poco on a horse, slid a noose around his neck and as he screamed for help kicked the horse out from under him. He jerked about wickedly, but it was no use. He was dying and I couldn't help him. After a while they still weren't sure Poco was dead, and they wanted their rope back, so they all took turns shooting him as he dangled in the air, laughing when they shot his privates."

Jimmy's face turned ashen, and he lowered his head shaking it in disbelief. "How'd ya get away?"

"I thought they were going to hang me, too. I was so scared I couldn't run even if I had the chance. Dared not touch my hatchet. I was just plain numb. As I stood there they coiled up their rope and told me to stay out of Calico or they would hang me on the spot. I guess they saw me as a victim, too. That's the last I ever saw of them."

"Do you think Poco stole the money they was talking about?" asked Jimmy, his eyes bulging out of their sockets.

"All I knows for sure is that he stole from me. He didn't deserve to hang though, not like that. From then on I learned to be real careful on the road. I stick to the shadows and ease off in to the brush if I hear someone coming."

Jimmy just nodded his head, knowing that Moses was giving him hard-earned practical advice. His mind started to drift off somewhere, but Moses continued speaking bringing Jimmy back into the conversation.

"Ya know," added Moses, "when it comes to dealing with six armed and angry whites, you have to be real careful. If I had mouthed off to them insisting I get my wife's ring back I'm sure I would have been swinging from a rope right next to Poco."

Suddenly Jimmy grew quiet and averted his eyes from his childhood chum. "I'm riding out this morning," said Jimmy in a low voice. "My horse is at the livery stable and I'm all packed up and saddled. I had planned on leaving yesterday, until I bumped into you crossing the street."

"What's the rush?" replied Moses, his mouth agape. "We just hitched up again after all these years!"

"It's nothing you said or did, my old friend, but I am in a rush. I ran into some trouble a few weeks back, and I think it best for me to keep riding east, at least until it blows over."

"What kind of trouble, Jimmy?"

"Not real serious trouble. I didn't shoot anybody if that's what you're thinking, but it's nothing you can help me with, either. I'll be back, maybe next spring I'm thinking, after visiting my family for a spell. Will you still be around?"

"Probably not. I am heading for Texas, and soon I hope. Certainly by the end of the month."

"Texas! The war's been over a long time, Moses, but Texas sided with the Confederacy. They still hang black folk down there for walking on the wrong side of the street. Hell...just for being black. I'm beginning to think I have been right about you all along...you are a bit touched in the head!"

Moses grew serious. "Listen, Jimmy. I'm a free man. Washington says so. And I am going to live free, for a long time I hope, and when the good Lord does take me home, I'll die in his arms a free man. I'll not have it any other way!

"Now don't you fret none. If need be, I can bow my head and say 'Yes, Massah,'" continued Moses, dropping his head and shrugging his shoulders in mocking fashion, "or I can turn around and walk away if I think that'll be all it takes to ease the tension. Violence will be my last resort however, and it will be measured against the consequences very carefully."

Moses paid for their meals, tipping the waitress handsomely for all the extra time the two spent jawing at the table, and walked Jimmy to the livery stable. Jimmy tossed a coin to the youngster who brought him his horse, checked to be sure his saddle bags, Spencer lever-action, and bed roll were secured properly, and mounted up. Then he leaned over the saddle and extended his hand once again to Moses.

"It was awful good seeing you again, Moses. I will look you up next spring if I am around."

"If you see my sister, tell her I think about her and her family often, and that they are in my prayers," said Moses while shaking hands one more time.

Without further talk, Jimmy lifted the reins and turned his horse east. "Adios Moses," said Jimmy as he dug his spurs into his horse's flanks.

Jimmy did not want to leave Ft. Smith, but he knew he had to keep moving. He also realized he better be thinking and behaving more like Moses. After what he did a few weeks back, he sure didn't want to end up like Poco.

The Return of the Laramie Kid

CHAPTER TEN

The Nelsons

Moses finished washing his hands, dried them off, and then looked back into the mirror. A smile came to his face as he remembered Dr. Roger's kindness and how his words of encouragement helped him deal with some troubling times. Indeed, it wasn't many weeks later, after leaving Ft. Smith, that he was confronted with one of those troubling times.

That is when he first met the Lone Ranger.

Moses had seen the flames from a campfire up ahead and stopped behind a fallen tree trunk to take a better look. He had learned his lesson south of Cairo. You couldn't be too careful these days. Bandits, bushwhackers, and others of ill repute often plied their trade on travelers, and a black man alone on foot could be an easy target for some men bent on robbery—or worse.

Moses could see one cowboy tending a cast iron skillet over the fire, a young man, maybe in his late teens or early 20s, wearing a home-spun shirt and woolen trousers. He was unarmed, although a Spencer was leaning up against a log within easy reach, and a gun belt with a pistol showing was lying atop a bedroll next to the butt of the rifle.

Moses could smell something tasty wafting through the early evening air, probably backstraps sizzling in that skillet he reckoned. A yearling buck mule deer was hanging from a nearby tree, its hide peeled back conspicuously along the right top side from the front shoulder to the rump. It was a fresh kill.

The scene seemed harmless and inviting, but that was before he noticed two horses hobbled along the creek, not one. And suddenly a shiver of fear raced up Moses' spine. Where was the other rider?

Moses slowly backed up until he was out of sight of the fire and then began to loop around the campsite. He was hungry, but not that hungry. He would cross the creek and then cut back up to the trail, making camp a mile or so down the trail where his fire would go unnoticed by anybody riding past.

At least that was his plan.

Click! "Mister, don't move. I have a Patterson Colt aimed at the back of your head, and I will shoot if you don't do exactly as I say."

"Okay," said Moses, startled at the sudden presence of another man.

"What are you doing sneaking around our camp?"

"I mean ya no harm," replied Moses, his tone a bit more relaxed. It was obviously a boy's voice that held the gun. "I'm just passing through and saw your fire. I was thinking about dropping in for a friendly visit, but had other thoughts when I saw that there were two horses. Didn't know if I would be welcome or not, and decided not to take the chance."

"You can turn around. Just keep your hands where I can see them and away from that hatchet. Where are you hailing from?"

Surprised at how young the boy looked, Moses looked him in the eye and answered him with respect, calmly and directly, like Dr. Rogers taught him. "I am coming from Ft. Smith where I lived for the past several months or so working in a medical clinic with Dr. Rogers."

"Oh yeah? Doc Rogers you say."

"Yes sir! He's a fine man. Do you know him?"

"I have heard tell of him. Did you ever fix a broken leg belonging to Bobby Nelson?"

"Why, yes," replied Moses, a bit relieved that maybe the two had something in common.

"I understand he got it tripping over his own feet while admiring a well-dressed lady crossing the street," replied the young gunman with a bit of a smile.

"Well, that might be what he told you," replied Moses in a low cautious tone, "but the truth of the matter is Bobby got thrown from his horse and hit the water trough next to the stable. Broke his lower leg in two places. We got it set right quick though, lucky for him. How's he doing?"

The boy slid his Colt back into its holster and smiled broadly. "He is doing just fine, thanks to you and Doc Rogers. Bobby is my cousin, on my father's side. You must be Moses."

Moses could feel the tension melt away from his arms and legs. He shifted his body weight and straightened up before exhaling a huge sigh of relief.

"My name is Nelson, Bill Nelson, and that is my older brother Brian back at the camp. We are just coming back from Ft. Smith ourselves. Our dad died last month, and we rode over to tell Uncle Mike the bad news and give him a daguerreotype we found of him and dad fishing when they were younger. We are going to be here for a day or two, resting the horses, before continuing on toward home."

Bill Nelson turned and headed toward the camp. "C'mon up the fire and have some venison. Brian shot a mule deer this morning when it meandered down to the creek for water. The backstraps should be about ready to eat by now. Do you happen to have any salt, Moses?"

Moses could tell that Bill was also relieved. And the fact that Bill called Moses by name indicated that he did not see Moses as a threat any longer.

"Yes sir, I have a packet or two of salt in my pack. Be glad to share it with you. I'm sorry to hear about your father. How did he die?"

Bill stopped dead in his tracks, looked down at the ground for a moment, then turned and looked at Moses through glistened eyes. "My brother thinks he killed him."

Bill slowly turned and continued on back to camp. Puzzled, Moses followed right behind not knowing what to think. When Brian saw the pair enter the clearing, he dropped the fork he was using to turn the backstraps and stood up, wiping his hands on his thighs.

"What's going on?" he asked. "Who's this?"

"His name is Moses. Don't reckon I heard your last name," said Bill turning to Moses.

"Sheridan. Moses Sheridan. How do you do."

"Moses is the orderly who helped set Bobby's leg. And he broke it as we thought...he fell of his horse...and then into a water trough!"

Brian smiled and welcomed Moses into camp. When Bill turned back to the fire to check on the backstraps, Moses realized Bill had lost a lot of weight recently. His pants did not fit right, and were gathered up and pleated around his waist and then held in place with a thin strip of rawhide.

Moses slipped his hand into his pouch and pulled a poke of salt from within and then handed it to Brian. The meat sure looked good and smelled even better. The salt was a luxury, something the Nelson boys appreciated after several weeks alone on the trail.

He was famished, but did not want to appear too eager. Once Brian handed Moses a plate of steaks however, he ate them without hesitation, washing them down with warm water from his canteen.

Moses took an instant liking to Bill and Brian. Two brothers taking care of business after their father's death showed Moses they came from a close-knit family. And that they shouldered the responsibility willingly.

Moses also sensed that something was eating at Brian, bothering him bad, and that impression continued when later Brian's appetite seemed to wane after only a few mouthfuls of venison. He just wasn't hungry, at least as hungry as he thought he should be. He, too, realized he was losing weight, and it was not from the long ride. He was always bone tired by the end of the day and sleep would come easy to him, but after only a few hours of shut-eye he would awaken with nagging thoughts of his father. It would take several hours of mulling over the details surrounding

Joe Nelson's death before he would once again drift off into the blackness.

Brian put his plate down and looked over at Moses who was leaning up against the log looking relaxed and sated. "What's a black man doing traveling alone in these parts?" asked Brian in an easy tone. "Lord, there are men out here who would shoot you for your boots, never mind because you have colored skin."

"I've been walking for over two weeks ever since departing Ft. Smith. City life is not for me. I need to be outdoors so I'm heading for Texas and hoping to get a fresh start. Maybe on a ranch."

"Moses," said Bill with a huge grin on his face. "You are in Texas, and have been for quite some time!"

Moses' eyes widened, and when he looked over at Bill to gauge his reaction, he saw that Bill, too, was laughing. Moses broke out into a wild roar of laughter himself, slapping himself on his thigh. "Well, I'll be dam..., uh, I'll be a danged pole cat. I'm in *Texas!*"

CHAPTER ELEVEN

Strangers in Camp

Taking the Nelson brothers up on their invitation, Moses unrolled his blanket and bedded down near the fire with his hatchet at his side. The trio was soon sound asleep, the coals from the campfire crackling and popping as the yellow and orange flames faded into the night.

Moses woke up once to see Brian sitting upright and poking at the dying embers with a stick, but Moses soon drifted back off into the darkness, wondering what was gnawing at Brian so fearsome it would rouse him from a much-needed night's rest.

The next morning Moses was the first one up. He went down to the creek to wash his face and hands, and then he scoured up and down the bank until he came up with a half-dozen duck eggs. Slipping them into his hat one by one, he left a couple for the mallard hen and returned to the campsite. The boys were up by now and had the fire blazing once again.

"I'll gather some more wood," said Moses as he slipped his hatchet from his belt, and off he went. In the meantime,

Brian and Bill took a quick swim in the creek and returned to the campsite just as Moses was greasing up the skillet with mule deer fat for the duck eggs.

"Add some venison to that fry pan while it's still fresh, will you Moses?" asked Bill. "I'm as hungry as I was last night. Is there any salt left?"

"Yes I will and yes there is," said Moses as he walked over to the deer carcass hanging nearby in the early morning shade. He had to peel back more of the hide as flies had already laid their eggs on the exposed flesh. Their buzzing annoyed Moses, but food was hard to come by, and you never wasted any of it if you could help it.

After breakfast, Brian sat away from the campfire by himself staring at the ground while Bill and Moses talked between themselves. Moses was a few years older than the Nelsons, but close enough to their age to have much in common.

"You seem to favor that hatchet a bit," said Bill as Moses adjusted the leather thong that held it fast to his belt.

"Most white folk see a black man packing a side arm," answered Moses as he stood up and righted himself, "and they get nervous. Some get downright mouthy, and once in a while you find one who actually thinks he should take it away from you. But a hatchet, well, is not much bigger than a buffalo knife, and is often viewed as useless against a Colt or a Spencer."

"You any good with it?" asked Bill quizzically.

"Pick a target and I'll show ya what it can do if called upon in a righteous manner."

"Okay," said Bill as he looked around the campsite.

"How about that log over yonder?"

"Too close," replied Moses. "See that dead knot on that tree over there, about four feet above the ground?"

"That's got to be close to 60 feet!" exclaimed Bill. "You're going to lose your hatchet in the brush."

Moses smiled back and motioned to Bill with his hand to stand out of the way. Then Moses slid his hatchet from his belt and stared at the tree as if he were about to set it on fire. Without saying a single word, he took one step forward and with a quick flick of his wrist unleashed his hatchet from his right hand. *Whoosh! Whoosh! Whoosh!* It rotated through the air with a slight whisper, striking the knot dead center.

Bill's jaw dropped, and even Brian stood up for a better view. "Can you do that all the time?" asked Bill.

"When it needs to be done, I can do it," replied Moses rather matter of factly. "It just takes occasional practice to keep my eye sharp, that's all."

Moses retrieved his hatchet and sat down next to Bill. Both of them were all smiles now.

"I'm sorry I pulled my gun on you yesterday," said Bill rather sheepishly. "I didn't know who you were or what kind of man I was up against."

"You can't be too careful these days," replied Moses as he turned to look Bill in the eye. I would have done the same thing so don't give it another thought."

Bill nodded his head and smiled back. Moses was easy to talk to, and Bill felt more and more comfortable around him as time passed.

Brian got up and walked over to Bill and Moses. "What are you two talking about?" asked Brian in a low tone and looking a bit lonely. He sat down next to Moses and stretched out.

"Oh, I was just telling Moses I made a mistake in judging him a bit too harshly yesterday when we first met."

"You have to be careful with my kid brother around," said Brian with a wide grin. "He can put the sneak on a puma. And that ain't no joke."

Snap! Suddenly, and without any other warning, two men walked into camp. A white man leading a white stallion and wearing a black mask over his face, and an Indian companion dressed in buckskins leading a brown and white pinto.

Startled, all three jumped to their feet. Brian glanced over to his rifle leaning up against the log next to the campfire. His and his brother's pistol holsters were lying atop their bed rolls—and out of reach!

Moses put his hand on his hatchet and stepped forward between the Nelsons and the two strangers, shielding Brian and young Bill from possible harm.

CHAPTER TWELVE
The Silver Bullet

"Stop right there. Who are you and what do you want?" demanded Moses, staring the masked man straight in the eyes.

"We're friends," replied the masked man, holding his arms out and away from his two pistols, "and we are not looking for trouble. We saw the smoke from your campfire from quite a ways off, and we're hoping to find the Nelson boys, Brian and Bill."

"Do not come any closer, stranger. You either, Injun. What do you want them for?"

"The whole county is on the lookout for them. Their father died well over a month ago, and the boys have not been seen since the funeral. We're all hoping the boys have come to no harm."

The Indian was mute, but there was sincerity in the masked man's straightforward reply. Still, Moses was not letting his guard down.

"If you're not looking for trouble, then why the mask?"

demanded Moses, his voice stern.

"The mask keeps my true identity a secret, but have no fear. I work with the law, not against it. I wore it when I spoke with Mrs. Nelson several days ago. She asked me to help find the boys and if I came across Brian to tell him no one blames him for his father's death. It was just a passing argument between a father and his firstborn, and she wants both her boys home safe and sound."

Brian started fidgeting about and looked first at his brother and then Moses before locking eyes on the masked man. "What else she say, mister?"

"She said your father left his muzzleloader to you in his will. The Billinghurst .36 caliber sidelock you took your first deer with when the two of you went hunting together along the creek that flows through the north end of the ranch. He put a notch in the stock, and told you there was plenty of room for more notches as you grew older and more experienced."

That clinched it for Brian. The masked man was telling the truth. Brian began to tremble with pent-up emotion as memories of the day he and his father argued bitterly surfaced.

"I don't deserve to go home," whispered Brian, his voice starting to quiver.
"I said some things to him I did not mean, and I said them in anger. I wish I could take them back, to tell Dad how sorry I am, but it's too late for amends now. Dad is dead... and I killed him."

Bill's eyes watered up. He knew how poorly his brother was taking their dad's demise. "Brian, Dad said some bad things, too. He had been in a sour mood for over a week, fretting over the ranch I guess and the calves and the leaky roof. It was inevitable you two would lock horns. He knew you wanted to leave, to strike out on your own, but he couldn't bear the thought."

Brian turned and wandered off toward the stream, his shoulders drooping and his hands stuffed in his pockets. He needed to be alone and think.

Moses watched Brian until he disappeared down the trail. "Let him go," said Bill turning to Moses. "He's been through a lot and needs to be alone for a spell. I think it's going to take a long time, however, before he can look himself in the mirror and smile once again. He really believes he pushed Dad to his death."

"Bill, do you mind if Tonto and I unsaddle our mounts and rest a spell? We have been on the trail for some time looking for you two boys."

"No, no absolutely not," replied Bill apologetically. "I, we, appreciate you and your Indian friend coming out all this way to find us. I'll stoke up the fire and put some coffee on. I'll fry up some mule deer steaks, too. I bet you are both hungry. It'll give us time to get better acquainted."

Moses relaxed his stance and for the first time dropped his hand away from his hatchet. He now trusted the masked man and his Indian companion and looked forward to learning more about these two strangers. And he wanted to learn more about the squabble Brian had with his father, too.

Everyone was hungry, and soon all you could hear around the camp were the sounds of knives cutting meat and forks stabbing that meat on metal plates, and coffee cups clanging one after another as each was set down empty on nearby logs and stones.

With the meal complete, the men started talking again. Moses was the first to open up. "Bill, I 'm sorry to see Brian agonizing over your father's death. He is not eating properly and he's lost a lot weight...his clothes just hang on him like a scarecrow...and he seems sad all the time. The longer it drags on, the worse it could get. Do you see where this is swimming around in your head, too? Tell me more about the argument between Brian and your father. Maybe I can figure something out."

Bill sat up and adjusted his legs so he could be more comfortable. Moses was right. The argument and Dad's death were gnawing on his bones like a porcupine on a sun-bleached antler. He had trouble sleeping once in a while, and it was interfering with his relationship with Brian, too. He needed to get this off his chest—and now was the time.

The Lone Ranger and Tonto stood up and were about to wander away from camp to give Bill and Moses some privacy when Bill stopped them. "No, don't go. Ma asked you to find us, and this will help explain why we have been gone for all this time. I don't want you to think Brian and I are disrespectful, but things happened right before Dad died that need to be taken care of, and the only way we knew how to do that was to leave home for a spell. We meant no harm to anyone."

Tonto looked over at the Lone Ranger, lifted the coffee pot, poured each a fresh cup, and then sat back down. Maybe they could somehow help the brothers, too.

"What exactly did they argue about?" asked Moses in a quiet tone as he handed his cup to Tonto. Tonto filled the tin with hot coffee and handed it back to Moses.

"Dad had been complaining that his back ached and his teeth hurt and he sometimes was having trouble breathing," explained Bill. "He wanted Brian to help him pull some stumps down by the creek, but Brian thought it was a ploy and told Dad he was not going to help him...not that day or any other day. Dad, in a fit of rage, told Brian to get out and stay out. He was no longer welcome at the ranch and could no longer call it his home. Brian told Dad he was nothing but an old fool...grabbed most of his belongings...and rode out. Nobody saw Brian again 'till the funeral.

"Later that day Ma brought Dad's lunch out to him. She wanted to speak to him about the argument, but found Dad sitting under a cottonwood tree soaked in sweat and having trouble breathing again. He looked pale and complained of a heavy feeling in his chest, like a horse was standing on him. She knew Dad was sick, real sick, but there wasn't anything she could do but stay with him."

"Did your father say anything to her?" asked Moses.

"Yeah, he told Ma he should not have been so hard on Brian. He knew Brian was feeling his oats and wanted to find himself, but Dad needed him at the ranch. Then Ma said Dad got a glaze in his eyes and started mumbling about the past. He remembered taking Brian deer hunting and watching Brian shoot his first deer, a mule deer doe. He said he was so proud of Brian and his eyes welled up a bit. Dad asked Ma to find Brian, he wanted to talk to him, but Brian had already left the ranch."

Suddenly all eyes were on Brian as he walked back into camp. "Everything my brother says is true except for one point," declared Brian loud and clear. "I also told my father if he ever came within arm's reach we would find out who was boss right quick. His eyes widened when I said that. He knew I meant business...and I would've thrown a punch right then and there if he came any closer to me."

Brian sat down on a log next to the fire, obviously spent from all the emotion. "Actually, Bill, I didn't know Dad asked Ma to find me. If I had calmed down and was not so pig-headed, I would have helped Dad pull those stumps that morning and he would be alive today. I got him so riled up that he worked himself to death. I killed him as sure as I am standing here in front of all of you right now."

Brian hung his head. "I never got a chance to apologize. I never told my dad I was sorry for what I said to him. He died thinking I hated him."

"Brian," said Moses in a hushed tone, "you did not kill your father. I learned from Doc Rogers that your father's shortness of breath, his backaches and his toothaches were all signs his heart pump was about to give out. That's probably why he was cranky and on edge those last few days. He knew deep down inside that something was frightfully wrong...and he feared he was dying. It would not have made any difference if you were still at home or had left the ranch to stay with friends. He would've died either way.

"An untimely death can eat a man up, I know," Moses continued. "As a husband, I know what it's like to lose your wife, and as a father, I know what it's like to lose a child. My Martha died during childbirth, bled to death in my arms as our newborn daughter cried uncontrollably in the middle of the bed. We were able to say good-bye to each other, but our daughter died before I could kiss her and hold her in my arms. I never got a chance to tell her that me and her mom loved her very much. She just suddenly stopped crying, and she was gone before I could bite the cord.

"Brian, what you do not understand is that your father was also sorry about the argument. He knew he was not feeling very good, and he feared the worse. He took it out on you, and later like you, he, too, wanted to apologize for his words. That's why he told your mother he wanted to see you. He was thinking about the good times you and he shared, like the two of you hunting, and wanted you to know that he was not mad at you...just proud. Can you imagine, Brian, your father was thinking about you in those ways as he drew his last breaths, and wishing he had time to say, "I'm sorry, son. I said things to you I did not mean to say."

Brian jerked his head up and looked at Moses straight in the eyes. Suddenly he realized that what Moses was saying was undoubtedly true. His eyes welled up, knowing now that he was not responsible for his father's death and that his dad was indeed as sorry about the argument as he was, and agonized about it right up to the end.

Brian walked over to Moses, shook his hand, and then got up and squatted next to Bill. "I need a swim. Care to join me?" The two brothers wandered down the trail to the creek and cooled off in the water for a spell before returning an hour later. Moses was sharpening his hatchet when Brian walked directly up to him. "Thanks, Moses, for setting me straight. I am beginning to see things differently now, and I think I am going to be okay. It is going to take some time, but I'm heading out today with Bill. I cannot wait to get home and see Ma again."

The Lone Ranger and Tonto were already saddling Silver and Scout, relieved that the boys were going home safe and sound. "Moses smart man, Kemosabe," said Tonto as he tightened the cinch on Scout. "He have way with words. He know how to help boy see truth."

"Yes, Tonto. Moses is also a brave man. He quickly placed himself between us and the boys when we walked into camp. He sensed danger and was willing to defend the boys, armed only with a hatchet. The West could certainly use more men like him."

Moses, Brian, and Bill soon walked over to the Lone Ranger and Tonto as the two tied on their bed rolls. As they shook hands, the Lone Ranger asked Moses what his plans were for the future.

"Brian and I are doubling up on his horse, and he's giving me a ride part way to the next town. They offered me a bed at their ranch, but they have some family fence mending to deal with now that their pa is gone. I will find work somewhere nearby so I can stay in touch and give them a hand should they need it."

The Lone Ranger reached down to his gun belt and pulled out a silver bullet. "On your approach to Colby, take the west fork to the Alexander ranch and give this bullet to Wilfred Alexander. He's always looking for good men, and the Alexanders will treat you with respect."

Suddenly, a loud ringing brought Moses back to the Alexander ranch. Reinette was hammering the dinner bell outside next to the kitchen. Breakfast was ready, and he was so hungry reminiscing about his past he could eat a dead rattlesnake—raw! But first he had to unlock a metal box he kept next to his bed for safe keeping, and peer inside.

Yes, the silver bullet was still there.

CHAPTER THIRTEEN
Riding Lessons

Clayton and Jason were already at the table wolfing down tall stacks of flapjacks and several long crispy strips of fried bacon when Moses walked through the door.

"I have a fresh pot of coffee brewing, Moses," said Reinette as she wiped her hands on a towel, "and there are more flapjacks and bacon if you give me a minute to set them on the table. These two boys eat like four full grown men! Where are the rest of the hands?"

"They're finishing up some chores, but will be along momentarily," replied Moses as he lifted a tin cup off a wooden peg next to the stove and peered into the coffee pot. "I expect them to be as famished as these two lads. Of course, Clayton and Jason spent most of yesterday hunting deer while we rode our tailbones moving the herd down to the creek and then over to the northern slopes. I think we will keep them there for the rest of the month. How did you boys do on those whitetails I told you about anyway? Did you see any deer, or did you spend the day swimming?"

Jason looked over at Clayton and then put his head

down, pretending to be more interested to what was on his plate than talking about yesterday's ill-fated deer hunting trip, especially with Reinette still in the kitchen.

Clayton wiped his mouth with the back of his hand and shrugged his shoulders. "We saw some deer, and we, I mean I, got a shot but missed. I need to talk to you later about that stretch along the river after breakfast, Moses. I thought that was open range?"

Moses sensed there was more to the story than a hunting arrow going awry. "Sure, Clayton, but first I needs to get some coffee in my gullet and some of those golden brown flat cakes. Reinette, do we have any of that maple syrup still around, the jug we traded for in town?"

Reinette laughed. "That syrup was gone in a week, Moses. Don't you remember?"

Just then the kitchen door opened and in came the rest of the ranch hands, all clamoring for coffee and something hot to eat. Reinette got busy serving while Clayton and Jason pushed themselves away from the table to make room for the others, and stepped outside in the early morning air.

"We have got to find out what is going on along the river," whispered Clayton as he pulled his hat down over his forehead. "Something just ain't right."

Daylight was coming fast, and you could almost see to the barn when the plodding of boot steps filled the air. It was Will, unusually late for breakfast. "You boys already eat?" asked Will as he whisked past the boys, pulled the door open, and went into the kitchen.

"Yup," replied Clayton as the door closed.

"Yup," echoed Jason. He turned to Clayton, and with

a nod toward the barn, asked in a low voice, "What do you want to do now?"

"Let's hang around here for a bit until Moses finishes his breakfast. Then I want to ask Gramps if he will teach me to ride Red Cloud like he did yesterday."

When Moses walked out the door a half-hour later, the sun was up and casting shadows across the coral. He caught sight of Clayton and Jason standing just inside the barn near the open door, and walked over directly to them.

"Okay, what happened yesterday?" he asked.

Clayton and Jason relayed the day's events to Moses, who listened intently until Bull's name entered the conversation. "I'm proud you boys stuck up for each other and held your ground against a bully, but ya have to be careful with Bull, very careful. He's big and mean-tempered, and I think he would just as soon punch ya in the face as shoot you in the belly. Do not agitate him without good reason!

"As far as that being open range, it always has been. But it's always been open to anyone who wanted to work it. I cannot imagine what Bull would want with that stretch. Maybe the water, but there's plenty of water this year. No... I also think there is something peculiar about his presence. You boys stay away from there for now and let me ask around town."

The conversation ended quickly as Will and the other ranch hands spilled out into the yard after breakfast. Will spotted Moses and walked over for a quick update on the cattle they moved yesterday.

Clayton spoke first however. "Hey Grandpa, how about letting me ride Red Cloud this morning? I want to learn to ride as fast and hard as you did yesterday afternoon."

Will put his head down, contemplating Clayton's request, and then turned to Moses. "You got some spare time?"

Moses stepped back a few steps and looked across the yard. Things seemed to be in order. Lopez, Vazquez, Tall Bear, and the other hands were already saddled up and heading out, but when they overheard Clayton's request, they rode over to watch what they expected to be a fine rodeo. Their other chores could wait until later in the morning.

"Yes, I sure do," smiled Moses. "I'll saddle Red Cloud up and bring him around pronto. This is going to be interesting to watch!"

Will turned to Clayton. "Listen up. Red Cloud is not like any other horse we have on the ranch," warned Will. "He's stronger and faster than any horse I've ever owned— smart, too. And cagey. He still has his manhood, and the juices always seem to be flowing. If he gets a whiff of a mare in heat, he will buck up and take flight with little warning.

"Now, he'll take your lead if you are quick to show him you're in charge. But if he senses fear from you or you act indecisively, he won't want anything to do with you. Stay alert. If he sees an opening, he'll take quick advantage and toss you to the ground without ceremony, understand?"

Moses brought Red Cloud out of the barn, all saddled and ready to ride. "Is he okay after yesterday's romp?" asked Will.

"Yup. The ride ya gave him tired him out a bit, but he needed to release some of that stored-up energy. If we don't work him regularly, he will be tough to control. Even so, Clayton, ya going to have your hands full this morning."

Will walked over to Red Cloud, stroked his near shoulder, and then ran his hand down the left foreleg. Red Cloud remained still, turning his head into Will's chest when Will stepped forward and adjusted the halter. "Good boy," said Will softly. "Good boy."

Clayton stepped forward, stroking Red Cloud's left flank, and then started to walk around behind him when Will grabbed him by the shoulder. "You don't want to do that right now, Clayton. Red Cloud is not sure what you're up to yet, and he might give you a swift kick in the nuts. Come around front and let him see you better. Let him get a good nose full of your scent. Let him lick your skin. Talk to him in low tones. You have to establish a trusting relationship with this animal, or you and him will be off to a rocky start, understand?"

Jason watched in amusement as Clayton and Red Cloud became acquainted. Clayton grabbed the reins and led Red Cloud around the barn and back, all the while talking slowly and quietly.

"Ready?" asked Moses.

"I think so," replied Clayton. Moving slowly Clayton slipped his foot into the left stirrup and then just as deliberately eased himself up into the saddle. Red Cloud turned his head, looked at Clayton, and...waited.

"How does it feel to be sitting on a lightning bolt?" asked Will and Moses simultaneously.

"I've ridden every horse on the ranch but this one," exclaimed Clayton enthusiastically. "I can tell he is all horse. He's coiled up like a rattler ready to strike! Good Lord he's powerful!"

"Where are you going to take him?" asked Jason.

Clayton slumped his shoulders and looked back

at Jason. "Oh, I don't know. Maybe just around the far meadow and back."

"Stay focused, Clayton. Ya looking a mite too cocky," warned Moses. But it was too late. Red Cloud, sensing Clayton's relaxed spirit and lack of direction, reared up on his hind legs and came down hard on his forelegs, nearly dislodging Clayton from his saddle. "Whoa!" exclaimed Clayton, pulling back tightly on the reins. "Whoa, Red Cloud!"

Wide-eyed, Clayton looked over to Will and Moses for an explanation, spreading his arms and opening his hands in a show of bewilderment—and inadvertently dropped the reins on Red Cloud's neck.

This time Red Cloud bucked up on all four legs several times before squeezing his front legs tightly together and lowering his head nearly to the ground. Clayton, barely holding on, slipped over Red Cloud's withers like an eel sliding out of a water bucket, and somersaulted to the ground, quite unceremoniously.

Clayton sprang to his feet, obviously embarrassed, and dusted himself off while trying not to wince or wiggle around too much. His pride was bruised more than his butt, but he wasn't about to show it.

"You okay?" asked Jason as he, Moses, and Will rushed forward.

"Get right back on him," yelled Will. "Right now!"

Again Clayton slipped into the saddle, and again Red Cloud tossed him to the ground. Again and again horse and rider fought for control until Will stepped forward. "I think you both have had enough for today. Walk Red Cloud around until he calms down, let him know you do not approve of his behavior, and then let Moses take over.

"You did fine, Clayton. I admire your tenacity, but it's going to be a while before you and Red Cloud become partners. You aren't sure where you're going, and he senses that. One minute you want him to turn right, and the next time you are trying to force him to go left. You give him his lead and then you pull back on the reins. He simply doesn't know what you want, and as a result he does not trust you...yet. But eventually if you stick with it, you will get there."

Moses, with his right arm crossed over his abdomen, his left elbow resting on his right hand and his left hand clenching his chin, shook his head and laughed. "Clayton, you have got a lot to learn! But I agree with Will...I think you was born to ride Red Cloud."

CHAPTER FOURTEEN

Boys to Men

The buckboard wagon creaked and groaned along the line of businesses, past the blacksmith and the livery stable, the bank, Western Telegraph, and the Land Office before turning north onto Main Street and then past the barbershop, Maggie's Emporium, and the Bell Hotel on the corner of Main and Jefferson. It had rained heavily during the night, and the streets were filled with rivers of red mud.

Saturdays always brought customers from the outlying ranches, and this Saturday was no exception despite the threat of more rain. Mrs. Temple and her daughter Judith waved good morning to Clayton and Jason as the two women tip-toed across a shallow rivulet and then up a slight rise to the boardwalk. There they stomped their feet to loosen the mud that clung to their shoes, and then continued on their way to Barnaby's Dry Goods, right next door to Doc Hayes' office. A new shipment of cloth had arrived, and they couldn't wait to see what colors and patterns would look best on each other.

Jake and Big Jim pulled the buckboard through the slop and the mud with little effort, stopping only when they reached Thomas' Hardware. As Clayton maneuvered the rig around the back of the store, they caught old man Winston pissing out the second-story window. Too lazy to use the chamber pot thought Clayton, as he stepped back and out of the way. A steady yellow stream arced 12 feet down from the open curtains and splashed on the ground in the alley below. No wonder the side streets reeked.

Moses had given Clayton and Jason a list of hardware supplies to purchase, including a large bottle of liniment for the horses, six pounds of one-inch tacks to help repair the roof in the bunkhouse, a pound of general-purpose four-inch nails, a roll of steel wire, a half-dozen steel traps to help dwindle the ranch's ever growing cougar population, and three 10-pound wooden kegs of black powder for blasting stumps along the river.

Next was a quick stop at Davis' Guns and Ammo for several boxes of .45 shells for Lopez, Blondie, Lefty, and Tall Bear, and two boxes of .45/70 cartridges for Moses' trap door Springfield. He was itching to take out a mountain lion himself.

While Mr. Davis was filling the order, Clayton and Jason admired the array of Colt and Smith & Wesson pistols on display inside a glass case. "Soon you and I will turn 18," whispered Clayton as he ran his hands across the top of the case. "Gramps said if we pass school and got a diploma we could have any pistol we admired. I have got a shine for the new Colt .45, the one on the left next to the used Paterson."

"Yeah, me too," replied Jason, not taking his eyes off the six-shooter. "I already got two handguns, Dad's twin cap-and-ball Colts that Mom left for me, and I wouldn't mind owning that worn Winchester lever-action but that Peacemaker is one fine shooter, too."

A dark shadow passed by the front window and stopped at the entrance to the shop. The boys casually looked up from the gun case to see who it might be, and when the door swung open, in walked Bull.

Startled, the boys backed up against the case...and winced. Not so much from the sudden appearance of Bull, but from the overpowering rot-gut stink of the man.

"I see you boys aren't deer hunting today," snarled Bull. "That means you learned your lesson...don't let it slip your mind."

Bull then directed his attention solely to Clayton and pointed his finger at his left eye. "Looks like your eye healed up just fine. Your father wasn't so lucky. I scarred him up good. Real good!"

Stung by the memory of Bull's fist, Clayton leaned forward and mockingly pinched his nostrils together. "I see you haven't learned your lesson about washing with soap and water, Bull. You still stink like a dead buffalo rotting in the sun!"

"Boy, I told you before not to sass me!" growled Bull again, furious at the insolence. He took a step toward Clayton, clinched his fists, and squared off to him. "Do I need to teach you that lesson once again?"

As quick as lightning, Davis pulled a 10-gauge coach gun from behind the counter, and with huge hands cocked both external hammers simultaneously. "I got buckshot in here Bull, and I will blow you to bits if you don't stop messing with my customers. Boys, here is your order. Be sure to thank Moses and the rest of the hands for their order when you get back to the ranch. Tell them I appreciate their business."

Caught by surprise, Bull immediately backed up and let the boys out the door. Then he turned around and faced Davis. "Okay! Okay! You can put that scatter gun away. I just wanted to scare those two. I only came in for a couple boxes of .45 Schofields for my Smith & Wesson. You got any?"

Davis put the shotgun back and limped over to the far shelves where he displayed the ammunition.

"Your leg bothering you today?" asked Bull, trying to make amends.

"Some," replied Davis. "When it feels like rain I can't bend my knee much. I get by, but it sure is painful to ride my horse without extending the stirrup four inches or so."

Two minutes later Clayton and Jason watched Bull head up the street toward the Half Dollar Saloon with two boxes of bullets clenched side by side in his huge left hand. "Clayton, praise the Saints, whatever possessed you to mock Bull? We're both unarmed, and he had us cornered in there!" whispered Jason angrily.

"Yeah, I know, but Bull had his back to Davis. When I saw Davis reach for that 10-gauge, I figured nothing bad was going to happen to us. Bull didn't know it, but we actually had *him* cornered!"

"There you go with that 'we' again! Let's finish off our list and get back to the ranch. From now on, I'm toting my .45 when we come to town. And what the dickens did that comment about your father mean? Did Bull have a run-in with him at some time?"

Clayton looked stunned and did not say a word. He just climbed up into the buckboard and released the brake.

The wagon next stopped at the supply store. Chicken

feed was not on the list, but Tall Bear mentioned a shortage to Clayton that morning as Jason was rigging up the horses. Four 25-pound bags should do it for now, Clayton figured.

And speaking of shortages, Clayton picked up several packets of Gayetty's Medicated Paper for the privy. Despite the occasional wood splinter, the flat sheets of medicated bum wipe had become more of a necessity over the years than a luxury item for the ranch hands. Dead leaves and clumps of dried grass simply did not get the job done anymore.

Then, a sack of flour, two sacks of cornmeal, a 50-pound burlap bag of Missouri potatoes, two 20-pound bags of raw coffee beans, and a couple pounds of salt were loaded onto the wagon and covered up with an Osnaburg canvas tarp. After lashing the tarp down tightly to the frame, using a frayed length of rope, Clayton went back into Frank's Feed and put a new bolt of rope on the billet and buried it under the tarp. He jumped back up into the seat, shook his head in disgust, and then went back inside Frank's for a new 25-foot chain he figured Moses would need to help pull those stumps. It, too, was not on the list.

Finally, they were ready for home. Clayton turned the wagon around, dodging two miners from up north trying to cross the street without getting wet or muddy. One miner shook his fist playfully at Clayton and then laughed. "Dang it son, I sure would hate to get runned over today. It's my 75th birthday, and I ain't had a bottle yet to help celebrate the blessed event!"

Clayton slowed the team to give them ample time to cross and smiled back, thankful he had never taken up drinking. It was the devil's brew, and those who imbibed on a regular basis soon became infected by its charms. A dismal life of despair and sorrow was sure to follow.

Before they could get out of town, however, the sky opened up with cracks of thunder and jagged bolts of lightning, and within a matter of a few minutes the wind began to howl like a pack of coyotes on the hunt, sending sheets of heavy rain slicing sideways across the street. Clayton had second thoughts about returning to the ranch and turned the team into the livery stable to wait out the tempest. No use taking a soaking if they could avoid one, especially with a wagon load of dry goods.

"You got any of your own money?" asked Jason as he jumped down from the rig. "I sure could use a hot cup of coffee and bite to eat. Let's go over to Sally's while we wait for the storm to let up."

Clayton just smiled at Jason. He knew what he was up to. Dancing Water was a waitress at Sally's, and Jason was sweet on her. Shy, but sweet on her nonetheless. This would be a good time for him to see her and maybe find out if she might be interested in him somewhat without having to actually talk to her.

Clayton also knew that Red Dog had taken a liking to Dancing Water. He was not shy and, in fact, was quite bold with women. Some would say disrespectful, but those voices might also be jealous. Tall, taller than Clayton or Jason, and muscular, Red Dog sometimes bragged after classes about his many experiences with the older girls living in town. Indians were generally not allowed in a white schoolhouse, but any family who worked at the Alexander ranch was given the opportunity to learn how to read and write—free of charge.

Miss Carlon would arrive each morning and teach the day's lessons in the one-room schoolhouse the Alexander's built north of the bunkhouse, and any child who failed to attend would get a visit from Will or Reinette. All in all there were nearly 18 students attending. Lopez's twin sons Pancho and Pablo were regulars, and for the most part so was Tall Bear's eldest son, Red Dog.

Jason pulled his rain slicker out from under the seat of the buckboard wagon and covered his head and shoulders with it as he ran for Sally's with Clayton struggling to keep up. Sure enough, once inside there was Dancing Water waiting on tables. She smiled when she saw Jason and Clayton pick a table in her section.

Jason was clearly relieved Red Dog was not present. Sure, they were friends and got along well together for the most part, but he did not want to get into a struggle with him over Dancing Water. At least not until he learned how she actually felt about him.

"Coffee?" smiled Dancing Water. "It's good and hot for a rainy day."

Jason looked up at her and smiled back. "Yes, please, and how about a rare steak and a couple of sunny-side eggs for me and a like order for Clayton? He likes his eggs over easy. We're both starved."

"Coming right up. I will be back shortly with your coffee, Jason. It's nice to see you today. What are you doing in town on such a miserable Saturday morning?"

"It's nice to see you, too, Dancing Water. We came to get supplies for the ranch, and were on our way back when the storm struck. We stowed the buckboard in the livery stable until the rain passes."

"Well, I am glad you did! I'll be right back with your coffee. Jason, do you take sugar with your coffee?"

"No thanks," replied Jason with a wide grin. "I'm already sweet enough!"

Dancing Water threw her head back and laughed. "Oh Jason, everyone knows that you are the sweetest boy in Colby!"

Jason eased back in his chair and smiled wide as Dancing Water took their orders back to the kitchen. Clayton looked over and poked him in the ribs. "She likes you, pal. She really does!"

Sally's was busy that morning as many cowboys and ranch hands came in to get out of the rain and get a cup of coffee and something to eat. Jason and Dancing Water did not have much time to talk after she brought them their breakfasts, but when the rain stopped and Clayton and Jason pushed away from the table, she made it a point to catch Jason's eye and wave good-bye. Jason tipped his hat in return, smiled, and headed back to the livery stable with Clayton walking alongside.

"Man," he said looking up at the gray sky, "don't you just love a day when it rains!"

CHAPTER FIFTEEN
Clayton's Father

Jason was in high spirits after seeing Dancing Water, making the two-hour ride back to the ranch seem short despite the wheel ruts and sloppy road conditions. Lefty, Tall Bear, and Lopez emptied out of the bunkhouse when they arrived to help unload the wagon while Jason unhitched the team and led Jake and Big Jim back into the barn.

Jason stayed in the barn with Tall Bear and Lefty while they finished putting up the new supplies. The kegs of black powder were stored by their lonesome in a water-tight shed a couple hundred feet behind the barn. Nobody wanted to take chances and no chances were taken.

Clayton could hear them telling jokes and laughing as he crossed the yard and went up to his room to get out of his wet clothes. He would have enjoyed the banter in the barn, but he was preoccupied with the morning's events, especially Bull's comment about his father. What was Bull referring to? Bull only recently showed up in town, maybe a year or a year-and-a-half ago, whereas Clayton's father had been dead over 10 years. Where could they have met, or was Bull trying to rile Clayton all the more by insulting his father?

Heck, Bull didn't even talk like he knew Clayton's father was dead, just that they apparently once got into a fight.

For the next several months Clayton could not get his father out of his mind. What kind of man was he? He heard the rumors while growing up how his father refused to work at the ranch when he came of age, and instead drifted from ranch to ranch and town to town working only when he was hungry or needed money. He could be gone for months at a time with no contact with friends or family, and then show up some afternoon riding a different horse. And when he was in town he would most likely be seen sitting outside one of the saloons all day long harassing passersby and flirting with the whores.

Late one evening on the way back from the privy, Clayton overheard Tall Bear and Lefty talking about his father from inside the bunkhouse. He stopped in the darkness and listened intently by an open window.

"Clayton has turned out to be a hard-working hand around here," declared Tall Bear after drawing smoke through his pipe. "He don't complain about the weather or the workload, and he's always willing to do his share without having to be asked. You know, for being the boss' grandson, he could get away by doing far less around here, but he ain't like that. Not one bit. I like the boy just fine."

"Yeah, you're right. I like him just fine, too," replied Lefty. "It sure is a good thing he did not turn out like his father. You didn't know him, Tall Bear, but John Alexander could be a son of a bitch when he wanted to be. He was a troublemaker on the ranch and couldn't wait to leave home when he was old enough to fend for himself. He married that pretty Sally Lister, moved to town, and then they had

Clayton within the year. I don't know how in hell she put up with him. Never home, carousing with the whores. Yet, she doted on him and never questioned him, at least in public, about how he made his money or who he spent it on. Even so, when he was with her and she with him, it was as if they had a marriage made in heaven."

Clayton was pleased that Tall Bear and Lefty respected his position at the ranch and how he carried out his duties, but learning that his father was not well liked at the ranch and that he appeared to be a notorious philanderer greatly disturbed him. It was no wonder then that Will and Reinette barely spoke of him, although it was clear they still grieve terribly for their sons and Clayton's mother even after all these years.

"You know," went on Lefty, "it is odd that John's older brother Jacob seemed to be just the opposite of a man. He became a deputy in town, and treated everyone evenly. He was well-liked and well-respected. Even the cowhands he threw in the tank for being drunk on Saturday night hardly ever had a bad word to say about him. He even helped me find work here at the ranch when I was down and out and plenty hungry. Too bad he got himself shot fighting those rustlers. Well, anyway, that's what we're told happened. The governor's office took over the investigation and it wasn't long thereafter that the shooting and the killing was forgotten. Nobody was ever charged for the crime."

Clayton always seemed to know that his Uncle Jacob was likeable and honest, and that his uncle's death was never clearly solved. What he heard Lefty say next however gave Clayton great pause, sending him into a wicked state of extreme agitation.

"What troubles me the most now, all these years, is the fact that John Alexander and Bull rode together up north."

Lefty's voice trailed off and was lost in the commotion that was circling around inside Clayton's head. How could that be true? Bull had threatened Clayton and Jason's lives on two occasions, and his continued presence in town was seen as nothing but trouble.

Clayton wanted to call Lefty out and tell him to shut up...or else, but he quickly thought better of it. Clayton knew there were rumors floating around about his father and uncle. Lefty, however, was supplying details that Clayton was not aware existed. Lefty was not a liar, yet he claimed Bull and his father were at one time one of a kind.

Clayton kept Lefty's conversation bottled up for several weeks while it gnawed greatly on his innards. Early one morning after yet another night of tormented sleep, he awakened Jason before dawn and told him the entire story including the bit about Bull riding with his father.

"How can that be?" asked Jason, sitting on the edge of his bed and rubbing his eyes. "Your father and Bull were friends? Partners? What would be the point?"

CHAPTER SIXTEEN
The Truth Be Told

"I saw Clayton's teacher in town today," said Reinette as she set the table for the evening meal. "Actually, I think she saw me first, as I left Miller's Store," she went on. "She met me crossing the street and asked if she might have a word with me, about Clayton. Moses waited with the buckboard as we went to the hotel and sat in the parlor. Mrs. Gustafason was kind enough to pour us each a cold glass of water from the well out back, and then gave us our privacy."

Will hung his hat on a peg in the hallway and turned to Reinette. "More trouble?"

"I am afraid so," she said. "Clayton has been asked to stop by during the day after his chores are finished to help out in the classroom and to be an inspiration to the students to finish their schooling.

"Miss Carlon, however, told me Clayton has been disruptive in her class several times during the past two weeks. Talking out of turn, laughing out loud at the younger kids when they make a mistake. He got into another fight with that Richy boy, and Big John O'Mally's eldest son had to break it up—again. Will, Clayton cut that boy's lip with his fist!"

"He's at that age, Reinette, when boys will be boys. He needs to sort out who he is and where he stands with the rest of the grown boys in town. I know that Richy boy. I don't doubt he had it coming. He needs to be taken out behind the powder crib and whacked a couple of times. That will straighten him out."

"I understand all that. My brothers were rebellious, too, but not like Clayton. He's been skipping his chores around here once in a while, and he told Moses he wasn't worth much around here 'cause he's too old to go to town by himself anymore and how he has to go with me and take the buckboard instead. He knows Moses can take care of himself; I don't know why he talks that way."

"I'm surprised Moses didn't give him a stern talking to right then and there," scowled Will. "It's a good thing he knew Clayton's father, or he might have!"

"And there's more," said Reinette, lowering her head. "He had a run-in with Sheriff Sweeney's new deputy, Mr. Ross, in town yesterday."

"I heard all about it from Moses just before I came into the house," replied Will, shaking his head side to side. "It seems old man Miller thought he saw Clayton pocket something, maybe some penny candy, and yelled at him just as Ross was walking past the storefront window. As it turned out, old man Miller was not sure what he saw, but Clayton spewed some choice words toward Miller, and let loose some profanity on Mr. Ross, too, 'for sticking his nose in where it don't belong'. Clayton walked away in a huff, and Miller and Ross just threw their hands up in the air not knowing what to do."

"Miss Carlon did say Clayton cussed at old man Miller and Mr. Ross, but both men didn't want to take it any further, out of respect for you I suspect. I guess she was really trying to tell me that Clayton's lack of respect for other people is getting worse with age, not better. I hate to say this Will, but Clayton is nothing like his father or his uncle...or you. I am, well, I am afraid I'm ashamed of him right now. He has quickly become a ruffian and a bully and only seems to care about himself and the here and now. And the worst of it is, well, I have come to believe it's all my fault...and, oh, supper's ready. Why don't you call the hands in to eat, and we'll talk some more tomorrow."

CHAPTER SEVENTEEN
A Promise No More

Reinette started a crackling fire in the cast iron stove and promptly slid a couple pots of coffee over the heat. She could use a cup of coffee herself, but first there was breakfast to prepare. Will would be down shortly as well as Clayton and Jason, and the ranch hands would be clamoring for a good breakfast, too, before they started their day's chores.

The fire in the stove started smoking a bit so she opened up the damper on the fire box and soon the flames were licking the metal plates atop the stove. Too hot, she said to herself, and closed the damper a pinch for a more even flame.

While waiting for the coffee to percolate, Reinette placed a slab of bacon on a wood board, sliced it into thin long strips with a sharp knife, and laid those strips across the grill. Next, she cut the Missouri potatoes left over from last night's meal into wedges, and then diced a half-dozen large skunk eggs freshly pulled from the patch down by the creek and several dried jalapeño peppers to add to the mix. She tossed her version of Texas home fries into a large skillet alongside several strips of bacon for grease, and placed it on one of the back plates to slow cook. Another skillet was greased and placed on the porcelain-lined bench above the stove until those who wanted fried eggs were ready to come in and sit down to eat.

"Coffee ready yet?" asked Will as he walked through the kitchen door, yawning and stretching his arms.

"Just about. Grab me a cup too, will you please? I haven't had my first cup, either. Let me put these biscuits in the oven, and I will sit down and join you."

But before she could relax for a moment with her husband, Red Dog came in from the bunkhouse and Jason walked down the stairs at about the same time. "Coffee on, Mrs. Alexander?" asked Red Dog.

"It just finished percolating. Grab your cups while I start cooking your breakfast. Eggs up for both of you, right?"

Red Dog smiled. He liked working for the Alexanders when they needed an extra hand. He always started out the morning on a full stomach. "Yes, please," he replied.

Jason followed suit and sat down next to Red Dog. Jason figured that Red Dog had to know about his budding relationship with Dancing Water, and was waiting for a signal from Red Dog to confirm what was fast becoming the obvious. He liked Dancing Water, a lot, and she seemed to feel the same way about Jason.

Red Dog lowered his head and gazed around the kitchen, and when Will and Reinette were not looking, he jabbed his elbow into Jason's ribs, hard, and smiled sarcastically. "That didn't hurt, did it? Dancing Water told me the other night when we were out for a walk that you were soft, like a momma's boy might be."

Trying not to make a scene, Jason fired back with his own elbow, nearly knocking Red Dog off his seat. "Mmm, you big war chief," Jason mocked, puffing out his chest. "Maybe it good Dancing Water walk with you, in case you need help finding way home in dark!"

"Jason, listen up," said Will. "Moses and Lefty are going to fix the roof over the bunkhouse this morning. He wants you, Red Dog, and Clayton to ride along the river and round up any strays that might be hanging out in the brush, and get them on down to the main herd. If you don't dally, it should not take you all day. It's going to be another hot one so I suggest you get started right after breakfast. Where is Clayton, anyway?"

"I heard him banging around in his room earlier. At least he's up," declared Jason.

Will and Reinette both detected a sarcastic tone in Jason's remarks, but held their tongues—at least for the time being. It was fast becoming obvious to everyone that Clayton had a chip on his shoulder, and that sooner or later things were going to come to a head.

Reinette diverted her attentions to the stove. There was no need for her to ring the dinner bell this morning as the rest of the crew suddenly burst through the door one after another, laughing and ridiculing each other as they went straight for the coffee before taking their usual places at the two breakfast tables. Reinette started cracking eggs as Lefty, Blondy, Tall Bear, Kip, and the others waited their turns to request an order.

"Lefty, how do you want your eggs this morning, with or without the shells?" she mocked with a serious tone.

"I'm so used to them with the shells," replied Lefty with raised eyebrows and feigned sarcasm, "that I don't think I could eat them any other way!"

Reinette smiled. She liked cooking for the men, and she made sure everyone had enough to eat. She and Will were equal partners at the ranch, and took both pride and pleasure at making sure everything went smoothly. Besides, she liked teasing the hands a bit. Moses and Lefty had been with them for more years than she could remember offhand, and Tall Bear, Blondy, and the others had grown on her too. She considered all of them family and made sure that if any of them went hungry while on the payroll, it was their own fault.

The men finished their breakfasts and dropped their dirty dishes in the wooden washtub, and were heading out to the barn when Clayton strolled into the kitchen. He grabbed a clean cup from the rack and proceeded to pour himself a cup when Reinette asked him how he wanted his eggs.

"If I wanted eggs this morning, I would have asked for them," scolded Clayton, shaking his head back and forth in annoyance.

Reinette placed both hands on her hips and fumed at his insolence. Will turned around to say something to Clayton, but Reinette looked at him and shook her head no. She would let it pass—for now.

Clayton grabbed a biscuit, broke it in two, and stuffed a couple strips of bacon between the two halves. He was about to turn and walk out the door with his coffee cup still in his hand when Will spoke up.

"Moses wants you, Jason, and Red Dog to look for strays this morning. Jason and Red Dog are already saddling their horses. Don't keep them waiting. It's not their fault you were late for breakfast."

Clayton turned around, putting his back to Will in an act of defiance. "Yeah, yeah, yeah. They can wait, or I will catch up to them later. It's not like the strays are going anywhere."

Will glared at Clayton's back. "You know Clayton, you don't have to help find strays this morning. Reinette has been talking about hiring a boy to help her in the kitchen. Maybe you are better suited to wearing an apron rather than that Colt you've been packing lately!"

Clayton spun around and faced his grandfather directly in a fit of rage. "I know why my father left the ranch when he was my age. It was because of you. You drove him away, and if you keep it up I'll follow in his footsteps." And with that brief exchange, Clayton opened the door and slammed it behind him.

Stunned, both Will and Reinette turned and looked at each other. "So that's what is bothering him," nodded Reinette. "It's his father."

Will got up and walked to the door. "Let's get to the bottom of this right now." He marched out to the barn and asked Jason to come back into the kitchen.

Jason knew Will's request had something to do with Clayton. When Clayton entered the barn a few moments earlier he hurled his coffee cup against one of the stalls and told him and Red Dog to hurry up and get their horses saddled. He was not about to wait for anybody this morning.

"What has got Clayton so riled up these past weeks?" asked Will as soon as the kitchen door closed behind Jason. "Does it have anything to do with him being late for breakfast so often?"

Jason removed his hat and sat down, squirming in his chair. "Clayton has been going to town after lights out and not coming back until after midnight. That's why he has been having trouble getting up in the morning."

"What is he doing in town at that late hour?" asked Will.

Jason looked over at Reinette and lowered his eyes in embarrassment.

"It's okay, Jason. This ranch is overrun with men, and I am not disturbed by their coarse language. Whatever you say I will not be offended by. Just tell us."

"He has been drinking a few beers with some of the local cowboys, and eyeing the girls that frequent the bars. But that's not what is eating him. He overheard a couple of the hands one night talking in the bunkhouse about his father, how he was a philanderer and a lazy saddle tramp. And how opposite a man his uncle seemed to be, honest and hard working, and why his uncle's death at the hands of cattle rustlers remained a mystery."

"Uh hah," nodded Reinette, her face betraying her deep sadness by Jason's words. She turned to Will, "I hoped it would never come out, but I guess I was wrong."

"Wait, there's more," Jason said. "He found out that his father once rode with Bull. Clayton hates Bull. Clayton and I have had a couple of run-ins with that son of a...no-good bully...that we have not told you about. We are both sure that it could eventually turn to violence. It's bad enough Clayton believes his father lacked character, but that his father was probably also an outlaw is what has got him so riled up. He blames both of you for not telling him the truth about his father, and believes it is somehow your fault his father, mother, and uncle are all dead."

Will and Reinette were devastated by Jason's remarks. Jason excused himself and started to leave when Will asked him to keep the conversation private. He and Reinette needed time to mull over this sudden turn of events before taking any action.

After they were sure Jason was out of earshot, Reinette came over and sat down next to Will. Looking forlorn and grief stricken, she folded her hands together carefully and laid them atop her apron before raising her eyes and looking over at Will.

"Will, when we buried John, I wanted our grandson to be safe. I wanted him to be able to sleep at night without worrying about strange noises in the dark. I needed to shield him from harm, and to do that I thought it best Clayton not follow in his father's footsteps. I made you promise me that, Will, and you kept your promise despite any reservations you may have had."

Will furled his brow and looked out the double kitchen window, thinking back to the funeral. Reinette was devastated over John and Sally's deaths, barely maintaining her composure during the viewing and burial, waiting instead until the last of the mourners had left the ranch to release her pent-up anger on him. Her words still cut deep:

Our grandson is not going to follow in your footsteps. He is not going into law enforcement like his father or his uncle, either. You hear me? I want you to promise me right now on our sons' graves that you will retire from the bench

from this moment on, and that you will not encourage
Clayton to become a peace officer. Please Will, I couldn't
bear the pain of losing Clayton, too! He is all we have left.

Will remembered lowering his head that evening and looking Reinette straight in the eyes, promising her with all his heart to honor her wishes—a promise he had kept all these years.

He gazed back at Reinette, still sitting next to him. Her hands were shaking now, and there was a quiver in her voice as she continued. "Clayton has become what I feared most, Will. A man with few principles and no direction in life, a drifter who only lives in the here and now. He only helps others if there is something in it for him. Will, Clayton is nothing like his father. How could he be? We, I mean I, did not allow Clayton to know his father, to know what he valued. I got in the way of him becoming a man, a good man like his father and his uncle.

"Will, I got what I asked for, but not what I wanted. At least not deep down inside. I didn't want Clayton to shy away from what is wrong with the world or to look the other way when trouble was brewing. But I didn't want him to become so principled it would lead him to his death, either."

Will nodded in agreement, not wanting to say or do anything that would get her even more upset.

"By comparison," said Reinette in low tones, "John was slow to anger, but quick to right a wrong. He was kind and forgiving, honest and truthful, yet tough as nails when the situation demanded it. I'm afraid Clayton has rarely demonstrated any of these qualities. He is at a crossroads in his life, and I fear we are going to lose him."

Will raised his finger to Reinette in an effort to silence her so he could now speak. "John and Jacob's encounters with men outside the law gave them their grit," he said, "and taught them that the difference between right and wrong is not always black and white. Clayton is just now beginning to learn those lessons. And they are hard lessons to learn."

"I realize now that I really wanted Clayton to be just like you and his father all along," said Reinette softly. "I just didn't want to lose him the way we lost John and Jacob. I made a mistake, Will, and am no longer holding you to your promise."

Reinette reached inside her apron and pulled out Will's tin star. "Can you forgive me?"

"You did what you thought was right at the time, Reinette. We both did. But despite our good intentions, it is still up to Clayton to pick the trail he is to follow. All we can do is pray he picks the right trail, like his father and uncle did when they were his age. Nonetheless, maybe it is time Clayton learned the truth about his father, and what it means to be a real man."

Will smiled and kissed Reinette on her forehead. Then he stood up, put his badge in his pocket, and walked outside.

CHAPTER EIGHTEEN

The Roundup

Jason and Red Dog were all saddled up, waiting outside the barn for Clayton, who seemed to be taking his sweet-ass time.

"What are you guys looking at?" Clayton snarled as he stomped past them. "You two better be ready to ride hard today 'cause I am not doing your share of the work." He backed his horse out of the stall, slid his Winchester into the scabbard, and led the gelding out of the barn. "Let's ride before the sun bakes us all like biscuits in an oven!"

Jason and Red Dog just shook their heads. They were becoming used to hearing Clayton run his mouth off in a fit of rage, as if he had a bad tooth aching to be pulled. Ever since he learned about his father riding with Bull, Clayton had withdrawn into himself only to lash out at anybody who dared get too close to pry into his private affairs.

The trio spread out and started rounding up strays as soon as they reached the river. A cow and a calf were in a finger of brush that extended 50 yards or so from the water, and another calf was bawling for its mother a hundred yards or so upstream. They located six more feeding on a rise just above the river and two more standing in the shallows as Jason rounded a bend in the river.

"There are a lot more strays than I figured on," said Jason as he pulled up alongside Red Dog. Suddenly, a yellow and orange cougar broke from cover, and weaving in and out of the brush, it scampered up a rocky hillside and then grabbing for more ground, disappeared over the top in a flash.

Startled by the sudden appearance of the big cat, Red Dog and Jason rode along the edge of a dry canyon to find out why the cougar was hanging around the water this time of day. When they topped a slight rise near the water they got their answer.

A brindle calf had become stuck in the mud, maybe a day or two ago, and could not free itself from the muck. Its bawling last night must have been heard for miles, tweaking the curiosity of a hungry cat on the prowl. Using the canyon for cover, the cougar quickly closed in and killed off the hapless calf and was in fact still feeding on the bloody remains when Red Dog rode into view.

"Clayton, over here! You are not going to like this!' yelled Jason. "Over here!"

When Clayton appeared, Red Dog drew his attention to the exact location of the half-eaten calf by waving his hat back and forth over his head.

"That is probably the fifth or sixth dead beef cow found this week on the ranch," said Clayton as he dismounted to inspect the dead calf. "Cougars are as thick as fleas on a dog this year. And there are damn few deer for them to eat. Any cow that gets sick and lies down or finds itself in trouble like this calf did is fair game, I guess. Who saw it first?"

"I did," replied Red Dog as he too dismounted for a better look-see. "Jason had his mind on other matters this morning to do his job proper like. He must have fallen off his horse when no one was looking 'cause he keeps rubbing his ribs like they are bruised and rolling his eyes like he is in some sort of a trance. Maybe you should send him back to the ranch by his lonesome. He ain't much good out here today."

Jason eased himself down out of the saddle and tied his horse up to some dead limbs before stepping into the shadows to take a piss. "Keep poking at me Red Dog, and you will find out just how sore I might be." Jason had a smile on his face when he turned back around and untied his horse, but all Red Dog heard was Jason warning him to back off or face the consequences.

"Well, good eyes anyway Red Dog," said Clayton smiling as his two friends continued to trade thinly veiled insults. "I guess there is nothing more we can do now 'cept shoot the next cougar we see. Or should I say shoot at 'cause I know neither of you can hit a wooden water bucket at 10 yards with a scatter gun, much less a wary cougar at 100 yards with a Winchester lever loaded up full!"

Jason sensed Clayton had come out of his foul mood. So did Red Dog. Without words, the trio began to lead their horses in single file to higher ground for a better look-see of the surrounding ground when suddenly another cougar broke from the brush uphill and ran stretched out and low to the ground across the open in a frantic effort to get to the nearby dry canyon for safety. The cougar had been resting with a full belly above the dead calf all morning long, but bolted when it thought its security had been compromised.

Clayton was the first to grab his rifle, but not much faster than Red Dog who also scrambled to find a clear line of fire. Shooting offhand, both men started sending lead in the cougar's direction, but with each round fired a puff of dirt exploded safely behind the fast-escaping cat. Indeed, the brass from Clayton's first round had not yet hit the ground when he yanked the trigger on a second bullet, and then another, and another, as if he was trying to outshoot Red Dog, who was rapid-firing his own Winchester at an equally blistering pace.

As Clayton and Red Dog jockeyed for a better shooting position, Jason dropped to his belly and took deliberate aim, leading the long-tailed critter by a half length. As the cougar zigzagged across the rocks and under the brush, using its long tawny tail for balance, Jason swung his sights in unison until the big male broke clear. A single shot caught the calf killer in midstride, blowing a hole clean through its vitals and sending it cart wheeling ass end over tea kettle and into the dirt.

Jason quickly ran toward the canyon to claim his prize as Clayton and Red Dog stood dumbfounded at Jason's incredible shot. They fired first and quickly, but first and fast are not as good as steady and deliberate, a shooting lesson both Clayton and Red Dog had yet to learn.

The hide was far from prime, but Jason skinned the mountain lion out anyway, not bothering with the feet or the head. He then loosely rolled up the green hide and laced it with a length of cord he kept in his saddle bags. He would need to cool the hide down and salt it soon or it would spoil in the afternoon heat.

"If we spot another cougar," said Jason with a broad smile as he approached Clayton and Red Dog, "let me do the shooting. Ammo is too expensive these days to waste on cowboys who can't hit a wooden bucket with a thrown rock much less a straight-shooting Winchester!"

Clayton and Red Dog just groaned, but did acknowledge the fine shooting they had just witnessed, each shaking Jason's hand as they walked back toward their horses.

Jason did not stuff the mountain lion's hide in one of his saddle bags right away, but first let his mount get a good whiff of the dead cat. Once his horse calmed down, he tied the pelt to his saddle so it could flop in the air and cool down before he mounted up to join Clayton and Red Dog, who were already looking for more strays.

As the morning gave way to high noon, they counted 23 stray cows and calves. "Let's push these over to the main herd," said Clayton as he pulled up alongside Jason, "and call it a day. It's getting too hot and the horses are feeling the heat. We can come back tomorrow and finish the job. There may be a dozen or more holed up along that stretch of cottonwoods up yonder."

They soon had the strays they found that morning moving along and had not gone more than a mile when they were met by Lefty, Blondy, and Kip. "You found quite a few, eh boys?" said Lefty as he rode up next to Clayton. "Anything happen? We heard quite a few shots ring out not long ago."

"Yeah, we shot a mountain lion that had been feeding on a dead calf down near the river," said Clayton as Lefty stood on his stirrups and stretched his legs.

"There you go with that 'we' again," chimed Jason as he rode into the conversation. "I shot the cat, and it only took one bullet. It was these guys who sprayed the hillside with lead, trying to get that cat to run faster for me I guess so I could better show off my rifle skills!"

Red Dog was silent as Clayton rolled his eyes and groaned.

The men milled around for 10 or 15 minutes, exchanging the passing events of the morning before Lefty, Blondy, and Kip took control of the beeves and headed them back to the main herd. That freed up Clayton, Red Dog, and Jason to ride back to the ranch, and they did so gleefully and at a leisurely pace.

CHAPTER NINETEEN

The Water Moccasin

They stopped to water the horses at Alexander's Crossing, a wide spot in the river where a series of shallow riffles allowed the horses to leisurely quaff their thirst, and after a brief spell they rode east along the bank to a familiar bend in the river where the river narrowed and the water ran cool and deep.

"You got any soap with you, Clayton?" asked Jason. "I need a bath real bad." Before he got an answer, Jason slid off his saddle, removed his boots, dropped his gold cross and chain into the nearest boot and then began stripping off his sweaty clothes. Clayton and Red Dog wasted no time disrobing, and suddenly all three were racing for the water's edge buck naked as the day they were born.

The foot race was a tie, or so it seemed, as together they jumped off a high point overlooking the water while screaming a war cry that each hoped would outdo the other. When they bobbed to the surface and began splashing each other in a fit of laughter, however, they heard a series of high-pitched screeches that would stampede a herd of cattle!

"Get out! Get out! Get out right now!"

They were not alone! There were three teenage girls huddled together breast deep in the shallower water near the shoreline. Clayton, Jason, and Red Dog had unwittingly jumped over the top of the girls when they hurled themselves into the river!

"Who are you?" asked Clayton as he swam to shallower water where he could easily touch bottom. "What are you doing here?"

"You just never mind who we are. Just get out and leave us alone. We were here first!"

"You may have been here first," smiled Clayton, "but this here is my grandfather's ranch, Wilfred Alexander, and you three girls are all trespassing."

"Phoebe Ann, don't get them all riled up. I doubt these boys have ever seen a live woman taking a bath before! You don't know what they will likely do next!"

"My name is Clayton, Clayton Alexander, and these are my two friends, Jason Gray Eyes and Red Dog. And we are not leaving. Now again, who are you and what are you doing here?"

"We are from back east, Ohio, and we sneaked across the Mississippi River last month to look for a lost member of our family, my uncle Ted. My name is Phoebe Ann Moses, and these are my two sisters, Elizabeth and Sarah Ellen. Now, if you do not mind, I would appreciate it if you would just leave. We will turn our backs if you are shy and embarrassed. We promise we will not gaze upon your naked form."

Clayton could not help himself. He had a grin from ear to ear as did Red Dog and Jason. "This is wild country, missy. No place for three girls traveling alone. How can you expect to take care of yourself if you run into outlaws or wild Indians?"

"Hey, leave the wild Indians out of this," remarked Red Dog rather defensively. "I can assure you ladies this redskin is friendly."

"You need not worry about us," replied Sarah Ellen. "We can all shoot straight, and Phoebe Ann can outshoot any man who causes us concern."

"Well, that's not a great accomplishment if you are thinking about outshooting either of these two," said Jason, baring his teeth with a huge smile as he pointed toward Clayton and Red Dog. "They can barely hit a wooden bucket at 10 yards with a stagecoach gun!"

Sarah Ellen leaned into Phoebe Ann and whispered into her ear, "He's cute!"

"Never you mind, Sarah Ellen," snapped Phoebe Ann. "We have a problem here, a conundrum that needs to be resolved, and right now. Clayton, we seem to be at an impasse."

"What do you mean 'we'?" laughed Clayton. "The solution is simple. This is our land and you must leave. If you are the ones that are shy and embarrassed, we will turn our backs so as to not gaze upon your naked form!"

Red Dog and Jason burst into laughter. They had the girls between a rock and a hard place, and the boys were not going to budge. What an exciting predicament! Red Dog started to walk toward the shoreline and into shallower water to test the girl's mettle when Elizabeth screamed. "Stay in the water, we can work something out here so nobody is seen without their clothing."

As the two groups whispered among themselves, a seven-foot serpent with a girth as thick as a grown man's thigh slithered off the banking on the far shoreline and slipped quietly into the water. Red Dog saw it first, and panicked. "Snake! Snake!" he yelled, pointing to the "V" shape in the water. Clayton and Phoebe Ann then saw it simultaneously and yelled out a warning. "Snake! Snake! Big snake! Get out of the water. It's swimming right at us. Get out of the water. Now! Run! Run!"

Modesty be damned! The girls screamed as they rushed to the shoreline and up the slippery banking in a state of pure fear. The boys were not about to become entangled with a water moccasin that big, and without looking back scrambled out of the river and up the banking toward their clothes and waiting horses.

Clayton was in the deeper water and as a result was the last to reach the shoreline. As he crawled up the steep bank he saw Phoebe Ann, who was just getting out of the water herself, out of the corner of his eye, and tried to steal a peek. But to his horror Phoebe Ann was also gazing in his direction, obviously trying to steal a peek herself!

Clayton quickly covered himself with his hand and scrambled up the banking, but not before catching a quick glimpse of Phoebe Ann's backside as she disappeared behind a veil of brush.

"Damn, that was a big water moccasin," screamed Red Dog as he pulled on his trousers. "I've never seen one so big!"

"Yeah, you looked scared out of your wits," laughed Jason as he mimicked Red Dog's frantic escape from the river by wildly flailing his hands and legs. "Your eyes were popping out of your head as you rushed swiftly past me trying to get out of the water before me. I don't blame you however. He was definitely a damn big snake! And he was swimming right at us with his white mouth wide open! Where in the hell did he come from? Let's finish dressing and then make sure the girls are okay. This is the last time I go swimming here!"

As Clayton was pulling on his boots, Phoebe Ann, Elizabeth, and Sarah Ellen came into view. "You guys all right? asked Phoebe Ann. "Anybody get snakebit?"

Clayton and Red Dog walked over to greet the three girls and to apologize for their ungentlemanly behavior. Soon they were all laughing off the event, thankful nobody got hurt and nobody felt too embarrassed.

Clayton happened to look over Phoebe Ann's shoulder as they spoke to each other and saw the big snake slither over the top of the banking and begin crawling in their direction. "Red Dog! Look! By the edge of the water. A snake! A big snake! It looks like the same one that chased us out of the river!"

Red Dog took a few steps forward and drew his pistol, as did Clayton. Shooting fast and furious, the two aimed and pulled their triggers at will, emptying each of their revolvers at the snake a mere 60 feet away. The ground was quickly pot marked as plumes of dirt and red dust rose two feet into the air with one round after another missing its mark. Six shots from each gun, and the snake slithered back toward the river unscathed. Phoebe Ann then stepped between Clayton and Red Dog, drew her Smith & Wesson, and fired once from the hip, taking the snake's head clean off!

"That's the way we do it back east" exclaimed Phoebe Ann rather proudly. "One shot...one kill."

Clayton stood still with his mouth agape.

As the girls and Clayton congratulated Phoebe Ann, Red Dog rushed over to inspect the snake. He picked up a forked stick and poked the snake to ensure that it was indeed dead. Even a water moccasin with its head missing can wiggle around a bit for a minute or two giving a good scare to anyone standing too close. And the head, especially one this size, though severed from the rest of the body, still holds enough venom to kill a horse if the horse is so unfortunate as to come in close contact with those fangs.

Red Dog jabbed the stick through the snake's head and with a glint of fire in his eyes impulsively tossed it toward Jason as punishment for ridiculing him a few minutes earlier. In an instant, Phoebe Ann pulled her Smith & Wesson from her holster and shot the snake's head in midair, blowing it to bits.

"Oh, I guess I touched on a raw nerve, Red Dog!" laughed Jason rather nervously. "And for the second time in less than an hour!"

Jason was beginning to see a pattern with Red Dog, one that made him feel increasingly uncomfortable the more time they rode together. If Red Dog was not the center of attention, he would do or say something to get people to look at him. And if he felt he didn't measure up or was being made fun of, then that something could border on violence. That's why he jabbed him hard in the ribs earlier that morning, and why he just tossed the snake head at him. "Good Lord," Jason muttered to himself, "we should change his name to Top Dog!"

When the snake's head exploded and hit the ground, Clayton once again looked at Phoebe Ann in amazement.

"Where did you learn to shoot like that!"

"Practice and lots of determination," she replied. "Mostly practice. I started shooting when I was 12 years old. We were poor, and the game I shot put food on the table and helped pay off the mortgage on the farm. I guess I became a good shot because I had to be a good shot."

"Where are you going from here?"

"Southeast to Haydenville first, and then farther west I guess until we learn some word about my uncle."

"What will you do for money, if you don't mind me asking. It's tough enough for a man to earn a living out here, but a woman, even three women, there just are not that many opportunities..."

"Clayton, I've been shooting all my life. Shooting is in my blood, and I've been taking care of myself and my sisters by hunting and selling the meat and hides, or every once in a while entering a shooting match for cash. Some men just can't stand the thought of a woman knowing how to shoot a gun and will gladly put up some money to prove me wrong!"

"Well, we will ride with you as far as the ranch," said Clayton, his eyes hoping for a soft smile in return. "I want to talk to you more about where you grew up and learn how you got to be such a first-rate shot."

"I would like that just fine," replied Phoebe Ann. "And I want to learn more about your grandfather's ranch. It sure is a fine looking spread."

The two carried on for several hours in easy conversation, each listening intently to what the other had to say. When they reached the road that led back to the ranch, Clayton, Red Dog, and Jason bid Phoebe Ann, Elizabeth, and Sarah Ellen farewell. Phoebe Ann promised to visit the ranch when they passed by the area on their way home. She sounded sincere, and Clayton was already looking forward to the time when he would see her again.

CHAPTER TWENTY
A Decade of Statehood

Texas was readmitted into the union on March 30, 1870, and the town of Colby planned a weekend celebration to honor that historical event. The mayor and Town Council would give speeches and award ribbons and fancy scrolled letters of commendation to those citizens who worked tirelessly all year round helping to make Colby prosperous and a better place to raise a family.

Mayor Jenkins would be presenting Bob Ward a commendation for bringing new business to town. Ward's first success was bringing a well-stocked apothecary operated by Chung Lee to town. His knowledge of certain herbs and medicinal concoctions was a blessing to those in the community, especially those good citizens who suffered from everything from headaches and hangovers to gout and tooth decay. Even old Doc Hayes referred his patients to Chung Lee when he thought one of Chung's potions might bring some relief to life's minor everyday illnesses.

Bob Ward's second success was cajoling the Bisbee brothers into constructing their new sawmill and dry kiln in Colby on the east end of town near the railroad line rather than Bing's Crossing, a small town 20 miles to the north. It was a major accomplishment, as the good citizens of Bing's Crossing had offered the Bisbee brothers several incentives to relocate their business to their growing town.

The Bisbee brothers were cutting their own timber from nearby virgin stands of white oak and other hardwoods and also buying felled logs from as far away as the Piney Woods to the east and then shipping them to Colby by horse-drawn wagon, ferry boat, and railroad car. Seasoned lumber stripped and cut to order was expensive and darn hard to come by in these parts until the sawmill opened its doors to local businessmen and area ranchers.

Indeed, there was no doubt the little town of Colby was growing, and it needed the products and services offered by both of these establishments to help fuel the expansion.

As with any growing community however, friction among its inhabitants was inevitable. Attorneys Ethan Brown from Boston and Perry Wilkinson from Buffalo argued criminal cases before the circuit judge, but also mediated civil cases between rival factions. Their resolution of the spat between the First National Bank of Colby and rancher Tom Evans over the purchase of 500 head of Texas longhorns earned both lawyers awards and helped save Evan's Circle Bar Ranch from a takeover by the bank, an outcome the bank and Tom Evans wanted desperately to avoid.

Miss Carlon was also to be honored that weekend. She volunteered her time every Sunday after church to give reading and writing lessons to those adults who for one rea-son or another never learned to read, much less write, their own name on a piece of paper.

As the town grew, reading and writing were becoming increasingly important, and a man learning how to write his own name, rather than scratching an "X" on a piece of paper, meant he could sign contracts and bills of sale and conduct other business transactions that would more likely hold up in court should a discrepancy surface. For those men who now needed to carry a sharp pencil in their shirt pocket, Miss Carlon's Good Citizenship Award was well deserved and long overdue.

The "Key to the Town" however would be awarded to the one person who best exemplified the courage of the unknown Texas Ranger who stood alone against a ruthless gang of outlaws who nearly took over the town almost 15 years earlier. Their brief reign of terror and senseless killings of civilians shook the south from New Orleans to the Alamo.

Nobody knew his real name, and few people even remembered what he looked like. By most accounts he was a young man, in his early to mid twenties, tall, maybe six foot, with short dirty blond hair and a scraggly handlebar mustache.

Some say he drifted in from up north near Ft. Laramie one day on a big red horse, a stallion with strong legs and a short fuse, while others thought he rode north out of Mexico or San Antonio. At first he seemed nothing more than a saddle tramp who passed his days camped outside one saloon or another sloshing down warm beers and carousing with the local whores.

Always unshaven and often smelling in dire need of a bath, he wore an old sombrero embroidered with eagles pulled tight over his forehead, a pair of well-worn leather chaps, and old scuffed-up cowboy boots fitted with wheeled Mexican spurs.

Despite his alley cat appearance, the stranger was quiet and polite to those who took the time to speak to him. There was an unnerving air of confidence about him that intimidated some of the drovers and unruly ranch hands that patronized the bars on and off during the day, but the local townsfolk and business owners grew to like him. He was an honest man who seemed trustworthy despite his disheveled exterior.

Whatever his name or wherever he hailed from, one thing is for certain. If the Kid from Ft. Laramie had not stood up to the gang of outlaws that Saturday afternoon, the town's life savings would have been stolen from the bank, and more honest citizens would have been executed by the band of thugs who were later identified as former members of Quantrill's Raiders, those very same bushwhackers who earlier butchered over 150 men and boys in the revenge raid on Lawrence, Kansas, in August 1863.

It was not until the shooting ended and all the gang members were dead or blowing bloody air bubbles out their noses that the townsfolk knew that the drifter who saved their town from certain financial ruin was an undercover Texas Ranger sent to Colby on a tip emanating from inside the statehouse, a tip that was aimed at bringing those members of Quantrill's gang to justice—dead or alive.

CHAPTER TWENTY-ONE
The Shooting Match

Clayton and Jason were up early Saturday morning with high spirits for the upcoming celebration. They immediately gathered up their archery gear, doublechecking their tackle and making last-minute preparations for the day's upcoming archery shooting events. They had spent the week with Red Dog refletching their hunting arrows and choosing the straightest shafts for the competition.

Each shaft was held up to their dominant eye, and slowly rotated. Any obvious bend or abnormal formation along the length of the shaft disqualified the arrow. They rested the business end of each of the better shafts on the palm of their left hand, and cradling the feathered end of the shaft between the thumb and forefinger of their right hand, blew on the fletching to rotate the shaft. A visible wobble anywhere along the length of the shaft also disqualified the arrow.

Later they would apply steam and moderate hand pressure to those disqualified shafts in an effort to straighten them sufficiently enough for target practice.

Finally, they dragged out Will's gold assay scale and compared several makeshift metal arrow tips to one another until they had a dozen or so that weighed nearly the same.

But even a hunting shaft that appears to be straight and rotates smoothly can still veer off course when shot from a bow. Clayton, Jason, and Red Dog practiced every day, shooting their best shafts into bundled hay targets positioned behind the barn before finally settling on those select few shafts that consistently grouped together in the tightest formations. By the end of the week they each had a dozen arrows that flew straight and true from their bows. And each claimed he could outshoot the other two in Saturday's competition.

That morning Will and Moses were also up early hitching up Jake and Big Jim to the buckboard and then loading up the bed of the wagon with clean clothing, blankets, and other incidentals for their weekend stay in Colby.

A woven picnic basket containing two homemade berry pies and two loaves of brick oven bread Reinette had baked during the week was secured under the seat. It was Reinette's contribution to the church food sale. Her pies and sourdough bread along with breads, pastries, and smoked meats from other parishioners would be sold over the weekend at the bazaar with all proceeds going into a fund to purchase a solid brass bell for the church steeple. They were nearing their goal, and Lord willing, they would meet that goal by sundown on Sunday.

Moses then stuffed a two-foot-long locked wooden box Will had never seen before under the seat next to the picnic basket and tied it down with a short length of rope.

"What's in the box?" asked Will as Moses jumped down from the wagon.

"It's a surprise, Will," replied Moses with a wide grin. "You'll find out soon enough though."

"Where did it come from?"

"If I told ya Will, it would no longer be a surprise, now would it?"

"Okay, I guess it can wait. Do we need anything else? I feel like we are forgetting something."

"My hatchet!" exclaimed Moses. "I almost forgot my hatchet. I'll be right back."

Moses strolled over to the bunkhouse to get his hatchet while Will crossed the yard on his way to the barn just as Clayton and Jason exited the ranch house with Red Dog in tow.

"I wonder if Will is planning on racing Red Cloud this weekend," asked Red Dog as Will disappeared into the barn. "Let's go ask him now and then get something to eat. I'm going to need all the strength I can muster today so I can prove to you and Jason that I am the best bow shot in all of Texas!"

"There isn't enough food in the kitchen to give you that kind of strength, Red Dog. Of course, you could try gnawing on the dead calf your father dragged into that patch of brush and scrub wood behind the barn yesterday. A belly full of ripe beef should help you shoot straight all weekend long!"

Red Dog just shook his head in mock sarcasm. As the trio entered the barn through the two sliding doors, morning's first light was just filtering through the open barn windows illuminating the horse stalls and tack room with soft yellow rays. Moses' horse was already saddled, but Will was nowhere to be found. Clayton called out his name several times, but got no answer.

"Where could he have gone?" asked Red Dog. "We just saw him walk into the barn. He seems to have a habit of disappearing in here. Let's saddle our mounts and lead them and Moses' horse outside. We'll have to catch up to your grandfather later."

They tied the three horses to the corral fencing next to Red Dog's waiting mount at about the same time Reinette stepped outside and began hammering the dinner bell. Five minutes later they were gulping down hot coffee and flapjacks and teasing each other with raucous laughter.

Will walked into the kitchen a few minutes later and sat down next to Reinette.

"We saw you go into the barn Grandpa, but we couldn't find you. Where did you go?" asked Clayton as he poured himself a second cup of coffee.

"I was there, you just didn't look hard enough," Will replied with a grin. "What did you want me for?"

"Well," asked Clayton, "are you gonna race Big Red this weekend?"

Will looked over at Reinette. "No, your grandmother and I are going to take in the sights and stroll about town. No racing, no shooting. Just a little watching, a little eating, and maybe I will have a beer or two with some old friends while Reinette is volunteering at the church."

Blondy and a few of the hands pitched in with the dishes and helped clean up the kitchen so Will, Reinette, Moses, Lefty, Tall Bear, and the boys could get an early start. Later they would play poker to determine who was watching over the ranch on Saturday and Sunday, and who was riding to town on either of those days to participate in the statehood celebrations.

Will and Reinette rode in the carriage while Moses, Lefty, and Tall Bear handled the buckboard with Clayton, Jason, and Red Dog tagging along behind on horseback. When they got near town, however, the boys split off and raced to Colby, eager to see what adventures awaited them. Their first stop? Sally's Home Style Cooking, of course, to see Dancing Water! Red Dog still took a shine to her and had not yet given up on catching her eye despite Jason's relentless pursuit.

Clayton seemed to have dealt with many of the issues surrounding the death of his father, mother, and uncle, but there was still an undercurrent of anger and mistrust about him. Maybe a weekend in town with his friends would help him see things in a better light, at least that's what Will and Reinette were hoping.

The Bell and Majestic hotels in Colby were already booked solid as was Mary Jane's Rooming House on Jefferson, but fortunately, Will had made reservations for everybody at the Colby House. Indeed, there was not a vacant bed in the whole town, and even the fallow field behind the livery stable was filled with tents, wagons, and makeshift lean-tos erected by visitors from as far away as Austin to the west and the Missouri border to the east. It was as if the town sent out invitations to all Texans, and half of them showed up in Colby to celebrate the 10 years of statehood.

As Will and Moses unloaded the buckboard, they were all surprised at how Colby had been gussied up for the festival. The smell of freshly cut wood permeated the air, giving a hint to some of the improvements made to the town. The boardwalk, for example, had been extended with new planking from the Town Hall all the way east to the livery stable and adjacent blacksmith shop on one side of Main Street, and from the church all the way to the last saloon on the other side of Main. A new boardwalk also intersected Main Street near the corner barbershop and then ran south along both sides of Jefferson to the very edge of town.

Lone Star flags fluttered in front of nearly every business, and red, white, and blue bunting was hung from the courthouse, the bank, Elsie's Rooming House, and several second-story balconies. Even the alleyways were cleaned up of debris and sprayed with lime to cut down on the smell of rotting garbage and stale urine. Colby not only looked good, it smelled good, too!

With strangers streaming into town every hour for the festivities, some of the local business owners were displaying their wares outside their storefronts on the new boardwalk. Several bolts of brightly colored cloth had been placed on tables outside Barnaby's Dry Goods along with a dozen bonnets of various styles. Several handmade dresses were threaded onto a long pole suspended from wrought iron brackets bolted to the side of the shop for passing customers to inspect and appreciate.

Davis' Guns & Ammo was sure to do a bang-up business over the weekend what with all the shooting contests scheduled. They had stocked up heavily on pistol and rifle ammunition and even had a case of shotgun shells available for the Church Charity Shoots scheduled for Saturday and Sunday afternoons. Two bits bought you a spot on the 12-man firing line where the paper target with the most holes within six inches of the center was awarded a hot meal from the church parishioners complete with homemade bread and desert.

Davis' was also offering the choice of a new Colt six-shooter or a Winchester lever-action to the man who best perforated a playing card with a pistol at 30 yards. This was the main event of the firearm competitions, and at two bits per shooter, Davis was hopeful some cash would flow in his direction.

Maggie's Emporium was also hopeful the statehood celebration would bring customers to her store, and to entice passersby to come in and browse around, she too displayed some products on the boardwalk, including a large selection of men's shirts and ladies blouses.

A glass jar filled with candy sticks, however, was the real draw, as each child that stopped to stare soon asked his or her parents for a piece of peppermint. And once the parents entered Maggie's to make that purchase, they would inevitably spend an hour or so poking through a wide variety of goods the Emporium had to offer.

Right next door to Maggie's was old man Winston's Leather Shop. He lived across the street and upstairs above Thomas' Hardware Store, the business Ezra Harding left his sons Thomas and Winston after his untimely death at the hands of a drunken cowboy. It seems the cowboy was shooting up the town late one night after a full day of heavy drinking, and a stray bullet went through a window in the hardware store and lodged deep in Ezra's hip. It could not be removed for fear of heavy bleeding although Ezra begged somebody to try anyway. He could not walk, and even strong whiskey could not kill the pain. Ezra died three weeks later of lead poisoning from that cowboy's errant bullet with Thomas and Winston at his bedside.

It was Winston's idea to open a leather shop as a hedge against the hardware store falling on bad times. It turned out to be a profitable move. As Winston's reputation as a cobbler grew, cowboys rode in from far and wide to get a custom pair of proper-fitting leather boots. He also sold tack to area ranchers and cowboys and often displayed everything from fancy saddles and leather chaps to holsters, scabbards, bandoliers, and leather wallets on the boardwalk in front of his store. And with the town growing, business was booming.

Of course shopping was not the only attraction in Colby that weekend. The Half-Dollar Saloon had nickel beer by the barrelful, and plenty of whores to pick the pockets of young cowboys in town for a good time after a month or so alone on the range. Two dollars was the advertised price, but only a fool paid more than two bits for a half hour upstairs with one of Millie's girls.

The Lucky Seven Saloon, not to be outdone, roasted a whole steer over a bed of mesquite coals in the adjacent alley. For two bits you got all the beef and salt potatoes you could eat plus a pitcher of cold beer. And if that was not enticement enough, they rolled the piano outside on the boardwalk for the entertainment of anyone within hearing distance.

CHAPTER TWENTY-TWO

Dancing Water

Dancing Water looked out across the floor of the dining area and immediately picked out Jason and his friends Clayton and Red Dog sitting at a corner table near the half-open window in the back of the room. She was hoping Jason would stop by to see her this morning and glanced over every time another hungry customer walked through Sally's front door to see if it was him coming in for a bite to eat.

Dancing Water was developing quite a fondness for Jason. He was certainly easy on the eyes, but more importantly he was kind to her whenever they were together. He never acted out and sought the center of attention as Red Dog had so often in the past, and he never ridiculed her when she thought she had something important to say.

She also admired Jason's desire to attend law school and knew in her heart that he would someday attend the university, especially since Clayton's grandparents had taken him into their home. Jason was fortunate to have friends like Clayton and his grandparents, and she could tell that Clayton's respect for Jason ran deep.

"Dancing Water, there are three new customers at one of the back corner tables. Can you get their orders for me?" asked Mary, another of Sally's waitresses on duty that morning. She knew Dancing Water had a crush on a young cowboy and figured it had to be one of those three young men she was smiling at.

Dancing Water smiled at Mary and wiping her hands on her apron, walked directly toward Jason's table. She could feel his eyes on her as she maneuvered herself between several tables and chairs. She could feel Red Dog's stare, too, but chose to ignore him, maintaining her eye contact with Jason instead.

"Any specials on the menu today?" asked Jason in a cheerful voice. "We're somewhat starved this morning since waking early and getting ourselves ready for the big week-end celebration. We've been practicing with our bows for a couple of weeks now and hope to do well at the archery contest. But we know we won't shoot that straight on a near-empty stomach!"

"Yeah, I should beat both Jason and Clayton," declared Red Dog with a sarcastic smirk. "They aren't poor shots, they just aren't as good as me!"

"How does beef steak, home fried potatoes, a couple of eggs, toast, and coffee sound?" asked Dancing Water, never taking her eyes off Jason.

"Yes, that will be fine," answered Jason. "I'll take my eggs sunny-side up and my steak medium rare, if that's okay."

"Me, too!" chimed in Clayton. "Sunny-side up and medium rare."

"Yeah, that will do me okay, too, Dancing Water,"

replied Red Dog as he slouched back in his chair. He was not getting anywhere with Dancing Water, and it was obvious she was taking to Jason more and more each time they met.

Dancing Water turned to go back into the kitchen with their orders. She liked Clayton fine, but Red Dog often annoyed her. She couldn't figure him out, and as time passed she cared less about trying to look into his heart. There was something twisted inside him, something that gave her a bad feeling at times, like he was trying to get between her and Jason.

Indeed, it was Red Dog who told her about the hotel fire that killed Clayton's mother and father and several guests years ago, and the rumors that Jason's Indian father, Gray Eyes, may have started the fire. Gray Eyes was lynched by an angry mob almost immediately after the fire burned itself out despite the lack of any hard evidence against him. When Jason's white mother passed away within the year, Jason lived with his religious aunt for a while before being taken in by Will and Reinette Alexander.

But Dancing Water did not find that information troubling, as Red Dog may have hoped. Indeed, Jason was an orphan, and that only strengthened the bond she was developing for him.

Dancing Water soon returned to the table with three breakfast specials and a pot of hot coffee. She smiled at Jason and wished him luck at the archery shoot before she was drawn away to wait on other customers. Sally's was busy this morning, and likely would be for the next couple of days as more and more people came into town to celebrate statehood with the citizens of Colby.

When it was time to leave, Jason glanced around the room hoping to get one more look at Dancing Water, but Red Dog gave him a shove out the door before he could scan the entire dining area. Dancing Water saw Jason, however, and was irritated with Red Dog's actions.

At 16, Dancing Water was more than old enough to take a husband, and she certainly had a fair number of suitors to choose from, but it was Jason with his good manners and quick-to-smile personality that she wanted to see right now. Indeed, every time she saw him she wanted to see more of him, and she was saddened when their brief meeting came to an end that morning.

Jason, Red Dog, and Clayton left Sally's and then walked their horses over to the livery stable, boarding their mounts there for the weekend.

"C'mon! Let's get going!" said Red Dog, trying to rush the others. "I want to get over to the church right away and see who we're shooting up against. Maybe Dancing Water will take a shine to me if I win."

Jason, irritated at Red Dog's antics at Sally's and now his remarks toward Dancing Water, snapped back at Red Dog. "You know, if you stopped showing off once in a while maybe a decent girl would take a shine to you. Of course, it will not be Dancing Water. She's mine now, and there is nothing you can do about it."

Jason and Red Dog were about to square off, but Clayton quickly jumped in and separated the two. "Okay, okay, let's just not get all worked up over this. We are here to have some fun, not get into a fist fight with each other. Let's get our gear and walk over to the church."

"Leaping lizards, look what's coming our way," whispered Clayton as he motioned ahead. Down the boardwalk strolled a young southern belle with an old black man in attendance politely holding a yellow parasol over her head.

She glanced ahead and saw the boys, but continued window shopping in their direction until the distance was closed to only a few feet. When she looked up, the boys were staring at her cleavage.

"Good morning mam'm," the boys said, bowing their heads and tipping their hats in friendly unison.

"What are you young men looking at? You keep your eyes where they belong!"

"Sorry mam'm, but we've never seen such a finely dressed lady before in our humble town! Why are you all gussied up?"

The belle smiled and lowered her eyes in false modesty, pleased she had so easily received such flattery from these handsome young men. A second up-and-down look at the trio, however, proved she wanted no further contact. Men of obvious poor breeding annoyed her.

"Why, what do we have here?" replied the belle somewhat sarcastically. "A handsome white boy of obvious poor stock, a half breed whose father I'm sure is in doubt, and a fearful redskin warrior, all armed to the teeth, I must add, with dreadful bows and arrows. Heavens, I must admit I am mortified at your appearances. You heathen ruffians stand aside, and let a lady pass!"

Without further adieu, Clayton, Jason, and Red Dog stepped aside and let the belle with her black servant continue on down the boardwalk. She was not quite out of earshot when

the three broke out in bawdy laughter, bringing further annoyance to the young southern belle.

She had not seen the last of them however. Not by a
long shot.

CHAPTER TWENTY-THREE
Miss Anabell

Firearms were a common sight on the streets of Colby and hardly a cowboy, rancher, miner, logger, or drifter was ever without a Colt or a Smith & Wesson on his hip and a Winchester lever-action secured in his scabbard. Even store proprietors and bankers kept a loaded pistol secured out of sight in a vest pocket or the small of their back when conducting business, and every saloonkeeper stored a double-barrel shotgun primed with 00 buckshot within easy reach behind the bar, just in case trouble brewed.

But archery tackle was not as common, and in fact, hunting with a bow and arrow was rarely practiced by anybody anymore other than local Indians of various tribes and young men with Indian friends who cannot yet afford a pistol or a rifle. The only exception was those who were captivated by the simplicity of the bow and arrow at a young age and then continued to shoot their bows on into their adult years.

As they became proficient with age, they eventually realized that under certain circumstances, bows and arrows have many advantages over guns and bullets. In the right hands, a stout bow matched with arrows of equal length and weight can shoot circles around the average cowboy shooting from the hip at ranges out beyond 30 yards or so. What the bow lacked in rapid firepower was more than made up for in deadly accuracy. Indeed, it only took one well-placed shaft to quickly drop an opponent to the ground.

The bow and arrow was also quiet. *Thifffft* is often all a deer—or a human adversary—heard before a sharp stone or metal-pointed stick passed through their vitals, with death from rapid blood loss occurring in as little as 10 or 20 seconds.

But the bow and arrow really shined on the blackest of nights. There is no doubt that pistol and rifle accuracy was improved under good lighting, however, an accomplished bowman drawing and shooting his bow instinctively could easily kill a man in the pitch dark. He seldom needed to see his adversary; he just had to sense his adversary's position to be effective.

Firearms were so commonplace that most gun owners scoffed at anyone, white or Indian, who relied solely on archery tackle for personal protection or meat gathering. So it came as a great surprise that Saturday afternoon in Colby when over 30 contestants signed up for the archery match held on church grounds.

Jason, Clayton, and Red Dog were not the first to arrive at the church however. In fact, by the time they had worked their way past the shops and mayor's office to the church grounds on the far side of town, quite a crowd had already gathered in the courtyard behind the church to witness the two primitive shooting events scheduled for that day.

Clayton spied Moses standing nearby in the shade talking with a couple of ranchers. When Moses caught Clayton's eye, Moses motioned the boys over. "Hey, I want ya to meet a couple of old friends, Bill and Brian Nelson. They work a spread about a day's ride from here."

Clayton was the first to stretch his hand out to Brian and then Bill. "Hi, I'm Clayton Alexander," he said with a broad smile. "Moses is our foreman at the Alexander Ranch. How did you meet Moses? And what brings you two way out here to Colby?"

After Jason and Red Dog introduced themselves and shook hands with each of the Nelsons, Bill spoke. "We met Moses on the trail from Ft. Smith several years ago. We camped together along a creek for a few days while Brian and I rested our horses. That's when we learned that Moses had helped doctor our cousin Bobby Nelson's busted leg back at Ft. Smith earlier that same month.

"Moses was horseless at the time," added Bill, "so when it was time to get back home, Brian doubled up and gave Moses a ride part way to Colby. We heard he got a job on a nearby ranch, but had not seen him since. A passerby told us there was to be a hatchet-throwing event this weekend in Colby, and we figured Moses would not be able to resist testing his skills. Brian and I just had to ride out to see if Moses here still had the eye."

Just then an elderly man dressed in a white shirt, black tie, and long black coat jumped out of the shine of the sun and onto a large flat rock for everyone to see. "All those ready to show off their hatchet-throwing skills, the first of today's target events, line up here on my right and pay us your two bits for the privilege," hollered Reverend Marstall. He was getting on in years, but was still spry enough to whip up some enthusiasm from the crowd.

"Good luck, Moses," said Brian as he patted Moses on the back. "I'm sure you will do just fine!"

Moses got in line, paid his two bits, and waited. Although he was well known around town and respected by many, there were also plenty of strangers in town for the celebration. Moses could feel their eyes and read the venom on their faces: no black man should be allowed to mingle with whites, much less participate in a church-sponsored event.

But Moses held his head high and smiled. Nothing pisses off a racist more than a successful black man. And Moses aimed at being the best with his hatchet that day despite the whispers of contempt from a few of the onlookers.

"Here are the rules," stated the reverend. "Bisbee's saw-mill donated four six-inch-thick slabs of a white oak sawed off a two-foot butt, then trimmed them down so they are all about the same size. We'll start off at a distance of 25 feet and give everyone a chance to throw before moving back 10 feet at a time until there is only one man left standing. Winner takes a gold dollar coin home, the church gets the rest.

"If the blade sticks in, you can stick around for the next round. If you miss, you can try once again at that range. You are, however, allowed only one miss during the competition. Miss a second time at any range, and you are out of the competition all together. Understood? Any questions?"

"Why Reverend, just one!"

Reverend Marstall turned around to see a young pretty girl with fair complexion and long blond hair painstakingly set up in large ringlets standing before him. She was looking at him rather coyly through a pair of stunning blue eyes while an older black man with graying hair stood behind her holding a yellow parasol over her head, ostensibly to shield her from the harsh rays of the late-morning sun.

The reverend was visibly shaken, some might even say stunned. He had not seen such dazzle on a woman since he was a young man some 50 years ago. He responded to the belle eagerly, and with a cheerful smile.

"And what might that question be, miss...miss..."

"Miss Annabel. Miss Annabel Preston from New Orleans, Reverend. I am traveling to San Antonio with my daddy on business. That's the sugar business of course. I'm sure y'all know of Preston Sugar. Well anyway, we heard that your quaint little town was holding a celebration of sorts, and thought we would stop by and see what all the excitement might bring us."

"Hey, look Clayton," muttered Jason, pointing to the girl in the formal yellow dress conversing with the reverend. "Isn't that the young belle we saw on the boardwalk earlier this morning? You know...the girl with the big..." Jason said as he cupped his hands over both of his nipples.

"It sure is," replied Clayton with a smile. "I wonder what she's up to? You can bet the reverend won't put up with her show-off ways today!"

Temporarily smitten by Miss Annabel's charms, Reverend Marstall soon came to his senses. Miss Preston, in addition to her long yellow dress that showed a little too much cleavage for the occasion, had on dainty lace gloves and matching pendulous earrings that sparkled a bit under her sun bonnet. Indeed, in this crowd of mostly ranchers, loggers, and hard-talking cowboys, she was definitely over-dressed—make that way overdressed—with finery not avail-able to women in Colby—and Miss Annabel knew it. In fact, she seemed to rather enjoy the attention she was receiving from the men...and the distain she sensed from the other women at the event as well.

"Why, Miss Preston, I am so happy you are gracing our celebration with your presence, but what is your question? You wanted to ask me something about the hatchet-throwing contest, did you not?"

"Why, of course, Reverend. Where are my manners? Lord forgive me! James, please move my parasol a bit so I can get a better look at this gentleman, this handsome man of the cloth!"

James dutifully lowered the parasol, giving everyone within earshot a better look at Miss Annabel. She now had the full attention of those in attendance, as she had planned.

Miss Preston pressed her hand on the reverend's arm, and spoke oh so very sweetly. "Sir, at Preston House, our plantation home built by my granddaddy years ago along the banks of the wild and beautiful Mississippi River, we do not allow our darkys to mix with us white folk, except for the maids and cooks of course, so I was wondering why y'all good Christian people of Colby choose to allow a darky to socialize so close to y'all...this being a church celebration and all. I mean, sir, why on earth would you let a strong and powerful black man with a sharp killing hatchet move about so freely while in your midst? Y'all must just be looking to meet the Lord sooner than expected!"

Before the reverend could reply, a bespectacled man in his late twenties dressed in a gaudy checkered suit raised his arm to get the crowd's attention, and spoke up. "Don't you worry yourself none now Miss Preston. We know how to handle those in Colby who don't know their place amongst good God-fearing white folk!"

The reverend looked over at Moses to see if he heard what Miss Preston and then the bespectacled yahoo had said, and once eye contact was made, the reverend looked away in painful embarrassment.

"Miss Preston, my humble apologies," replied Reverend Marstall in a sarcastic but gentlemanly tone. "We are all God's children, and I am sure that with your fine Christian upbringing you can find it in your heart to forgive us sinners whose humble appearances bring you so much discomfort."

Miss Preston smiled with all the sweetness she could muster and looked around so she could soak up the praise and adulation from the crowd gathered before her, not realizing of course that the reverend was actually poking fun at her by mocking her southerly charms.

"Now step closer to me girl," demanded the reverend, "and gather up your hanky. You have some slimy dark matter dangling from one of your nostrils. It is rather unbecoming of a lady of your stature."

Caught off-guard, Miss Preston flushed and turned her head aside, obviously quite embarrassed, as she searched unsuccessfully for her hanky. The crowd seemed to get a chuckle out of the sudden turn of events and moved in a bit closer, as if they knew by instinct there was more fun to come at Miss Annabel's expense.

"Why Miss Preston," crowed Marstall loudly for all to hear, "it does appear to be a little snot about to slip into your mouth!" The reverend then turned his head aside, covered his mouth, and feigned a bit of gagging.

"Please, folks. Does anyone have an old rag for Miss Preston's snot?"

The crowd now began to giggle a bit at Miss Preston, putting her under a rich cloud of further embarrassment. A few of the ladies in attendance started to clap in appreciation of Reverend Marstall's dramatic performance, enjoying the comeuppance Miss Preston was receiving most deservedly from a respected man of the cloth.

Miss Preston finally pulled a lace hanky from deep inside her bosom and wiped her nose, passing it from one nostril to the next in a most dignified and refined fashion.

"Ah miss, all you need to do to rid that snot is pinch off one nostril with your finger and blow hard through the other nostril, like this!"

Stunned by the comments emanating from somewhere within the group of onlookers, the reverend and the belle both looked toward the unfamiliar voice and saw an old man dressed in fringed buckskins cleaning his nose in just such a manner and then wiping his dirty fingers on his pant leg. "That's how ya do it in Texas, Miss Sugar!"

Miss Annabel looked at the mountain man with vile distain as the crowd laughed at the old man, giving her a reprieve of sorts from the staring eyes. But her reprieve was short-lived.

"Oh, Miss Preston, you didn't get it all," said Reverend Marstall with great flair. "There's a wet spot on your bosom."

With the crowd of onlookers now laughing uproariously and without guilt or embarrassment, Miss Preston looked down at her bosom and, seeing nothing, lifted her dress with both hands and stomped off into the crowd.

"I guess New Orleans sugar is not so sweet," said Bill Nelson loud enough for everyone to hear. "In fact," added Clayton, "I will wager that Preston Sugar is only good for making tarts!"

Of course, not everyone was amused with Reverend Marstall's unique manner, or the manner in which he put Miss Annabel in her place. Nonetheless, the crowd too had been subdued by the reverend's clever and insightful rhetoric, and no more racial epithets were hurled from the crowd of onlookers that morning.

As the men began to line up for the hatchet-throwing competition, Reverend Marstall caught Moses' eye and gave him a wink before melting back into the crowd. Moses smiled and lowered his eyes to the ground to think about what just happened.

His longtime friend Reverend Marstall had used humor and ridicule to diffuse a tense situation. It was also a strategy Doc Rogers used at Ft. Smith when dealing with rowdy cowboys in need of medical attention. Although always an option, physical confrontation was not always the best answer, a lesson that was now permanently ingrained in Moses' brain.

CHAPTER TWENTY-FOUR
Dueling Hatchets

Finally, it was time to see who best could hurl a hatchet. There were 18 ranchers, cowboys, and other ax aficionados who paid their two bits and took their turns first at 25 feet and then at 30 feet. None of them missed at either distance, but when the line was drawn at 35 feet, hatchets started falling short, or if the toss was long enough, the blade failed to penetrate the white-oak slabs. Only 13 men were on the line at 40 feet, and that number fell dramatically at 45 feet and again at 50 feet.

At 60 feet, there were only two men left standing, Moses and Jack Ryan, that grizzled and near toothless old-timer who mocked Miss Annabel earlier, who bragged that he was a direct descendent of the famous mountain man Jim Bridger after the first hurl. Standing not quite five-and-a-half feet tall and weighing in around 200 pounds, Jack did not seem to be the mountain man type, despite the fringed buckskin shirt and breeches, his long and unkempt fiery red hair, and the bone-handled knife he called "grizz" sticking out of the top of his right sided calf-high deerskin boot.

Something was missing, and Moses couldn't quite figure out what it was, at least not at the moment. Maybe it was the bear claw necklace. It looked, well, like it might have been store bought. Or maybe it was his ragged, over-sized felt hat. Pulled tightly over his ears, it made his asymmetrical face with wide-set eyes appear more rounded and quite pudgy.

Moses and Jack stepped up to the line, and to speed things up, they agreed to hurl their hatchets simultaneously at the two-foot-wide white-oak slabs, much to the delight of the crowd.

Moses and Jack now stood side by side, eyed each other up and down...and hurled. *Whoosh, whoosh, whoosh, whoosh, whoosh, whoosh...CRACK! CRACK!* Both spinning hatchets hit their respective marks with resounding ear-splitting accuracy.

Moses rubbed the silver bullet tucked away in his front pocket and stepped up to the line to oppose Jack, and again and again their hatchets slammed into the oak slabs first at 65 feet and then again at a distance of 70 feet. They were on fire, and they knew it!

As the two men lined up at 75 feet, a formidable distance for both men, Jack turned to Moses. "Ya knows, Moses, you're damn good with your throwing," he said after spitting out a wad of tobacco onto the ground. "I'd wager you and me woulda made a good team years back when I was young and spry, especially if you could cook. By any chance, can ya cook as good as ya hurl?"

Moses broke out into a wide grin. He liked Jack, and he also began to think they would have made a good pair years ago trying to carve out a living from the wilderness.

"Yes, I can cook," replied Moses, looking old Jack straight in the eye. "Of course, I would have to depend on you to bring down a deer or an elk once in a while. Ya know, you'd have to do more than your share of the meat gathering if ya wanted me to fire it up right and tasty."

"By cracky, I like the sounds of that, Moses," said Jack as he slapped him on the back. "I'll do the shootin' and *you* do the cookin' and we'll make out just fine. Might even stuff our pockets with some gold dust once in a while, too, if you was willing to pan a secret river up north with me in hostile Indian territory."

Moses did not want to comment on doing any panning for gold, Indian territory or not, and changed the subject. "Where'd ya get your hatchet?" he asked, admiring the rough workmanship of the blade and the intricate Indian markings on the handle.

"I took it off a dead redskin after the big ruckus at Little Big Horn. I was a scout for General Custer back then. I told the general the Sioux were cagey, but he paid me no never mind. He was whatcha call a fancy pants. Needless to say, I got caught up in the battle, ran out of bullets early on, and then got shot in my leg. A young Sioux brave sent an arrow clean through my thigh. Didn't hit anything important, though I bled plenty until I was able to wrap my shirt sleeve around the hole, stopping the blood. It still pains me once in a while when I lay on the wet ground to sleep.

"I tried to stand up then and keep fightin', but I got run over by a horse. I played dead then, but I did see Custer go down. He threw his empty pistol at a charging Sioux brave, but it didn't do him no good. That young brave ran the general through with a lance, and that's what killed him, that no-good son of a bitch. Killed him dead.

"After the battle, the Sioux came in and started cutting up the dead. They ran a sharp stick through both of Custer's ears so he could listen better to them in the afterlife. When they found me still alive, they whooped it up quite a bit and were about to open my guts when one of them recognized me. I lived among them for two years, had a squaw and a couple of kids that fell to the fever. I knew Crazy Horse, and had in fact hunted buffalo with him several times. I guess they thought that killing me would bring them bad medicine, so they put me on a horse, not mine of course, it had been killed from between my legs, and let me ride out with all my body parts still attached. I grabbed this here hatchet on the way, keeping it for a souvenir. Mine got lost somewhere in the grass, and I didn't want to look around for it. I just wanted the hell out of there. Yup, Moses, I fought the Sioux at the Battle of the Little Big Horn and lived to tell the truth about it."

Moses didn't know quite what to say. Jack could spin a yarn, and a fine one at that, but that is just what Moses thought it was—a yarn, a make-believe story that was as far from the truth as the stars were from the ground they were standing on.

The spectators were crowding the shooting lane, jostling each other back and forth for a better view, and were anxious to see who was the better of the two, Moses or Jack, with occasional shouts of encouragement for both men emanating from both sides of the lane. Several men also stood on stumps and wood benches positioned behind the line for a better view of the proceedings.

Clayton, Red Dog, and Jason were standing in the crowd next to the Nelson brothers, clearly enjoying the contest. "Is

Moses any good at this distance?" asked Jason. "Seventy-five feet is a long toss."

"We've seen him hurl at 60 feet with bull's-eye skill," replied Bill Nelson, "but 75 feet may be his limit. That old-timer in buckskin is good, too. It's gonna be close, but I'm betting on Moses."

The crowd hushed as the two men stepped up to the line, wound up, and hurled their blades at the white-oak slabs 75 feet away. *Whoosh, whoosh, whoosh, whoosh, whoosh, whoosh...CRACK! CRACK!*

Incredibly, both rotating hatchets slammed into their respective white-oak slabs with abject ear-splitting authority. The crowd burst into cheers and loud applause, bringing broad smiles to the faces of both men.

Jack, however, did more than just smile. He started dancing around and throwing his hands up in the air. He was enjoying the attention he was receiving to the point where some thought he was showing off. And that was causing him to lose favor with some of the spectators.

But Moses saw Jack differently. He saw a lonely old man who stretched the truth about his accomplishments in the wilderness and on the battlefield. He probably was no relation to Jim Bridger, never trapped beaver in the Rockies, never panned for gold, never killed a grizzly bear with just a knife, and certainly was not the lone survivor of the Little Big Horn.

Somewhere in his past, however, he did learn to hurl a hatchet with amazing speed and accuracy. This was probably one of the few skills he possessed that allowed him to honestly feel good about himself.

As they retrieved their hatchets and started the short walk back to the shooting line, the old man started to rub his throwing arm. He was not used to hurling his hatchet so many times and at these distances in a single day, and his arms were weak from lack of use. Jack turned to Moses and, in a rare moment of honesty, said, "Dang, it looks like I'm about to win something! It will be the first time I ever got to claim a prize for being good at something, other than being a famous mountain man that is."

Moses knew Jack was playing games with his head, trying to get him to think he was destined to lose, but Moses was confidant he was still on target and hurling better than ever. He also knew that Jack was tired. He was starting to breath hard just walking the short distance to and from the white-oak slabs. The hot sun was also taking a toll on Jack. He was sweating profusely and had asked for a bucket of water to slake his thirst and to pour some over his body to help cool himself down.

The two men stepped up to the line, looked each other over one more time, and without further fanfare...hurled. *Whoosh, whoosh, whoosh, whoosh, whoosh, whoosh, CRACK! TWANG!*

The look on Moses' face told it all. His hatchet rolled blade over handle perfectly and slammed dead on into the white-oak slab. Jack's hatchet, however, had ricocheted off the edge of the slab and rolled onto the ground several feet past the target. Jack had missed, and the look on his face was pure disappointment.

It took a minute or two for Jack to realize the outcome. He turned to Moses and shook his hand vigorously. "Ya beat me fair and square, partner. Congratulations on a fine hurl."

As the crowd applauded both men, Clayton, Jason, Red Dog, and the Nelson brothers surrounded Moses, congratulating him on his win, and then shook Jack's hand with equal enthusiasm. It had been a fine display of frontier gamesmanship.

Moses saw Reverend Marstall approaching him and Jack who were now standing near the white-oak slabs and talking to several onlookers. Moses walked over to the reverend and whispered something in his ear. The reverend looked at Moses, nodded his head up and down, and then went back into the church. He unlocked his office door and rummaged through several storage boxes crammed with clothing, household utensils, family heirlooms, and other treasures donated by parishioners until he found what Moses had in mind. He immediately left his office and returned to the festivities outside.

As the reverend worked himself through the crowd, the bespectacled man in the gaudy suite bumped into him. "Excuse me, Reverend."

Reverend Marstall didn't want to pay any attention to him. Why, he wondered, were racists so often social misfits and misguided white trash? He acknowledged the bespectacled man's apology with a nod and continued on through small groups of spectators until he jumped up on the large flat rock, and held his hands out to quiet the crowd. "Moses Sheridan, please step forward."

Moses eased up in front of the reverend and removed his hat.

"I declare you the winner of the town of Colby's Hatchet Hurling Event. Moses, here is your prize, a gold dollar coin."

Moses thanked the reverend, raised his hat high, and bowed his head in response to the thunderous applause. He was quite taken back by the response, erasing for the time being memories of the racial epithets hurled at him earlier in the day.

Before the onlookers could disperse however, Reverend Marstall again held his hands out to quiet the crowd. "Jack Ryan, please step forward."

Puzzled, Jack looked around to see if anyone in the crowd understood what the reverend wanted him for. Nobody seemed to have an answer, so he eased himself through the crowd and stood in front the reverend.

"Jack Ryan, the town of Colby also wants to recognize your skill with a hatchet."

Reverend Marstall reached into his vest pocket and produced a medal with a silver bar attached to red, white, and blue cloth stripes and a silver star dangling underneath. He then reached out to Jack and said, "Congratulations on a fine showing!" as he pinned the medal on his shirt.

Jack was stunned. And for the first time in many years, he was speechless. He had spent most of his life trying to convince strangers and friends alike that he was somebody special, somebody with extraordinary skills—generally to no avail. But today he had won applause and adulation from a group of strangers for ridiculing a racist and for hurling his hatchet the best he could.

Years later, Jack told his daughter it was the proudest moment of his life. He finally got what he always wanted, respect, and he got that by simply being himself.

CHAPTER TWENTY-FIVE

Brocken Arrows

Onlookers and contestants alike took advantage of the break between the hatchet and archery contests to mingle about and exchange recent news concerning their neighbors. Who had been sick, who was getting married, and who had become a new grandmother or grandfather was of interest to many. And for those who had loved ones pass into the hereafter, there was some grieving to do in the graveyard adjacent to the church where wild flowers were placed on headstones and questions concerning the cause of death were raised.

It was the courtyard behind the white clapboard church where the largest crowds gathered. There were plenty of tables and chairs available plus four long tables draped with woven cloth coverings where various dishes prepared by some of the parishioners were available. Blackened pots of young carrots, creamed onions, salt potatoes, and of course chili—hot chili—were on every table, as were various salads, breads, and desserts, including Reinette's homemade fruit pies.

The main course was a young steer slowly roasting over an open-pit mesquite fire, its drippings igniting with short-lived balls of flame and gray puffs of smoke as each drop hit the smoldering coals. The cook and his helper basting the steer with a secret proprietary hot sauce were employees of the Double Bar Ranch, whose owner, Jimmy Vachel, not only donated the steer, but was also participating in the archery shootout.

The church deacons teamed up and removed the white-oak slabs used for the hatchet-throwing event and replaced them with bales of dried grass bound tightly. They positioned the targets on the edge of church property to the south rather than the open lane on the north side so that an errant shaft would sail harmlessly away from the gathering crowd of onlookers.

Clayton, Jason, and Red Dog were getting anxious to get the shooting match underway. They strung their bows and began to warm up by practicing with a few arrows. A tall man with a strange accent brought out his bow, an odd-looking contraption that was nearly six feet in length. Sir Thomas was from some town on the other side of the Atlantic Ocean. He called it an English longbow, and he shot it quite accurately, although Red Dog thought it was too long to shoot easily from horseback.

Vachel also shot a few practice shafts. Tall and lanky with long gray sideburns, Vachel had been an archer most of his life, preferring to hunt with his bow rather than a rifle. He could wrap his hand around his three-shot groups, a level of proficiency not yet possessed by Clayton or Jason.

The Reverend Marstall fumbled for his watch, but it was not in his vest pocket. It must have broken loose from its chain and unbeknownst to him fell to the ground sometime earlier in the day. Or maybe he left it in his office earlier. He would search for it later. In the meantime, he stepped up on a four-legged wood stool, and as if on cue, a crowd of onlookers encircled him to hear what he had to say.

"The archery shoot-off will begin shortly," he declared. "All those willing to test their skills should line up here on my right and pay your two bits for the privilege."

Red Dog, Jason, and Clayton rushed to the head of the line and paid their money. When they turned around to make room for the next contestants, Will and Reinette were standing by with Red Dog's father, Tall Bear, waiting to wish them all luck. They were conspicuously absent during the hatchet hurling, and missed seeing Moses take first place.

Reverend Marstall then extended his arms to quiet the crowd and get their undivided attention. "Here are the rules, gentlemen. You will start at 15 yards and shoot three arrows at a five-inch bull's-eye attached to the middle of a bound grass bale. If a single arrow fails to hit the bull's-eye, you will immediately be disqualified, even if it is your first shaft. You will move backward in five-yard increments until there is only one archer standing. Deacon Jones will be the only judge, and his word is final. No exceptions. Where is Miss Annabel? I hesitate to say this, but are there any questions?"

His comments earned him a few laughs from the spectators. Nonetheless, a few did look around to see if the young southern belle was standing somewhere nearby.

"If not, let's begin!"

Clayton, Jason, and Red Dog would be shooting together at the first target.

"Will, I know you need to talk with Moses," confided Reinette, "so I'll watch the contest with the Wilkinsons and meet you in the courtyard afterward."

Will nodded in agreement just as Moses joined them.

"Congratulations, Moses," smiled Reinette. "We missed your performance, but everybody is talking about it on Main Street. You're becoming quite popular!"

"Thanks, Reinette. It was quite an experience. I didn't realize how much fun I was having until after it was all over. I still find it hard to believe I actually won. My arm is a bit sore...but I'll manage. I'll tell ya all about it later."

"I'll be looking forward to it, Moses," replied Reinette. And then she touched Will's arm before joining the Wilkinsons.

Will and Moses walked slowly out of earshot from the rest of the crowd of spectators. Nobody seemed to take notice.

"Did you get a chance to talk to Sheriff Sweeney yet?" asked Moses once they were sure they were alone.

"Yes. We talked for about an hour in his office while Reinette shopped. Moses, you were right. Bull is one tough hombre. According to Sweeney, he received a couple dozen or so telegrams from Texas Ranger headquarters all over Texas, including San Antonio, and several more law offices in Missouri, the Oklahoma Territory, and as far east as New Orleans.

"Bull has been in and out of eight or ten jails for everything from public drunkenness to armed robbery. And listen to this! He walked into a gun store outside of San Antonio a few years back and asked to see a new Colt. When the proprietor's son handed him one, Bull pistol-whipped the kid until he was nearly blinded by the assault!"

"Why did he do that?"

"It seems Bull wanted a box of shells so he could test

fire the gun outside behind the shop. The kid said he couldn't oblige him without first getting his daddy's say-so, and Bull went berserk saying the kid sassed him. The only thing that stopped Bull from killing the kid was the kid's dad. He came back from the bank just in time and clubbed Bull in the head with an ax handle several times and then went to work on his face, breaking his nose and knocking a couple teeth out. The kid's father finally swung on him with an uppercut to the groin, and Bull went down like a pole-axed mule. Bull spent 18 months in the county jail for assault and had to give the kid his horse and saddle for restitution."

"It doesn't seem to take much provocation to set him off, does it?" said Moses as he looked around to make sure no one was listening in on their private talk. "He's a stallion that needs to be gelded, and by the sounds of it, that's exactly what it took to beat him into submission at the gun store!"

"Yeah, he can sure take a beating...and give one, too, without much warning. Sweeney got a telegram from Mexican authorities advising him to approach Bull with extreme caution. It seems Bull stuck a knife in a vaquero's back 10 years ago during a bar fight over a whore, paralyzing him from the waist down. Bull spent five years in prison before they escorted him to the Texas border for "good behavior." If he ever returns to Mexico, and they catch him, they'll hang him on the spot.

"Oh, there's more, but you get the picture."

"Yeah. This guy is dangerous. Crazy dangerous. Did Sweeney say anything else, maybe something about those rumors of Bull riding with your son?"

Will dropped his head and looked down at the ground for a second. "Yes, there seems to be some truth to those rumors, but Ross, Sweeney's new deputy, came into the office and we had to cut our discussion short. I plan on talking to Sweeney some more after the archery shoot-off. I want you there with me.

"Oh, by the way, congratulations on your win. Colby is quiet these days, but you never know when your skill with a hatchet might be called upon again!"

A loud round of applause diverted Will and Moses' attention to the archery contest. They walked over to get a closer look-see and learned that Clayton, Jason, and Red Dog were still in the running after each of them hit the bull's-eye three times at 35 yards. Only eight shooters remained in the contest, including Sir Thomas and Jimmy Vachel.

At 40 yards, four more shooters were disqualified, including Clayton, who missed the bull's-eye with his third arrow. Now it was down to four.

Before the next round began, Tall Bear rolled out a wagon wheel and propped it up against one of the dried-grass bales. This was not your average wagon wheel however, but one modified by the blacksmith especially for the archery shoot-off. It had an open four-inch center where the axle once ran, but the spokes were covered with metal plates.

"If your arrow does not pass through the axle opening," explained Deacon Jones with a big grin, "it will splinter on the metal plates protecting the wheel spokes and you will be disqualified. I sure hope you all packed plenty of arrows...'cause you are going to need them!"

The gallery had swelled to over 100 onlookers, and when Deacon Jones explained the new rules, they moved in a bit closer for a better look.

"Now, each of you will shoot three arrows at the wheel, with the winner being the one who sends the most shafts through the axle opening without breaking. If there's a tie, we will step back another five yards and shoot another round. Are you ready?"

Jimmy Vachel was the first to give it a try. He unleashed three shafts in quick succession...*THIFFFFT*...*THIFFFFT*...*THIFFFFT*...and all three passed through the axle opening with ease. Jason looked a bit worried after that performance, but he, too, sent three shafts one at a time and seconds apart...*THIFFFFT*...*THIFFFFT*...*THIFFFFT*...through the center of the wagon wheel with plenty of room to spare.

Sir Thomas was next. He stared at the axle hole for several seconds before nocking an arrow. Then he brought his longbow to full draw, and as soon as his draw finger touched his check he released a feathered shaft...*THIFFFFT*...*CRACK!* His shaft slammed an inch above the axle into one of the protective metal plates shielding the spokes and splintered into a dozen or more pieces.

He turned around and with a big smile, congratulated Vachel and Jason on their fine shooting before stepping back and out of the way to take in the rest of the match as an observer. Even though he had two shots left, he could not tie Vachel and Jason with their perfect rounds.

Vachel walked over to Sir Thomas. "That was still good shooting, my friend. I wouldn't want you shooting at me at 45 yards. I'm afraid you would skewer me right easily! Why don't you visit my ranch for a few days after the celebration is over? I would love to learn more about your longbow."

Sir Thomas smiled and nodded his head. "This archery shoot-off was bloody good fun. Yes, I would like to see your ranch. Maybe we can hunt some stags with our bows or maybe one of your big cats."

"Good. Then it's settled. We'll ride out together Monday morning!"

At 73 years of age, Sir Thomas had nothing to prove, and nothing to be ashamed of either. He rather just enjoyed the camaraderie and the competition. Yet Will thought there was something odd about this sudden friendship with Vachel, almost as if the two men had met before and didn't want anyone to catch on.

Red Dog was last, and he looked plenty nervous. He walked up to the line knowing that all eyes were on him. He stared at the center of the axle hole for several seconds. Then in one fluid motion he brought his self-bow up to chest level and without hesitation released a feathered shaft...*THIFFFFT*...right through the center of the axle... followed by two more in quick succession...*THIFFFFT*... *THIFFFFT*...both as accurate as the first.

He turned to the crowd and was humbled by the applause he received from several of the white men. Not every white man, or black man, or Mexican for that matter, was a racist.

Tall Bear eased through the crowd to get a better look at his son. He showed no emotion, but inside, he was proud. Very proud. Tall and muscular, Red Dog had become a man before his very eyes. Good with a horse, an excellent shot with a rifle and now with a bow and arrow, Red Dog would have made a fearsome warrior in past years. His grandfather, Buffalo Hump, who at times went on raids against the Comanche's, would have been proud, too.

"Okay now. Let's give the shooters some room," ordered Deacon Jones as he moved the contestants back five additional yards.

Suddenly that wagon wheel looked mighty small. This was a long shot with a bow and arrow at a very small target. There would be absolutely no room for error.

Again, Vachel was the first to shoot, and again, he sent three shafts in quick succession through the open center of the wagon wheel...*THIFFFFT...THIFFFFT...THIFFFFT...*with such precision the shafts were each touching one another.

"Jason, you shoot next," declared Deacon Jones.

Jason was beginning to show some strain. This was a tough shot for anybody, but Vachel made it look easy. Jason's first arrow slid through the center hole with ease, as did his second shaft. Maybe it was nerves, maybe it was overconfidence, maybe it was fatigue, but Jason's third shaft *clanked* into the metal two inches above the open axle, sending wood splinters in several directions.

Disheartened, Jason gazed first at Vachel for his reaction before turning his head in Red Dog's direction. Showing no emotion, Red Dog simply stared back at Jason and stepped up to the line. He knew he finally had a chance to beat Jason at something important and win favor with Dancing Water.

"Okay, quiet down everyone," ordered Deacon Jones. "Okay, Red Dog it's your turn to shoot. Take your time."

All eyes were now on Red Dog as he pulled a shaft from his quiver and snapped it onto his bow string. Then in one fluid motion he came to a full draw and released his first feathered shaft at the wagon wheel...*THIFFFFT...*it flew

189

straight and true through the axle opening...as did his second shaft with equal precision.

It was the third shaft that upset Red Dog. He knew he could beat Jason and tie Vachel with this shot. In his head he in fact had already beaten Jason, but his heart felt differently, telling him he wasn't good enough.

Red Dog nervously took his eye off the axle hole for a split second as he brought his bow to full draw, and instead of another smooth release, he plucked the string, causing the shaft to bob up and down like a cat chasing a mouse all the way to the wagon wheel.

Red Dog watched with dismay as the wooden shaft hit the metal surrounding the axle opening with a resounding *clang*, scattering wood splinters all over the ground and ending his chances of impressing Dancing Water.

Vachel, with his years of experience with the bow and arrow, clearly won the contest. He shook hands with Jason and Red Dog and complimented them on their fine shooting before Reverend Marstall quieted the crowd to bestow upon Vachel his prize—a gold dollar coin.

"Jimmy Vachel, congratulations on your incredible shooting!" declared the reverend. "I must ask you one question, however. How far can you shoot your bow with that kind of accuracy?"

"Jason, Clayton, Red Dog, and Sir Thomas and the others are certainly worthy adversaries," answered Vachel with a twinkle in his eye. "I have found that the hungrier I get the better I shoot. I once took a mule deer at nearly 100 yards because I hadn't eaten in three days. Now, my belly is aching hungry today, but wagon wheels aren't much good to chew on. So, as to just how far I can hit the center of that there wagon wheel, well, I think I shot about my best today."

Sir Thomas, Clayton, Deacon Jones, Will, Moses, Tall Bear, and the others laughed at Vachel's response, and when he held the gold coin high in the air, they applauded him for his prowess with the bow and arrow.

Red Dog however was nowhere to be seen.

CHAPTER TWENTY-SIX

The Grifters

"Who won the archery contest?" asked Sheriff Sweeney when Will and Moses entered his office.

"Jimmy Vachel, Steve," said Will.

"He sure did," echoed Moses as he closed the door behind them. "He shoots that bow of his better than most cowboys shoot their Colts."

"Why, I do declare. I know that face and voice from somewhere!"

Moses spun around. There behind bars was Miss Annabel Preston and some bespectacled dandy standing behind her in a gaudy suit. Her father, Moses surmised!

"Do you know these two?" asked Sweeney in a surprised tone.

"Yes, I'm afraid I do," replied Moses. "And I'm just as surprised as you! That's Annabel Preston and her father from New Orleans. He owns Preston Sugar. She told everyone at the hatchet-throwing contest that they stopped in Colby en route to San Antonio on business. Or so she says anyway. What's going on?"

"Oh, they stopped here on business all right," said Sweeney with a smirk. "I received a telegram an hour ago about these two. They're not father and daughter, they're man and wife. And they don't own Preston Sugar or any other company in New Orleans. In fact, nobody in New Orleans ever heard of Preston Sugar. They're carpetbaggers, Moses, and they're here in Colby to swindle anybody they can dupe. Their real names are Ed and Rosemary Cochran, and they hail from Goshen, a small hamlet in Pennsylvania near Harrisburg."

"How on earth did ya find all that out?" queried Moses.

Sweeney walked over to the cage and looked Ed and Rosemary straight in the eye. "It seems here that while Miss Annabel got the attention of the crowd by parading about in her fancy yellow dress and singling you out as a dangerous black man, her partner here, Ed, was picking the pockets of our fine citizenry. At some point, he bumped into Reverend Marstall and lifted his gold watch and chain without the good reverend's knowledge.

"Of course we wouldn't have known that if it weren't by accident. Mrs. Temple and her daughter Judith just happened to notice the watch while they were shopping at Barnaby's Dry Goods. These two grifters were trying to trade the watch for something or another. Mrs. Temple recognized it as belonging to the reverend, and told my deputy."

Sweeney turned around and went back to his desk. "Reverend Marstall is coming by shortly to identify his watch, the one his daddy gave him when he took up the collar, and to help me identify the rightful owners of all this other property we found in Ed's saddle bags."

Sweeney then emptied the contents of a grain bag onto his desk. There were several jewelry pieces, including a necklace and a broach, a green poke filled with silver and gold coins, two wallets stuffed with cash, one wallet emptied of all its contents, two more watches, and a set of false wooden teeth.

"How in the dickens did he lift those false teeth without the owner gagging?" chuckled Will. "I hope they were in the owner's pocket and not his mouth!"

"I think they belong to one of the miners in town for the celebration," smiled Sweeney. "If he's sober I'm sure he misses them by now. After Reverend Marstall drops by I'm going to walk about town and see if I can locate him. I'll have my deputy look around, too."

"By the way, whose horse is that tied up out front?" asked Will.

"Why, that's Ed's horse and saddle, the one with the saddle bags stuffed with stolen property, why?"

"Because that mare belongs to the Nelson brothers. They've been looking for it all day. They thought it wandered off by itself. They feared they would have to double up for the day's ride back home, and will be right glad you recovered it for them."

"Damn! They stole the horse, too!" Exasperated, Sweeney stomped outside to make sure the horse stayed secured to the hitching post and then came back into the office shaking his head in disbelief. "You just don't know who you can trust these days, do you?"

Moses suddenly felt the sting of Miss Annabel's racially charged remarks she levied on him yesterday lifted. She was no longer a southern belle, rich and refined, with a fine plantation house on the banks of the mighty Mississippi River and prominent social status among other well-to-do New Orleans sugar plantation families, but rather a fraud all wrapped up in stolen finery, worthy of nothing more than contempt from most decent folks. Simple white trash, that's all she really amounted to.

"One more thing, Sheriff," asked Moses. "Where's the old black man that accompanied Miss Annabel all about town? The one who dutifully held the parasol high over her head? He could have been part of the charade, too, don't ya think?"

"No, I spoke to him already, Moses. He, too, was taken in by Miss Annabel. She promised him a position in the kitchen on the Preston plantation when they got back to New Orleans. I guess he's an excellent cook, but when he found out the truth about her and Ed he tossed her parasol in the manure pile behind the stable and walked away."

"Reinette was thinking about hiring help for the kitchen," chimed in Will as he looked out the window. "If you see him again, ask him if he's willing to work inside for us. Give him directions to the ranch if he is, and we'll let our rowdy crew judge his culinary skills."

Moses moved to close the heavily reinforced wooden door that separated Sweeney's office from the barred cell so he and Will could talk privately with Sweeney. At first he resisted the temptation to flash a broad and contemptuous smile at Miss Annabel, but before he latched the door he did ask her if she would like a hanky "cause it shore looks like ya could use one!"

Miss Annabel just stared at Moses until the door was shut tight, as if her eyes could fry him like a piece of liver on a red-hot stove.

"What else did you hear about my son John and Bull riding together?" asked Will when Moses stepped away from the door.

"Not much more than what we already discussed, Will," replied Sweeney. "John and Bull rode together up north for about a year. They both got into some trouble with the law, fighting mostly, but on one occasion John punched a store-keeper square in the mouth for allegedly cheating him on some merchandise. John spent the night in jail, but that's all that happened. The storekeeper refused to press charges the next morning, telling the deputy it was all an honest mis-understanding, which tells me that John was probably right about the storekeeper doing some cheating.

"I tried to find out some more, but it seems John stopped going by his Christian name. The locals started calling him Mexican Jack for his penchant of wearing a sombrero, Mexican wheeled spurs, and a double bandolier of rifle bullets, and the name stuck. His Spanish was more than passable and the folks soon took a liking to him. It might help if I had a picture or a hand drawing of your son when he was a young man. I don't think I ever met him up close to give out a solid description."

Will and Moses looked at each other, but did not say a word.

CHAPTER TWENTY-SEVEN
The Judge Packs a Pair of Navy Colts

Sunday was the last day of the town's celebration, and it was also the day of the pistol and rifle-shooting contests. These events were sure to draw the biggest crowds, and hopefuls from miles around were quickly gathering at the church eager to show off their shooting skills.

Clayton and Jason were most interested in the pistol competition, with each having it in his head that he was actually capable of winning the event.

"Where's Red Dog?" asked Clayton. "I thought he would be here by now."

"I haven't seen him since yesterday after he lost the archery shoot," answered Jason. "I wouldn't be surprised if he already rode back to the ranch alone."

Suddenly a single shot rang out, and Clayton and Jason stopped talking. "Now that I have your attention," roared Reverend Marstall after he slid his pocket Colt back into his vest with a big smile, "we can begin today's shooting events.

"First off, however, we have an important announcement to make. Mayor Jenkins and the members of the Town

Council will you please come forward and join me?

"Folks, please give Mayor Jenkins and the Town Council a warm welcome."

Polite applause followed. Marstall then stood aside, allowing all eyes to fall upon the mayor.

"Fifteen years ago our town was saved from sure destruction by an unknown Texas Ranger," declared Mayor Jenkins. "He alone and without fear foiled a gang of seven ruthless outlaws from a bank robbery that would have surely bankrupted most of the businesses and private citizens of Colby. Several people lost their lives that day, and the body count would have been higher if it were not for the courage of that young man.

"In commemoration of that day and the events that followed, the Town Council once a year bestows upon an individual who best represents the courage and selflessness of that undercover Texas Ranger the Key to the Town.

"Sheriff Steve Sweeny, please step forward."

Sweeney, who was talking to his deputy, was caught off-guard somewhat by the mayor's booming voice. He turned his head and made instant eye contact with the reverend, who flashed back a bright smile.

"Sheriff Sweeney," repeated the mayor, "please come up and stand next to us so everyone can see who you are. Folks, please give our sheriff a warm welcome."

Sweeney didn't know what was going on, and he looked a bit embarrassed by all the fuss Mayor Jenkins was making. Nonetheless, he removed his hat and stood next to the mayor, Reverend Marstall, and the members of the Town Council on a slight rise above the onlookers.

The mayor then held out a fancy wood box in front of Sweeney. "Sheriff, please accept this Key to the Town of Colby as a token of our appreciation for all your efforts in keeping our citizens safe and out of harm's way."

Stunned, Sweeney could only stand there, soaking up the applause from familiar faces as well as the visages of strangers. He bowed his head several times in thanks for the unexpected honor. Only two onlookers seemed perturbed at Sweeney's award: Bull and gun shop proprietor Davis.

"Now we're going to see who's the best pistol shot in these here parts," declared Reverend Marstall.

"C'mon Reverend," said some freckled-face kid in the crowd, "you know it has to be me!"

Marstall at first nodded his head at the kid and then shrugged his shoulders as if to say "maybe yes, maybe no!" Marstall continued. "Here are the rules. Each contestant will fire six times at a single playing card set out at 30 yards distant. To qualify for the shoot-off, you need to put at least five holes in that card. Moses Sheridan and I will be the sole judges in the event anyone thinks he nicked the card, and nicks will count. Now, who wants to give it a try for two bits?"

Almost 60 cowboys, ranch hands, store keepers, card-sharps, miners, and others stepped up and got in line. And for the next two hours they laid their money down and took their chances at the shooting range. In the end, only three made the cut, and one of them was the freckled-face kid.

Clayton and Jason missed as many times as they hit and were quickly eliminated. They were both stunned when they saw their scores and left the shooting line without saying a word to each other.

"The rest of you may as well get out now 'cause I'm the best there is!" boasted the kid with the freckles. "After all, I'm the only one who hit six out of six!"

Marstall was getting annoyed with the kid, but didn't let it get to him as Miss Annabel had the previous day. "Do we have any other shooters?" he asked as he looked around.

"Yes!" said a voice from the crowd. "How about giving Will Alexander a chance to shoot? Everybody knows he already has the reputation for being the best shot around!"

Clayton and Jason stood on their tiptoes and scanned the crowd to see who was doing all the talking. To their astonishment, it was Red Dog!

"What is he up to now?" asked Clayton.

"He lost face in the archery shoot yesterday, and today he has to be the center of attention to make up for it," Jason replied. "He's mad, too, and I think he's trying to embarrass your grandfather just like he was embarrassed after losing to Vachel. You know, the more I see of Top Dog, the less I like him."

Marstall turned to Will, who was standing with Reinette and Moses in the nearby shade, and held up his two outstretched hands. "What do you say, Will? Do you want to give it a try?"

"Why ask that old man?" yelled out the kid. "He hasn't packed a gun in nearly 10 years I'm told. He probably can't see the card much less hit it!"

That got a laugh from a few bystanders, those that did not know Will personally.

"Who is that kid?" asked Reinette, a bit miffed by the insolence. "I've never seen him before. He certainly is a cocky lad."

"That's the Miller's oldest boy, Mark," replied Moses. "He has the reputation for being a fair shot, but with a loud mouth. He and Clayton haven't gotten along ever since old man Miller accused Clayton of stealing something from his store some time ago."

Red Dog spoke out again. "Will Alexander is still the man to beat folks." Several people turned around to see who was talking, but Red Dog slipped away and joined Clayton and Jason standing near the outskirts. He felt a chill, as if he was not welcome, but he quickly shrugged it off.

Suddenly another man stepped away from the crowd. "And I am the man to beat him. In fact, I am the only man here that can beat Wilfred Alexander. Neither of his sons could ever shoot straight, and his grandson can hardly hold his Colt steady enough to hit a barn much less a playing card!"

Clayton, Jason, and Red Dog each looked at each other in disbelief. It was Bull!

Clayton's face turned sundown red, and Mark, the freckled-face kid, suddenly backed up and shut up.

"Moses, get the wood box from the carriage for me. Please." begged Reinette. She then turned to her husband. "When I gave you back your badge, Will, your pistols went with it. I asked Moses to bring them here for you so you could enter this contest if you had a hankering to do so. I had a wood box made special for the occasion. Will, it's time you strapped them back on."

"What do you say, Will?" asked the reverend. "This could be quite a shooting contest the likes of which has never been played out here in Colby if you agree to take these two to task!"

Moses walked up to Will and handed him the box. Inside were two custom 1851 Navy Colts with engraved ivory grips.

"I cleaned them both up and shot them several times this morning before breakfast. Reinette asked me to in case you wanted to do some shooting today. I found them both to be incredibly accurate! I loaded each cylinder with fresh powder and equally weighted lead balls, snugly capped each cylinder and then smeared the chambers with pork fat. Each hammer is resting between chambers."

Will didn't want it to appear that he was goaded or shamed into entering the pistol match. He threaded two right-hand holsters onto his gun belt, positioning one over his left hip and the other off the left side of his stomach, and buckled the belt.

"I am humbled by the fact that Red Dog and young Mark Miller believe I am still a crack shot. Thanks, boys, for your respect.

"And Bull, now that you have told everyone how good you are with a gun, I can only surmise that it must be true even though nobody has ever seen you touch off a single round. Frankly, I am inclined to believe you're all smoke.

"I accept the challenge, but here is the hitch. I am an old man who can barely ride a horse anymore. Heck, my wife drove me here in a carriage, so if you two outshoot me it's nothing to be very proud of really. You merely outshot an old man well past his prime. Big deal.

"But, if by chance I show both of you what this pair of Navy Colts can really do, here and now, then you both should be embarrassed for letting a crippled old man like myself pistol-whip the two of you in broad daylight and full public view. Rather pathetic, wouldn't you agree?

"One more thing. If I lose this shooting match, then the winner must donate any winnings back to the church, including the gun Davis offered up as top prize, agreed?"

Miller and Bull immediately agreed to Will's terms and moved over to the firing line while Will paid the reverend his two bits.

Clayton felt a tug on his left arm and turned to see who it was. "Phoebe Ann! What are you doing here!"

"I heard about the shooting contests, but it looks like I arrived too late to enter. Just as well. Your grandfather has certainly outmaneuvered the Miller boy and Bull. No matter what the outcome, he wins. Now I know where you get your charm and dogged determination from."

Clayton couldn't believe Phoebe Ann was standing next to him. She looked more beautiful than ever in the dappled sunlight. He thought back about how they met at the swimming hole, and how she steadfastly refused to put up with his shenanigans. And later, when she feared not the snake, she proved she could shoot when she shot the head off that serpent tossed high in the air. And damn, the gal could really shoot!

Clayton reached down and touched her hand. She squeezed his hand and then put her arm around his waist. "I missed you, Clayton Alexander. A lot."

"Me, too, Phoebe Ann. I was beginning to think I would never see you again." He turned his head and kissed her... and she kissed him back. And neither one of them cared if anybody saw them.

Marstall took Will's money and then Bull's before announcing that there would be no need for either to qualify. Mark Miller had waived them both to the line.

Four aces were attached to wooden stakes hammered into the ground 90 feet distant.

"Miller, you will be shooting first at the ace of diamonds," stated Reverend Marstall, "followed by Bull at the ace of spades leaving Will to target the ace of hearts. Glass balls tossed high in the air will be used as a tie breaker, should they be needed. Good luck to each of you."

Miller looked less cocky than he did a few minutes back. He sure didn't count on Will Alexander strapping on a pair of black powder Colts, and he sure in hell didn't think Bull would dare show his face amongst all these townsfolk—he simply was despised by most.

Miller dropped six metallic cartridges into the cylinder of his Colt Peacemaker, cocked the hammer, and aimed for a brief second before touching off six .45-caliber rounds one after the other.

Moses ran down and read out the results: "One shot hit the diamond in the middle, two more just outside the diamond, and three nicks. Six hits altogether."

Bull was next. He loaded his Schofield Smith & Wesson Model 3, swiveled his hips, and turned his right shoulder into the target. Without taking his right eye off the center of the playing card, he cocked the hammer and raised his .45 to eye level. Then in carefully timed intervals, he fired six times at the ace of spades.

"Six hits with no nicks," reported Moses. "Two holes dead square in the center spade."

Shooting last gave Will confidence. He knew what he was up against, and instinct told him he would not be out-shot today.

He stood square to the target, hips parallel to the playing card, and bent over slightly at the waist. Then in one quick motion he drew his first pistol, and palmed six shots from the hip in rapid succession. The barrage from the Navy Colt was deafening.

But before anything could be said, Will told Moses to throw six glass balls into the air. Moses complied, and when the six were high overhead, Will drew his second pistol and shattered each globe one at a time before any one of them could hit the ground. A roar of astonishment erupted from the crowd. Will Alexander had just proven what townsfolk had known instinctively for years. Judge Alexander was a crack shot, the best anybody had ever seen!

"Bring the cards up, Moses," ordered Marstall, "and let's see how they did."

All eyes went to Will's ace of hearts. "I count six holes," reported Moses. "Five through the red heart in the center of the card, and one just outside that heart by a horse hair."

"I declare Will Alexander to be the winner," said Reverend Marstall, "and this gold coin is his reward."

"That's incredible shooting, Mr. Alexander," said the Miller kid, his eyes as big as a hoot owl. "I didn't think it was possible...to put that many holes in the center of a playing card I mean."

"That's because you're a stupid kid," bellowed Bull. "A worthless know-it-all."

"Yeah, maybe, but you didn't do much better than me, Mr. Bull!"

"If you guys are impressed with Will Alexander's shooting skills today, you should have seen him shoot when he was in his prime," boasted Reverend Marstall. "Back then *all* six shots would have been touching, and the ace of hearts would have only had a single ragged hole dead center resembling a rosebud."

Bull looked Will straight in the eye and was about to say something. Will squared his shoulders and looked back at Bull directly, almost daring him to make a move. Bull knew better and after a long pause, averted his eyes. Then for just a brief moment Bull focused his eyes on Will again and muttered, "Your rose is my rose."

As he turned to walk away, Bull found Clayton standing square in his exit path. For a moment Jason and Red Dog thought there might be trouble, but Bull looked away again and nonchalantly walked around him without incident. Bull had just been publicly pistol-whipped and wanted nothing more than to wash his embarrassment away with a bottle of whiskey...and a half hour with one of Millie's whores.

Clayton, Jason, and Red Dog all examined Will's playing card. It wasn't just good shooting, it was great shooting. Too good for the average cowboy. Too good for someone who hadn't packed a gun in nearly a decade.

"Are you thinking what I'm thinking?" asked Jason as the trio walked away from the crowd.

"Yes, I am," replied Clayton.

"Do you remember that afternoon your grandfather caught up to the runaway buckboard," asked Jason, "and saved your grandmother from wrecking? Do you remember the Mexican clothes he was wearing, the Mexican saddle he was riding, and how smoothly he rode Red Cloud?"

Phoebe Ann suddenly rejoined the group, telling Clayton she needed to find her sisters.

"Walk with me back to town?"

"Absolutely!" replied Clayton enthusiastically.

Thoughts of his grandfather being a Texas Ranger, the famed undercover Texas Ranger that thwarted the Colby Bank robbery nearly 15 years ago, started to circle around inside Clayton's head. The possibility that his grandfather was the same Texas Ranger that captured the escaping ringleader, a murdering thief named Robertson, and then brought the no-good back alive to Colby for a public hanging, would have to wait for another time.

Clayton had other ideas, more interesting ideas, to contemplate at the moment.

CHAPTER TWENTY-EIGHT
Back at the Ranch

It took over a week before the ranch could settle down and get back into a regular work routine after the weekend celebration. Lefty, Blondy, Tall Bear, and the others told stories again and again after supper about their experiences in town. These stories often ended in raucous, bawdy laughter that permeated the walls of the bunkhouse well into the evening. Indeed, the men needed a vacation from the ranch, and the weekend certainly rejuvenated their spirits.

Even Moses seemed to have a spring in his step as he came into the kitchen for his meals. He and Reverend Marstall had worked together over the weekend in great harmony. Moses admired the manner in which Reverend Marstall handled Miss Annabel's conniving nature and the adolescent outbursts of Mark Miller. It reminded him of Dr. Rogers and his use of humor when dealing with anxious patients. Moses even began attending church services on Sundays and took up reading the Bible when his chores were finished for the day.

After supper one evening when the ranch hands had retired to the bunkhouse to play cards, Reinette came to Will with a second piece of berry pie and a cup of hot coffee.

"What do you think of Clayton's girlfriend, Phoebe Ann?" she asked as she sat down next to him. "I mean, she seems nice enough, and I like her, but I'm not sure she's the right kind of girl for Clayton."

"How so?"

"Well, she certainly is a pretty girl, but quite independent, don't you think? I mean, she goes where she wants to go without supervision, she fends for herself and her sisters without complaining, and Lord knows she can handle a gun better than most men. She seems to have little fear of traveling about the countryside with just her sisters for company, and she certainly seems ready to face any troubles she encounters along the way. Yes, she can take care of herself, but..."

Will put down his fork and looked at Reinette with a warm smile. "Maybe an independent woman is just what Clayton needs to keep him in line. In fact, that's probably exactly what he finds so attractive about her. I know that's the type of woman I fell in love with..."

Reinette straightened her shoulders, cocked her head a bit, and smiled a bit defensively before raising her head and looking at Will directly. "Just what is that supposed to mean?"

"All I'm saying Reinette is that Phoebe Ann is a lot like you! That may be why Clayton seems to be so infatuated with her!"

"Oh, hush Wilfred Alexander...I mean, I never quite thought of it in that sort of way...hmm, maybe you are on to something."

Reinette stood up, walked across the kitchen, and then turned around to face Will.

"That doesn't alter the fact that Clayton sometimes still

seems to have a chip on his shoulder. Even this morning he sassed me after breakfast. I thought you were going to have a talk with him about that?"

"I intend to. It's gone on long enough, and in fact, right now is as good a time as any. Why don't you tell Clayton and Jason I want to see them out in the barn."

CHAPTER TWENTY-NINE

The Secret Room
and the Secret Within

Will waited outside the barn until he saw Clayton and Jason walk out of the ranch house and look over in his direction. When he was sure they spotted him, he disappeared into the bowels of the barn.

Clayton and Jason stepped up their pace when they saw Will, but when they walked through the double open doors of the barn, Will was nowhere to be seen. They scrambled down the aisle between the stalls calling out his name, to no avail.

C-R-E-A-K. That sound came directly from the corner stall in the back of the barn. Clayton and Jason rushed over, but all they saw was a sliver of light shining through an open slot. They stepped into the stall, and upon closer inspection discovered what appeared to be a false wall to the stall and an open slot revealing an unhinged panel door left partially open.

"Grandpa?"

"Come on in, boys," came the answer, "and please shut the door tightly behind you. I don't want anybody else to know where we are."

Clayton and Jason walked through the door, pulled it snug behind them, and then stepped into a large room tucked out of sight from elsewhere in the barn where they found Will seated at a workbench busily cleaning his Navy Colts.

"I never knew this room existed," said Clayton, eyes bulging with wonder. "Jason, Red Dog, and I always played in the barn when we were kids, especially on rainy days, and never once did we suspect there was a secret room hidden within."

"Only your grandmother and Moses know about the existence of this hideout. And now so do the both of you. I don't want anybody else except Red Dog to know however. Nobody, understand?"

Clayton and Jason nodded their heads in agreement as their eyes darted back and forth about the room. "So this is where you disappeared to every time I went looking for you. I'd see you go into the barn, but when I looked for you, I couldn't find you!"

"That's right, Clayton. I needed to keep this place a secret, even from you and Jason. I will explain more later."

"Okay, but what is this place, really?" gushed Clayton as he continued to explore the forbidden room with his darting eyes.

"Keep looking around, and then you tell me," replied Will, smiling now that he seemed to have triggered Clayton and Jason's inherent curiosity.

There were several lever-actions standing upright in an open gun cabinet secured to the wall, including a Henry lever-action and more than a dozen pistols hanging on pegs adjacent to the gun cabinet, along with several boxes of ammunition of various calibers stored on nearby shelves. In addition, there were several muzzleloaders, rifle scabbards, pistol holsters, flags, gun belts, swords, and other objects decorating the room.

"This place looks like a fortress or a museum," replied Jason, in awe as deep as Clayton. "Wait a minute Will, is that not the Mexican saddle you had on Red Cloud when you caught up to Grandma Reinette and the runaway buckboard several months ago? And that blue shirt. You were wearing that shirt that day, too, weren't you?"

"That's right, Jason. You have a good eye, an eye for detail, and a good memory, too."

"The one thing that seems to really stick in my head though is the way you rode Red Cloud," gushed Jason. "He was galloping at full speed over rough terrain that day as you picked your way down off the hill, but your shoulders were square and you remained tight in the saddle. It was an incredible sight. I've never seen any cowboy before or since ride so taunt, so perfectly, and with such determination, as if the devil himself were at your heels. You ride like a Comanche warrior!"

"Jason's right, Grandpa," echoed Clayton. "Who taught you to ride like the wind?"

"John Coffee 'Jack' Hayes," replied Will directly, "soon after he became a Texas Ranger. He taught me how to ride, and ride hard like my life depended on it. In all my days since I've never run across a better horseman. He understood horses and their ways and could train a wild stallion into doing almost anything he wanted him to do by simply being patient and deliberate in his actions.

"Captain Hayes also taught me something else just as important. A good horse needs a good rider. When you ask a horse to do something, you must be pure of heart and clear in your intentions. No ambiguity, no doubt. Only then will a stallion trust you and give you all that he has to give.

"If not, if you don't know what you're doing or why you're doing it, he'll buck you right off, it's that simple; like Red Cloud did to you Clayton the day you tried to ride him outside the coral."

C-R-E-A-K! Suddenly Red Cloud's head appeared through a small door in the far wall.

"Yes, Red Cloud has a secret passageway to this room, too," laughed Will. "He likes to keep me company when I'm out here alone. Unless you're standing on the far side of the coral, you can't see this door. And that's why I only allow Moses to enter the corral, and why Moses is the only other cowboy on this ranch who can ride Red Cloud. Red Cloud has learned to trust Moses implicitly, as I have ever since Moses stepped foot on this ranch looking for work many years ago."

Clayton had so many questions. "Everybody knows the Texas Rangers can ride like there's no tomorrow when called upon, like you Grandpa. And rumor has it that at one time you rode with the Rangers. Is that true, Grandpa? Are you a Texas Ranger? Are you the Texas Ranger that caught the outlaws robbing the bank years ago, the one whose memory the town has honored every year since by giving to someone with his kind of grit the Key to the Town?"

"I've had the honor of riding with the Texas Rangers on one or two occasions," replied Will as he lowered his eyes, "but not as a Ranger. No, I am not and never have been a

Texas Ranger. And I'm definitely not the undercover Texas Ranger who broke up the robbery by killing those outlaws that day and then brought the ringleader Dwight Robertson in for a hanging, either."

"But Will, you sure shoot like one!" blurted out Jason. "After that shooting lesson you gave Bull and Mark Miller, you're the talk of the town. How'd you learn to shoot like that?"

"Not only did Jack Hayes teach me to ride," replied Will, "he taught me how to aim, shoot, and reload—all from horseback, too. Once you learn how to shoot a man in the head while galloping at full speed straight at him, hitting a stationary playing card at 30 yards isn't much of a challenge. And as for those glass balls, there's a trick to that kind of shooting. Someday I'll show you how you can do it, too. It's really easier than taking the center out of a playing card."

Clayton and Jason looked at each other in utter amazement. All these years they saw Will Alexander as a kindly old man, wiry and agile as a big cat and tough as nails when need be, but easygoing nonetheless. Not much seemed to ruffle him, even when Bull looked him straight in the eye after the pistol-shooting contest. Bull was looking for trouble, but Will stared him down and forced Bull to walk away.

For a second or two Clayton began to admire his grandfather, but then he remembered those ugly stories of his father being a drunk and a philanderer and, worse, riding with that no-good slob, Bull.

Suddenly furious, Clayton lashed out at Will. "Yeah, well it's too bad you never took the time to show my father how to ride and shoot like Jack Hayes instead of running him off the ranch. Maybe he wouldn't have burned up in the hotel and maybe he'd still be alive today!"

Stunned by the sudden outburst, Will knew it was time to tell Clayton, and Jason for that matter, the real truth about Clayton's father. Something he should have told him long ago, but kept mute because of the promise he gave to Reinette the day they buried their son, John.

Clayton turned his attention to several of the black and white photographs that hung from the wall. "Is this you in the photograph with Sam Houston?" he asked. "How did you know Sam Houston?"

"Read the caption!"

"Wilfred Jacob Alexander (right) and Governor Samuel Houston (left) at the statehouse, 1859. Alexander, age 37, is one the youngest state judges ever appointed to the Texas bench."

Clayton had calmed down a bit, but still seemed ready to explode at the slightest provocation. "What is that around Houston's neck?" he asked Will. "It looks like a crude necklace of sorts."

"Houston told me he spent time with the Cherokee Indians as a boy in Tennessee, living with Chief Oolooteka on Hiwassee Island, a fact not widely known at the time," said Will. "Chief Oolooteka eventually adopted Sam into the tribe, giving him the Cherokee name Colleneh or "the Raven." Houston later married into the tribe. He wore that necklace, a gift from his Cherokee family when he left Tennessee, on and off for several years in remembrance of those times."

Clayton moved along the wall, examining photographs and other memorabilia, including that of his uncle Jacob, when he came across another black and white picture that caught his eye.

"Who's this?" he asked with more curiosity. "It looks like a young Deputy Sheriff Sweeney on the courthouse steps with another deputy. The deputy is packing twin Navy Colts and has a Henry lever-action in the crock of his arm. The picture is dated July 1865. That's the same date the attempted bank robbery took place. Wait a minute, that deputy is a Texas Ranger. I can tell by his badge. Is he the one that broke up the gang?"

Will sat up straight and leaning forward spoke softly to Clayton in carefully measured words. "Look closer at the deputy, Clayton."

Clayton moved his head closer to the photograph and with squinted eyes studied the deputy carefully. Suddenly he reeled back, turned around, and pointing at the deputy in the photograph with his right hand, yelled at Will.

"That's you in the photograph. That's you!! You told us you weren't a Texas Ranger, and there you are, standing with brass balls next to Sweeney! And those twin custom-ized Navy Colts with engraved ivory grips. Those are the same ones Moses handed you at the pistol shoot. And that Henry rifle, is that the same rifle you have stowed away in the gun cabinet?

"*You* are the Texas Ranger that took down that killer Robertson and his gang. Why have you kept it such a secret all these years? Why?"

"I am not that Texas Ranger, Clayton. There was only one Texas Ranger in this family, and he is buried in the cemetery behind the ranch house, in the corner plot along the picket fence."

"That cannot be. That's where my father is buried!" replied Clayton, yelling as if he caught Will in yet another lie.

"Why are you lying to me?" demanded Clayton. "That's *you* in the picture!"

"Take a close look again, Clayton. I mean a closer look. That's not me in the picture. That Texas Ranger is my youngest son, John."

Clayton looked again at the photograph and then back at Will before falling back against the wall, mouth agape, trying to sort out what he thought he knew about his father, what he just heard his grandfather say, and what he saw in the photograph.

Jason, silent up to now, stepped forward and put his arm on Clayton's shoulder. "Clay, what your grandfather is trying to tell you is that the man that saved the town's bank nearly15 years ago was your father. Your father was an undercover Texas Ranger...the Laramie Kid!"

Clayton sat down and looked over at his grandfather. Then he put his head in his hands.

"Clayton, my grandson—your father—was not a drunk or a womanizer," said Will in gentle, hushed tones. "Your mother knew what your father was doing, and she supported his efforts to bring law and order to Texas. He was good at his job in part because he knew your mother trusted him.

"People often didn't recognize your father, even those who grew up with him, because he was a master of disguises. He wore a Mexican sombrero over an embroidered short jacket when he thought he would blend in better with the Spanish-speaking townsfolk, or other times he dressed up like a tinhorn gambler with fancy white-cuffed shirts and a black derby hat to better fit in with cardsharps and crooked gamblers. The white hat he's wearing in the picture became his favorite. It was given to him by Sam Houston himself just before he passed away. John added a sidewinder hat band later that very same day, and wore it proudly."

Clayton glanced over at the white hat perched on a shelf next to the gun cabinet. A pair of cowboy boots stood next to the hat on the same shelf. Clayton stood up to reach for the hat, but then changed his mind and sat back down.

"What really happened that day of the robbery," asked Clayton. "I have heard all kinds of rumors, some of them brutal. Did my father really kill six outlaws and then capture Robertson single-handedly?"

"Yes!" replied Will. After the hanging, John sat down with me, several witnesses, and Ned Buntline, a young dime novelist, and over the next several days hammered out the course of events in great detail and exactly as they occurred. It was first published in the Colby Tribune. Later that year Beadle and Adams published his account as part of a longer narrative. There is a copy around here somewhere, wrapped in salmon-colored paper, if you want to read it."

CHAPTER THIRTY
Finally, The Truth Comes Out

Clayton found the book, opened it to the short story, and began to read.

THE KID FROM FT. LARAMIE, by Ned Buntline

The Kid from Ft. Laramie became suspicious when...

When Clayton finished he put the book down and walked over to the picture of his father standing on the courthouse steps with Deputy Sweeney. Now he could see the physical resemblance between his father and his grandfather, and he wondered if he had any of those same physical traits.

Jason quickly picked up the book and began to turn the pages. When he was finished reading about the bank robbery, he looked up at Clayton. "Clay, your father was a hero. Not only could he ride and shoot, he was also one tough son of a bitch doing it. Don't you wish you could ride and shoot like him?"

Clayton looked over at Jason and then spoke to Will. "This is going to take some time to sink in, a lot of time really. Up to now I believed my father was a no-good, an outlaw, and a bully no better than Bull, a worthless saddle tramp. And I thought you were at fault. And now this..."

"Your grandmother made me promise on your father's grave that we would not allow you to follow in your father's or your Uncle Jacob's footsteps, Clayton. That meant law enforcement. Reinette could not bear to lose you after burying both of our sons. But we both realize now that the strategy to keep you safe and out of harm's way was wrong. We should have told you everything you wanted to know about your father as you were growing up."

Jason put down the book and walked over to the wall of memorabilia. "Who is this standing next to Clayton's father?"

"What is he wearing?" asked Will.

"Fringed buckskin britches and a turquoise calico shirt," replied Jason looking back at Will. "He's also toting a pistol on his left hip, can't make out what brand or caliber it is exactly. It looks well-used but not fancy like those Navy Colts of yours. He also has a knife tucked into his boot, and there's a bow and a quiver of arrows hanging off a nearby peg."

Will stood up and joined Jason to see what picture he was referring to. "Why, that's my son John and one of his best friends, Gray Eyes, your father, Jason. That was taken a year before the Colby Hotel fire."

"My father? I didn't know any photographs of him existed!" beamed Jason. "So that is what he looked like!"

"If you look around I think there are a couple more photos of him here somewhere. I have some of his clothing here too, given to us by your mother before she passed away. She wanted us to pass them on to you when you were old enough. I guess now is as good a time as any."

"We kept all of this a secret from you, too, Jason. Your father sometimes passed pertinent information to John and then to me. Nobody suspected he was an informant for the Texas Rangers, and I needed to keep it that way."

"Why?"

"Because your father's death is somehow tied to both of my sons' deaths. I just don't know how, but my instincts as a judge tell me it's so. I am convinced now more than ever that pressure is mounting, and somebody is going to open his mouth and slip up. And they are going to do it soon!"

"What does the fire have to do with all this?" Jason asked.

"I believe the fire was deliberately set, and before the smoke cleared your father was conveniently blamed for the carnage—and then quickly hanged before the real arsonist could be brought to justice."

"IIow do you know that?"

"Jason, your mother told me," Will replied.

CHAPTER THIRTY-ONE
The Conflagration

The flame started out small, but with a little help it soon began to hiss and crackle against the far corner of the storage room wall, catching it afire along with some folded linens piled on a shelf just above the floor.

The arsonist then closed the door to the storage room, giving him time to sneak down the stairs and out onto the street before anyone saw him...and before the fire could reach the two oak powder kegs loaded to the gills with dry powder and smothered in several pounds of pine pitch.

Gray Eyes' wife Louise heard an odd commotion in the adjacent storage room and then heard creaking stairs as if someone was descending catlike down the steps and out onto the street. She parted the curtains and peeked outside through the open window just in time to see a man dressed in dark clothing miss a step and tumble off the boardwalk, get up, and then hurriedly hobble across the street before disappearing into a long dark alleyway.

Suddenly, she caught a whiff of wood smoke. The open window had created a draft in the bedroom and was sucking in smoke from somewhere under the locked door.

"Gray Eyes, wake up. I think I smell smoke!"

"What!"

"I think I smell smoke. Get up!"

Gray Eyes rolled out of bed. He too could now smell smoke. But before he could react further, a thunderous explosion rocked the second floor of the hotel.

POW! The pine pitch had caught fire and finally ignited the oak kegs of dry powder, blowing the door off the storage room and collapsing bone-dry rafters up and down the hallway all the way to the floor.

"Mommy, what was that noise? I'm scared Mommy!"

"The hotel is on fire, Jason. We have to get out right now. Give me your hand. Leave your things, and follow me. Hurry!"

Gray Eyes opened the door to their hotel room and peered down the hallway. It was already engulfed in flames, and there was a huge section of the roof missing. Gobs of burning pitch were splattered everywhere helping to spread the fire. He ran across the hall and beat on John's door.

"Fire! Fire! John, get up! The hotel is on fire!"

Gray Eyes kicked in the door to see John trying to get out from under a pile of broken timbers.

"Help my son, Gray Eyes. He's still in his bed!"

"I got him. Let's go!"

"I can't. Sally is pinned down. Get out, now, and please take my boy with you! We'll be right behind you!"

Gray Eyes wrapped young Clayton up in a couple of old blankets and backed out of the room. The heat in the hallway was intense, and thick smoke was billowing out through the hole in the roof like a chimney. Gray Eyes knew he had little time to waste. He quickly picked up Jason with his right arm, wrapped him up in the other blanket, and together with his wife ran down the hallway to the back stairs and out onto the street.

The explosion had awakened half the town, and a water brigade was already thankfully underway. Screams could be heard inside the hotel as the fire raced through the building.

A young cowboy dressed only in his skivvies tried to jump from a second-story balcony when the flames broke into his room. He got tripped up however, and failed to clear the railing. He landed on his head, snapping his neck and killing him instantly. An older woman, scantily clad in typical barroom fashion, came out of the room behind the young cowboy and watched in horror as her client hit the street. She turned around and started back into the room when yet another explosion rocked the building, quickly engulfing her in hellish hot flames. She withered for a moment in the intense heat, arms flailing over her head in a desperate attempt to put out the fire, and then collapsed onto the balcony a blackened corpse.

Gray Eyes knew the hotel would soon be lost. Wasting no time, he immediately handed the boys off to a kindly old lady who shepherded them away from the blazing hotel fire. Then he and his wife submerged the blankets in the nearby water trough and ran up the stairs and back into the building where they could hear Sally screaming.

"John, Sally, where are you? You have got to get out! Now! The whole building is about to collapse."

John ran to the door of his room and grabbed the wet blankets from Gray Eyes and Louise.

"I can't. Sally is pinned mighty hard. Help me get her out!"

A heavy oak timber used as a carrying beam had fallen across the bed after the explosion. It barely missed John, but crushed Sally's legs tightly against the floor.

"Get me out! Get me out!" screamed Sally. "I don't want to die. John, please get me out! I am so scared. Please help me. Please! Please!"

Sally's legs were pinned below the knees, and the flames were getting closer. Her bed clothing suddenly caught fire, searing her flesh with intense heat. John wrapped a blanket around her legs and extinguished the flames, at least for the time being.

"Where's Clayton? John, where's my son?" screamed Sally.

"He's safe outside," answered Gray Eyes. He and Jason are both safe!"

"Get me out! Please, I'm on fire! My hair, it's on fire!"

John together with Gray Eyes and Louise tried to move the beam off Sally, but to no avail. It was wedged too tightly against the wall and floor and other debris in the room.

The sudden realization that they could not free Sally was overwhelming.

"It's no use, John. You have got to get out, save yourself, for the boy's sake."

"Oh, Johnny, please don't leave me! God, oh God. Please save me!"

John turned to Gray Eyes and Louise. "Go! Now! I'm not leaving!"

John then grabbed the other blanket, lay down next to Sally, and pulled the blanket over the both of them. "I love you, baby. I'm not leaving you. I love you. I love you."

And John held her tight in his arms with her face against his chest. She stopped screaming as the flames engulfed them both.

With timbers crashing all about them, Gray Eyes and Louise, both in tears, fled down the hallway to the back stairs and safely out into the street.

Devastated by the death of their friends, Gray Eyes and Louise collapsed on the far side of the street, hacking to rid their lungs of all the smoke. Nobody asked them if they needed any help. Nobody asked about their son. Nobody asked about their friends. Nobody consoled them.

Nobody except Sarah, the kindly old lady.

All together, 13 people died in the Colby Hotel fire, including two toddlers. Angry and heartbroken, the good church-going folks of Colby were aghast at the destruction of the hotel and nearby business establishments, as well as the pungent order of burned flesh that permeated the town.

A mob soon gathered demanding answers. They quickly pounced on Gray Eyes, blaming him for the conflagration. And why not, they reasoned. He was just an Indian, and since only he and his family and a friend of their son's escaped unharmed, he must have set the fire; so before the sheriff could launch an investigation, they strung him up in a fit of rage before sundown that very same day.

The good Christian folks of Colby later congratulated themselves on a job well done, a job that needed to be done.

Thank the Lord.

CHAPTER THIRTY-TWO
A Time For Reflection

Clayton and Jason settled down and slowly began sifting through the memorabilia stored in the secret room. Will sat silently, answering questions as they arose, but not offering any other information. He could tell that Clayton and Jason were both struggling with the facts surrounding their fathers' lives and untimely deaths, especially Clayton.

For the next week or so Clayton just moped around the ranch. He kept to himself mostly but was usually on time for his meals. He even helped Reinette once or twice in the kitchen and smiled back at her when she thanked him for his efforts.

One morning after breakfast Reinette had a chance to talk with Will about something that had been keeping her awake on and off for several nights. She wiped one of the tables clean, poured two cups of coffee, and then asked Will to sit down beside her.

"Will, do you think the talk you had with Clayton and Jason did any good?" she asked, her voice quivering. "Clayton hasn't sassed me since, but he's not the same, either. I'm afraid he's just independent enough to leave the ranch, Will, and we won't see him again despite him finally hearing the truth about John being the Texas Ranger who foiled that bank robbery and the suspicious circumstances surrounding the fire that killed his mother and father. Where will he go? How will he survive? Will, he is still a boy!"

Will sensed the fear in Reinette's heart and clasped her hands with his. That's when he noticed she was crying. "He's no longer a boy, Reinette," Will confided softly, trying to reassure her. "Clayton is growing into a man. A fine young man! But he has a lot stuck in his craw right now, and he needs time to sort out all the facts before he can get on with his life. For the past several months he has been blaming us, mostly me I guess, for running his father off the ranch. He's also been tormented by the events surrounding Jacob's death and the words he heard about his father riding with Bull. That's all my fault, too, I guess.

"That talk in the barn set his head a twirling, that's for sure, and he doesn't really know what to believe. And just as importantly, he doesn't know how to behave around us. Should he be thankful we finally told him the truth about his father? Should he still be angry with us for waiting so long? If he accepts the truth about his father, does that mean he's been a fool to believe otherwise? How does he reconcile that with his recent behavior on the ranch?"

Will finally picked up his cup of coffee and took a long drink. "What will he do? I don't know. He could cut and run, but I think Clayton has more character than that. We'll have to wait it out. I know he's been talking a lot with Jason around the ranch. Yesterday, they grabbed their bows and went deer hunting in the afternoon along the river. I suspect they did more talking than they did hunting though.

"And to top it all off, he now has a girlfriend. She has extended her stay in town, and Clayton has seen her a couple of times. Moses told me. I also know he's more than just interested in her. She could be good for him, help him see the sun through all the storm clouds."

Reinette patted Will's hands and smiled. "You're right, Wilfred Alexander, Clayton does have character, and he will eventually do the right thing. We just have to be patient and give him all the time he requires." Reinette wiped her eyes with the corner of her apron and then stood up. "In the meantime, I've got chores to do. Is Moses still going to town today for supplies? If so, give him this list for me, will you? We percolated the last of the coffee this morning, and I need sugar and flour and a few other items if I'm going to keep our ranch hands happy and well fed!"

"I will see to it right away," said Will as he finished his cup of coffee and headed for the door. He stopped halfway across the kitchen and walked back to Reinette, who was using her apron as a pot holder to take the nearly empty pot of coffee off the stove. He softly touched both of her shoulders, kissed her on the neck, and turned to walk out the door.

Outside, Will saw Moses coming out of the barn and gave him the grocery list from Reinette.

"Yup, I plan on leaving shortly. You need anything yourself?"

"No, don't think so. Oh, wait a minute, I am running low on powder and lead for my Navy Colts. See what you can do. I believe those guns are going to see some action real soon, and I need to keep my eyes sharp and my hands steady.

"And oh, one more thing. Please stop at the Western Telegraph and send this message to the statehouse. You can read it, but wait for a reply. Stay at the hotel overnight if need be. We'll talk about it later."

Before Moses could ask what was going on, Will turned and walked away.

Moses slid Will's telegram into his front slash pocket. Then he tucked Reinette's list into his shirt pocket and pulled out the list he had already compiled, adding Will's request for powder and bullets to the paper before stuffing it back in his pocket.

Moses finished his chores and then went into the barn to hitch Jake and Big Jim up to the buckboard for the trip to town. As he was about to jump on board, Clayton stepped out of the barn. "Mind if I tag along, Moses?" asked Clayton as he held up his open hand to keep Moses from leaving without him.

"Not at all, Clayton!" answered Moses somewhat surprised. He replied quickly, and with a friendly smile. "I could use some companionship on the road to town and some help loading these supplies when we get to Colby. Hop up and let's get started."

Clayton always liked Moses' open manner and with some enthusiasm, climbed up on the seat. "I have a few things I would like to do in town."

Moses climbed up, grabbed the reins, and released the brake. For the first mile or so Clayton spoke little, but Moses sensed that Clayton wanted to talk more than he wanted a ride to town.

Moses decided to break the ice. "Will told me he showed you and Jason the hidden room in the barn. He also said he told you about your father being a Texas Ranger and how he chose to die with your mother in a suspicious fire. Damn, I'll bet that tidbit of history struck you like a bolt of lightning on a sunny day, huh?"

Moses looked over at Clayton to gauge his reaction. Clayton had pulled his hat down a bit and then lowered his head to hide his face. He sat there for a few minutes, then sat straight up, tilted his hat back, and looked over at Moses.

"Yeah, it did. It struck Jason pretty hard, too. At least he now knows the truth about his father not starting the fire. That's always gnawed at him like hunger pangs that won't go away."

"You heard the truth about your father, too, Clayton," said Moses as he slapped the reins gently against Jake's and Big Jim's backs. "He was an honest man doing a dirty job, a job few men have the guts and skills to face... especially alone."

"Yeah, but what about Bull?" replied Clayton as he turned and faced Moses head-on. "What the hell was my father doing riding with that no-good son of a bitch? I mean, Bull is a dangerous man. No telling what he will do next. He just don't care if he lives or dies, but he's willing to find what you are willing to do to stay alive. The bastard thrives on fear."

"I don't know why your father chose him as a saddle mate, Clayton, but I bet he had his reasons, and they were good ones, too. To be frank, that relationship bothers me a bit, too. All that comes to mind is John, your father, was working him over for information, maybe about your uncle Jacob's death at the hands of those cattle rustlers."

Clayton turned his head away and looked out over the prairie. He liked Moses. Moses seemed to understand what

Clayton was thinking, what he was feeling, without being judgmental or sarcastic. It was as if he and Moses were trying to sort things out from the same side of a barbed wire fence.

As the buckboard rolled along, Clayton realized his instincts were accurate. He could trust Moses and in fact could confide in him some of the recent events that he was finding so troublesome.

"Why did my father stay in the hotel and elect to burn with my mother?" asked Clayton in a voice fraught with anxiety and uncertainty. "He would still be alive today if he had left, knowing that there was nothing he could do to save her. Nobody would have blamed him."

"Your father was deeply in love with your mother," began Moses in a low, even tone. "He would have never been able to forgive himself if he had left her in that hotel room to burn up all by herself. She begged him to stay, and out of love and without reservation, he did."

Moses pulled back on the reins, bringing the team to a halt in the middle of the road. He then laid his left hand on Clayton's shoulder and looked him straight in the eye. "Your mother was terrified of the fire, of dying, but mostly she was terrified of losing your father, the love of her life. Clayton, I know this is difficult to understand, but your parents shared a love so deep it transcends death. There is a God, and there is eternal life after death that they now share together, and they are looking down at you knowing in their hearts that you will sort all this out and then do the right thing. This crisis will pass Clayton, and you will be stronger for it."

Moses slapped the reins, and the buckboard continued on down the bumpy road toward Colby, jostling Moses back and forth on the seat like a jackrabbit outrunning a coyote.

Clayton on the other hand sat up straight, and with his feet on the footboard and his hands locked behind his head, he smiled, beginning, it seemed, to take the bumps of life more in stride.

CHAPTER THIRTY-THREE

Bull and the Hatchet

The remainder of the ride to Colby was uneventful. Moses gathered up Reinette's supplies first and then stopped at the feed store, the blacksmith's shop, old man Miller's general store, and finally Davis' Guns and Ammo for the rest of the supplies. A bell chimed when Moses and Clayton entered the shop and closed the door behind them.

"Hi boys!" greeted Davis as he came out from the back room. "I haven't seen much of you since the statehood celebration. What can I do for you this fine afternoon?"

"We need a couple of boxes of .45s, two pounds of black powder, and some soft lead for making bullets," replied Moses. "Can you fix us up?"

"Sure can!" Davis pulled two boxes of metallic .45s from a nearby shelf and then picked up a bag of soft lead pieces from the floor next to one of the display cases. "I keep the powder in a shed behind the store, you know, for safety's sake. It will just take a minute or two, but go ahead and look around a bit. You might see something else you need, like a new Colt six-shooter or a Winchester lever-action. I just got a new shipment in from Fort Laramie. A new Colt is a mite more powerful than that hatchet you are so attached to, Moses."

When Davis returned with the powder, Moses noticed that Davis' limp seemed to be more pronounced and brought it to Davis' attention. "Your leg hurt more than usual today?" asked Moses. "You've had that gimp a long time. How'd you get it anyway?"

"Ah, it acts up whenever rain is near," lamented Davis. "And yeah, I guess I have had it for a long time. I fell off the boardwalk one dark night, nearly broke my neck. I was drinking heavy all that day and didn't realize until the next morning that I had splintered my lower leg. I should have had a doc set it up straight and proper, but a bottle from the bar eased the pain and I let it heal on its own. Doc Hayes said he could break it again for me and fix it so I don't limp no more, but there isn't enough whiskey in this town for me to let him do that to me. Nope, I can live with it just fine. Don't need no more pain."

Moses and Clayton paid Davis in cash for the gun supplies, thanked him proper, and turned to leave.

"Say hi to Lefty, Blondy, and the rest of the boys for me when you get back to the ranch, Moses, will you?"

"You bet!" replied Moses as he and Clayton walked out the door. Once outside, they stared a bit at each other as they climbed up into the buckboard. Neither of them missed Davis' remarks on how he broke his leg.

"Let's sit on those words for a spell," said Moses after looking around to make sure nobody was within earshot. "Sometimes the truth reveals itself in mysterious ways. Will should hear all about this when we get back to the ranch, too. In the meantime, I forgot, I've got one more stop to make. It will only take a minute or two."

Clayton nodded in agreement. "Drop me off at the Colby Hotel first, will you Moses? I want to see Phoebe Ann. I'll meet you at the saloon across the street in 10 minutes and buy you a beer for the ride home."

"Okay Clayton. Ten minutes. Don't keep me waiting!"

Clayton rushed inside and found Phoebe Ann on the back porch talking with Dancing Water. Phoebe Ann jumped up when she saw Clayton step onto the porch landing and gave him a big hug. "What a surprise! We were just talking about you. What are you doing in town so early in the day?"

"I rode in with Moses to help pick up some supplies for the ranch. We're heading right back, but I wanted to stop in and ask if you had any plans for this Sunday. I would like to take you on a picnic."

"Oh, I would love to!" gushed Phoebe Ann. "Elizabeth and Sarah Ellen are assisting the Nelson brothers for a couple of weeks while their mother heals from a fall she took in the barn. In the meantime I'm staying with Dancing Water. You can pick me up there."

"Great! Dancing Water, what are you and Jason doing on Sunday? Would you like to join us?" asked Clayton, his eyes darting over to Phoebe Ann's. He was just being polite and was relieved when Dancing Water said that she and Jason had already made other arrangements. He wanted to be alone with Phoebe Ann, and by the look on her face, she wanted to spend the afternoon alone with Clayton, too.

They finished making their plans, and Clayton raced across the street to the saloon. Moses was already at the bar, finishing his first beer, when Clayton plopped down beside him, all smiles.

"Hey barkeeper, how about a beer?" ordered Clayton as he pulled some coins from his pocket.

"I already paid for your beer," declared Moses. "Let's grab a table and sit down." Clayton complied by picking up his beer and moving over to a round table in the corner of the room near the stairway where they could talk with more privacy.

"What do you think about Davis' remarks he made earlier?" asked Moses. "Do you think it's possible he's the arsonist who started the hotel fire that killed your mother and father?"

"There isn't really much to go on," replied Clayton thoughtfully. "So a man with a limp admits to falling off the boardwalk in a drunken stupor several years ago. That doesn't prove anything."

"But I must tell you I'm suspicious," Moses countered. "We need to learn more. If he did set the fire, we have to find out why he did it. What was there to gain for him, or was it just for revenge? Did he target someone in the hotel that night? Was the fire a cover-up for another crime, an undisclosed offense that we have as yet no knowledge of? Was he working alone?"

"Oh, what's the use," lamented Clayton. "The trail's as cold as winter snow. Besides, what can I do about it now?"

"Well, it's something to wonder about," said Moses. "I'll be right back. I got to water my horse."

"What?"

"I've gotta take a leak!"

Moses walked out back to the piss house where he could relieve himself into a cracked wooden trough that funneled most of the urine outside to a sand pit behind the saloon. On a busy night the piss house reeked of hot steaming urine, but the bartender had splashed some pine juice on the floor and down the trough just a short time ago to help kill some of the putrid odor. It still stunk, but it was a mite better than pissing outside for any passing pedestrian to witness.

In the meantime Clayton was sitting alone sipping his beer with his back to the wall when in walked Bull. Bull had recognized the buckboard outside and entered the bar hoping to find Clayton and Jason alone.

"Alexander, I thought I told you and your half-breed Indian friend to stay the hell away from the river. I caught you two there once before, and last week I saw the two of you bow hunting deer along the banks."

Bull's voice was stern, ugly stern, and he sprayed spit when he talked. Several cowboys and miners leaning on the bar picked up their drinks and moved back toward the front of the saloon near the swinging doors should they need to make a quick escape to avoid trouble. And trouble seemed inevitable.

The two whores working the saloon made it upstairs without incident and now leaned over the railing to watch the battle that was sure to unfold.

Bull grabbed a couple of chairs and smashed them one at a time against two of the oak timbers that supported the balcony above. The girls screamed and stepped away from the railing and then fled over to the top of the stairwell where they were out of harm's way but could still see what was going on.

"You don't learn so well, do you boy? Last time I broke your face, this time I think I might just pop an eyeball out and swallow it with a mug of warm beer. How would that suit you?"

Clayton was trapped. He could scoot up the stairwell to the whores' business rooms, but there was no way out from up there. He would have to keep his wits about him and confront Bull.

Bull closed the distance to Clayton and pointed a grimy finger in his direction. "Your old man didn't learn so good, either. More than once I had to give him a good whooping. One time he sassed me real bad in front of some ladies, so I suckered him with my pistol barrel. He hit the floor like a dead beef cow and didn't move for over an hour."

"Damn, Bull, my dad had a thick skull," retorted Clayton with a wide grin. "Your pistol-whipping didn't drop him to the floor. He probably passed out when he caught a whiff of your rancid breath! Right girls?"

The whores at the stairwell couldn't help it, and broke into giddy laughter. They knew Clayton spoke the truth about Bull's sour breath.

"Don't sass me boy!"

"Don't sass you? You know what I think, Bull? I think you're hiding something in the hills above the river. Something you don't want anybody to know about. In fact, the more I hear you bellow, the more I'm convinced of it.

What is it Bull that you don't want me to see?"

Furious, Bull pulled his Smith & Wesson and squared his sights on Clayton's forehead. Bull opened his mouth and was about to issue another ultimatum to Clayton when *whoosh, whoosh, whoosh, whoosh, whoosh...CRACK!* Moses hurled his hatchet just in time at Bull's head, grazing his skull and knocking the big man off his feet. Bull hit the floor with a resounding *THUD* and didn't move.

There were cheers from those witnesses standing near the front swinging doors, and the bartender bought a round of beers for everyone in celebration. When Bull finally came around, with the help of several pints of pine juice collected from the leaky trough in the piss house, Bull was more than a mite bewildered. He was dazed and confused and couldn't speak—not a single word.

Moses leaned over Bull and tapped him on his head with the blade of his hatchet. "The next time you threaten any of my hands, keep this blade in mind. I will gladly perform a public gelding on you right then and there in broad daylight, and nobody, and I mean *nobody*, will ever call you Bull again. Understand?"

Humiliated, and reeking of urine and pine juice, Bull eventually staggered outside, climbed on his horse, and rode out of town holding a wet rag against the side of his head. He had taken a public beating, a beating he might have deserved, a beating he would not soon forget. And by God somebody was going to pay for it...but not just now.

In the meantime, Moses and Clayton were checking the horses before they headed back to the ranch. "Thanks for stepping into the ruckus back there," proclaimed Clayton with a wide grin and a slap on Moses' back. "I'm not sure what Bull's true intentions were, but I was sure glad to see that hatchet of yours sailing through the air. Bull didn't know what hit him until he woke up on the floor, and by then it was too late for him to do much of anything 'cept get the hell out of town!"

Moses was all smiles, too. "Bull could have killed you back there, and honestly I don't know why he didn't drop the hammer. He had you square in his sights, that's for sure, but something held him back. Something mighty important. Even so, I'm not so sure you'll be so lucky next time."

On the way out of town Moses stopped at the telegraph office and picked up the reply Will was waiting for. After reading it, he folded the telegram in half and slid it into his vest pocket.

He didn't say anything to Clayton about either telegram.

CHAPTER THIRTY-FOUR
The Picnic

Sunday morning couldn't roll around fast enough for Clayton. After breakfast he quickly finished his daily chores and then headed for the bathhouse for a good hot soak in one of the wooden tubs. Soon he was all gussied up in fresh underwear and clean-smelling clothes. He even splashed on some of that fancy rose water he confiscated from Jason's room before hitching up the mare to the carriage.

"Don't forget your picnic basket," yelled Reinette as she ran across the yard with it draped over her right arm. Phoebe Ann is Dancing Water's guest and even though they are friends it might be a bit of an imposition for her to pack a lunch for the two of you, so you bring the vittles. I am sure she will appreciate your thoughtfulness. Your eating tools are wrapped up in those red and white napkins, and I see you already have a blanket to sit on. Inside there is cold chicken, potato salad...no onion, some fresh biscuits left over from this morning, a jar of berry jam, two big slices of berry pie, and a pail of coffee."

Clayton pawed through the reed basket for a quick look-see, closed the lid, and stuffed the basket under the carriage seat.

"Thanks, Grandma!" he gushed, and gave Reinette a kiss on her forehead before slapping the reins on the old mare. Reinette smiled and smoothed her apron with both hands as she watched Clayton leave the ranch. He was feeling more like himself, Reinette surmised. And now so was she.

Phoebe Ann was sitting on the porch with Dancing Water when Clayton pulled up. She was about to say something about lunch when she spied the picnic basket tucked under the seat and instead quickly hopped into the carriage, not waiting for any help from Clayton, and waved good-bye to Dancing Water. Clayton also waved to Dancing Water as he turned the carriage around in the yard and then slapped the reins.

"Where's Jason?" asked Phoebe Ann as she settled into her seat.

"He'll be along shortly," replied Clayton. "He's finishing up his chores and then he is attending church with Moses. He should be around shortly."

"Good. Dancing Water is baking fresh bread this morning, enough for Jason to bring back to Reinette later on today. Do you think she'll like it?"

"Let's see. Jason likes Dancing Water and Dancing Water likes Jason, therefore Grandma will certainly take kindly to anything Dancing Water does for Jason, so, yes, I am sure Grandma will be thrilled that Dancing Water took the time to bake her a few loaves of bread. I know they won't last long with our hungry crew!"

Phoebe Ann was pleased and flashed a big smile at Clayton as he slapped the reins. "Giddy up Molly. Giddy up." And soon Dancing Water was a mere speck of color on the porch.

"It's a nice day for a ride on the prairie, don't you think Phoebe Ann?" asked Clayton. "You can see for miles and miles over the open prairie with no end in sight, like the state of Texas goes on forever and ever.

Phoebe Ann reached over and touched Clayton's free hand and then without hesitation leaned over and gave him a kiss on the cheek. "Yes, it is a nice day, Clayton. A very nice day for the two of us to spend together!"

They rode and talked for almost an hour before arriving at a deserted section of the river, far from where he and Jason had their encounter with Bull. There they spread out the blanket under a shady tree and talked for hours as they ate their lunch. Thunderheads passed over head, blocking the sun on occasion and threatening them with an afternoon cloud burst, a common occurrence this time of the year.

"And that's when Will told me who my father really was," said Clayton, "an undercover Texas Ranger who saved the town's savings years ago and then skedaddled before he could be properly thanked. Even today only a few people know that it was my father who brought Robertson to justice."

"And all along you thought he was a drunk and a womanizer," replied Phoebe Ann in a conciliatory tone, "a man who rode partners with Bull, someone many believe to be an outlaw. It must be some sort of relief to finally learn otherwise, that your dad was an honest, brave man. A man to be proud of, not vilified."

Clayton lowered his head and started picking the leaves off a small branch. "Yes, it's good to know the truth, to know that my father put his life on the line to help others, to know that he was fearless in going after thieves and murderers.

"Nonetheless, Jason and I are thinking about striking out on our own, maybe to San Antonio or even north into Oklahoma Territory. We're both tired of the whispers and the secret talk that follows us wherever we go. The gossip that belittles us for being the sons of perceived misfits and undesirable men."

Phoebe Ann stood up to stretch her legs and then sat down on a log Clayton had dragged over near the blanket for just such a purpose. She looked away, across the river, and then back at Clayton. She started to speak but hesitated, as if she wasn't sure she should speak at all. She folded her hands across her lap and then changed her mind again and spoke up.

"Clayton, are you sure leaving Colby is the right decision for you and Jason? I mean, the town's perception of you and your father, and Jason and his father, will not change unless you step up and show them differently. Show them, prove to them, that your fathers were both honorable men."

Clayton tossed the leafless branch up into the air and watched it settle back onto the ground. "Up to just recently I was embarrassed by my father. I didn't want to be anything like him. Now I find out that he was nothing like what I had been told he was all these years."

"Do you know what I think?" asked Phoebe Ann, gently, so as not to push him away. "I think you have come to admire your father. And you want to be just like him, but can't admit it to anyone because of the disrespectful way you've been acting. And now that I think more about it, this could be the underlying reason why you and Jason want to leave town. Clayton, your father and uncle, as well as Jason's father, deserve your respect, not your condemnation."

Clayton exhaled loudly and raised his eyebrows. "I hadn't thought about it in quite that manner." He then stood up and started to walk away.

"Where are you going? asked Phoebe Ann, fearful she had intruded too far into Clayton's privacy.

"I'll be right back. I have to water my horse."

"What?"

"I have to pee."

Jason walked into the bushes to relieve himself and then stripped down and ran for the river. He screamed as loud as he could as he launched himself feet first into the water. When he bobbed to the surface he could see Phoebe Ann standing up next to the log, looking quite flabbergasted.

Treading water, Clayton hollered, "Come on in, Phoebe Ann, and cool down. The water's nice!"

"Naw, I don't think so," laughed Phoebe Ann. "You're naked, and I'm not swimming with you when you don't have any clothes on."

Clayton swam toward shore, and when he could touch bottom he walked at her until the water was just below his waist.

Shocked, Phoebe Ann suddenly began to stammer. "That's a big snake, Clayton!"

Clayton lowered his eyes and shrugged his shoulders. "Shucks, Phoebe Ann, I'm just a regular guy."

"No Clayton, that's a big snake! Believe me!"

Clayton was surprised at Phoebe Ann's hysteria. "Phoebe Ann…"

Before he could finish the sentence, however, he saw Phoebe Ann pointing to the water behind him and yelling, "Snake! Big snake, Clayton. Water moccasin!"

Clayton spun around in the water and looked behind him while at the same time starting for shore, eyes bulging and legs kicking in a frantic effort to get out of the water before the snake could bite him. By the time he reached his gun, he could hear Phoebe Ann laughing. He dried himself off with his shirt and slipped on his skivvies before walking back to the blanket.

"Very funny, Phoebe Ann. You scared the hell out of me!"

"I know. I'm sorry. I just couldn't resist teasing you when you were, ah, so vulnerable."

Clayton sat down on the log next to Phoebe Ann, and she gave him a kiss on the cheek. "Clayton, I've never slept with a man, and I don't intend to until my wedding night. I'm so sorry if I gave you any indication otherwise."

Clayton was definitely confused. "I'm sorry if I offended you, Phoebe Ann," he stammered. "I wouldn't do anything to hurt your feelings. I just thought..."

"Clayton, I said I don't intend to sleep with any man until my wedding night. But there are other things we can do, besides doing that, if you know what I mean."

"Ah, not exactly, Phoebe Ann."

"Come, lay down next to me on the blanket, silly, and I will show you exactly what I mean."

CHAPTER THIRTY-FIVE
The Decision

Clayton arrived back at the ranch well after dark. He unhitched Molly and then fed and watered the mare before leaving her in the coral to cool off for the night. The light was still on in the kitchen, so when he finished putting up the harness and backing the buggy into an empty stall, he headed off in that direction.

"How was your picnic, Clayton?" asked Reinette when he stepped out of the darkness.

"We had a grand time, Grandma," smiled Clayton. "A grand time. Oh, I left the picnic basket in the buggy. I'll get it in the morning."

"How good a time did you have?" asked Will with a twinkle in his eye.

"Oh, you leave him alone, Wilfred," scolded Reinette. Then she slapped him on the shoulder for still smiling before turning to Clayton. "Do you want something to eat, Clayton? There's still a piece of berry pie left in the tin. Will already voiced his need for a second helping, but…"

Clayton turned in his seat and faced Will head-on. "I'll split it even with you Grandpa" replied Clayton, "if you will sit for a spell. I need to talk to you about something."

Surprised, Reinette poured two cups of coffee, put the pie between Clayton and his grandfather, and then handed Will a knife. "You split the pie in half, Wilfred, and let Clayton choose which piece he wants!"

Will eyed the pie carefully and with great fanfare cut the last slice of berry pie exactly in half. Clayton and Will laughed, as one piece looked as big as the other, and then each wolfed down their pie and coffee.

"I was thinking, Grandpa, about the hotel fire. Where is the evidence stored? Sheriff Sweeney claims someone turned in bits of a blackened oak powder keg smeared in pitch found across the street the next morning after the fire. Apparently the explosion tossed those fragments high into the air and they landed quite a distance away. Sweeney also said they found Gray Eyes' bow, quiver, and several arrows smeared with pitch under the boardwalk. He surmised Gray Eyes hid the black powder earlier in the day and then used flaming arrows to kindle the fire that led to the explosion. That doesn't make sense to me and Jason. Gray Eyes, Louise, and Jason were all in the room when the fire erupted."

"Well, it should still be in the courthouse, why?"

"I was thinking about taking a look at that stuff, you know, with a fresh pair of eyes. Maybe something will come to light?"

Will looked at Clayton for a second and then asked Reinette to fetch him a pencil and a piece of paper.

"Take this note with you and hand it to the clerk," said

Will. "You should have no problem viewing the evidence. Let me know what you think, okay?"

Clayton picked up the dirty dishes and dropped them into the wooden sink. "I will. Good night Grandma."

Will couldn't resist one last comment about the picnic, hoping to get a sultry clue from Clayton's reaction. Clayton didn't bite. As he opened the kitchen door to step out into the yard, he turned around. "I didn't bring any shame to you Grandma." And then he closed the door behind him.

CHAPTER THIRTY-SIX
The Laramie Kid Rides Again

The night air was invigorating, and Clayton stopped briefly in the middle of the yard to breathe deeply and gaze high up into the night sky. There seemed to be more stars that ever, bright points of light that shined down from every direction. Indeed, Texas has more stars overhead than any other state in the Union.

He wondered if his mother and father were looking down on him from heaven, and if they were, what they thought of their only son and how he had conducted his life so far. As he reflected, he realized that for the past week or so he was feeling like himself again—physically strong and confident with pointed, barbed-wire intellect. It had been a long time since he felt like that. And it felt good. Real good.

Clayton was lost in his thoughts for a minute when he saw a lantern flickering behind the bunkhouse and soon found Jason coming from the latrine. "Damn, it stinks in there. So, how did your picnic with Phoebe Ann go? Did you see her naked?"

"A gentleman doesn't reveal those things about a lady, Jason."

"Yup, just like I figured, nothing happened. That's because Phoebe Ann is a real lady and as sharp in the mind as a thistle. You'll have to marry her before you can bed her, Clayton. You're lucky to have paired up with such a classy woman."

"Yeah, I think so too. She's going to ride over to the Nelson's in the morning to help her sisters Elizabeth and Sarah Ellen care for mother Nelson. She'll be gone a few weeks I suspect. Phoebe Ann sure has a good heart for other peoples' troubles."

Jason nodded his head in agreement. "What are you doing up so late?"

"I'm going to the courthouse in the morning. I want to take a second look at the evidence gathered after the fire. It just don't set with me right, and I want to find out why. Your father didn't kill my father and mother. But someone seems to have gone to a lot of trouble to make everyone think that's what happened."

"I tell you, Clayton," interjected Jason, "the whole episode keeps my stomach sour sometimes, especially at night. I hear the whispers in town, and it eats at me like a rancid piece of meat. Let me know what you find out."

Clayton was up and dressed at pink light and quickly headed right out to the barn. He gathered up his saddle and riding gear, walked straight into the secret room, and headed out into the corral through the hidden hole in the wall.

With pride and determination, he whispered to Red Cloud as he placed the bit in his mouth. Then with deliberate and measured moves, he saddled the stallion. Red Cloud looked at Clayton several times, but stood firm his ground and offered no resistance. Clayton stoked Red Cloud's neck after tightening the cinch and then led him back outside and into the corral, tying him to the gate.

Wasting no time, Clayton turned around and hurried back into the secret room. He chose an 1851 Navy Colt, dried each empty cylinder with a soft cloth, and then loaded and primed five cylinders, leaving the hammer to rest solidly on the sixth—an empty tube. Then he stripped off his clothes and quickly donned his father's shirt and hemmed trousers.

His trousers were black cotton canvas with a cinch-back, v-notch back waistband, suspender buttons, a single back pocket with slash front pockets, and curiously enough, a well-worn watch pocket. He paused to ponder that idiosyncrasy for a moment. Nobody ever spoke of his father depending on a pocket watch to learn the time, and he never saw his grandfather with a pocket watch, either.

He shook the thought from his head, and after snapping the black galluses over his shoulders, he slid the vest over his shirt and slipped his feet into his father's boots. To his utter astonishment, Clayton found his father's clothing fit him perfectly.

Mindful to latch the door to the secret room behind him, Clayton rushed out into the yard, untied Red Cloud's reins, and led him across the yard. This time he knotted the reins and draped them over the saddle horn. Red Cloud held his ground while Clayton rushed into the kitchen, and after scoffing up some biscuits and cold leftover coffee, Clayton led Red Cloud to the family cemetery behind the ranch house. The sun, now a soft red orb just peeking over the tree line, illuminated the cemetery with a soft angel-like glow.

Clayton respectfully opened the gate and knelt down beside his father's tombstone. "Dad, I'm sorry if I offended you and Mom. I doubted your honesty Dad, your integrity, and because of that I treated Grandpa and Grandma poorly. I took it out on Moses, too.

"Mom and Dad, I'm so ashamed of myself. But I know the truth now, and I'm aiming to find out who started the fire and why. And I'm going to bring them to justice Dad, just like you would have done. I'm so proud now to be your son, and I hope someday you will be proud of me, too."

The sound of a horse's approaching hooves snapped Clayton out of his dreamlike remorseful state. It was Jason leading the roan, Smokey.

"I've been up half the night thinking, and have come to realize that I have to ride with you, Clayton, and clear my father's name. I'm no longer the crazy half-breed son of Gray Eyes, the murderous Indian who burned up half the town, killing 13 citizens.

"No, my name is Jason, Jason Gray Eyes, and I'm the proud son of Gray Eyes, the trusted Indian who rode honorably with John Alexander and the Texas Rangers, and the only son of his beloved white woman, Louise, Louise Harding from New Haven, Connecticut, who had to endure the shame wrongfully bestowed upon her by the good Christian folk of Colby."

Clayton looked up at his blood brother and lifelong friend. He wasn't surprised to see him, and he wasn't surprised to see that he was wearing his father's flat-brimmed hat with a straight-sided crown and rounded corners. The turquoise beads in the hat band matched the long-sleeved cotton calico shirt that his father once treasured, the very shirt now worn by Jason Gray Eyes. The sweatband had the name "Stetson" embossed in the leather, and with a slight tug on the hatband, it, like the rest of his father's clothing, fit the only son of the once-proud war chief Gray Eyes perfectly.

Jason's trousers, however, did not identify him as a native warrior, but were instead similar to Clayton's—black cotton canvas with cinch-back, v-notch back waistband and black galluses, trousers he thought his white grandfather, a Yankee lawyer from Connecticut, would wear in trying times like these.

"I see you also picked out a cap-and-ball Navy Colt," remarked Clayton.

"I figured if an 1851Navy Colt was good enough for Will, your father, and Wild Bill Hickok, it ought to suit me just fine. Now, are we riding to the courthouse or are we going to jaw till the sun's blazing hot and high overhead?"

Clayton smiled. "Yes, 'we' are riding, and I wouldn't have it any other way, Jason, Jason Gray Eyes."

And with that declaration Clayton stood up and placed his father's white felt cowboy hat with its distinctive rattle-snake hatband atop his head, and snugged it down. It fit perfectly.

Red Cloud suddenly stepped forward, and with a whinny nudged Clayton with his forehead. Clayton reached up and stroked Red Cloud's face and neck in response. Red Cloud had finally accepted Clayton, and now they were both ready to ride together.

Clayton placed the reins around the saddle horn, put his foot in the stirrup, and confidently swung his right leg up and over Red Cloud's back. Red Cloud stood still as

Clayton settled into the saddle, but Clayton could feel the power of the stallion as he then reared up on his hind legs and with forelegs grabbing for air, whinnied before dropping all fours back to the ground. He reared up one more time and then with his great head swaying up and down and chomping at the bit, Red Cloud waited for Clayton's next command. Clayton pulled back on the reins to settle Red Cloud down and give Jason Gray Eyes time to mount the roan Smokey. When both men were ready, Clayton touched Red Cloud's flanks with his Mexican spurs.

With coiled muscles, Red Cloud immediately dug his hooves into the ground and sprung forward to take the lead. Each rider leaned low over the saddle as their mounts galloped past the bunkhouse and down the line of trees that led to the open prairie and Colby beyond the horizon. They did not jockey for position like they did when they were boys as this was not a race to see who was best. Indeed, they were not in competition with each other for they were now men sharing the same goal: to uncover the deadly arsonist who set the Colby Hotel afire and bring him to justice. And they would not rest until the job was done.

When they reached the open prairie Clayton took charge and gave Red Cloud his lead. By urging him on faster and faster, he hoped to learn his and Red Cloud's upper limits. Just what kind of horse was Red Cloud? Could he count on Red Cloud when trouble was at hand? Could he handle Red Cloud if he started to act up? Could he ride Red Cloud like the wind on a tale end of a summer storm? Could he ride with wild abandon as his father and grandfather were known to do? Well, ride he did!

"Giddy up, giddy up Red Cloud! Giddy up!"

And to Clayton's utmost shock, Red Cloud responded to these urgings with thunderous speed. Clayton could feel the immense power stored in Red Cloud's muscles as the stallion maneuvered his way across the prairie with uncanny care and precision, picking up speed with each bound and tossing crimson colored dirt and debris behind him like a swirling cyclone. Red Cloud could sense Clayton's purpose and determination and settled into an exhilarating, blistering pace that Jason and Smokey could not maintain.

When Jason turned Smokey and broke off the run more than a mile from the ranch, Clayton slowed Red Cloud down to a walk. He had an ear-to-ear grin when Jason rode up alongside.

"I knew Red Cloud had speed, but that burst was more than I could have imagined!" declared Jason shaking his head in disbelief. "I'll wager he could have kept that pace all the way into town. You ride him as good as your grand-father! Will and Moses are right...Red Cloud is one hell of a horse, and Clayton, you were born to ride him!"

CHAPTER THIRTY-SEVEN
Revealing Evidence At The Courthouse

The pair continued on into town, content in their belief that they were on the right trail, and went directly to the courthouse. Clayton showed the clerk the note from Will, and she immediately took Clayton and Jason upstairs to a second-floor storage room. She unlocked the door and led them to the box of items marked "Colby Hotel fire."

"You can look all you want, but nothing can leave this room," she ordered. "There's also a bow, quiver, and five arrows stored on the upper shelf," she added, pointing to the top shelf nearest the window. "Be careful as they are still covered with pitch."

After she left, Clayton and Jason started pawing through the evidence box the clerk left on the table—bits of powder barrel, fragments of tar balls—but nothing of interest caught their eye. But when Jason brought the bow, quiver, and arrows over to the table for closer inspection, something didn't appear quite right.

"What kind of wood is this?" asked Clayton. "I've never seen anything like it growing around here! It has a distinct orange hue."

"It's horse-apple," said Jason as he turned the bow around and around in front of his eyes, "and it grows along the Red River and elsewhere if you know where to look. White folks call it Osage orange. My people have been using this wood for many years to make bows. It's highly prized for its strength and durability and its ability to cast an arrow accurately at great distances. Red Dog's bow is carved from this wood. So is mine.

"Clayton, do you remember the picture of my father your grandfather showed us in the secret room? The first one I asked him about. My father was wearing fringed buckskin britches and the turquoise calico shirt I'm wearing today. He was also toting a pistol on his left hip. It appeared well-used, but for some reason we couldn't quite make out the brand or caliber. Do you remember?"

Clayton took his eyes off the bow and furrowed his forehead before settling his eyes on Jason. "Yes, I do remember that photograph. Something bothered me about it, too, now that you mention it. For some reason, it didn't seem authentic. Like, I don't know, like it was..."

Jason raised his hand up and interrupted Clayton. "See these marks on the bow, here on the right side above the grip?"

"Yeah...so?"

"They're made when you release the arrow. Whoever shot this bow was left-handed. When you bring back the arrow with your left hand, you must tilt the bow to the left to help keep the shaft resting on the riser and the top of your fist.

"Now, remember the photograph of Gray Eyes? He was wearing his pistol on his left hip, indicating he was left-handed, or so it would seem. But my father was right-handed, as am I. My mother told me this when I was just a child. Something does not make sense with that photograph, Clayton. Do you agree?"

"Yes, I agree. Let's go back to the barn and look at the photograph again. We should talk to Red Dog, too. Maybe he can shed more light on these markings we see here on the bow and compare it to the other photographs of your father Will has tucked away in the secret room."

"I agree. We should talk to Red Dog...soon."

Clayton put the bow, arrows, and quiver back on the upper shelf, put the box of evidence back where the clerk found it, and left the courthouse after thanking the clerk for her assistance.

"Let's get something to eat before we head back to the ranch," said Jason as he rubbed his stomach. "I haven't had anything to eat since last night!"

"I don't think you'll starve to death before we get back to the ranch, but sure, okay, maybe we can stop at Sally's for a quick plate of whatever she has hot on the stove. If that's okay with you of course. Dancing Water is sure to be working, and we don't want to get in her way, do we, and interfere with her work duties?"

Jason shook his head back and forth, in feigned concern. "No, of course not, but we won't bother her much because we're only going to be there for a few minutes.

Besides, that will be just enough time to ask if Red Dog is in town this morning."

As luck would have it, Dancing Water was not working at the moment. "She brought Red Dog his breakfast, but then had to leave suddenly to run an errand," said Mary as she cleaned off a table. "I'm covering her section until she returns."

Red Dog had not finished his breakfast and was still sitting at a table near a window by himself. He reluctantly motioned Clayton and Jason over to his table.

At first Jason and Red Dog were uneasy with each other. What was Red Dog doing at Sally's anyway? Was he showing off for Dancing Water? Was he trying to court Dancing Water again? Jason had to know.

Red Dog was waiting for more criticism from Jason. He knew Jason often derided him, calling him "Top" Dog behind his back whenever he thought Red Dog was showing off or looking for more attention than he deserved.

Nonetheless, Clayton and Jason sat down with Red Dog and quickly brought him up to date on the secret room and the long discussion with Will.

There was too much at stake for petty differences to interfere with something as important as finally discovering who really set the fire that destroyed the Colby Hotel. And all three knew it.

"Humph! It's hard to believe that we used to play in the barn on rainy days when we were kids," reminisced Red Dog, "and never once did we stumble into that secret hide-away. Do you remember the day we became blood brothers, mixing our blood together in the hayloft? How old were we? Ten or eleven?"

For a moment or two Clayton and Jason chuckled at those long-lost days, but they quickly turned the conversation back to the present. There were serious issues to discuss.

"I think you're correct in believing those marks on the bow's riser where made by a left-handed archer," declared Red Dog, "but the photograph in the secret hideaway baffles me. Why does it look like Gray Eyes was left-handed when in reality he was a right-handed man? I must see this photograph with my own eyes to understand this more."

"Let's go now then," pressured Clayton as he stood up to leave. Jason tossed three bits on the table to pay for all their meals, pushed his chair back, and stood up.

"You should leave something extra for Dancing Water, Jason," demanded Red Dog. "You know, a tip. She is after all your girlfriend, not mine."

CHAPTER THIRTY-EIGHT
Back At The Secret Room

The ride back to the ranch was uneventful although Clayton thought it odd that Red Dog failed to notice that he was now riding Red Cloud. Never even mentioned it. Jason did catch Red Dog staring at Red Cloud when he didn't think anyone was looking, and when Red Dog rode up ahead for a spell, Jason pulled up alongside Clayton. "He's jealous," shared Jason.

"What?"

"Red Dog is jealous you're riding Red Cloud. That's why he hasn't said anything to you since we left Sally's."

Clayton nodded. "Yup, if Red Dog is not the center of attention, he gets a bit mad and becomes sullen, like he is now. He's still our blood brother though."

When they reached the ranch, Moses came out of the barn to greet them. "I'll take care of your horses for you boys. What did you learn at the courthouse?"

"We came away with more questions than answers, Moses. Is it clear to slip into the secret hideout?"

"Yes. I'm the only one here right now," replied Moses.

"Will and the rest of the boys are checking brands in the main herd. What's going on?"

"Come with us into the secret room," replied Clayton as he led Red Cloud into the corral. "We need to talk to you. And thanks, but I will take care of Red Cloud myself. I rode him, and I will take care of his tack and then feed and water him."

A half-hour later Clayton, Jason, Red Dog, and Moses were all examining the black and white pictures of Jason's father.

"Were there any other markings on the bow you examined at the courthouse?" asked Red Dog.

"No, none that I recall anyhow," replied Clayton.

"No, there were none," answered Jason. "In fact, now that I think about it, it's strange that my father didn't make his mark on his bow, or his quiver of arrows, either."

Red Dog looked closely at another photo of Gray Eyes cradling his bow. "Humph! Well, he put his initials on this bow, something Indians don't do. It must have been his white wife's influence that led him to cut 'GE' on the riser, color the letters with a black substance—probably campfire ash—and then seal it with melted beeswax."

"Wait a minute," said Red Dog with a sense of urgency. "Let me see that first photo again, the one where your father is wearing a pistol on his left side."

Clayton handed the photo to Red Dog. "Look at the riser on his bow. There is no 'GE' on the riser, but a crude number '36'!"

Clayton took the picture and brought it up to his eyes for closer scrutiny. "That's not the number '36' Red Dog, that's

'GE' in reverse! Somehow somebody made this picture look backwards. Where did this photograph come from, Moses?"

"Young Sheriff Sweeney told Will and I it had been passed around town to prove that the bow and pitch-covered arrows belonged to Gray Eyes. Knowing the truth, however, somebody else must have planted the bow and pitch-covered arrows and then claimed they were used to start the fire in the hotel that night...from a safe distance, perhaps from the alleyway. Later they came to understand their error and had to make the left-handed bow fit Gray Eyes, so they doctored up this photo after the hanging and offered it as proof they executed the right man!

"Whoever realized that the bow belonged to a left-handed shooter must know a lot about Indian bows, a lot more than the average cowboy. If we find who doctored up that photograph to make Gray Eyes look guilty," reasoned Moses, "that person could lead us to the real killer. But who could doctor up a photograph?"

Red Dog sat there for a minute and then stood up. "I know!" he boasted loudly. "There's been a traveling photographer staying in Clarkson's Fork this past week. We should pay him a visit as soon as possible...tomorrow is not too soon. Once the word gets out that we have been examining evidence at the court house and asking a lot of questions, the real killer might wise up and disappear.

Clayton and Jason looked at each other and nodded in agreement.

"I have never seen that clerk before," stated Clayton. "She could already be spreading the word about our interest in the Colby fire, even innocently. And who knows who could be listening. I agree with Red Dog. We don't have time to waste."

Red Dog stood up. "Humph! Maybe the photographer can tell us more about this backwards photograph," he added. "Since tomorrow is Sunday, we should have no problem tracking him down. He will most assuredly be asking folks to pose in their best church clothes after morning services. He may even sell a few copies of those photos to them for keepsakes."

CHAPTER THIRTY-NINE
Mathew Brady

The next morning after a quick breakfast Clayton, Jason, Red Dog, and Moses filled Will in on their findings thus far. Reinette poured everyone coffee from a fresh pot and then sat down to listen.

"Looks like we got more than one suspect," said Will, bewildered at the sudden turn of events. "First Davis, although admitting he broke his leg by falling off the board-walk after a day of heavy drinking doesn't mean he set the fire. We don't even know if he broke his leg the same night as the fire, or a month before or after the fire. Nonetheless, he fits the description Louise gave us about the man who fell off the boardwalk after scrambling down the hotel stairs that night. Indeed, it seems he could have set the fire. We'll have to try to eliminate him as a suspect.

"What's even more distressing though is the fact that the sheriff could be messed up in this. Why on earth would he have given Moses and me this doctored photograph? Did he know it had been doctored?"

Reinette leaned forward and chimed in. "He may not have known if Gray Eyes was right- or left-handed, or cared for that matter. Who's left-handed and works here at the ranch? I'll tell you. It's Blondy, but that doesn't come to mind very easily, does it!"

"Reinette has a point," said Moses as he stood up to grab a warm biscuit. "The sheriff could have just accepted the photograph as the God's truth, as we did up until today!"

"We won't find any answers to these questions sitting here," declared

Clayton as he drained the last drop of coffee from his cup. "Jason, Red Dog, and I are riding over to Clarkson's Fork this morning to have a talk with a photographer. Maybe he can tell us how that photograph was doctored up—or maybe even who did it!"

"Humph, that's a good idea, Clayton," agreed Red Dog, rising from his chair and poking his finger into his chest to emphasize the point, "but keep in mind that I thought of it first...not you!"

Clayton looked over at Jason, who turned his head and looked at Moses. Nobody said a word as the three got up from the table and walked briskly to the barn and their waiting mounts. After they closed the door behind them, Moses turned to Will and said, "I'm afraid if those three don't sort out their differences soon, there'll be trouble between them. Big trouble."

Will and Reinette nodded in agreement and then set about to clean up the kitchen. "I'd like to say 'boys will be boys,'" said Will as he filled the wooden sink with dirty dishware, "but in this case they're all young men. A split-up now could last a lifetime."

Two hours later Clayton, Jason, and Red Dog rode into Clarkson's Fork just as the Sunday services were letting up.

They had no trouble finding the photographer, bent over a black box-like device strapped atop a tripod with his head draped under a large black cloth. He appeared to be looking into the box. A most curious position.

Suddenly he jerked his head out from under the cloth, and peered over the top of the camera. He was a frail looking man, maybe a few inches over five feet, with a thick thatch of black wavy hair parted on the right and then combed straight back, and a combination black mustache and goatee barely visible under a pair of wire rim glasses and a straight English proboscis. A black vest hung loosely over a long-sleeved white shirt that was rolled up over bony arms furthering the appearance of a spindly gentleman, maybe in his late forties.

He stuck his head back under the cloth, made some adjustments to the box, and then slowly eased his head back out like a turtle emerging from its shell. He positioned a dusty black derby on his head and looked at the middle-aged couple about to have their picture taken. "Please, everyone hold still," he asked wringing his hands together nervously, and suddenly a flash and a puff of smoke rose above the crowd gathered around him. He then began anxiously pulling and sliding black panels in and out of the black box all the while thanking everyone profusely for their patience.

Clayton and Jason were amazed at the number of people who wanted their picture taken. They stood by for almost an hour until it seemed the photographer was finished. "Everyone can pick up their photos at the hotel next Saturday morning," he stated in a somewhat high pitched voice. "I'm sure you will be more than pleased at the results.

"Now, what can I do for you boys?" asked the photographer. "You've been standing patiently nearby for almost an hour. Do you want a picture of yourselves taken?"

"We rode all the way over from the Alexander ranch out near Colby," declared Clayton, "to ask you if you could help us understand this photograph."

Jason handed the photographer the black and white print of his father.

The photographer examined it carefully and then asked, "What do you want to know about it?"

"That man in buckskins is right-handed," said Jason, "but the picture seems to be doctored up to make him appear to be left-handed. And we can't seem to make out the make or caliber of his pistol, either. It looks like a Smith & Wesson, but that part of the picture is a bit fuzzy."

"Well, I can tell you that this is a fine photograph. It was obviously taken by an expert photographer, one of the best in the country I reckon. I know his work well. As to the 'doctored' part, there's a trick to making a photograph look this way. It's done in the processing of the black panel I pull out of the camera, and then flipping the negative.

"Now, as to the gun being fuzzy, that's also done after the picture is taken. You simple wave a magic wand over the negative...why do you boys want to know all this, anyway?"

Clayton stepped forward. "We'd like to know who took this picture, if possible. You said he might be the best around. Can you tell us who he is and where we can find him? It's important."

"You sound almost desperate young man. The photographer's name is Brady, Mathew Brady."

"And where can we find him?" asked Jason.

"Boys, you're looking at him! My name is Mathew Brady. Pleased to meet all three of you!" And then smiling, he reached out and shook each of their hands.

With mouths agape, Jason, Clayton, and Red Dog stood silent for what seemed to be an eternity. Then Clayton spoke up.

"Did you take this picture?"

"I sure did, many years ago, in fact a year or so before the great Colby Hotel fire."

"How can you be so sure, Mr. Brady?" asked Jason. "That was quite a few years back."

"A photographer never forgets a picture he's taken. Never. It's burned into our brain with thunder and lightning 'till the day we die."

"Did you do the doctoring, too?" asked Clayton.

"Yup, I sure did. We call it burning and dodging. Do you like it?"

Jason showed Brady the photograph again. "This man in the calico shirt is, was, my father. Why did you make him out to be a left-handed Indian when in reality he was right-handed, like me?"

"After the Colby Hotel fire, I was asked to do this doctoring to a couple of photos I had taken a year earlier of this Indian and then turn those pictures over to the sheriff. If I remember correctly, his name was Gray Eyes. It seems your father, and I say this with great humility and sorrow Jason, was accused of starting the fire. A mob hanged him before an investigation into the incident could be conducted.

I don't know why they wanted me to doctor the photos however. I was just told to give them to the sheriff."

"This is important Mr. Brady," said Jason in a low forceful tone, "did the sheriff ask you personally to doctor the pictures of Gray Eyes?" Brady's eyes began darting fearfully back and forth between Jason, Clayton and Red Dog as if he were anxiously trying to read their state of mind.

"No, it wasn't the sheriff. Let me think now, it was a rancher who owns a big spread outside of Colby. Let me think...he was a tall man with an attitude as I recall. Vachel was his name...Jimmy Vachel. That's who asked me to, as you say, 'doctor' the three pictures. He paid me right up front, too. Four dollars apiece. He wanted them real bad and real fast, and then gave me another dollar to forget all about our transaction. It's been so many years I'm sure he won't begrudge me remembering that small detail. Especially since Gray Eyes was your father."

"Thank you, Mr. Brady," replied Jason. "That helps clear up some of our concerns."

"Glad to help."

They stood there in front of the church for a while making small talk. Then another couple with twin boys asked Brady to take their picture for the family album. He readily obliged, and as he went about preparing for the shoot, Clayton, Jason, and Red Dog walked across the street to the Lone Star Cafe for a bite to eat—and to talk more about the photograph.

It didn't take them long to start wondering what role the sheriff might have played and why on earth Vachel wanted the photograph doctored.

Red Dog wasted no time. As soon as their orders were taken, he spoke up. "Vachel won the archery contest during the town's celebration days. He obviously knows a lot about shooting bows and arrows, and I'm sure that he would know the difference between a left- and a right-handed bow. And he would have eventually realized that the bow and pitch-covered arrows purported to belong to the fire starter belonged to a left-handed bowman, and that bow could not have belonged to Gray Eyes because he's right-handed."

"That makes perfect sense to me," replied Jason. "The mob lynched the wrong man, and he had to cover it up before anyone discovered the truth. And that included doctoring the earlier photo of Gray Eyes."

Red Dog countered. "Humph! But for what reason? What did he have to gain?" Clayton leaned forward across the table. "I think I know why. Vachel's ranch borders the property along the river where you and I hunted whitetails. The same property that Bull so forcefully protects. The same open range that Vachel has been running his cattle on lately."

"Yeah, I recollect the day we had the run-in with Bull," said Jason. "Clayton, do you remember how he rode up the bluff afterward where his horse was hobbled and met up with another rider who suddenly appeared out of the shadows? He looked familiar to us, but we couldn't make out his identity."

"I sure do," replied Clayton bitterly. "It looked like they were arguing over something, and then he and Bull rode off in different directions. As I recall, there was also something odd about the manner he filled the saddle, as if his right leg did not fit the stirrup properly."

Suddenly Clayton and Jason looked directly at each other with eyes blazing, and together blurted out, "That's because he has a broken leg! He can't bend his knee so he has to lower the stirrup on that side to fit his stiff leg. That was Davis! It had to be! He was the rider who had the argument with Bull that day!"

"Are you sure?" asked Red Dog. "If so, then why don't they want you up there? There must be a mighty good reason. What are they hiding, and how does Vachel figure in to all this?"

"Let's go back and ask Brady if he knows anything about Davis or Bull," declared Clayton as he finished cleaning his plate. "Maybe he can shed some light on their relationship with each other and if they have had any doings with Vachel."

After paying their tab, they walked back across the street to talk with Brady, who was just finishing up his last session with a newly married couple.

"Now what can I do for you boys?" he asked as he prepared to pick up his camera and stow it in his wagon.

"We have a few more questions Mr. Brady, if you don't mind," replied Jason.

"Sure, fire away!" he replied, eyes darting back and forth somewhat fearfully."

"Have you ever seen Vachel with the sheriff or a man named Davis since the fire?"

"I haven't seen Vachel or the sheriff since Vachel paid me for those photographs. I don't know anyone going by the name of Davis."

"What about a big man named Bull?"

Brady suddenly stepped forward and put his finger in

Jason's face. "You stay away from that man," replied Brady with a hostile tone. "He's a dangerous soul who'll stop at nothing to get what he wants. I've never seen him with the sheriff, but I have seen him with a man who has a stiff right leg, like he might have broken it some years before. Neither one of them would be what I call the friendly type."

Brady quickly regained his composure and apologized for his angry outburst. "I'm sorry. I had a run-in with Bull last year," explained Brady almost under his breath. "He wanted to know about that same photograph you boys are inquiring about today. I would have told you about it earlier, but I didn't want to get you boys involved with him. There's no doubt he'd throw a punch to get his way."

Clayton rubbed his jaw. "I know that to be a fact, Mr. Brady. What did you tell him?"

"I told him the same thing I told you," stated Brady, "but I regretted it sometime later. There's something else you should know about Bull. The afternoon stage from Morganstown was robbed again two weeks ago by over a dozen riders, and the description of one of the bandits given by a surviving passenger fits Bull perfectly.

"Look lads, how about if I give you three a photo of yourselves, one that you might look back on fondly in years to come?"

Clayton looked at Red Dog and Jason. "Why not? How much?"

"I won't charge you a nickel, and I'll forward a picture to the telegraph office for each of you on a midweek stage. Maybe you could put out a good word for me when I come to town in a month or so?"

Neither of them had ever seen their likeness, except by looking in a mirror. Red Dog readily agreed, and with a bit of laughter, Clayton and Jason swiftly followed suit.

Brady then posed the three of them together using the church as a backdrop and three metal stands to help them stay still, and took their picture. Clayton and Jason drew their Navy Colts and squatted, looking rugged and confident. Red Dog however stood behind them with his arms folded across his chest, proud and defiant. Little did anyone know at the time that that photo session would be the last time the blood brothers would be seen together in apparent harmony.

In less than a month, one of them would be dead.

CHAPTER FOURTY
Judge Alexander Reinstated

It had only been a week or so since Will sent the telegram to the statehouse when there came a knock on the ranch's front door.

"Will!" said Reinette loudly. "There's a gentleman here to see you."

"I'm in the office, Reinette. Bring him in."

Will was shuffling papers when Reinette opened the door and ushered in a well-dressed gentleman complete with a white dress shirt, silk cravat, and black waistcoat. He was puffing on a cigar clenched between his teeth and holding a briefcase under one arm. "Hello, Will. Long time no see!"

Will's jaw dropped, and then a smile erupted on his face as he stood up to shake the visitor's hand. "John! John Bastion! I had no idea! When I got the reply to my telegram, it said someone would be in contact, but I had no idea it would be you! How the hell are you! Damn, I haven't seen you in, what, 25 or 30 years? Could it really be that long?"

Will came around his desk and gave Bastion a hearty handshake. Then he put his left hand on Bastion's right shoulder and turned to his wife. "Reinette, this is John Bastion, Judge John Bastion. We grew up together, rode together a bit in our younger days, and later were both sworn in to the bench at about the same time by Houston himself. I'm sure I've talked to you about him plenty in the past."

"Why, yes Will, you have. It is so very nice to meet you, Judge Bastion," beamed Reinette.

Judge Bastion shook Reinette's hand with a wide and generous smile of his own. "Pleased to meet you, Mrs. Alexander. Very pleased!"

"Oh, please. If you have known my Wilfred all these years, you can call me Reinette."

"Why thank you! And me, call me John. Please!"

"Reinette, John and I spent many an evening talking about law and the future of Texas in our younger days," chimed in Will enthusiastically. "You might have seen each other once or twice in the statehouse, but I don't believe either of you were ever formally introduced."

"No," replied Reinette thoughtfully, "I don't think we've ever met."

"It's always seemed to be a small world, but this meeting is, well, I'll be damned! John, it's so great to see you again! What have you been up to?"

"I moved to the panhandle right after I was formally sworn in, but before you wed, and since then I've been in the service of the great state of Texas. I have kept tabs on you somewhat, Will. In the course of the last several years, there are a few items that've come to my attention that you need to know about. I'll explain later in full detail."

"Well, here sit down, John. Would you like a brandy?"

As Bastion sat down, he relaxed with an audible sigh of relief. "No, not right now, Will. Thanks. I want to keep my head clear for a while."

Reinette sensed that Will and John's reunion had more to do with business that rekindling an old friendship. "Have you eaten recently, John? We just finished our supper, but I have some leftover venison roast I could warm up right quick with salt potatoes, gravy, and some homemade buttered biscuits."

"That would be fine, Mrs. ...I mean, Reinette. I am hungry. Actually, very hungry. I took the stage to Colby and then rented a horse and buggy at the livery stable. I made one quick stop to purchase an extra box of .45s—a lone man on the road needs to be careful these days, a full wheel is often not enough if trouble shows up—paid my respects at the sheriff's office, and then rushed on. I was excited to see Will again, before nightfall, and simply didn't take the time to eat in town."

"Then why don't I let you two get reacquainted while I fix you a warm plate," said Reinette. "Will, I'll bring you both a pot of coffee and a couple of slices of berry pie when John's supper is ready."

Reinette closed the door behind her and rushed off to the kitchen to prepare a home-cooked meal for John. In the meantime Bastion sank deeper into the chair. "Reinette is a gracious woman, Will. I can tell from just meeting her she must be special. Maybe after I eat, which, by the way, I really appreciate your hospitality 'cause I'm about ready to eat a mule, you can show me around the ranch."

"John, you didn't come all this way unannounced and late in the day to compliment my wife and taste her cooking, or to take a tour of my ranch for that matter. What's going on?"

Judge Bastion straightened himself up in the chair, opened his briefcase, and then stood up holding an official-looking document in his hand.

"Your telegram came at a most important time, Will. First, stand up and raise your right hand."

"What?"

"Please, Will. Stand up and raise your right hand."

Will obliged.

"Wilfred Alexander, do you solemnly swear to uphold the laws of Texas to the best of your ability, and to...just say 'I do,' Will."

"I do!"

"By the power vested in me by the governor and the Texas legislature, you now have been officially reinstated as judge for the Third District, state of Texas. Congratulations, Judge Alexander!"

Will was somewhat flabbergasted. He hadn't seen his friend for half a lifetime, and within 10 minutes of their reunion, he finds he's again been sworn in to the bench.

"When we got your telegram requesting to be reinstated, it couldn't have come at a more opportune time, Will. It was as if providence had been called to intervene on both our behalf's.

"I had to come in person. We couldn't respond to you in writing for fear every bandit on the wire would be tipped off."

"Tipped off? To what?" Will settled back into his leather chair and folded his arms, taking a somewhat guarded stance. He needed to hear what his friend John, or was it Judge Bastion, had to say. What in the hell was going on?

CHAPTER FOURTY-ONE

Death Revealed

"Let me get right to the point, Will. We, and by 'we' I mean the state of Texas, have a problem on our hands, one that's been brewing for quite some time...and we need your help."

"What kind of problem? What kind of help?"

"How well do you know the ranchers around here, or more specifically, what do you know about a fella named Vachel?"

"I know all the ranchers within a 30-mile radius of Colby. They're all hard-working, honest folk, at least for the most part. As far as Vachel, he owns a large spread a bit to the east of town," replied Will. "Has quite a few hands on the payroll. Keeps to himself mostly. Why?"

"What about an Englishman that goes by the name of Sir Thomas? He fancies having royal blood in his veins, or so he claims. He also fancies himself an English bowman of sorts. He's in his early seventies and is a personable chap, at least when you first meet him."

"I don't know him all that well, John. I know he competed in an archery contest we had during the weekend we celebrated Texas' return to the states. I have a favorable impression of him. Why?"

Judge Bastion leaned across Will's desk and lowered his head, as if to weigh his next words very carefully, before lifting his brow and looking Will straight in the eyes. "How many times has your grandson, Clayton, been caught snooping around the river boundary to Vachel's ranch, and how many times has he been knocked on his ass by a big, mean son of a bitch that goes by the name of Bull?"

Will was caught by surprise. Complete surprise! "How do you know all this, and what does any of it have to do with my grandson? And how in the hell did you even know I have a grandson anyway, much less his name?"

Will was suddenly starting to get a bit defensive and a little hot under the collar. Bastion seemed to know an awful lot about the surrounding ranchers, one in particular, and his grandson's problems with Bull.

"I repeat. How do you know all this, and what does any of it have to do with the problem the state of Texas has, a problem you say you need my help with?"

Bastion realized he was coming on a little strong and backed off a bit. "Will, I was part of the team that investigated your son Jacob's death and the deaths of his deputies at the hands of those cattle rustlers. We know that the cattle were sold to some Mexican ranchers who took the herd back across the border themselves. The money was never recovered, but we have since learned that Vachel was the brains behind those killings, the killings of other cowboys and ranchers, stagecoach holdups, and more cattle rustling for quite some time since.

"It's a criminal enterprise that's operated unchecked for too many years, but we're finally closing in on them. They seem to operate from Vachel's ranch, but don't pull any shenanigans within a couple days' ride of any of his holdings. They even go over the border to steal Mexican cattle and bring them back to Texas to sell to the very rancher who had his herd pilfered by other Mexicans in the first place. That's what makes it so hard to pin any robberies on him. He operates a fair distance away where nobody knows him and deals with ranchers and others who, habitually or otherwise, have larceny in their souls."

Will started to rise from his chair. "How come nobody told me this before? That Vachel was behind the cattle rustling and my son's death? And that he's still rustling and directing stagecoach holdups?"

"You were on a need-to-know basis, Will. But wait. There's more." Will sat back down and ran his hands through his graying hair. "What do you mean there's more?"

"We just learned that Vachel was also behind the Colby Hotel fire, the fire that killed your son John and his wife Sally along with several other visitors to the hotel. An Indian informant that we were relying on named Gray Eyes was blamed for the fire and lynched before the law could intervene, before we could save his life actually."

"Once again, John, how do you know this, and how long have you known it? Damn it, John! Stop playing games. Out with it. All of it!"

"Okay, okay. Will, we have an agent working for Vachel. A well-trained and trusted undercover Texas Ranger with lots of experience. He recently got word to us that a certain one of Vachel's hands confessed one night over a bottle of whiskey to starting the Colby Hotel fire and that he was under direct orders from Vachel to do so. We could arrest that cowhand right now, but it would only be his word against Vachel's. Worse yet, his arrest would only serve notice to Vachel that we're on to him."

"Do you have any idea why Vachel would want to burn down the Colby Hotel?" asked Will.

"I do now, Will. Your son John was doing plenty of snooping around Vachel and his ranch, and Gray Eyes was passing what John learned about Vachel back to us. We think Vachel caught on and had the fire started to kill your son and Gray Eyes before Vachel's criminal enterprise could be exposed. A well-established and very lucrative criminal enterprise I might add."

"Do you have any other evidence? If not, an awful lot of what you say is dependent on the word of your undercover agent. Why should anybody believe anything he has to say? Who in the hell is he anyhow?"

"You've met him, Will. Several times. If I told you his name, you'd trust him as much as we do. Right now, his identity is protected by silence. Only my secretary Rose O'Brien knows who he is, and she's instructed to reveal his name only upon my death... and even then only if the agent requests it."

"Nonetheless, the time has come. It is now imperative for you to know who it is." Judge Bastion then pulled a piece of paper out of his briefcase, wrote something on it, and handed it to Will.

"You're right, John, I do know this man...and I do trust him. Implicitly."

"For the time being, his name must not go past this room. Not to your wife, your grandson, or any cowboy you deem fit to wear a badge as a Texas Ranger."

Will nodded his head in agreement, and then scratched a match on the side of his desk and lit the paper afire. He held it in his hand as long as he dared and then dropped it on the floor, allowing the flame to extinguish the name on the paper.

Just then there was a knock on the door. It was Reinette. "Supper is ready. Are you two old friends ready to eat?"

CHAPTER FOURTY-TWO
Texas Gold

Bastion was indeed hungry and finished his plate with barely a word or two between bites. "Thanks, Reinette," he said as he pushed his plate away. "That's the best home-cooked meal I've had in months."

"I'm glad you liked it, John," replied Reinette. "I hope you left room for dessert!" She then brought over a couple of pieces of berry pie warmed on the stove, and a pot of coffee to wash them down with, and placed them on the table in front of Will and John. "I'll be in the sewing room if either of you need anything else," said Reinette as she picked up the dirty dishes.

Will and John took notice of when Reinette closed the door behind her and then continued their earlier conversation in hushed tones.

"Why don't you get a big posse together and take Vachel into custody at the ranch?" asked Will in a rather direct and matter-of-fact tone. "He certainly wouldn't be expecting it."

"We don't have enough hard evidence to convict him at a jury trial. We need to catch him in the act, Will, and that's the main reason I'm here and why the state of Texas is asking for your help."

Will was visibly frustrated. "I want the people responsible for killing my two sons in the worst way, John. And any way we get them is fine with me. But I also know that we have to do by the rule of law. We've waited a long time for justice to be served, and by 'we' I mean Reinette, Clayton, Jason, and me. But with you here today and this recent unveiling of long-buried facts, there's hope, and I don't think we'll have to wait much longer. How can I help?"

John pulled a map from inside his briefcase and spread it out over the table. "The army is escorting a shipment of three million dollars' worth of gold bullion from New Orleans to Austin, and it'll soon be passing through Colby. We have let it be known that the wagon train will cross the river on your property on its way to town, right here, at the only shallow area within miles.

"It's an ideal ambush point, and I'm sure Vachel will see it that way, too. What he doesn't know is that the gold shipment will have a little surprise in store for him ...50 additional armed soldiers shadowing the shipment. As soon as Vachel shows his face, they'll swarm in from both sides of the river. He won't stand a chance."

"How do you know he'll take the bait?"

"Vachel's already ordered six new heavy-duty wagons from the blacksmith, each built to handle heavier than usual loads with stronger axles and thicker floorboards. The wheels are also bigger in diameter and reinforced with eight extra heat-treated oak spokes per wheel. We believe he plans on transferring the gold to these stronger overland freight wagons to help him make a clean getaway."

"John, three million in gold bullion is a lot of gold, but how is he going to spend it? Every banker and lawman in the state will be on the lookout for that much gold. He won't be able to show a single bar without drawing suspicion."

"Vachel already has that figured out. They plan on taking the gold to Mexico and then putting it on a ship bound for England. That's where Sir Thomas comes in. He may have royal blood running through his veins, but it isn't blue. He's going to pay Vachel two million dollars for the entire shipment once it crosses the border. He makes a million bucks without hardly lifting a finger, and Vachel gets to spend his share without anyone knowing where he got the money."

Will looked directly into Bastion's eyes. "So what do you need me for?"

John turned the map around so both he and Will could examine it together. "Will, what can you tell me about those riffles?" John asked as he pointed to a wide section of the river. "Our information is that they can be tricky to navigate."

"Well, that's Alexander's Crossing, and you're correct. It's the only good place to take a heavy gold-laden wagon across the river for several miles up- or downstream. The bottom there is solid, mostly gravel and small stones, making it easy for the wagons to cross at that point.

"You have to be careful though, as the slow-moving water can be deceptive. The currents do swirl there, and over time a huge cavernous hole has developed downstream and along the edge of the riffles about two-thirds across on the west side. If you take the wagons too close they'll surely slip in over the lip. It's about 30 feet deep there, and in the past, inexperienced drivers have lost a wagon or two. There's not much you can do about it once you start to go. The horses will certainly drown, and it'll be hell getting the gold back out of the river."

"Will, our drivers are young army boys with little experience crossing rivers, much less these dangerous riffles. I fear they might lose the wagons in the crossing even if we've already arrested Vachel and his gang. The state of Texas would like to hire you and six of your best and experienced men to guide the army wagons across the river.

"Now, if we round up Vachel, then they can take the gold across through the riffles safely and at their leisure. I don't want to lose a young inexperienced soldier and a team of horses unnecessarily. However, if our plan backfires, I want your drivers to purposely take the wagons downstream of the riffles and into the hole, shoot the horses, and let the gold sink in the river. I don't want Vachel to get that gold under any circumstances."

Bastion slid his hand off the map and looked up at Will. "What do you think?"

Will rubbed his jaw a bit and then again looked John straight in the eye. "It's a good plan, a solid plan. I'll see if Lefty, Blondy, Kip, Tall Bear, and a couple of others will volunteer. I doubt they'll turn down the opportunity."

"Tell them the army will pay each driver a month's wages for every day he works, and this will be at least a three-day job. When we hire good men, we pay them promptly and without reservation."

Will nodded in agreement as John folded up the map and slipped it back into his briefcase.

"It's getting late, John. Why don't you spend the night and we can talk more in the morning. Maybe stay a few days. Heck, we haven't seen each other in all these years, it would take a lot more than a few days to catch up on all the news!"

"I was planning on staying in town tonight, Will, but I'm not as spry as I used to be, and it's a long ride back to town, so, yes, I'd like to take you up on your invitation. Besides, I want to meet the guides."

"Good. I'll ask one of the hands to put your horse and buggy up in the barn and then bring your bags into the guest room. Tomorrow I'll introduce you to some of the ranch hands I think would make good guides, and you can explain to them what you want them to do. My grandson, Clayton, and his two friends, Jason and Red Dog should be back from Clarkson's Fork later in the day. They may have some more information about Vachel and his gang."

"Good. I need to hear what they have to say." Bastion started to leave the room, but stopped and turned around.

"And Will, the state of Texas has one more favor to ask of you. We'll discuss it later."

CHAPTER FOURTY-THREE
Outside Vachel's Compound

Clayton, Jason, and Red Dog were mute as they left Clarkson's Fork that morning, but Brady's words were bouncing around inside their skulls like bullets ricocheting off a stone wall. They knew they were close to finally discovering who set the Colby Hotel on fire and just as importantly, for what purpose.

Jason rode up alongside Clayton and then kept pace with Red Cloud. "You know, we know Vachel is certainly implicated in the fire, but what about the sheriff? He accepted a fake photograph from Vachel. And Davis? His gimp leg is a dead giveaway, or so it seems. What in the hell was he doing on the rise that day we had the run-in with Bull?"

Clayton looked over at Jason and shook his head back and forth. "We keep rehashing the same information over and over again. Nonetheless, we seem to know more today than we knew yesterday, yet we're still in the dark. At this point we seem to have more questions than answers. I think it's time we took a closer look at Vachel's ranch. Maybe we can get a better idea of just what the hell is really going on up there!"

Red Dog rode up along the other side of Clayton. "Humph! What are you guys talking about? Me?"

"No, we're not talking about you, Red Dog. We're thinking about riding up to the bluffs above the river and taking a closer look at Vachel's ranch. That's where Jason and I had our first run-in with Bull. Are you in?"

"Why, don't you want me to go?"

Clayton looked over at Jason, and they both just shook their heads in bewilderment.

A few hours later they were easing their horses through the brush that grew along the river's edge and up a hill where they could dismount and glass the surrounding terrain without exposing their position to watchful eyes.

Red Dog began to remove his chaps.

"There're rattlers up here, Red Dog," cautioned Clayton. "I'd think about leaving those on...you know...just in case."

Red Dog hesitated for a minute while he pondered Clayton's remarks and then reluctantly took his advice and left his chaps in place. He followed Clayton and Jason up the hill to the nearest high point.

Once in place, they removed their hats and peered over the edge of the rocky outcropping. Clayton scanned the terrain below with his field glasses, the same pair he found hanging in the hidden room behind the horse stall, the same ones his father used when he was a Texas Ranger. At first nothing caught his eye as he scanned the treeless landscape before him. Then a puff of gray smoke caught his attention.

"We have to get closer," whispered Clayton. "I think I just found the whereabouts of Vachel's ranch house."

The trio dropped behind a grassy mound and then duck-walked 75 yards closer to the smoke. This time when they peeked their heads over the rim they could make out the entire layout of the ranch.

"What can you see?" asked Jason.

"The main ranch house is fairly run down with a broken window facing the front yard. The porch roof looks porous and is missing several shingles. A couple of ranch hands are sitting on a bench out front, just talking it seems. There's a stream running along the far side of the compound, with plenty of green pasture out back for several horses. The barn's not as big as ours, but it seems to have a long coral leading to another barn and a few outbuildings. One of them is definitely a blacksmith shop. That's where the smoke is coming from."

Clayton handed the field glasses to Jason. Can you make out any of those three men standing in front of the barn?" he whispered. "The one in the dark suit looks like Vachel."

Jason focused the lens on the three men. "Yup, that's Vachel all right." "Do you see who he's talking to?" asked Clayton.

"I'll be, it looks like Davis! That son of a bitch!"

"Let me see," whispered Clayton, holding out his right hand. Jason passed the glasses back to Clayton without taking his own eyes off of the three men standing in front of the barn.

"You're right, Jason. That's Davis. Acting all friendly like. Who's the third man? He, too, looks familiar. Like I should know him. He has a strange hat and seems to be wearing a fancy vest and polished knee-high leather boots.

He certainly doesn't look like a ranch hand, that's for sure."

Red Dog reached over and tugged at the strap around Clayton's neck. "My turn."

Clayton obliged without saying a word. Red Dog focused the binoculars on the third man, lowered the glasses, and looked directly at Clayton and Jason. "You will not believe who is standing down there big as all get out. It's Sir Thomas, the Englishman who nearly beat me at the archery contest. What the hell is he doing here?"

"Red Dog, do you recognize anybody else down there?" asked Clayton.

"I see maybe two dozen or more men just fiddling around," replied Red Dog, not taking the glasses off the compound. He continued scanning the yard and outbuildings. "I don't recognize any of them though. They're all strangers, even for these parts. You'd think that maybe you'd have seen one or two of them in town on a Saturday night at a bar or doing business with one of Millie's girls."

"Exactly!" replied Clayton. "These are all new cowhands. New to us anyway. Why would Vachel hire so many new men?"

"Look! Over by the blacksmith shed," said Jason. "They're wheeling out a wagon. A big wagon! Let me see those glasses again.

"Something looks mighty peculiar about that wagon," said Jason in a barely audible whisper. "Wait. I see what it is. They've installed four sets of leaf springs under each corner of the wagon. Looks like four or five leaves per set. They're planning on hauling something very heavy with that rig. Very heavy."

"We've seen enough," Clayton whispered back. "Let's get back to the horses before we're spotted. I don't want to have another run-in with Bull. At least not right now. We don't see him down there, and that means he could be up here somewhere looking for someone who doesn't belong. Open range trespassers, as he calls them."

The trio started to retrace their steps single file, but at the last minute Red Dog changed his mind and jumped down from one rocky ledge to the next in an effort to beat Jason and Clayton to the horses.

It was a strategy he'd soon regret.

CHAPTER FOURTY-FOUR
Goliath Does His Death Dance

Clayton stopped and turned to Jason, who was only a few steps behind him. "What the devil is Red Dog doing?"

"He's trying to beat us back to the horses," replied Jason hurriedly. "If he's not the center of attention, he just has to do something about it, doesn't he?"

Red Dog continued his reckless descent, knowing he had caught Clayton and Jason off-guard. One more ledge and he'd be on flat ground. Then it would be just a short sprint to the horses, an easy victory over Clayton and Jason.

Goliath was sunning himself on that bottom ledge and felt the vibrations of Red Dog's rapid approach. With no place to go in short order, Goliath had no recourse but to coil his entire length in a defensive posture and with his forked tongue flicking in and out trying to gather in a scent, shake his tail back and forth to warn the intruder away.

But the warning went unheeded.

Or maybe Red Dog simply didn't hear Goliath's death rattle.

As soon as Red Dog landed on the ledge, Goliath struck his left leg just below the knee with a resounding *WHACK!* The attack nearly knocked Red Dog to the ground.

"Aiheeee!" screamed Red Dog. "Snake! Snake!"

Red Dog instinctively jumped back in an effort to distance himself from the serpent, but it was to no avail. Goliath's fangs had sunk deep and then become entangled in the thick, soft leather of Red Dog's chaps and the stringy fibers of his tattered canvas pants underneath. Goliath tried to withdraw his head but couldn't extricate his fangs!

Clayton and Jason heard Red Dog's screams, looked down, and saw Red Dog struggling to remain standing as Goliath began wriggling his body in a frantic effort to free himself from Red Dog's chaps.

"Damn! Look at the size of that damn snake!" yelled Clayton. "We gotta get it off him, fast!"

Goliath began to panic, throwing his body back and forth to free himself. The sheer weight of the snake's whip-lash was enough to knock Red Dog down, but he instinctively scissor-spread his legs, putting his right leg to the rear, and braced himself in a desperate effort to keep his balance—and to get the snake off him.

"SNAKE! SNAKE! Hurry! Get this thing off me! Please! Please!"

Red Dog's heart was racing and his blood pressure was soaring. He knew, deep down inside, that the venom from a rattlesnake this size could kill him in less than a minute. He was about to pass out from sheer fear as Goliath continued to wiggle back and forth, his huge tail now slapping the ground like rolling thunder. But the more Goliath twisted his body the more entrenched the entanglement. Indeed, his twisting efforts to escape did nothing more than tighten the canvas fibers underneath the soft pliable leather surrounding each fang. He was hopelessly stuck. He was tiring, and somehow, instinctively...Goliath began to sense his own doom.

Clayton and Jason arrived at the same time and as quickly as their legs could carry them, but their own fear of the nine-foot-plus reptile nearly paralyzed their response. "Red Dog, don't move. There could be more snakes nearby."

With both eyes bulging out of their sockets, Red Dog didn't need advice—he needed quick action to save his life. He picked up a small rock and threw it at Goliath. It struck the serpent on the head, but the force was insufficient to knock the snake off. Sensing more danger, Goliath doubled his efforts to escape and with a gigantic thrust of his tail, threw his 90-plus pounds of sinew and muscle to one side, knocking Red Dog to the ground.

"Aiheee!"

Clayton and Jason looked for a weapon, something heavy to kill Goliath with, but all they could see were small, flat rocks. "We gotta grab that fucking snake by the head and yank it off Red Dog," yelled Clayton. "Once we grab it, don't let go or it'll surely bite us, too!"

Red Dog didn't hear Clayton; he couldn't, for he was in a state of morbid panic. The action before him suddenly turned to slow motion, a life-saving advantage, for it allowed him to perfectly time his attack on the snake. When Goliath twisted his head to the left, Red Dog reached down with his left hand and grabbed Goliath behind his gigantic triangular-shaped head, and with his right hand unsheathed his long-bladed hunting knife.

Goliath began to shake violently, but the adrenalin flowing through Red Dog gave him incredible strength, enough power to squeeze Goliath's neck so tightly the veins were rising from his hand. Without letting go of his grip, Red Dog slipped the blade between his leg and Goliath's twisting body and severed Goliath's head in one quick and decisive upward motion.

Clayton and Jason were aghast at Red Dog's actions. "Don't let go of his head, Red Dog," they chimed in unison. "He can still bite you!"

Clayton unsheathed his own knife and stepped forward. "Don't move, Red Dog!", and quickly slipped his own knife into Goliath's open mouth. With one quick upward thrust, he then pushed the blade through the top of Goliath's head. "When I say, 'let go,' do it and I'll toss the head out of the way."

"Let go!"

Red Dog released his grip, and Clayton tossed Goliath's massive head safely onto the rocks.

"Don't go near it," cautioned Jason. "It's still flicking its tongue...it can still bite!"

Red Dog was awash with sweat, and his hands were shaking like a half-dead leaf in a wind storm. But he was alive!"

"Did he bite you?" yelled Clayton.

"I don't know!" screamed Red Dog, spittle spraying everywhere.

"Sit down then, and let us take a look," ordered Clayton.

Jason and Red Dog rolled up Red Dog's canvas

trousers, but couldn't see where Goliath's fangs had broken any skin. They then inspected his chaps and found that both of Goliath's fangs had broken off inside the leather when Clayton forcefully plied his knife. The thick leather chaps had indeed protected Red Dog from harm.

There was a huge sigh of relief from Clayton and Jason. They, too, sat down to let their breathing return to normal. And when they it did the tension began to dissipate.

Clayton glanced over at Red Dog who was sitting with his head in his hands staring at the ground. A flood of memories chronicling their lives together suddenly flowed into Clayton's consciousness, beginning when they were kids wrestling in the barn and fishing in the river to the time they spent herding cattle and racing their mounts against the wind. Red Dog was always strong and agile, yet despite these traits he had almost lost his life.

Clayton looked over at Jason and then back to Red Dog. He realized that they weren't kids anymore, and that death can come when you least expect it. Indeed, the decisions we make every day, even the seemingly innocent ones, can have a deleterious effect on our chances of surviving another day if we are not careful. Why was it so important for Red Dog to beat us back to the horses? What was he trying to prove?

"That was quick thinking on your part, Red Dog, to use your knife," said Clayton as he removed his hat and wiped the sweat off his brow. "When I first saw that snake on your leg, and how big he was, I thought for sure you were a gonner. I've never seen a snake so big, never even heard of one that size!"

Jason shook his head back and forth as he relived those first few images in his head. "Red Dog, maybe next time you'll stick with us and not go off by yourself. You don't have to prove your manhood to us."

Red Dog just stared at the ground. He was still shaking from the close call he just experienced. "I haven't seen such a large snake either. When I looked down at his eyes, all I could see were my ancestors calling me home."

"Well, you can tell them to wait now," laughed Jason as he slapped Red Dog on the back. "You're the bravest man I've ever seen. I don't think I could've done what you just did, grabbing that big, ugly son of a bitch with just your bare hands. Incredible!"

Red Dog smiled a bit and then looked over at Clayton, who looked to be coming out of shock himself. Red Dog could feel the color beginning to return to his face.

"Wait here, Red Dog. Rest and I'll get the horses," said Jason. "I wouldn't walk around too much though. I'll wager that's not the only snake living in these rocks."

CHAPTER FOURTY-FIVE
One More Scare

"What do you want to do with the snake?" asked Clayton. "Your horse won't let you drape the carcass over the saddle, or your bed roll, for that matter. And it definitely won't fit in your saddle bag. That's one very big snake. I'll bet it weighs nearly 100 pounds!"

"I want to bring it back to the ranch to show my father and your grandfather and some of the other ranch hands. I have a large canvas sack used to haul two grain bags at a time tied to my saddle bags. I reckon the snake will fit in that sack. I'll then tie my lariat to the sack and drag the rattler behind me all the way back to the ranch."

Red Dog didn't notice that Jason had already gathered up the horses until Jason coughed. Clayton stood up and grabbed the canvas bag off Red Dog's horse and then held it open so Red Dog could pick up the dead rattler and drop it in. When he touched the snake, however, it quivered, sending Red Dog into a fit.

"Aihee, it still lives!"

"Just nerves, Red Dog," said Clayton in a calming tone.

"Your snake is long dead. Don't pick up his head however to put it in the sack. I'd be very careful with it. Use a stick instead and roll it into the mouth of the bag. It can still strike hours after you cut it off."

Soon they were all riding back down to the river, with Red Dog dragging his dead snake behind him in the canvas sack.

When they reached a shallow section a mile or so down river, Red Dog dismounted and secured his lariat around the horn of the saddle.

"What are you doing?" asked Clayton impatiently. "We're still several hours' ride from the ranch, and I want to get there in time for supper."

"I've got to wash the blood off my arms and hands and the stink off my clothes before I get back to the ranch," said Red Dog still looking exhausted over his ordeal.

He walked over the stream bank, disrobed, and jumped into the clear water. The coolness of the flowing current further calmed Red Dog, soothing his body and his mind. He sat down in the river and rubbed sand on his skin until Goliath's blood was gone. Then he stepped ashore, grabbed his breeches, and tossed them in the water. He scrubbed them as best he could and then stepped back into them.

Clayton and Jason had dismounted but didn't want to jump in the river with Red Dog, although a good soaking wouldn't have hurt either one of them after all the hot dusty days on the trail.

"Clayton, grab that dead branch next to your feet and hand it to me without Red Dog seeing what you're doing."

"What are you up to, Jason?"

"Watch this!"

Jason took the branch from Clayton, eased up to the river bank, and when Red Dog wasn't looking in his direction, launched the black and twisted branch at Red Dog, yelling "SNAKE! SNAKE!"

Red Dog caught a brief glimpse of the twisted branch out of the corner of his eye and heard it splash into the water, for a brief second or two thought it was indeed another snake. He panicked and rushed out of the water, but before he set foot on the near shoreline he realized it was only a prank played on him by Jason.

Red Dog now believed the feud between him and Jason was still roiling around inside Jason, despite his comments to the contrary. Without saying a word, Red Dog finished dressing and mounted his horse.

"It was funny when you tossed the dead water moccasin's head in our direction, why isn't this funny now?" challenged Jason as he slipped his foot into the stirrup.

"Give it up, Jason. C'mon, Red Dog's had enough to do with snakes today, and frankly so have I. There're much more important issues we have to deal with than who did what to whom several months ago."

Jason quieted down and then issued an apology to Red Dog. "I guess it wasn't funny after all, Red Dog. I'm sorry. It was just a harmless prank, and I meant nothing sinister. Let's go home and get something hot to eat. Maybe we can all have a good laugh over this when our bellies are full."

Red Dog grunted and waved Jason off, but it was obvious to Clayton that Red Dog was visibly shaken by Jason's antics. The big rattler had almost killed Red Dog an hour earlier, and it wasn't likely Red Dog would be laughing about it anytime soon.

CHAPTER FOURTY-SIX
Inside Vachel's Compound

Vachel inspected the freight wagons and was pleased with the work completed by his men. The installation of four sets of heavy-duty leaf springs and larger reinforced wheels nearly doubled the carrying capacity of each wagon. They should have little trouble transporting three million dollars in gold bullion to Mexico.

"There're other problems we have to be concerned with," chimed in Davis, "not the least of which is spare parts for the wagons. We've driven cattle back and forth several times, and we all know the trail can be hard on man, beast, and equipment."

"We'll have another freight wagon in the convoy to carry eight extra wheels, two dozen or so spare heat-treated oak spokes, four additional axles, and several tubs of axle grease for the breakdowns we're bound to experience," stated Vachel. "In addition, Henry the blacksmith is packing all the fixings he needs to replace horseshoes, wagon tongue pins, wheel rings, and other metal accessories plus several sheets of leather for harness fixings. Once we're on the trail to Mexico, we can't afford to stop for any great length of time and have to keep on the move as much as possible."

"You seem to have thought of everything, Vachel. I like that. It lets me rest easier in the evening after the lanterns go out," Davis commented.

"Once we get out of this open country, the cattle we're driving to Don Carlos will help conceal the wagon tracks. The army, or what's left of them, will never find us," boasted Vachel. "Barring any misfortune, I reckon it'll then take us no more than 10 days to get to the border, and less than that to get to the coast."

"I've received word from Don Carlos. He and his vaqueros will meet us at the border, take control of the herd, and then escort us to the saltwater coast where the frigate HMS Arrow will be lying at anchor and waiting for our arrival," added Sir Thomas. "Even the Mexican Army has been taken care of and will allow us safe passage by simply looking the other way...for a small and reasonable fee. You'll be paid the agreed-upon share only once the bullion is on board, not at the border, as I stipulated earlier, and I will set sail for England immediately on the first high tide."

Vachel nodded in agreement. "It looks like all we have to do now is steal the gold!" said Vachel matter-of-factly. "Let's go inside where we can talk privately. Davis, go get Bull. I think he's still in the blacksmith shop. He needs to know exactly how we're going to pull this off."

When Bull walked into the ranch house, Vachel and Sir Thomas had their heads bowed over a map of the territory. "Bull, what do you know about Alexander's Crossing, here on the map?"

"It's the only suitable wagon crossing for miles up and down the river," reported Bull. "The water is shallow with a series of slow riffles no more than a few feet deep. It has a good solid bottom and the banks are easy to navigate. The only problem, and it's a big one, is the deep hole on the downstream edge where the riffles narrow. You get a wagon caught in there, and it'll sink into a 30-foot abyss. It'll be hell retrieving a wagon full of gold from that drop-off. In fact, you'll probably have to leave it there and let the army fool with it after we've gone."

"There won't be much of an army left when we get done," smiled Vachel, "but I do understand your concerns. Alexander's Crossing is an ideal ambush point, and we need to take advantage of it. The gold will be heavily guarded, but nothing we can't handle ourselves. After all, it's not like this is our first Union robbery!"

"Yeah, but if all goes well it very well could be our last!" laughed Davis!

"It better not be your first attempt or your last attempt at a Union robbery," warned Sir Thomas, his voice growing louder with each utterance. "If the bullion doesn't arrive here by sundown on the day after the robbery, I'll be on my way to Mexico to have a word with Don Carlos and his vaqueros.

Vachel looked over at Sir Thomas and to avoid a needless confrontation, simply waved him off. "Okay, here's the plan. The army doesn't want that gold to drop into the chasm anymore than we do. My guess is that they will drive the wagons across the riffles one at a time, just to be safe. We'll let the first couple of wagons roll without incident. That'll help build their confidence. Help them relax a bit. Now, when the last wagon gets halfway across, we hit them from the front and the rear simultaneously. If need be, we shoot the horses drawing the wagons...even the last wagon if it's still in the river. That gold isn't going anywhere then, except to Mexico with us.

"I'll tell Kirby to hold off until he hears my signal...a blast from my 12-gauge. He'll ride full speed at the front of the wagon train and cripple the lead wagon."

Vachel turned back to the map. "Bridges will be hiding in this dry creek bed a couple hundred yards downstream and ride in from the rear after Kirby's men begin their attack. This should cause mass confusion and split the Union forces. They'll be unable to protect both ends of the wagon train. Hell, with any luck, they'll probably end up shooting each other!"

"Yeah," said Davis, "but our forces will also be split!"

"That's true, but we'll be attacking the center of the convoy from both ends while the army is riding away from the convoy trying to stop the attack! In fact, there's nothing stopping Kirby from riding across the river to help Bridges, putting what's left of the Union forces in a pincer. It'll be a bloodbath, to be sure!"

"There's another problem," said Davis as he stood up. "Sheriff Sweeny told me he's going to organize a posse to help escort the gold to the bank in Colby. He's rounded up a dozen or so men, men that can shoot, and they'll ride out to meet the army at the river."

"I thought they might, and in fact I hope they do! The bank is flush with cash this time of year, and with most of the able-bodied men riding out to protect the gold ship-ment, the bank will be an easy target.

"Bull, I want you to take 15 or 20 men and nonchalantly work your way into town on Saturday, the day we expect the gold to cross the river. The townsfolk have been used to seeing you and some of the others on and off on a regular basis, and your presence should be no cause for concern.

"What! Are you crazy?" yelled Davis. "You want to rob the Colby Bank at the same time we're attacking the gold shipment?"

"Well, not exactly," Vachel corrected. The bank will be expecting the gold shipment after closing hours. Bull will walk into the bank just as they are about to draw the shades for the day, and relieve them of all their cash. There'll be nobody in town to stop them."

"Nobody?" asked Davis contemptuously.

"Nobody! It'll be a complete surprise."

CHAPTER FOURTY-SEVEN
The Traitor

As Vachel was ending the planning session, there was a knock at the door.

"Who is it?" demanded Vachel.

"It's Kirby. I have someone here who says he knows you and wants to talk to you...alone. He says he's riding with the wagons carrying the gold."

Vachel motioned to Bull to open the door.

"Lieutenant Barrows! I wasn't sure we'd see you again!" exclaimed Vachel, all smiles. "Do you have any news for me?"

The lieutenant looked nervously around the room. "It's okay, Lieutenant. You can trust these men. Where's the wagon train?"

The lieutenant removed his spotless white gloves one at a time and without bundling them, slowly pushed the pair up and under his utility belt. "The wagons should arrive at the river on Saturday, the day after tomorrow. They plan on rolling the bullion across at first light, but there's a problem."

"What's that?" asked Vachel.

"It's a trap. They suspect you're going to try to take the gold at Alexander's Crossing, and they're prepared to defend it at all costs. If need be, they'll drive the gold into a deep hole downstream of the riffles to keep it out of your hands."

"Why are you telling us this?" asked Davis sarcastically. "We certainly don't need you to tell us the army is going to fight back. And we certainly don't expect them to just hand over the bullion to us...unless we ask them real polite like!"

Bull, Vachel, and Kirby broke out in raucous laughter, which embarrassed the young lieutenant.

"What's in it for you, Lieutenant? I mean, you don't look to be much over 20 years," asked Bull.

"I may be young to you, but I'm old enough to know that I'm not going to get rich riding with what's left of the 7th Cavalry. I just want a small percentage of the take, and then I'll skedaddle and be out of your and the army's sight forever."

"What else do you know about the army's plans?" asked Vachel. "If they're expecting trouble, they might just delay the crossing."

"No, they're under contract to get the gold to Colby and then on to Austin. Colonel Warner told me he's hiding six marksmen in each wagon carrying bullion. These guys are all crack shots and will cut your riders down one by one in quick fashion if you should be, and now these are his words, 'so stupid as to even try taking the gold away from him.'"

"Is that it, Lieutenant?"

"Pretty much. There're no more than 35 officers and men guarding the columns of gold. And all of them, in my estimation, lack discipline and are easy pickings!"

"Good!" said Vachel as he stood to shake hands with the lieutenant. "Thanks!"

Vachel turned to Davis. "Please take the lieutenant here over to the cook's shack and get him a hot meal. But first, cut him out a fresh mount from that bunch we just stole from the army. He has a long ride back to the convoy ahead of him."

The lieutenant turned to walk out the door.

"Oh, Lieutenant, one more thing," said Vachel. "You might want to drop back some when the convoy nears the river so one of my men doesn't shoot you by mistake. We'll meet back here after we take command of the bullion to divvy up the take.

"You know," added Vachel, almost as an afterthought, "I could use a good man like you in my outfit. Maybe after I pay you for your information you'll consider riding with us on a permanent basis? It's a lot more lucrative than the few dollars you get a month riding for the army."

The young lieutenant beamed. "I'd like that, sir!"

After the door closed, Bull turned to Vachel. "What information? He didn't tell us anything. C'mon! Give that young shave tail a job? I don't trust him! Not one bit!"

Vachel just smiled. "He just told us the army doesn't really think we can overtake the convoy and steal the gold. They're overconfident, way overconfident, and that's to our distinct advantage. I told you, it's going to be a fucking blood-bath, Bull!"

In the meantime Davis led the young lieutenant out to the corral. "Pick out a horse, Lieutenant. Any horse you like."

The lieutenant leaned up against the corral and stud-ied the 20 or so horses milling around before pointing to a gelding that seemed to have more spirit then the next. Before he could utter a single word however, everything went black.

He never heard the shot that blew the back of his head off.

CHAPTER FOURTY-EIGHT

Wagons, HO!

Colonel Mark Warner had been handpicked to command the wagon train carrying the gold bullion. Decorated for his exploits during the Civil War, one of his strengths was his knowledge of men. He could read the mind of the unwary like a schoolmaster understands Shakespeare.

And one man the colonel read perfectly was young Lieutenant Barrows.

"Is Barrows back yet?" asked Warner. "Where the hell is Barrows?"

"He hasn't yet returned from his scouting mission, Colonel," replied the colonel's aide, Captain Jackson. "He left at first light two mornings ago and should have been back by now. I've had riders out looking for him, but no sign of him yet. Do you think he deserted, sir?"

"I pray so," replied the colonel with more than a hint of disgust in his voice. "He's a slippery son of a bitch, and I don't trust him...not one bit. He asked way too many questions about Vachel and his gang, even praising their trickery at one point. I have little doubt he's in cahoots with Vachel, or wants to be. In fact, I'm counting on it!"

"How much does he know about this mission, Colonel? And how much does he know about Captain Hickson's forces shadowing the convoy?"

Barrows knows a lot less than he thinks he does, Jackson. He knows nothing of Hickson's forces because I didn't enlighten him to those facts. And he knows nothing of the armament stored in two of the wagons. I told Barrows that I had six sharpshooters assigned to each wagon carrying bullion. What I didn't inform the young lieutenant is that those army-trained sharpshooters all have the last name—Gatling.

"Now, let's get the men to uncrate a half dozen of those six-barreled Gatling guns and set them up in each wagon carrying bullion. I'm sure the lieutenant's lack of solid information will do nothing but give Vachel false confidence, that we are an unprepared contingent of inexperienced cavalry. Lambs ready to be slaughtered. If Vachel takes the bait, and I have little reason to think he won't, then Barrow's misleading piece of hogwash is to our distinct advantage. It's going to be a bloodbath, Captain. A fucking veritable bloodbath!"

"Excuse me, sir. Captain Hickson is waiting to see you."

"Send him in Corporal".

Captain Hickson served with Colonel Warner during the Civil War. The two men thought alike.

"Colonel, my scouts tell me the river crossing is near at hand. We haven't yet had any contact with Vachel or his gang, but we suspect they'll be setting up their ambush soon. We've stayed a few miles out to the north of the convoy. I don't believe we've been spotted."

"I doubt very much you've been spotted. Captain, fetch me the map of the river crossing."

"Yes sir."

The colonel spread the map out over a table and pointed to the river crossing. "As I see it, there are two places Vachel can hide his men from view," stated Warner. "Here on the west side of the river where he can launch a frontal attack, and here on the east side in this dry creek bed where he can come at us from the rear once the fighting starts. What are your thoughts on the matter?"

"I think a frontal assault would be a good diversionary tactic for Vachel, Colonel," said Hickson after some careful thought. "Using a minimal force to tie us up, we would have most of our troops busy defending the wagons that have already crossed while he attacks the rear of the column with his main forces from our blind side.

"However, if we could plant two Gatling gun emplacements and four soldiers armed with Springfields protecting each gun here and here, along the east edge of the river, using those wagons waiting to cross as cover, we would have ample time to set each gun steady and conceal it from view. The element of surprise would be ours then, not his, and a carefully aimed barrage of 200 rounds per minute per gun from those Gatling's should cut Vachel's exposed forces to pieces. Just like at Black Creek, Colonel. Those charging Rebs never had a chance!"

"And your forces, Captain?"

Hickson pointed his finger at Alexander's Crossing on the map and then ran his finger downstream. "With your permission, I'll take my mounted unit to this point during the night and swim across under the cover of darkness. We don't need a solid river bottom like the wagons carrying bullion do, and then we'll be in position to attack Vachel's frontal forces at first light. We'll also be in good position to thwart any of Vachel's riders that happen to get around those Gatling guns."

"One more thing, Hickson. The sheriff is riding out from Colby with a posse of able men to help escort the gold from the river to the bank. They most certainly will want to join you at the river. Please discourage them. This is an army operation, and I don't want any civilians killed or injured unnecessarily."

"Yes, sir!"

"Sir, you have some visitors from Will Alexander's ranch. They say they're willing to guide the wagons through the riffles and across the river."

"Send them in, Corporal."

Colonel Warner and captains Hickson and Jackson shook hands with each of the volunteers—Lefty, Blondy, Kip, Big John, Pete, and Tall Bear.

"Gentlemen, the army appreciates your help in this matter. I assume Judge Bastion informed you of the risks, and your presence here tells me you accept those risks."

The six cowhands each shook their head in the affirmative.

"Raise your right hand. Do you solemnly swear to uphold the Constitution of the United States of America, so help you God, and to obey all orders given to you from this command?"

"Yes. Yes, sir!"

"Good, you are now each army property and rightfully under my command. Let's get down to the facts. I need each of you to guide a wagon heavily laden with gold bullion across the river at this point on the map."

Lefty spoke up. "We know that crossing like the back of our hands, Colonel. We've crossed horses, cattle, and wagons there dozens of times, and none of us has lost a team to the deep pool that lies just downstream of the rifles."

"I need you to understand that the gold must not be taken. If need be, I want you to drive the wagons into the chasm and then shoot the horses. Under no circumstances is Vachel to get his hands on that bullion. Understand?"

"Loud and clear, Colonel."

"Now, gather around this map and we'll share the plan Captain Hickson and I just conceived."

The six men looked at several contingencies and eventually agreed on the plan initially proposed by Colonel Warner and Captain Hickson to protect the gold—and to catch the outlaw Vachel in the act.

Nonetheless, even the best-laid plans can go awry.

CHAPTER FOURTY-NINE

Red Dog's Moment In The Sun

Clayton, Jason, and Red Dog rode up to the ranch house late in the afternoon. Moses met them at the barn and helped them with their horses.

"What's in the bag, Red Dog? You look mighty proud of it!"

"Don't go poking around the bag right yet," cautioned Red Dog with a big smile.

"What's in it then? Is it that dangerous, or do you have a bag of dried cow patties to share with the other hands?"

"Moses, it's the biggest rattler I'll bet you've ever laid eyes on! And the last time I opened the bag he was still twitching a bit and flicking his tongue even though his head has been cut clean off!"

Curiosity got the better of Moses. He untied the bag real careful like and peeked inside. "Yowee! That is one big snake!"

"Go ahead, Moses. Dump the critter on the ground.

I want to measure him neck to tail and get a better idea of what he weighs."

"You mean head to tail, don't you Red Dog?"

"No, Moses. I'm not going to touch that snake's head for a long while, till it's dried out. I bet he's still got enough poison in his fangs to kill a dozen horses!"

"How'd ya get him?"

Clayton was walking toward the coral leading Red Cloud, and turned to Moses. "Moses, you won't believe his story. But it'll be true, every word of it. I'm a witness and so is Jason! Let's feed and water the horses and then we'll tell you all about it!"

When the horses were taken care of, Clayton, Jason, and Red Dog walked back out of the barn to see Will, Moses, and what appeared to be a friend of Will's standing near the snake.

"Red Dog! That's one helluva snake!" said Will as he shook Red Dog's hand. "How'd ya get him? Oh, wait a minute. I forget my manners. Judge Bastion, this is my ranch foreman, Moses Sheridan, my grandson Clayton Alexander, and his two friends Jason Gray Eyes and Red Dog. You met Red Dog's father earlier, Tall Bear."

Each of the ranch hands stepped forward one by one, looked the judge square in the eye, and then firmly shook his hand.

"Good to meet all of you," said Bastion, pointing his boot at the serpent. "That's the biggest rattler I've ever seen, Red Dog. He looks mean and frightful even dead and stretched out like that!"

Before Red Dog could comment, Reinette came out to

ring the dinner bell, saw the snake, and came over to take a closer look. "Oh, Lord," she exclaimed. "Did you boys get him around here?"

"Red Dog got him way out of town, Grandma. Don't fret none," said Clayton, trying to calm her fears.

"Well, what're you going to do with him now?" asked Reinette with her hands on her hips. "He's going to rot soon if something isn't done right away!"

"After we eat I'm going to skin him and salt the hide," replied Red Dog, "and then cut the meat up into small chunks. We'll fry him up in pork fat and have him for supper. I'll tan the hide later and use some of it for backing the limbs on my new bow. The rest I'll fashion into hat bands, with the first one to honor my father.

"But first, I want to put him on the grain scales. I'll wager he'll go 90 pounds, maybe even a hundred, even without his head and all the blood he left on the ground, which was considerable. What do you think he'll go, Moses?"

"Your guess is mighty close," replied Moses scratching the back of his head. "Get the scales!"

It took three men to position the snake, but when they did Goliath tipped the scales at just a horse hair under 92 pounds and measured nine feet two inches neck to tail.

"You going to tell us how ya got him now, or are ya gonna wait until somebody comes in with a bigger one!" laughed Moses. The rest of the onlookers then broke out into a lighthearted laughter all their own.

"I'll tell you all about it while we get something in our bellies," smiled Red Dog. "I could eat that snake raw right now, but Reinette's stove has something tasty waiting for us right now. I can smell fresh biscuits and hot gravy from here!"

Red Dog was suddenly in great spirits, in part of course because of all the attention he was receiving. He proudly told the story in the kitchen, and no one interrupted one word of what he had to say—not even Jason.

CHAPTER FIFTY
One More Favor

Later that afternoon, Will and Judge Bastion met with Moses, Clayton, Jason, and Red Dog in Will's office where they brought each other up to date on Jimmy Vachel and his gang. They shared everything, except the true identity of Judge Bastion's informant. His name was not revealed.

Judge Bastion started the meeting. "It seems pretty clear to me, and by 'me' I mean the state of Texas, that Vachel is the leader of a gang of outlaws responsible for killings, robberies, stagecoach holdups, bank heists, and various other misdeeds in this part of Texas for years, and that Davis and Bull are part of that gang. The Englishman who calls himself Sir Thomas is as big a thief as Vachel, but not yet a proven murderer."

"Who set the fire that killed my son and his wife and several other townsfolk at the Colby Hotel that night remains less a mystery," stated Will. "We think the fire was started purposely in order to kill John Alexander, my son, and his confidant Gray Eyes. John was investigating Vachel's activities and Gray Eyes was passing his findings on to Judge Bastion. Who started it? Well, the order probably came from Vachel, but either Davis or the sheriff actually torched the building. Bull was cleared a long time ago. Another one of Vachel's riders could have also set the fire, but a name hasn't yet surfaced.

"I agree", says Jason, "and when they realized that the left-handed bow allegedly used to start the Colby Hotel fire couldn't have belonged to my father Gray Eyes because he was right-handed shooter, Vachel had an earlier photograph doctored by Brady to make Gray Eyes appear left-handed... and thus guilty of starting the Colby Hotel conflagration."

"What else do we know, or think we know?" asked Moses.

"The man seen leaving the Colby Hotel at the night of the fire slipped on the boardwalk and probably broke his leg. Davis has a limp from a broken leg. Doc Hayes could break and reset the leg, but Davis will have nothing to do with it. We don't know when Davis broke his leg. We do know however that he's been seen with Bull on at least one occasion, and he's been seen at the Vachel compound."

"We also know that Sir Thomas has been seen at Vachel's ranch," added Red Dog, "along with dozens and dozens of new faces. We also know that Vachel's had several wagons upgraded so they can handle much heavier loads. It looks inevitable that he'll try to steal the army's gold at Alexander's Crossing. It's the most logical ambush point along the army's preplanned route to Austin."

"In truth," said Judge Bastion as he stood to stretch his legs, "all we really have is speculation and hearsay. We may be overlooking some important facts, or we could've misinterpreted the facts as we see them. One thing's for certain though, Vachel's a criminal, and the gold bullion passing through Colby on Saturday, the day after tomorrow, is a rich target too tempting for Vachel to pass up. We nab Vachel in the act of robbing the U.S. Army, and we'll eventually learn the truth about several robberies and killings, including the culprit that started the deadly Colby Hotel fire so many years ago!

"That's why I have one more favor to ask of you Will, I mean Judge Alexander. Vachel's smart and slippery, but he's also greedy, and I'd not put it past him to rob the army's gold convoy *and* the Colby Bank on the same day. I'll be riding with Sheriff Sweeney and his posse to help escort the gold from Alexander's Crossing to Colby. That leaves the town virtually defenseless.

"I need you to deputize a small cadre of new Texas Rangers to keep an eye on the bank until the army shows up with the gold bullion for deposit. The plan is for the army to rest and regroup in Colby for a few days before they begin their next push for Austin. I want them to have a bank to put their gold in for safekeeping while they make those final arrangements. Do you have anybody in mind, Will? Any volunteers?"

Will looked around the room, making eye contact with Moses, Red Dog, Clayton, and Jason. Clayton was the first to stand and raise his hand, followed quickly by all the others.

"I never had a doubt!" exclaimed Will as he slid open a desk drawer and withdrew a silver Texas Ranger badge for each of them. After a brief swearing-in ceremony, he pinned the first badge on his grandson, Clayton John Alexander. "Clayton, this is one of the proudest moments of my life, and if your father and uncle were here, they, too, would be beaming in delight. Congratulations."

After the rest were awarded their badges, Will and Bastion pulled Moses to one side. "Moses, I remember the day you arrived at the ranch looking for work. You showed me a silver bullet given to you by the Lone Ranger, a stalwart protector of law and order, as a reference to your character. I wish he were here today to see how far you've come. Moses, there's not a better man in this room to wear that badge. Congratulations."

Judge Bastion then stepped forward to shake Moses' hand. "I believe you're the first black Texas Ranger, Moses, in this district and maybe in all of Texas. And if the Lone Ranger and my longtime friend Judge Alexander are as good at judging character as they say they are, I know you'll not be the last. Congratulations."

Moses lowered his eyes and for a moment was visibly shaken by those words. "Thanks, Will, and thank you too, Judge Bastion. I will always wear this star proudly."

As he turned to walk out of the room, Moses reached in his pocket and rolled the silver bullet back and forth between his fingers...and smiled.

CHAPTER FIFTY-ONE
The Celebration

The air was cool outside, thanks in part to a setting sun and a southwesterly breeze. Clayton, Jason, and the others milled around in the yard talking about the Vachel gang and the gold shipment when Phoebe Ann and Dancing Water rode up.

Clayton and Jason helped them down from their horses and then tied the reins to a hitching post alongside the barn.

"When did you get back into town?" asked Clayton, beaming from ear to ear.

"Yesterday afternoon."

"You both have been gone quite a spell," said Jason feigning a scowl. "How is Mrs. Nelson doing?"

"She's coming along just fine," replied Phoebe Ann. "Elizabeth and Sarah Ellen were a big help feeding her, bathing her, and helping her get in and out of bed and back and forth to the latrine. Brian and Bill helped as much as they could, in between their own chores and keeping the ranch running. They're both men however and not accustomed to seeing to their mother's personal needs.

"Did Elizabeth and Sarah Ellen return to Colby with you?" inquired Clayton matter of factly.

"No," replied Phoebe Ann, "and I don't suspect they will anytime soon, either."

"Why not?"

"Brian has taken a shine to Elizabeth and Bill has been making eyes at Sarah Ellen. They both asked my sisters to stay on a spell, just in case their mother has a setback."

Clayton looked at Jason, then at Phoebe Ann, and broke into a big smile. Phoebe Ann smiled back and they all broke into gleeful laughter.

"I'll be staying at the hotel in town for the time being. I stopped at Sally's yesterday afternoon and Dancing Water told me you were riding Red Cloud and that you have a couple of leads on the Colby Hotel fire. How'd all that come about? And now I find out you're a Texas Ranger!"

"A lot's happened in the time you were gone Phoebe Ann," said Clayton with a big smile. "Let's go for a walk. I'm anxious to tell you more about it."

The pair walked out past the front gate and stood there nearby talking for over an hour, later returning to the barn as darkness grew near. "Judge Bastion is riding back to town tonight. You should ride back with him, for safety's sake. There's no telling what Vachel might be up to, and I'd sleep better knowing that you're with him."

Phoebe Ann and Dancing Water nodded their heads in agreement.

"We'll see you both Saturday morning then at the hotel, or better yet, why don't we all meet at Sally's for breakfast?"

"I'll be there because I'm working in the morning," said Dancing Water, "but what about Red Dog? Will he be there, too? I haven't seen him yet tonight."

Clayton and Jason looked around but did not see their blood brother Red Dog. He seemed to have disappeared, maybe into the barn.

Red Dog was not in the barn but had drifted off alone into the darkness near the corral. It seemed no one missed him, and that made Red Dog feel like he didn't belong, a feeling he sometimes struggled with, even though tonight he was deputized along with Clayton, Jason, and Moses. He knew this was something his father would be very proud of when he returned from helping drive the gold bullion across the river at Alexander's Crossing.

Red Dog turned his back on the festivities and leaned up against the corral, holding his hand out for Red Cloud.

Red Cloud's response caught the attention of Moses, who now saw Red Dog standing alone in the shadows. Moses had been watching Red Dog struggle with his identity for several months now. Maybe this evening was the perfect time to step in and say something to Red Dog, maybe open a few doors for him.

Moses moved out of the light now emanating from the porch lanterns and into the darkness with Red Dog. "You look lonely tonight, Red Dog, more lonely than usual."

Red Dog was caught off-guard by Moses' assessment. He didn't think anybody really noticed his plight.

"You're a red man trying to fit into the white man's world, my young friend. Why do you choose to be alone on a night like this, a night of honor and celebration, a night you'll surely remember for the rest of your days?"

Red Dog looked over at Moses, a man everyone on the ranch respected. Even in town, Bull begrudgingly gave way to Moses. Indeed, there were a couple of times Red Dog wanted to talk to Moses about personal matters, but he never seemed to muster the courage. This evening was different, and he needed to get something off his chest.

"You fit in with the whites, Moses. They like you. They trust you. But me, I always seem to be the outsider, especially with Clayton and Jason."

"What makes you think you're an outsider?" asked Moses.

"Take tonight for example. Neither Clayton nor Jason shook my hand or congratulated me on becoming a Texas Ranger. They shook each other's hands and slapped each other on the shoulder, but they more or less cut me out. When Phoebe Ann and Dancing Water arrived, they just went off by themselves."

Moses put his head down for a second or two, then turned and faced Red Dog head-on. "Clayton and Jason are your friends, Red Dog. They're not running from you; rather, it's you who pushes them away. Tonight for example, did you take the initiative and be the first to congratulate them? Did you walk over and greet Phoebe Ann and Dancing Water?"

"No, I guess not."

"You told us that Clayton and Jason rushed to your aid when you were struggling with that big rattler. They risked their own safety, their own lives, because they feared for your safety, your life. And they did this in spite of the chip you seem to have on your shoulder, your desire to always be 'top dog.'"

Red Dog nodded his head, listening intently.

"If you want a friend, Red Dog, you must first be a friend."

Red Dog lowered his eyes. He knew Moses was right. It was just that he wanted to be accepted, and to be accepted, he thought he had to be like them, a white boy.

Moses sensed Red Dog's dilemma. "You don't have to be like them— just be yourself. Once you learn to like yourself, Red Dog, others will like you, too. After all, you're Red Dog, proud son of Tall Bear, proud grandson of Buffalo Hump, a Lipan Apache who once rode against the Comanche...and proud blood brother of Clayton Alexander and Jason Gray Eyes."

Red Dog slowly raised his head, looked right at Moses, and then lowered his head and smiled. "Those are powerful words, Moses. I see now why you have so many friends. You understand people's feelings."

Moses and Red Dog joshed about being Texas Rangers for the next 10 or 15 minutes, laughing a bit over the big snake, both relieved Goliath was indeed dead, before turning in the for the night.

Tomorrow was sure to be a big day for both of them.

CHAPTER FIFTY-TWO
The Premonition

Reinette was conspicuously absent from the celebrations and barely made eye contact with Clayton when everyone stormed into the kitchen for an after-dinner snack of berry pie and coffee after the swearing-in ceremony. Something was definitely on her mind, and Will picked up on it right away. Later that night when the two lay side by side in bed, Will asked her what was bothering her.

"I know I released you from your promise to keep Clayton out of law enforcement, but tonight when I saw him with that silver star pinned to his vest, I began to shake all over. Will, I had a dream last night, a dream that a new Texas Ranger was going to die soon. And now I find out that my grandson has become what I always feared most...a Texas Ranger like his father.

"Will, I am so dreading Saturday."

CHAPTER FIFTY-THREE
Saturday Morning On The Praire

The sky was as dark as the inside of a coffin when Captain Hickson's detachment reached the river a couple miles south of the riffles. One by one and without hesitation the horses entered the tepid water and swam to the west side without incident. In some cases soldiers immersed themselves in the slow-moving water and held on to the saddle horn as their mount made its way across the river while others stayed in the saddle with their boots in the stirrups and their carbines held high overhead.

"Sergeant Wilson," whispered Hickson. "See that all the troops are present and accounted for and then have each man check his carbine and pistol and reload if necessary. We don't want any misfires when the fighting begins."

"Yes sir!"

"And keep the chatter down. Let's not give up the element of surprise, at least not yet."

"Yes sir!"

The night air was warm, with only a slight breeze to help dry the men off. Nonetheless, each soldier checked his weapons, drained the water from his boots, and then remounted to await further orders.

"Captain, all present and accounted for."

"Thank you, Sergeant. Let's keep to the banks of the river for the next mile and then swing wide to the west. We want to rendezvous a mile west of the riffles by pink light."

"Yes sir!"

"Double file! Ho!"

An hour later the detachment halted below a slight rise. Hickson and the sergeant crawled to the top and glassed the terrain in front of them. The eastern sky had gone from black to pink and was now glowing with purple and red streaks across the horizon. Dawn was only minutes away.

"Look! Over there!" directed the Sergeant. "I can see several men on horseback silhouetted against the sky!"

Hickson swung his binoculars over in that direction. "Yes, I see them too! It looks like Vachel has taken the bait! They don't see us and that's good. They're not expecting us...at least not yet. When they make their move on the wagons, we'll ride to their southern flank and attack."

The convoy had already reached the east shore of the river, and while it was still dark, the soldiers set up two Gatling gun emplacements in the brush, each supported by a four man crew. Corporal Reed manned the first gun and Sergeant Peabody the second. This was Reed's first battle-field experience with a Gatling, and although well trained had trouble inserting a 30-round stick magazine into the slot atop those six rotating barrels. Peabody recognized Reed's nervousness, and without saying a word calmly set the clip for him. Then as soon as it was light enough to see, the first gold-laden wagon entered the water.

"I can't swim," said the young soldier sitting next to Blondy.

"Why don't you ride my horse across? You won't be any help if we have to ditch this wagon in the deep water. Just stick with the horse; he'll get you safely to the far side."

"Thanks, but my orders are to stay with the wagon, and that's exactly what I intend to do."

Blondy nodded in approval and then pointed the way as the young soldier deftly drove the horses away from the deep hole.

The second wagon guided by Tall Bear was halfway across the river when the first shot rang out. It was Vachel's 12-gauge signaling the others to commence the attack. Vachel planned to remain safely hidden in the brush just downstream of the riffles until the battle was over.

At the blast of the shotgun, Tall Bear slapped the reins again and again while hollering "giddy-up, giddy-up!" The horses responded immediately and broke into a gallop, spraying white water high and wide as they raced across the shallows. Tall Bear had all he could do to keep the horses from taking the wagon into the deep hole, but he succeeded in getting the bullion safely to the far side. He pulled his rig up next to Blondy's as the troopers ripped the Osnaburg canvases down exposing a fire-breathing Gatling gun secured in each wagon, loaded and ready to fire.

"Keep your heads down, boys," one of the troopers hollered. "These guns only know how to do two things...shoot... and shoot a lot!"

Tall Bear and Blondy secured the brakes on both wagons and then dropped below the seat with their lever-actions pointing out over the top of the horse's heads... and waited.

"This is it, boys," yelled Kirby. "Let's give 'em hell while we take their gold. Shoot every Blue Coat twice...we ain't leaving any witnesses behind!"

As Kirby's men began their attack, it was Kirby himself who fired the first shots. The flashes from his pistol were clearly seen by Hickson before he heard the shot, and he wasted little time responding.

"Sergeant, have the men form a skirmish line to the right."

"Yes sir!"

When all 50 mounted soldiers were so lined up with their horses chomping at their bits, Captain Hickson gave the order.

"Bugler, sound the charge!"

Kirby was too caught up in the battle to hear the bugler, at least the first few notes. He was suddenly confronted with two Gatling guns spitting out a measured 200 rounds of 300-grain lead slugs per minute at him and his men. *THUMP! THUMP! THUMP! THUMP! THUMP! THUMP!* The bullets were ripping through Kirby's ranks like hot knives through freshly churned butter, tearing limb from limb and flesh from bone. The first four riders each caught lead in their bellies, dropping them to the ground along with two of their mounts that were also shredded apart by the hail of gunfire. The other two mounts veered off to one side as the next six riders caught slugs in the head and chest, killing each one instantly.

The next wave of outlaws suddenly turned north in an effort to avoid the hellfire of the Gatling's, but the Gatling's kept spewing out bullets, one of which tore the left leg of one of Kirby's riders clean at the knee. The rider looked down in horror, but before he could scream, a single rifle bullet from Blondy's Winchester blew his lower jaw off and spun the outlaw from his saddle.

Blondy and Tall Bear then finished him off with several more shots from their Winchesters. Then they turned their sights on the gut-shot robbers trying to crawl to safety. They did not make it.

Kirby was aghast at the damage those twin Gatling guns were creating and was about to turn back himself when he finally heard the bugler's notes. He looked to the south and saw a single line of 50 Blue Coats charging his way with sabers drawn and lead flying. Two more bandits fell in front of him from army carbines, and the rest of his men were frozen in a state of sheer pandemonium.

"This was supposed to be an easy raid," Kirby muttered to himself, but it was anything but that. Kirby stood up in his stirrups to get his men's attention and with a rebel yell, *REMEMBER CHANCELLORVILLE,* charged the two war wagons on the edge of the river. It was their only hope of salvaging the raid, he reckoned.

To his utter astonishment, two more wagons had crossed the riffles during the initial attack and were now positioned to the left and right of the first two wagons already in place. There were now four Gatling guns blazing hot lead toward his men. And shoot they did, with over 2,000 rounds in the next few minutes bringing death and destruction to both man and beast.

The cavalry were now also wreaking havoc on Kirby's men, who were falling from their mounts left and right with multiple bullet wounds to their chests and legs. None of these men were alive when they hit the ground.

What was left of Kirby's men were now in a state of absolute panic, but following Kirby's lead and riding straight at the blazing Gatling guns. Three more men were riddled with hot lead by the time Kirby's men broke through the line of wagons with Hickson's cavalry hot on their heels.

Surprisingly, Kirby's charge caught Kip in midstream with his wagon of gold bullion. An errant bullet sliced through the lead horse's abdomen, and it hunched its back in pain.

Kip knew what he had to do. "Soldier, cut the horses loose as soon as I hit the deep water. We can't leave this wagon in the shallows for Vachel's men to steal."

With a crack of his whip Kip turned the horses upstream toward the chasm. "Heyah! Heyah!" The team broke into a gallop, spraying white water over the top and both sides of the wagon when without warning the lead horses and two front wheels caught the edge of the riffles and slipped into the chasm.

"Cut the horses loose, soldier!" yelled Kip, but his worlds fell on deaf ears. The soldier had taken a bullet to the chest from Kirby, and now Kirby was drawing down on Kip.

"You're as good as dead!" yelled Kirby. "Welcome to hell!" What Kirby failed to take notice of was the Gatling gun in the back of the wagon. The four soldiers had already stripped the Osnaburg canvas free of the rigging and had swung the great gun at Kirby and his fast-approaching hoard of men.

THUMP! THUMP! THUMP! THUMP! THUMP! THUMP! The six barrels were rotating as fast as a young corporal could turn the crank, and bullets were leaving those barrels at over 400 rounds per minute. The first 20 rounds flew harmlessly over Kirby's head, but the next 20 cut the outlaw riding up behind him in the upper torso, removing his right arm in surgical fashion and then puncturing a hole the size of a man's fist through his lungs.

Kirby looked over in horror as his friend's blood squirted out the stump of his right shoulder as well as his nose and mouth and then looked over at Kip, whose Colt was pointing in his direction.

"Welcome to hell yourself!" Kip screamed as he centered his aim. Time seemed to stand still for the next few seconds as Kip slowly squeezed the trigger. He knew he would only have one shot, and he had to make it good before Kirby cut him down. He kept his aim steady, the hammer fell, and the .44-40 slug caught Kirby square in the teeth, flipping him off his mount and into the water in a faceless, bloody heap.

Kip and the troopers jumped from the wagon as it began to sink into the abyss. They couldn't save the horses however. Struggling to free themselves from their harnesses, the two geldings nearest the wagon were the first to go under. With eyes bulging and nostrils flared, they tore at the water in a futile attempt to reach firm footing, but the gold bullion in the bed of the wagon was dragging everything steadily toward the bottom of the river.

The two lead horses seemed to sense their fate, but that didn't stop them from struggling for their lives. For a second one of the horses caught the edge of the riffles with a forefoot, giving both animals hope, but the gravel soon crumbled underfoot, and with the wagon now on a steady downward spiral into the abyss, both horses disappeared below the surface frantically churning the water with their flailing front legs.

The wagon sunk upright to the very bottom, but the dead horses floated up toward the surface held in place by the very harness that sealed their doom. There they stayed bobbing back and forth grotesquely in the current only 15 feet below the surface.

Kip and the troopers swam easily the short distance to the riffles, but stayed low in the bloodied shallow water as the last of Kirby's men fell to the barrage of gunfire.

Bridges' men on the east side of the riffles were faring no better. When Vachel's 12-gauge lit up the early morning sky, Bridges readied his men and then anxiously waited for Kirby's attack to get underway. He hoped it would draw soldiers from the rear of the wagon train to the west side of the river, leaving the tail end of the convoy vulnerable. It didn't quite work out that way.

Bridges soon heard some small-arms rounds penetrate the still morning air, followed quickly by the rapid fire of the Gatling guns, and knew from experience that the army was not caught by surprise.

Nonetheless, it was now or never, and he urged his men out of the dry creek bed, and with a mighty war hoop of his own led the attack. As he neared the wagons, he could see the rotating flashes of a Gatling gun sending lead in his direction. He instinctively hunkered down over the saddle, but it was a useless maneuver for a string of .45/70 shells ripped into the horse's head and Bridges' head and neck, killing horse and rider simultaneously.

Both ground placement Gatling guns were firing as fast as Reed and Sergeant Peabody could turn the cranks now, spilling blood and bone on the open prairie the likes of which even the most callous of cavalry men couldn't easily stomach. Heads and appendages were tossed skywards, appearing like so many glass balls exploding in midair at an exhibition shooting match. Indeed, it seemed no soldier could miss his mark that morning as one outlaw after another felt the sting of hot lead and fell dead to the ground.

Corporal Reed was frantically trying to load another 30 round clip into the Gatling when two of Bridge's men broke through the hail of gunfire, and rode straight at Reed's gun emplacement. Reed locked eyes on the first rider as he fast approached the Gatling, shooting two measured pistol rounds at Reed. Both missed. The outlaw then took a third passing shot at Reed, grazing his shoulder, just as he and his mount leaped over the gun emplacement.

Although stung by the bullet, Reed again tried to insert the clip, but fear overcame him when he saw the second of Bridge's men bearing down on him. Caught out in the open, Reed wanted to run but simply could not, and fell back against the gun carriage to await his fate. The outlaw sensed Reed's vulnerability, took careful aim and shot the Corporal twice in the chest. Blood spurted out of Reed's mouth as he gasped for air, then turned his face away from the escaping outlaw and dropped dead to the ground.

Of the nearly 50 outlaws that sprung out of the dry creek bed that morning, less than a dozen made it as far as the river. The rest were chopped up and sent to hell compliments of Colonel Warner and the U.S. Cavalry.

Those that made it past the Gatling guns and the line of troopers positioned along the edge of the river couldn't stop their forward progress. They knew they'd entered the jaws of eternity and kept riding across the river in a desperate attempt to escape with their lives. There they were met head-on by Hickson's men galloping in hot pursuit of Kirby's dwindling ranks.

Suddenly faced with complete annihilation, the remaining outlaws threw down their weapons and raised their hands over their heads to surrender, including the bandit that killed Corporal Reed.

As the soldiers took control of the melee and bound the outlaws, Blondy yelled out to the troopers. "Vachel! There's Vachel! He's getting away!"

Tall Bear sprang from under the seat of the wagon and leveled his sights on Vachel's gelding. It was a perfect shot, taking Vachel's horse out from under him and knocking Vachel unceremoniously to the ground. When Vachel stood up to run, two mounted troopers scooped him up in midflight, each soldier grabbing an arm, and brought him back to Colonel Warner kicking and screaming.

"You should have killed me, Indian!" Vachel muttered in disgust.

"It's not for me to decide your fate," replied Tall Bear, his Winchester cradled comfortably in his arms, "but for that of a judge and jury. Rest assured, you will most certainly hang if for nothing more than your exploits today."

When the wounded were attended to and the dead bandits piled up, the total body count was staggering. Two troopers sadly lost their lives and 16 were wounded, two gravely, but they would all recover in the weeks ahead. Six army mounts and 35 outlaw horses were left prostrate on the prairie and a dozen or so of those had to be euthanized.

Only 11 outlaws including Vachel survived that morning out of nearly 75 that came to Alexander's Crossing to steal the army's gold. Two weeks later they all were hung in Colby, one at a time, and their bodies dumped somewhere on the open prairie where the coyotes could have their fill.

Colonel Warner was one of the soldiers gravely wounded that day. He stood fast by the Gatling guns all during the attack, shooting several bandits, including two square in the head, as they raced past the guns. The last shot fired that morning came from a dying outlaw who targeted the colonel from close range. He knew the battle was lost, but with his last breath he nonetheless still squeezed off a round. Indeed, there is never any honor among thieves and murderers.

When the shooting stopped, Judge Bastion and Sheriff Sweeney's posse crossed the river to see if the army could use any help mopping up the last of the bandits. Ordered to stay out of the battle by the colonel, they still got their licks in by dropping a couple of bandits that were running scared from those deadly Gatling guns. Their escape plan might have worked except that they rode smack-dab into the sheriff and his posse and were immediately shot dead off their mounts.

CHAPTER FIFTY-FOUR
News From Colbey

"Colonel, the sheriff and his posse are here to see you."

The colonel extended his hand and motioned to the corporal to bring them in.

"We set the trap and Vachel took the bait!" strained Colonel Warner from his hospital bed. "Thankfully there were only a few army casualties, but it was indeed a blood-bath for Vachel. We killed nearly all Vachel's men and captured Vachel himself as he tried to make a getaway. And just as importantly, we saved the gold...although Lieutenant Simpson will have to figure out a way to extricate those gold bars from the bottom of the abyss. How did the battle look from your position?"

"We watched from a distance the brutal effect those Gatling's had on Vachel's men," replied Judge Bastion. "They had no idea of the sustained firepower those guns generate! Indeed, the battle seemed to be over 20 minutes or so after the first shot. I think Vachel's men, at least those that survived, learned this morning that it takes more than riders and guns to steal gold from the United States Calvary!"

The colonel smiled.

Sheriff Sweeny stepped forward. "Congratulations, Colonel. Vachel's gang is finished. I doubt there're enough men at the ranch to keep the criminal enterprise going. There's certainly no leadership. We've seen the last of that bunch, thanks to you and your men."

Corporal Batchelder poked his head back into the tent. "Colonel, there's a young lady here to see you. She claims to know Judge Bastion and the men you hired to help take the wagons safely across the river."

Judge Bastion looked at the Sheriff and shrugged his shoulders. "I have no idea who that would be Colonel!"

Colonel Warner extended his hand and motioned the corporal to bring her in.

"Hello Judge Bastion."

"Phoebe Ann! What in heaven brings you all the way out here from Colby?"

"Judge, 20 riders or so rode into town in twos and threes this morning, led by Davis the gunsmith and Bull, Vachel's strongman. They don't seem to be interested in doing much except keeping their eyes on Main Street. Judge Alexander thinks they are planning to rob the bank, probably when it closes at three o'clock, and there are only a few men left in town to stop them."

"Who's there now?" asked the sheriff.

"Just Judge Alexander and the four Texas Rangers he just swore in: Clayton Alexander, Red Dog, Jason Gray Eyes and Moses Sheridan."

"I'll gather up the men, including the six that guided the gold wagons for you, and head right back to town," exclaimed the sheriff.

"This is still an army campaign, Sheriff. I can use you here to help guard the prisoners. Corporal, get me Captain Hickson right away!"

"Yes sir"

"We'll bivouac here while we retrieve the bullion," declared the colonel, "then clean up the battlefield and bury the dead. Where the hell is Hickson?"

"Right here, sir!"

"It seems the battle isn't quite over, Captain. Gather a strong detachment with fresh mounts and let this young lady lead you directly to Colby. It seems some of Vachel's men might be planning on robbing the bank when it closes this afternoon. You'll have to ride hard and fast to be there by three o'clock."

"Yes sir!"

"I don't like the looks of this one bit. Damn! Corporal, better round up those six guides after all. Tell them they're still on the payroll and I want them to follow the detachment to Colby. They'll be under Captain Hickson's command."

"Yes sir."

"Corporal, one more thing. Get Miss Moses a fresh mount. She'll guide the detachment to Colby."

"Miss Moses?" called the captain. "I've seen you some-where before. I remember. Yes, I'm sure now. It was at a shooting exhibition we had at the fort a few months back, but you didn't go by that moniker!"

"Sir, my given name is Phoebe Ann Moses, but my stage name is Annie, sir. Annie Oakley. Now, let's ride. There's not a moment to lose!"

CHAPTER FIFTY-FIVE

The Calm Before The Storm

Clayton, Jason, and Red Dog walked across the yard to the barn, fired up a couple of lanterns, and entered the secret room. Clayton and Jason rummaged through their father's clothing while Red Dog attended to the horses.

Clayton chose an old sombrero embroidered with eagles, a pair of well-worn leather chaps, and old scuffed-up cowboy boots fitted with wheeled Mexican spurs. Jason picked only one item...a turquoise shirt.

Clayton then pulled his father's Henry lever-action down from the wall, grabbed a full box of .44 rimfire shells off a nearby shelf, and inserted shell and after shell into the round tube magazine till it fit no more. For good reason, he did not lever a live round into the chamber. He stuffed the rest of the .44's into his front pockets.

Next, a small .31 caliber Pocket Colt was slipped between his shirt and britches and into the small of his back. It fit right snugly, giving Clayton an extra measure of security.

Last, he strapped on a brace of .36 caliber cap 'n' ball 1851 Navy Colts that his father once wore. He "half-cocked" the first pistol to rotate the cylinder and dried all six chambers with a soft cloth. Then he fired off six fulminate percussion caps to clean each chamber of any moisture and oils that may have accumulated over time to lessen the odds of a misfire.

Pointing the muzzle straight up, Clayton now loaded each chamber with an equal measure of black powder, being careful to leave enough room to seat a ball, followed by a greased felt wad over the powder column.

Next, he placed an 86-grain round ball in the mouth of each chamber, leaving the sprue mark facing forward. Then he rotated each chamber under the rammer and used the loading lever to seat the bullet firmly atop the powder column.

He repeated this process, loading six cylinders in all with 36 rounds.

When he finished, he dropped two of the loaded cylinders back into the Navy Colts, slipped a percussion cap over each nipple, and eased the hammers down between chambers. A groove in the hammer engaged a peg in the rear of the cylinder, preventing the hammer from accidently striking a percussion cap and firing the gun off prematurely.

Then he smeared pork lard across the face of each cylinder to prevent a spark from jumping over to one or more of the adjacent cylinders and setting the whole load off in his hand.

Clayton slid the four extra greased cylinders into his coat pockets...two in the left pocket and two in the right.

"I'm ready," he said as he looked over at Jason.

"Yeah, me too. Or just about!" replied Jason as he loaded a Winchester 73 to the gills from a partial box of .44-40 ammunition sitting on a lower shelf and then stuffed the remainder of that box of shells into his two front pants pockets. Thirty-four rounds were more than enough he figured.

Red Dog whistled once, indicating that their horses were saddled up, grabbed his bow and quiver full of hunting arrows, and slung them over his right shoulder. Jason and Clayton looked at Red Dog and then each other rather quizzically. "Guns make too much noise," Red Dog uttered.

Even so, he still slipped a loaded Winchester 73 into his scabbard and a handful of shells into his pockets.

They led their horses outside through the corral where they met Will and Moses, who were already mounted and ready to ride. As they rode past the front gate, the eastern sky was glowing with purple and red streaks across the horizon. Dawn was only minutes away.

As they rode toward town, Will spoke to the Rangers unaffectedly. "We'll eat a hearty breakfast at Sally's and then take up positions on both sides of the street near the bank. I'll wait it out in the sheriff's office.

"If Vachel takes the bait, most of his men will be at the river crossing right about now. The gold is their main target. If a few of Vachel's men do show up in Colby, I suspect they won't try anything until three o'clock, if they try anything at all."

Nonetheless, they tied their horses up at different hitching posts near the bank and then headed towards Sally's for a quick breakfast. Phoebe Ann met them on the boardwalk however, and by the look on her face Will knew something was wrong.

"Six strangers just rode into town," said Phoebe Ann a little apprehensively. "I don't recognize any of them, but by their chatter they all know Bull...and Davis, too!"

"Where are they now?" asked Will.

"Over at Millie's"

"It may not mean anything," replied Will, "or it could be the calm before the storm. Let's take our positions around the bank like we planned, and see what happens. Just be careful out there until we know for sure what's going on."

Soon three more riders rode past the bank. Each man looked intently at the front doors and then rode on to Millie's. Over the next four hours, six more rough-looking riders went past the bank on their way to Millie's. And each rider couldn't seem to take his eyes off the front of the bank as he rode by.

Will was clearly concerned now. He summoned Phoebe Ann to the sheriff's office.

"Phoebe Ann, there's trouble brewing for sure. I need you to ride out to Alexander's Crossing and find the army. Ask for Judge Bastion and tell him there are too many strange men in town for it to be a coincidence. He'll know what to do. You must ride hard and fast. There's no time to waste!"

Phoebe Ann went out the back door and in minutes was riding out of town at a gallop. Will went up the street, found his deputies, and told them to sit tight while Phoebe Ann rode for reinforcements. Then he returned to the sheriff's office where he could keep a better eye on the main streets.

For the next several hours Will could hear the boisterous behavior emanating over at Millie's with bottles breaking, men fighting, and occasionally a few pistol shots ringing out. The din seemed to be getting louder and louder as time went by.

At one o'clock, Will grabbed two 12-gauge side-by-side doubles off the rack, a couple boxes of buckshot, and hurried over to the bank.

"Will! What's going on? Are we going to be robbed?"

Mr. Estes had been president of the Colby Bank for over seven years. He fought at Gettysburg and could handle a gun with the best of them. More importantly perhaps, he was a soldier at heart and no stranger to violence.

"It looks like a couple dozen or more men might be planning on doing just that, Bill. They are part of Vachel's outlaw gang, and they know that the sheriff and his posse left early this morning to rendezvous with the army and its wagon train full of gold bullion. Their expressed purpose is to help escort that gold to Colby. They won't be here until three o'clock though."

"Then let me have one of those shotguns and a box of buckshot, Will. I'm going to send the tellers home early and close the bank. I'm also going to reset the timer on the vault. That'll make it tougher for them to get any money should they break in."

"Good. I've got four men stationed outside on both sides of the street. If Vachel's men come looking for trouble, then trouble they will get!"

Bob Timmings, the bank's assistant manager, came out of his office with a handful of papers locked in his fist. "I'll stay with you, Bill. I have a stake in this town, too. How about giving me that other shotgun and a box of shells, Judge? I'm not as good with a gun as Bill here is, but I can hit what I aim at and I'm not afraid to pull both triggers at the same time!"

"Okay, Bob. Pull the shades and then barricade the front and back doors. Don't let anyone in after I leave. I'll knock and speak out if I need to come back in."

An hour later two men left Millie's, mounted up, and rode slowly uptown toward the bank. Clayton recognized it for what it was—a scouting mission. They wanted to know how well the bank was protected.

Clayton levered a round into the chamber and then dropped another rimfire cartridge into the top-loading tube magazine. He was fully loaded now, but realized he had to be careful. The gun was cocked and there was no safety, unlike later Winchesters where a half-cock mechanism prohibited the hammer from falling on a live round. He eased the hammer back, and it rested on a live round. A sudden bump and the rifle could fire.

As the riders approached the bank, Clayton threw back his sombrero and stepped out into the middle of the street. At first the two riders disregarded Clayton as being nothing more than a half-drunk Mexican, until they caught a glimpse of his silver star.

"Stop right there and turn around," ordered Clayton. "The street's closed until further notice."

"Says who?" challenged the younger man with a bit of sarcasm.

Clayton cocked and raised his rifle in one fluid motion and pointed it right at his head. "Says my old friend Henry."

"Well sonny boy," laughed the older man, "you can't get us both before one of us drops you dead in the street, now can you?"

"I wouldn't be so sure about that, mister" said Clayton

calmly as he redirected his aim. "I may or may not be fast enough to shoot you both, but one thing's for certain old man. You won't live long enough to find out because I'm going to shoot you first and right between the eyes!"

Clayton's response certainly rattled the old man.

"Now, why don't the both of you turn around and go back to Millie's, right now...or I'll be sorely tempted to try to kill the both of you where you stand."

The old man held steady, not knowing what to do.

"Your move!" said Clayton forcefully.

The younger man raised his reins as if he were going to leave the scene and rode his horse a fair distance across the street, but then suddenly turned around and faced Clayton head-on.

"No kid, it's your move!"

"No, don't shoot," said the elder man raising his hands over his head. But his surrender was meant to be a distraction, for at that precise moment the younger man went for his gun.

THIFFFFT! From out of the blue an arrow sped down from a distant rooftop and sliced through the younger man's heart, leaving the broadhead sticking out of his lower torso an inch or two just above his right hip. The younger man looked down at the blood spurting from his chest and glanced over at the old man before tipping off his saddle stone dead. When his body hit the street with a THUD, his horse reared up and galloped back to Millie's.

Red Dog peered down from the rooftop. "I got you covered, Clayton." Then before Clayton could respond, Red Dog eased back out of sight.

Clayton ordered the older man off his horse at gunpoint and then had him drag his companion off the street. After tying the outlaw's horse to a hitching post, Clayton marched the aging outlaw over to the sheriff's office.

"I didn't hear any shooting!" said Will as he locked the outlaw in a cell.

"Red Dog took him from the rooftop with a perfect bow shot. I got the body off the street and out of sight real quick."

"We're spread pretty thin," said Will sounding more than a bit worried. "Moses and I will cover the front of the bank. Bill Estes and Bob Timmings are barricaded inside with shotguns. You, Jason, and Red Dog pull back closer to the bank."

"Okay."

"What time is it?"

Clayton reached in his pocket and pulled out a watch. "It's just a few minutes before two o'clock. Why?"

"Because if Phoebe Ann got through, help should be arriving soon. By the way, where did you get that watch?"

"I found it in the secret room behind the stall in the barn. Why?"

"I forgot all about that timepiece. Reinette and I gave that to John, your father, as a gift on the day he was sworn in as a Texas Ranger. I guess it's yours now."

CHAPTER FIFTY-SIX
Bull and Davis Team Up

"Hey, that's young Pete's horse. What's it doing in front of Millie's all covered with blood?"

Bull and Davis caught the passing remark and stepped out of Millie's to examine the horse. The horse was fine, but there was plenty of red frothy blood on the left side of the saddle, saddle blanket, and saddle bag, plus more fresh blood on the horse's left hindquarter.

"Did anyone hear any shooting?" asked Davis.

Nobody had.

Then a Mexican vaquero spoke up. "He's dead senor. I saw him fall off his horse with an arrow sticking out of his hip."

"Where were you when this happened?" asked Davis.

"I just walked out of the hardware store and saw a man with a silver star and a rifle standing in the middle of the street. He told the two men the bank was closed for the day and they had to go back. Words were exchanged, and then I saw your young friend with an arrow in him fall dead to the ground."

"They're on to us," reasoned Davis. "Even so, they cannot have more than a handful of men guarding the bank.

Every other able-bodied man rode out early this morning to help guard the gold. If I'm right, then this'll be the easiest bank job we've pulled yet.

"What time is it?"

"It's two-thirty," said Bull. "Why?"

Davis turned around and looked directly at Bull. "'Cause I think it's time to hit the bank. Right now!" he said with a grin.

"Everyone else listen up. The first man that makes it inside the bank gets a double portion, and another double share for every Texas Ranger you kill getting there!

"Now, here's the plan," explained Davis now with a quiet, determined voice. "We can't just ride over to the bank; they'll cut us up good and proper. Instead, we'll outshoot them from the ground. They won't expect a full-frontal assault, so that's what we'll give them.

"Ryan, Tommy Rudzinski, Pat O'Leary, and what's your name...you standing at the window with the fancy Colt on your hip."

"Me?"

"Yeah, you. What's your name?"

"Shawn. Shawn Williams."

"Okay Shawn Williams, follow Ryan and the others down the west side of the street. Get as close as you dare, find some cover...and wait. Shoot the first Ranger that sticks his neck out.

"Zack, you and your brother Ezra take Ed Rawlings and his brother Paul down the east side of the street. Take your time, make it look natural like. We don't want to alarm any townsfolk until it's too late for any one of them to do anything about it.

"Some of the rest of you boys pick a side of the street, and don't be shy. There'll be plenty of shooting for everyone.

"In the meantime, Bull and I and a few others are going to sneak around to the back side of the bank. The Rangers will be so busy out front that we might just be able to sneak in the back. Any questions?"

Nobody spoke up.

"Oh, one more thing," cautioned Davis. "Don't leave any witnesses in the upright position. Ammo is cheap; shoot everyone twice."

Shawn followed Ryan, Rudzinski, and Pat down the left side of the street until they got to the office of the Cattleman's Association. They looked over to the east side of the street and watched as Zack, his brother, and the others worked their way into position. Suddenly, two quick shots rang out—*Bang! Bang!* Davis surprised a young drifter heading toward Millie's, and when he refused to answer Davis' call, Davis shot him dead, once in the chest and once in the head.

When Rudzinski looked back up the street, he saw Jason drawing a bead on him with his Winchester. Rudzinski wasted little time and fired first with his Colt. The slug passed very close to Jason, lodging in a wooden corner post an inch over the top of his head.

"Clayton, there's at least four bandits on the west side coming up the street at us," yelled Jason as he dropped down for cover.

"I see them," yelled Clayton. "Can you get a shot at them?"

Jason didn't respond with words. Instead, he raised himself up a bit and looked down the barrel of his '73. When Rudzinski tried to get a better look-see at Jason, Jason let loose with a quick barrage of four rounds, one of which struck Rudzinski in the neck, spinning him around and into the street. Jason took careful aim and finished him off with single shot into his chest.

Jason kept his aim toward the Cattleman's Association office and waited. Ryan got nervous and tried to break down the office door with his shoulder, but the locked door wouldn't budge. Scared, he started to back up, looking for more cover, when Jason's Winchester barked again, sending a fusillade of four more 200-grain .44-40 bullets at him in quick succession, the metallic casings tinkling like rain drops on the boardwalk. Each lead bullet found its mark, with three perforating Ryan's intestines and one cutting through his windpipe. He collapsed on the boardwalk drowning in his own blood.

"Reload Jason!" yelled Clayton. "The other two aren't going anywhere. I've got a bead on them!"

Ed Rawlings and his older brother were having second thoughts about the bank, and when they thought Jason was reloading, they turned in the direction of Millie's to slowly ease themselves out of the action.

Red Dog drew his bow, and when Rawlings stepped off the boardwalk, he sent a hunting arrow zipping in and out of Rawlings' abdomen. Rawlings felt the sting, looked down, and saw blood gushing out from under his shirt. He turned to run, somewhere, anywhere, but there was no place for him to go. He collapsed to the ground not realizing he was bleeding to death.

When his brother stooped over to help Ed, Red Dog sent a second feathered shaft down from his perch on the opposite side of the street striking the elder Rawlings in the rib cage. The razor-sharp tip sliced through two ribs, cutting the aorta just above the heart. The elder Rawlings keeled over graveyard dead before his younger brother bled out.

Will, Moses, Jason, and Clayton were now trading shots with bandits on both sides of the street. All the windows of the Cattleman's Association were smashed from gunfire as were most of the storefront glass panes on the east side of the street. The boardwalks on both sides of Main were littered with the dead and dying.

Will turned to Moses. "I don't know how long we can hold them off. There's a lot more firepower from Vachel's gang than I figured on! Have you seen Davis or Bull?"

"No!"

But Davis had seen them. And Davis also saw Red Dog moving along the rooftops on the opposite side of the street picking off Vachel's men one after another like they were chickens on the roost.

He turned to Rudy. "Get to the other side of the street and find that Indian. He's on the roof somewhere. Find him and kill him!"

At six foot four inches and 275 pounds, Rudy was not as agile or fleet of foot as Red Dog. But he managed to cross the street without getting shot.

And soon he would also manage to sneak up behind Red Dog without getting shot.

Suddenly there was an explosion at the rear of the bank that blew a hole big enough to let a grown man through.

"Jenkins, get in there and see if anyone is left alive," ordered Davis, but when Jenkins stepped through the opening, Estes met him with a full charge of oo buck.

Davis jumped through the hole and in turn shot Estes in the chest and then yelled at another one of his men to charge through and open the front door. Bob Timmings heard Davis give those instructions and dropped to the floor on his knees. With shaking hands, he cocked both hammers of his 12-gauge, raised the gun to his shoulder, and when the outlaw showed himself, Timmings squeezed the two triggers simultaneously. Fire belched out of both barrels, and 16 pellets of oo buck hit the would-be bandit in the face and neck, severing his head completely from his torso.

"I heard you Davis," yelled Timmings. "If you want the money that bad why don't you first come on in and pick your friend's head off the floor!"

Davis thought better of that idea and ducked around the side of the bank where he caught Will and Moses trying to get in the front door.

"Bill, Bob, you guys all right?" yelled Will through a broken pane of glass.

"Estes is dead, and I killed one of the bandits, yelled Timmings. "I'm all right though."

Davis aimed his Colt at Will's back and started to squeeze the trigger when he caught sight of Clayton and Jason diving into the hardware store for cover. Davis didn't hesitate but lowered his pistol, circled around, and entered the hardware store through a side door.

"Drop your guns, both of you!" screamed Davis.

Clayton and Jason turned around.

"I said drop 'em. Now!"

Clayton looked over at Jason, and they both let their guns fall to the floor.

"I don't know why Bull didn't kill you two a long time ago," shouted Davis, "like I ordered him to."

Clayton thought of his pocket pistol nestled in the small of his back and then thought the better of it, at least for now.

"So you two are in this together!" blurted out Clayton.

"Yeah, but you'll never live long enough to tell anyone," replied Davis more calmly now and with a wide grin. He raised his pistol and was about to draw a deadly bead on the two Texas Rangers when Bull burst through the same side door.

"Where in the hell have you been?" barked Davis. "We got at least a dozen men killed in the street!"

"I got pinned down by these two," shouted Bull in response. "But the tables are turned now, aren't they Clayton! This is the time I've been waiting for...the time to beat the two of you until you're so broken and bloody nobody will recognize you. Not even your grandmother, Clayton."

Davis smiled. "After you break them up bad," said Davis sadistically, "I want to dose them in coal oil, set them afire, and watch them wriggle in the flames. I want to hear Clayton scream like his mama did when I set the Colby Hotel on fire. I want to see Jason's eyes bulge like his daddy's did when I talked the good folks of Colby into hanging him for starting that fire."

"So that's why you and Vachel had to doctor those

photographs you gave the sheriff," said Jason. "You knew my father was not left-handed, but you couldn't afford to have any suspicious eyes fall on you!"

"That's right! Pretty clever, huh?"

"There's still one thing I don't understand, Davis. Why'd you ever throw in with Vachel? You were a respected businessman. Huh? Was it just greed?"

"Why? Hell, kid, I'd do anything for my big brother. Yeah, that's right. Jim and I are blood brothers. Real blood brothers. Same mother, different father, and I have no idea who mine was!"

"Davis, we're wasting time talking!" screamed Bull. "These two aren't worth it. Get over there and blow that vault before more Rangers show up. Let me torture these two a little before I shoot them. You owe me the privilege... and they owe me the satisfaction."

Money can be a powerful motivator, and once Davis thought about it for a second, he holstered his pistol and slid back out the side door. He didn't get 10 feet when two mea-sured shots rang out. *Bang! Bang!* He stopped for a second, smiled, and then continued running toward the bank.

"There goes Davis!" yelled Moses, who took a wild shot at the fast-disappearing outlaw. "What the hell was he doing over there? That's where Clayton and Jason were taking cover, and that's where those two shots just came from!"

"Wait here, Moses," said Will. "I'll find out."

Will entered the side door carefully, with pistol drawn, and silently walked up behind Bull.

"Bull!" he yelled.

Bull spun around on his heels with his pistol in hand,

still smoking, and faced Will head-on.

"Shoot him!" yelled Clayton and Jason. "Shoot him!"

Will looked first at his grandson and then at Jason—and holstered his pistol.

"How long have you been a Texas Ranger, Bull?"

CHAPTER FIFTY-SEVEN

Reinett's Prophecy Comes True

"Ho!"Captain Hickson reigned in his mount and raised his gloved hand over his head as the detachment came to a halt on a slight rise above Colby.

"I hear gunfire," said Oakley as she pulled up alongside Hickson. "We're too late!"

"I pray not! Sergeant Wilson!"

"Yes sir!"

"Two columns, single file!"

"Yes sir!"

"Bugler, sound the charge!"

Down from the foothills came Hickson and the U.S. Cavalry at full gallop. Entering Colby from the south, they rode up Main Street, dispersing Vachel's remaining men with shouts and gunfire. Shawn Williams dropped to the ground and took aim at the lead horse soldier. It was a foolish maneuver. *THIFFFFT!* Another one of Red Dog's deadly missiles took Williams through the neck. He grabbed his throat in an effort to breathe and stem the flow of blood, but a horse soldier's follow-up bullet to the chest ended his efforts. Williams died right there in the street, clutching his throat and gasping for air as the cavalry rode past.

Davis reacted to the blare of the bugle as if his world was about to come to an end. He ran up the street and dove headfirst under one of the buildings to escape detection. He crawled over to a wood floor support and lay motionless. All he could see were horse's legs and the boots of the troopers as they rounded up the rest of Vachel's men. For the first time since he was a small boy, Davis could taste fear.

The soldiers rode right up to the bank's front doors. From his vantage point, Davis could hear the soldiers talking to Alexander. He knew now the attempt on the Colby Bank had failed. He knew he had no choice but to bide his time and make a break for it—or he would sure as hell hang for his misdeeds.

"I assume you're Judge Alexander," stated Captain Hickson as he extended his open hand. "Judge Bastion said I would find you here!"

"That's right, Captain. And this is Clayton Alexander, my grandson, Moses Sheridan, my ranch foreman, and Jason Gray Eyes, our newest Ranger."

"Where's my son?" asked Tall Bear, his bright red turban headdress fluttering in the breeze as he stepped out of the crowd. "Has he been hurt?"

"No, he hasn't been injured. Red Dog's been manning the rooftops with his bow and arrows. I don't think we'd be standing here right now if Red Dog hadn't picked off so many of Vachel's men."

Red Dog heard his name called and walked to the

edge of the roof to look down at the crowd gathered way below. The fight was over, and he was happy. He caught his father's eye and the eyes of his blood brothers and with a wide smile, raised his hand to greet them when Rudy got up behind Red Dog, grabbed him around the neck, and pushed an eight-inch knife deep between his ribs.

"Aihee!"

Red Dog winced in pain and turned his head to face his attacker. Rudy just smiled and with much disdain, pushed Red Dog off the roof.

His fall appeared to be in slow motion. Tall Bear and his blood brothers watched in horror as Red Dog tumbled head over heels off the roof, twisting and rolling in midair in some grotesque attempt to right himself before he struck the street below with a resounding *thump*!

Everyone heard his legs break.

Everyone heard his kneecaps snap.

Everyone heard his pelvis crack.

Everyone heard bone fragments as sharp as a barber's razor slice through tendons, sinew...

And everyone heard Red Dog cry aloud in sheer agony.

For a moment the crowd was stunned as if frozen in time. Tall Bear reached his son first and put his hand under Red Dog's head. "Red Dog, are you..."

"Please father, don't move me. It's no use. It's my end of days. But it's good that I rest here with you for a moment or two, before I die. To see you one more time father, to thank you for your love and your wisdom."

Tall Bear nodded. "I'm proud of you, my son. You've

fought bravely in battle, protecting many others so that they may live. You gave your life freely, Red Dog, and there's no greater gift a warrior can bestow upon his friends."

Red Dog looked deep into his father's eyes and smiled at his words.

"Rest easy now my son for soon your spirit guide will take you to the council fire where you will meet the Great Spirit, the maker of all things. Tell him your name is Red Dog, proud son of Tall Bear and grandson to Buffalo Hump, a Lipan Apache who once rode against the Comanche. Ask him humbly for his wisdom."

Red Dog looked again into his father's eyes. They were weeping. He looked for Clayton and Jason, and found their eyes to be filled with tears.

"I am Red Dog, proud blood brother to Clayton John Alexander and Jason Gray Eyes. I must go now my brothers, but know forever in your hearts I am grateful. You have helped give my life meaning, and know forever in your hearts I go in peace."

Red Dog's eyes did not blink again.

Red Dog felt his father's hand caress his face.

Red Dog listened as Clayton and Jason and Moses and Phoebe Ann and others he barely knew pleaded with their God to let him live.

Red Dog watched as his friends began to weep at his passing.

He saw all this and more as he drifted above the crowd that had gathered in his name, and he wanted to console them. He wanted to tell his friends that he was going to be all right.

Red Dog slowly drifted off into the land of visible darkness. A land that was warm and inviting. A land where there was no pain, no fear, no hunger, no regrets, no anger—only compassion and love.

Red Dog looked up and saw his mother, and she held his face in her hands...and kissed him.

Red Dog looked up again and saw his mother's mother and his father's mother, and they each in turn held his face in their hands...and kissed him.

And then Red Dog looked up again and saw his father's father, Buffalo Hump.

"Welcome Red Dog, proud son of my son, Tall Bear. Follow me, my grandson, for we are all waiting to greet you at the council fire and watch with pride as you sit and feast with us and tell us of your journey."

Red Dog looked up again and saw the faces of his people, faces of friends and relatives long past. He recognized them in his heart and knew their names even though some had passed before he came to be.

Red Dog looked up again and saw a bright light beckoning him.

"Welcome, Red Dog, proud son of Tall Bear, proud grandson of Buffalo Hump, proud blood brother to Clayton John Alexander and Jason Gray Eyes. Know now and forever your struggle is over."

Then Red Dog looked up and saw the face of the Great Spirit. So handsome. So very handsome.

"Come, Red Dog, and take your rightful place next to me at the council fire.

"Come Red Dog, and I will explain all the mysteries of life to you. Come Red Dog, and be at peace forever."

Then the Great Spirit held Red Dog's face in his hand... and kissed him.

"Welcome home, my son."

CHAPTER FIFTY-EIGHT
A Father's Revenge

"Somebody please get a blanket and cover this brave Texas Ranger," pleaded Captain Hickson reverently. "And then spread out and get that coward who knifed this man and pushed him off the roof."

"We already caught him, Captain!" reported Sergeant Wilson. "He was hightailing it up the hill behind the blacksmith's shop when two troopers caught up to him on horseback. He's none too happy."

Rudy looked scared, as well he should. He had nothing to say, however.

Captain Hickson turned to Tall Bear. "I promise you I will personally bring this man to trial and see him hang."

"Thank you, Captain. But white man's justice takes too long and does not always rule in favor of the red man," replied Tall Bear, his eyes burning with pain and hate.

Moses moved closer to his friend and put his hand on Tall Bear's shoulder. Moses was about to say something conciliatory to Tall Bear, something soothing, but before he could utter a single word, Tall Bear reached for Moses' hatchet. With a screaming war hoop, Tall Bear hurled the hatchet at Rudy, bound tightly by strips of rawhide a mere 20 feet away—*Whoosh! Whoosh! Whoosh!...Crack!*

Red Dog's father had buried the blade squarely in Rudy's skull, killing the son of a bitch instantly.

No one said a word.

CHAPTER FIFTY-NINE

A Son's Revenge

Davis crawled to a low spot under the building, where he could see the street, and witnessed Rudy's death. Shaking with fear and against his better judgment, he crawled out from under the building, dusted himself off, and calmly walked toward a tethered horse. Nobody paid any attention.

He led the horse down the street a bit where he casually mounted up and headed south out of town. Davis then chuckled to himself, thinking he was quite clever, when Blondy yelled out. "Hey, that's Davis, and he's stealing my horse!"

Clayton looked over and caught Davis' eye. Davis thought Bull had disposed of Clayton, and again he trembled in fear. Clayton had every reason to kill him for starting the Colby Hotel on fire and killing his parents—and then bragging about it.

Clayton ran to Red Cloud and mounted up with a single jump.

"He's mine, but I'm empty and need another gun! Jason, toss me yours!"

Red Cloud knew instinctively what was about to be

asked of him. He bunched his muscles, reared up on his hind legs, and with a snort dropped to all fours. Then he dug his hooves into the dirt and sprang forward, tossing loose red soil behind him like a prairie windstorm.

Clayton extended his hand as he passed by Jason. With an underhand throw, Jason tossed Clayton his freshly loaded Navy Colt and yelled, "Get the son of a bitch!"

Davis already had a good head start and was well on his way out of town by the time Clayton holstered the Navy Colt. Nonetheless, Clayton laid low over the saddle and urged Red Cloud on. "Giddy up, Red Cloud. C'mon, you can do it. Giddy up!"

Red Cloud knew in his heart that this was a race he must not lose. And with untapped energy he lengthened and quickened his stride. Faster and faster he ran, picking up speed with every step. Clayton soon caught sight of Davis riding hard at the edge of town and urged Red Cloud on to a full gallop. Breathing rhythmically and with nostrils flared, Red Cloud responded, giving it all he had.

The distance between Davis and Red Cloud began to shorten. Davis looked back in terror and urged his mount on. But Blondy's gelding was tired from the long ride to Colby from Alexander's Crossing and was fast becoming winded. Davis dug his heels into the gelding's ribs, but it was to no avail. The gelding was already running as fast as it could. Flecks of blood began to fly from the gelding's nostrils, staining Davis' jacket and white shirt red.

Davis drew his pistol and fired one shot back at Clayton. It went wild. He cocked the hammer again and yanked on the trigger, but this time the hammer fell on an empty chamber.

Davis was in trouble, big trouble, and he was scared. Real scared. He turned the gelding into a steep canyon and then down a rocky path where speed was less a factor in his escape. But Red Cloud still gained and was soon running side by side with the gelding.

Clayton stood on his stirrups and was about to jump onto Davis, knocking him from his saddle and onto the ground, when he thought the better of it. Instead he pulled Jason's Navy Colt from his holster...and shot the gelding in the head. Dead on his feet, the horse somersaulted tail over head, spilling Davis head over tail and onto the ground in a rumbling heap.

Clayton quickly dismounted, grabbed Davis by the collar, and rolled him over on his back. Wide-eyed and trembling with gut-wrenching fear, Davis covered his eyes and cried out for mercy. "No! No! Please! No!"

Clayton laid the barrel of the Navy Colt several times back and forth across Davis' face, blinding one eye and breaking his nose over and over again until blood flowed freely.

"Mercy?" screamed Clayton. "You want mercy? What mercy did you give my mother when you set the hotel on fire? Huh? What mercy did you give my father when he stayed with her till the end? What mercy did you give Gray Eyes when the mob strung him up? Huh? When did you ever show anybody mercy?"

Davis was hysterical and began sobbing uncontrollably. He knew he was about to die.

Now with both hands trembling and eyes ablaze, it was time for retribution. Clayton placed the muzzle of the Navy Colt between Davis' eyes...and slowly cocked the hammer until it *clicked*!

"Fuck you!" he screamed—and pulled the trigger.

The blast echoed off the rocks and past the foothills and over the prairie and all the way back to Colby. The bullet however had just grazed Davis' blood-soaked head, striking gravel on the far side of the canyon. Missing on purpose, Clayton looked down at Davis' quivering body with a broad smile.

Davis had clearly pissed his pants.

CHAPTER SIXTY

Your Rose Is My Rose

Judge Bastion and the Texas Rangers were gathered in Judge Alexander's office two months later for a meeting when a sudden knock came at the door.

"Who is it?" asked Will.

"Hubert Honeywell, sir."

"Hubert!" exclaimed Judge Bastion as he jumped up and opened the office door. "Please come in! I was afraid you weren't going to make a showing! Rose told me she was having trouble getting a message through to you."

Mr. Honeywell politely removed his black hat, stepped forward, and slowly closed the door behind him.

"Yes sir, I got the telegram this morning."

"Hubert, I want to formally introduce you to Jacob and John Alexander's father, Judge Wilfred Alexander. I think you've already met everyone else in the room."

Honeywell looked about the office and nodded as he made eye contact.

"Judge Alexander, please meet the best undercover ranger in the state, Hubert Honeywell. This is the man I told you about in this very office a short time ago. He's the man who infiltrated Jimmy Vachel's gang and was instrumental in bringing him and his outlaw gang to justice."

"Yes, I remember that day vividly," replied Will.

"Will, he's also the same Ranger who discovered the men responsible for Jacob's murder and the Colby Hotel fire that killed your son John, his wife Sally, and several others."

Washed up and clean shaven, Clayton, Jason, and Moses hardly recognized the man. He stood before them with his hat held tightly in both hands, dressed in polished boots, creased trousers, a white shirt, a black silk cravat, a short waist jacket —and a Texas Ranger badge pinned to his chest.

Bull leaned forward and extended his right hand. "How do you do, Judge Alexander. We met briefly in Colby at the pistol competition. It's a pleasure to meet you this evening on a more formal basis."

Judge Alexander stood up and shook Bull's hand. "Mr. Honeywell, the pleasure is all mine. I can't thank you enough for all you've done for me and my family. I owe you a great debt of gratitude."

"Sir, I knew both of your sons and counted them among my closest friends. I rode undercover with John for several years before the fire. We were quite a team, bringing more than a few bandits to justice. Nobody ever figured out we were both Texas Rangers.

"When I heard he died in a suspicious fire, and that Gray Eagle was falsely accused and then hanged for the crime, I knew I had to get involved. I had to find the real killer or killers. But to do that I had to stay undercover. Judge Bastion helped create quite a cover story for me.

Indeed, from Mexico to New Orleans I'm still known as a real bad hombre."

"You had everyone in these parts thoroughly convinced of that!" replied Will as he slapped his thigh and laughed.

Hubert stepped forward and stood in front of Clayton.

"Clayton, I once held you in my arms when you were only a few weeks old. You have grown into a fine young man and a tough Texas Ranger. Your father and mother, and your Uncle Jacob, would be right proud of you today."

Clayton stood up, threw back his shoulders, and faced Honeywell.

"Clayton, I'm sorry I had to land some punches," added Honeywell, "but if I hadn't, Davis would've surely shot you himself. I couldn't let that happen."

Clayton looked Honeywell straight in the eye and for a moment just stared at him.

"Honeywell, you are one mean son of a bitch."

Then Clayton smiled and extended his hand in gratitude.

"You had me convinced one of us would eventually have to kill the other, right up till the moment you and Davis held me and Jason at gunpoint. I was sure glad to see Grandpa come up behind you then with his pistol drawn and cocked, but flabbergasted when he suddenly holstered his Navy Colt. I had no idea until just then who you really were!"

Jason then stood up and extended his hand, too. "Mr. Honeywell, thank you for avenging my father's death."

"I've also known you since you were very young, Jason. Your father and I shared many campfires on the trail, and today I can see his resemblance in you in both body and spirit. Without him, I would've had trouble passing on information to John and Judge Bastion, information that eventually led us to Vachel and his gang. As the word gets out of your father's role with the Texas Rangers, I'm sure that those good folks of Colby who did nothing to stop the murder of your father will hang their heads in shame."

Jason started to say something, but choked up.

Honeywell turned to face Will once again. "When did you figure out I was a Texas Ranger, a man you could trust?"

"After our pistol-shooting contest," replied Will. "I sensed the inherent goodness in you that afternoon when you whispered to me "Your rose is my rose!" Later I mulled those words over and over again until I thought you might be referring to Rose O'Brien, an old friend of mine and Judge Bastion's secretary. When Judge Bastion confirmed your identity, I began to rest a lot easier."

"I wanted you to know how sorry I was for the loss of both of your sons and your daughter-in-law, Mr. Alexander," replied Honeywell. "I wanted you to know that the state of Texas was committed to finding the real killers. And I needed to let you know who I was in case this didn't turn out so good."

Judge Alexander nodded and solemnly lowered his head.

Honeywell then looked over at Moses. "You hurl a mighty hatchet, my friend. My head still rings once in a while when I think about that day. Thank goodness you were off a tad."

Moses' jaw dropped. "I gave it my best! Good Lord, Mr. Honeywell, I almost killed you!"

"Well you didn't, and that's all that counts today,"

replied Hubert, grinning as he rubbed the side of his head. "I had to bully you and Clayton in order to maintain my cover. Sometimes I took things a bit too far I'm afraid. Even so, you stood your ground for Clayton, and I admire that. Of course, if I had known you were a man of the cloth I might've behaved differently. How long have you been a preacher?"

Moses laughed. "I've been studying the Bible with Reverend Marstall for quite some time. I was ordained just this morning!"

"And this coming Saturday he will perform his first duties as Reverend Sheridan," piped in Jason with pride. "He's going to perform a triple marriage ceremony. Dancing Water and I are getting hitched along with the Nelson brothers. Bill is marrying Elizabeth Moses and Brian is taking her sister Sarah Ellen as his bride. It's going to be quite a Saturday afternoon. Would you honor us and be a witness to our wedding?"

"Yes, I would like that—very much."

The men talked into the late hours of the evening, sharing details about Vachel and his gang that shed even more light on the role Hubert Honeywell—Bull—played in bringing the gang to justice. Clayton listened intently to every word and soon found himself admiring the undercover Texas Ranger he once loathed.

CHAPTER SIXTY-ONE

Good-Bye

Reverend Sheridan stood silent before the wedding party and their invited guests for a moment, and then spread his arms out for everyone to see. "Jason Gray Eyes and Dancing Water, William Donald Nelson and Elizabeth Mary Moses, and Brian Richard Nelson and Sarah Ellen Moses, I know pronounce each of you man and wife. Gentlemen, you may kiss your brides!"

With a loud roar and plenty of applause, the newly-weds kissed each other and then walked in tandem down the aisle and over to the Grange Hall for a triple wedding celebration the likes of which will not likely be seen anytime soon in Colby.

Reverend Marstall blessed the meal and then Reverend Sheridan rose with glass in hand to say a few words. "May God bless the friends and relatives gathered here to celebrate the wedding vows of these three young couples. May their union be fruitful and bring everlasting happiness. I also offer a toast to our lost comrade, Red Dog, whose sacrifice helped make this day possible."

"I'll second that!" replied Clayton as he and Phoebe Ann were the first to raise their glasses. Then more glasses were raised and a rousing cheer echoed throughout the hall.

After a fine Texas barbecue complete with a yearling roasted steer, the tables and chairs were pushed back for dancing and merrymaking. Even Will and Reinette took to the floor for a waltz or two and as partners in a grand Virginia reel.

As sundown approached, Bill and Brian Nelson were the first to leave to parts unknown on their honeymoons followed soon thereafter by Jason and Dancing Water. They were moving to New Orleans where Jason was enrolled at Tulane University Law School. Will and Reinette had given them a horse and carriage as a wedding gift to help them make the transition to city life a little more palatable.

"Jason, here's the rest of the money you earned since you moved in with us," said Reinette. "We deposited a portion of your earnings into the bank for you each month, hoping this day would someday be a reality. Will and I added an additional $500 to the kitty."

Reinette then leaned forward and with watery eyes kissed Jason on the forehead. "Now you two better get going before it gets too dark to travel safely."

Jason thanked her and then wasting little time, slapped the reins. He wanted to leave the scene before anyone other than Dancing Water could see that he was crying.

Clayton and Phoebe Ann watched the carriage disappear down the street and then turned and walked hand-in-hand back to the Grange. They stopped where they could be alone.

"What are you going to do now, Phoebe Ann?" asked Clayton.

"I'm going to stay here in town for the night and ride out in the morning with Mrs. Nelson. I'll remain with her at the Nelson ranch until my sisters return from their honeymoons. Then I'm heading for Greenville, Ohio. I heard that a man named Frank Butler is challenging all comers to a shooting match. I think I'll see to him about that. What about you?"

"My bags are already packed. I'm leaving tonight."

Phoebe Ann looked down for a moment and then turned to face Clayton. "I'm going to miss you, Clayton John Alexander." And then with tears in her eyes she embraced him with open arms.

"Will I ever see you again?" asked Clayton, hoping she would say yes.

"You can count on it! I'll be visiting my sisters often enough, hoping to become 'Auntie Phoebe' soon enough, too. I'll make sure to let you know so you can come and visit us."

They stood there locked in a tight embrace when the clop clop clop of two horses broke the silence. It was Hubert on horseback and Reverend Sheridan leading Red Cloud, already fitted with a Mexican saddle and a familiar Henry lever-action secured in a scabbard.

"You ready to ride, partner? There's a man in San Antonio that needs a jail cell!" informed Hubert, disheveled and dressed in dirty clothes once again. "Your father's belongings are in the satchel."

Clayton grabbed the satchel, stepped out of sight for a moment, and then returned wearing his uncle Jacob's shirt, an old sombrero embroidered with eagles pulled tight over his forehead, a pair of well-worn leather chaps and a pair of old scuffed-up cowboy boots fitted with wheeled Mexican spurs.

As he was about to mount up, Moses spoke up. "Clayton, stick this in your pocket for good luck. It was given to me by the Lone Ranger many years ago before I worked for your grandfather. It certainly has done just fine by me, and I hope it does the same for you."

Clayton reached out and Moses dropped the silver bullet into his palm. He looked at it for a moment and then looked at Moses. "Thanks, Moses. Thanks a lot! I'll always carry it with pride."

Red Cloud bobbed his head up and down, raring to go as Clayton slid into the saddle and pulled back on the reins. He looked at Phoebe Ann one more time, tipped his Stetson with a smile, and then reluctantly touched Red Cloud's flanks with his spurs.

"Adios, amigos!"

Phoebe Ann and Moses watched as Clayton and Hubert rode quickly out of town past Will and Reinette and the other wedding party revelers. Clayton slowed Red Cloud long enough to tip his hat to his grandparents before spurring Red Cloud onward.

Mrs. Wilkinson, who was standing next to Reinette, asked her who the young man was, the one with the sombrero, the one riding tall in the saddle. She thought he looked familiar.

"Didn't you recognize him, Edna? That was my grandson!" replied Reinette proudly. "Texas Ranger Clayton John Alexander.

THE END